IN THE EYE OF THE
OF THE
HAWK

REX BARTON

authorHOUSE®

AuthorHouse™
1663 Liberty Drive
Bloomington, IN 47403
www.authorhouse.com
Phone: 1 (800) 839-8640

Cover Design: Antoinette Barton and Joe Frank

IN THE EYE OF THE HAWK is a work of fiction by the author. Many of the incidents
written about may be real. The events, timelines, boundaries, borders, names, dates,
whether actual or not, and people—living or dead—are entirely coincidental.

Published by AuthorHouse 04/24/2017

ISBN: 978-1-5246-8743-4 (sc)
ISBN: 978-1-5246-8741-0 (hc)
ISBN: 978-1-5246-8742-7 (e)

Library of Congress Control Number: 2017905476

Print information available on the last page.

This book is printed on acid-free paper.

Scripture quotations are taken from the NIV (New
International Version) of the King James Bible
New Testament in Modern English. Published by Tyndale
House Publishers, Inc. Wheaton, Illinois
And Zondervan Publishing House, Grand Rapids, Michigan
The Life Application Bible is a registered trademark of Tyndale House
Publishers, Inc. and Copyright: 1988,1989,1990,1991

DEDICATIONS

I dedicate *In The Eye Of The Hawk* to all the hard working people in Law Enforcement, Fire Departments, Military, Coast Guard, and the Medical teams around the world who attempt to give life and freedom even when it may be temporarily gone. Thank you. God bless each and every one of YOU! It comes at a very steep cost. I know.

To Antoinette, my wife, whose loving kindness, continued encouragement, first round editing kept me going in times that were tough and fearful. My writing took on a life of its own, and you allowed me the experience of finding my words and loving me, no matter what. I know how hard it must have been reading our life over on every page. Mattered not the pain, losses, tears, nights of fear, and caring for the wounded and broken parts. I Love you and need you always. Thank you!

Julianna, your reading of each chapter prior to the publishers and editors, gave me hope and encouragement to write the next chapter. You helped in research, and that was much appreciated. Love you always. Thank you!

Sally Franz—for encouraging me to start and after each page, you would say, "keep writing." Those two words inspired me to write well into the nights until finished. Thank you!

Talon, you helped me put it all together. From checkpoints to edit and corrections. Thank you! See you in Book II, III, IV, and beyond.

Special thanks to the Office Depot. Thank you, Chris and the entire team, for all your help. Getting stuck in a program or needing supplies, you all made such a great difference. You helped me continue along the writing trail. We have many more projects to go.

CONTENTS

"For God so loved the world that he gave his one and only Son, that who so ever believes in Him shall not perish but have eternal life" (John 3:16).

CHAPTER 1

THE BLOOD ASSASSIN

Circa 1969

Any month on the Central Coast is a good month. The sun always seems to shine; the smell of fresh sea air blowing in from the Pacific Ocean is refreshing. Even, many different flowers are still in bloom in the freeway median. That's how it was in October of 1969. The other thing that was high was Hawk's adrenaline because, on this day, he was involved in a 'high speed' chase, Northbound on 101 Freeway at speeds over 100 mph. He was in the chase of his life after one of the FBI's most wanted killers. Hawk's patrol unit was running with red lights and siren. Ahead of him was a 1969 silver Pontiac GTO. The driver was a Larry Blood, a known assassin with a long rap sheet of kills. Everything from pet dogs to horses. Even husbands wanting partners or wives killed. Police and fire department officers; known criminals and politicians. It mattered little to Larry Blood. If you were on his list, you were already dead. The money for the kill was already in his offshore bank account just waiting for his pick-up time. These are not Hawk's words, but that of Agent Kevin King of the FBI who alerted Hawk's team at their briefing the previous afternoon. Blood was in their area, and if they spotted him, they were to notify the FBI immediately of his location and stand down. The FBI did not want any more murders on their watch.

An appropriate last name for one of the world's most wanted and deadliest killers ever known. *How did he make it this long without being detected and brought to justice? Why didn't our government, or any government for that matter, put this sick dog out of his misery?* Hawk thought. And now, here he was, chasing one of the most wanted killers on HWY 101 through his town, Santa Barbara, California.

Flashback

After the morning briefing, Hawk checked his patrol unit for an assault rifle, ammo, flack-jacket, first aid, emergency gear, and then the radio. The last thing on his list, but one of the most important, was checking the tires and fluids of the patrol unit. Having been a sports car driver and racer in Europe, while in the military, Hawk was keenly aware of the importance of safety. Too many patrol cars were rendered useless and out service because of the lack of simple checks.

As a Deputy Sheriff in his county of over 150,000 people, it was critical that he or any law enforcement officer be where needed if called for help. Nothing worse than a call back to dispatch that Unit 7 is out of service due to a flat tire, or out of oil, or the engine light is on, and the car won't start. Lives are at stake, and simple solutions like checking the obvious are critically necessary and mostly forgotten. Hawk couldn't live with himself if he had to tell someone who just lost a home in a fire or lost family, "Sorry I couldn't get here sooner, but my car wasn't running very well."

At the briefing, Hawk was given a notification to go south to the Ventura/Santa Barbara County line and take a report of an attempted burglary from earlier in the day. He left the county garage after checking his unit out thoroughly and headed south to the attempted burglary caller's residence.

The unit in the field at the time was busy with a traffic fatality and was unable to make contact and take the burglary report when first called in. An attempted burglary was not the same as a burglary in progress, and that's why there was no real urgency to take the report.

Hawk pulled up to the address, got out of the patrol car, and walked up to the front door. As he walked up, he heard some muffled noises inside and decided to knock fairly hard on the front door. The voices he heard was a man telling someone to shut-up and a woman's voice saying, "Please no," and then crying. Hawk knocked two times more and listened. The next sound was somewhat familiar to him. A crack, like someone's neck having been twisted around or a stick broken. Then a heavy object like a body being dropped to the floor. Next was the back door being opened and the screen door slamming shut. Hawk knew something wasn't right, so he started moving faster toward the side of the house where a dog was barking in an enclosed fenced side yard and the deep throaty sounds of a muscle car starting up. The dog was safe enough, and Hawk pulled his service revolver out of his holster and carefully looked through a tall hibiscus plant toward the sounds of a car burning rubber. It was a newer silver GTO.

Taking a compulsory look through what was the kitchen window, Hawk saw the naked body of a young woman lying on the kitchen floor. Opening the gate, and then the back-kitchen door, he ran to the victim's side to check for a pulse on her neck and wrist. Nothing. She was dead, mostly from a broken neck. Her head was twisted grotesquely to one side. That was the hideous crack that Hawk had heard while standing at the front door listening. Looking down at the naked body of this young girl, Hawk could not help but notice how beautiful she was and now her body was lifeless.

What Hawk saw made him emotionally sick and angry. All the signs were there telling him she had been beaten, tied up, and violated in the worst way. It was also apparent that she didn't give in to the

REX BARTON

abuse that easily. There was blood under her fingernails; some of her fingernails were broken off. Her legs were bruised, as was her face and arms. Numerous lacerations were apparent everywhere. She had struggled to live until the final moment when the perpetrator snapped her neck and ran out the back door. Was this the Larry Blood that the FBI was talking about? Every sign pointed to that, including the silver GTO speeding off down the driveway.

Hawk holstered his weapon while running toward the front door to his patrol car. Hawk and his team were told in a briefing by the FBI not to engage this guy, but Hawk had a fresh murder on his hands, and he determined this was going to be this dude's last. Hawk wasn't thinking of killing him yet, but those thoughts did become paramount in his mind as he watched Blood's GTO careening off cars speeding north on 101 Freeway, attempting to escape yet another murder. A senseless murder of a beautiful young woman who had her entire life ahead of her. Next to her body was a bath towel with blood on it. Before jumping up and running out the front door, Hawk took a moment to cover her nude body. Even though she was dead, she deserved respect. This was now a primary crime scene, and many people would be walking in and out the residence. A question crossed Hawk's mind as he was running to his patrol unit: *How did dispatch get this so wrong? Attempted burglary?* He would ascertain the answer later.

Hawk opened the patrol car driver door with his left hand, fastened the seat belt next, and with his right hand, started the engine and turned on the red lights and siren. He shifted into reverse and backed out of the driveway with his rear tires smoking. At the appropriate moment, Hawk then pulled the automatic shifter down to drive, with his foot still on the accelerator, and turned the wheel. He was now headed out the drive and onto the two-lane road in pursuit of the GTO.

Hawk's tires were as hot as lava, and he was up to speeds of 80 mph on a little two-lane road just inside the Rincon, Ventura County line. He could see the aftermath of the silver GTO's direction. Several cars had been sideswiped while the driver was maneuvering around them, cutting the angles a little too close. As Hawk sped by, he looked for injuries and radioed for assistance. He related to dispatch to send units to the accident scenes and alerted the Highway Patrol of his 1020 (location), Northbound on 101, in pursuit of the silver GTO wanted by the FBI.

"10-4 Unit 7, stand-by!" were Hawk's new orders. Not this time. They didn't have all the facts yet. Hawk's foot bent forward all the way to the floorboard, causing the speedometer needle to hit the stop post hard.

Dispatch: "This guy is driving like a maniac, bouncing off cars and the median cement retaining wall. Tell the Hwy Patrol to follow, not to barricade at this time. Too much traffic heading north. 10-4 Unit 7, stand-by please for the WC (Watch Commander)."

A few seconds later, Hawk listened over the radio and heard the following message: "Unit 7, back it off right now." It was Numb-nuts of course, Hawk's watch commander.

Then Hawk heard another very familiar voice of the Undersheriff on the dispatch radio: "Unit 7, turn to 1410."

1410 was a private radio frequency that allowed dispatch to talk with any patrolman without interfering with other emergency traffic calls or civilian ears.

Hawk: "Unit 7 standing by on 1410 now."

Dispatch: "Hawk, this is the Undersheriff."

Hawk: "Yes, sir."

Dispatch: "Can you safely effect a stop or not?"

Hawk: "Yes, sir, I can once this guy is above El Capitan and on the open hi-way. Minimal traffic today northbound above Goleta. Right now, it would be impossible."

Dispatch: "What is your speed, Hawk?"

Hawk: "In excess of 110 mph, sir. If this guy bounces one more time off any more cars or trucks, he is done. His front end is hanging on by a screw, and I don't know what is keeping his doors shut. The GTO looks like a total wreck right now. However, I can shut him down, sir.

Slowing down will not slow him down. He just killed another victim. A young girl back at the address I was sent to for the burglary report."

Dispatch: "Watch yourself, Hawk."

Hawk: "10-4. Switching back to standard."

Three minutes later, Hawk radioed dispatch, "Unit 7 approaching El Cap turn-off now, light traffic." Three minutes at speeds in excess of 100 mph was an eternity and Hawk knew the entire Sheriff's Department was sitting on pins and needles.

Hawk: "10-4 Unit 7."

Dispatch asked a couple of minutes later: "Unit 7, 1020 now?"

Hawk: "Still at 110 plus, approaching Refugio."

Dispatch: "10-4 Unit 7, FBI is here and wants you to shut it down now."

Hawk: "With all due respect, dispatch, tell the FBI … you know what... Click-click."

At the dispatch office, Sheriff Lamb and Agent King were having the following conversation:

"This officer is the best there is, Agent King. He is a marksman with honors and FBI-trained. He has prior race car training, nerves of steel, and more than capable of taking your guy down," Sheriff Lamb said.

"Sheriff, I understand, but we will have a chopper in the air any minute now, and I will take over. Stand your man down before anyone gets hurt out there," Agent King replied.

"Agent King," the Sheriff replied, "are you at all familiar with our county? Do you realize there is nothing but open space and national forest from his location all the way to San Francisco?"

Agent King was silent; he was in thought, weighing all his alternatives, if any.

Dispatch: "Unit 7, alert the Hwy Patrol and our units in Santa Ynez that we are now headed northeast on Mountain road. Still, excessive speeds. If he stays on this road, we can affect a stop with a couple of patrol cars or a big tractor in Santa Ynez."

Hawk: "OK, Sheriff, have your man continue to follow. The chopper is of little help in the national forest. Let your deputy know we will be overhead to assist any way we can."

Dispatch: "Good. Unit 7, FBI chopper will be your 1020 (location) in about fifteen minutes and will remain overhead."

* * *

The setup:

- GTO and Patrol unit speeding nearly out of control on a dirt road headed toward Santa Ynez. This is a single lane dirt mountain road with a mountain on one side and a sheer cliff drop of 100 feet or more on the other side.

- The GTO has avoided crashing to this point, but getting close to going over the edge due to rear tire slides at his current speed of 70 mph and a dislocated front end and side panels. Hawk could see his wheels wobbling in the rear. This GTO was ready for Destruction Derby day.

* * *

Dispatch: "Unit 7, I am going to push this guy over the edge. Have a clearing coming up. We can end this right now, 10-4 Unit 7."

Hawk was pushing the patrol car up to within eight feet of the rear bumper of the GTO at 70 Mph and more. Dirt and small rocks were still hitting the window of the patrol car, creating blind spots. It was time for Hawk to affect the maneuver or risk disaster himself. He then shoved the gas pedal all the way down to the floorboard. His patrol unit lunged forward one more time, hitting the GTO's rear bumper on the right side of the quarter panel.

There wasn't much room on the road for a full pit maneuver hit, but just enough. It was all Hawk needed. The GTO slipped to the right. As predicted, Blood over-corrected and began sliding left toward the mountain side of the dirt road. No room there either and another over-correction caused the GTO to slide right again, only this time he was sideways on the road. Hawk watched as his last over-correction took him and the GTO off the road and down the hill. The GTO started its roll and flipped over and over, crushing the top of the car, ripping the driver door off its hinges. It must have rolled half a dozen times before coming to a stop on its side wedged between a stand of boulders. This GTO would never run again from a police unit. It would never run again, period. The engine was ripped out from under the hood and resting several feet from the car at the bottom of the hill.

Looking down from within the window of the patrol car, Hawk couldn't see the driver anywhere. Too much dirt, debris, smoke, and a little oil and gas fire from where the engine once was.

Hawk gently applied the brakes until the patrol unit came to a sliding stop. Once stopped, he put the patrol unit in reverse and backed the unit up to where the GTO went over the embankment.

In order to grab his shotgun out of its holder, Hawk had to push the safety lock button on the gun holder in a view to release the shotgun. With his right hand, he pushed the button, grabbed the shotgun, changed hands, and then pulled the car keys from the ignition. After throwing the keys under the seat, Hawk took off—running back toward the mark where the GTO went over the side. The emergency lights were still flashing. Hawk figured it would be a good marker for the FBI chopper and any Sunday drivers wondering down the road.

Without thinking or slowing up, Hawk leaped over the edge of the road and soared down the cliff face a good twenty or more feet. Luckily, Hawk was still on both feet when he landed. He slid downward very fast—down the embankment—toward where the GTO laid silently on its rooftop.

Hawk was used to sliding down mountains of water surfing. This slide was just a little harder to land on if he should fall. He made sure he didn't.

Not sure what he was going to encounter once he reached the bottom where the GTO was lying, Hawk's body was tense, muscles bulging from the extreme driving and leap of faith down the mountain. The entire chase was like being back at La Mann's France. Racing was in Hawk's blood.

As Hawk bounded down the face of the cliff, his eyes were looking from side to side for the driver of the GTO, expecting the body to have been thrown from the vehicle or still rolling down the mountain. Hawk was ready for anything; half sliding, half running until he reached the bottom of the hill. Before hitting the GTO with his body in order to stop his forward momentum, his eyes were set on the rear window and peering inside of the car for a body. Hawk figured it was possible that this guy might still be alive, but he had to be badly hurt. Hawk was not going to take any chances—not with this perp's record. He had a wife and kids at home waiting for him. Unfortunately, this guy had the devil waiting for him.

Using the cover of the big boulders, Hawk slowly made his way around the car, not taking his eyes off of the GTO for one second. Nothing. Nothing there. Hawk looked down inside the car through another broken side window, with the shotgun barrel first and his finger on the trigger. *Should this idiot reach up somehow and grab the barrel of the gun, he would first feel the heat of the projectile speeding down the barrel, and then the blast itself. By that time, it would be too late. He would feel nothing but dead. Where the hell is he? Lord, help me find him fast.*

Looking around the rocks and under the car, there was nothing. The only sign a human was even here was the trash that came out of the car on impact. There was no body; only smoke, dirt, and more debris floating in the air—debris everywhere.

There had been enough time for the FBI Chopper to be here. *Where the hell was it?* Hawk still didn't hear a sound other than a small stream that was fifty or so yards away from where he was standing. Scrub pines and Monterey pines littered the landscape along with rocks and brush. Hawk figured if this fool were lucky enough to have made it out alive somehow, he would be armed and dangerous. There was no way he could have climbed back up the cliff to hot wire the patrol unit. He may be able to pop the trunk and take the assault rifle out, but not likely.

Where is this guy, God? Now in a low crouch, protected by a few rocks, Hawk kept surveying the landscape all around. *What did I miss? Where are you, Blood?* he said to himself.

The perp would have water and shelter by the trees, but running anywhere in his condition would be slow going. One step, one very slow step at a time, Hawk made his way around the car, expanding the circumference by thirty yards or so. *He is somewhere here, I know. I can feel him. He is watching me!*

As Hawk proceeded in his search, he realized he was now an open target, being half-way from the boulders and the trees in his circumference walk. Hawk was looking, looking, looking for anything that moved or was out of place, or even a blood trail. Scanning up the hill again, he saw it. There it was—a piece of clothing stuck on a sagebrush limb, ankle high. It was a third of the way back up the hill. Hawk kept on scanning the cliff and northward toward a few trees. When he reached the sagebrush limb with the article of material, he then spotted the blood trail going off in the direction of the pine trees and further on toward the water. The piece of bloody cloth hanging on the sagebrush limb and the blood trail showed Hawk that that was where Blood had been thrown from the car on one of its rollovers.

Hawk had lost some time circling the wreck, looking for the perp but it was necessary to get it right and not get in a hurry or sloppy or killed. After all, it is not every day that a deputy gets a chance to go one-on-one in a confrontation shoot out with a hired assassin. Although, Hawk liked his odds better and better. *Just don't get careless, man. Stay alert be ready. You can do this, Hawk, and bring this sick animal down,* he said to himself. *Help me, Lord,* he said again. This was not going to be easy. This guy was still loose and now on the run. Hawk didn't know how this perp could have escaped the GTO roll over and not have been crushed, but he did.

They were in a canyon that probably opened up somewhere down below a good three miles or more. If Blood could make it down to the road and stop a car, then someone else was going to be killed today. And that would be on Hawk because he thought if the perp went over the cliff, all would be done. *This guy is tougher than most. Almost as tough as me,* he thought. The only difference was that Blood had real kills with his marksmen ship badge, where Hawk had real targets and a lot of God saying no in his ears. *What would God say now if I had this murderer in my sights or if I had to draw on him?* Hawk thought but quickly reminded himself, *No time for What If's, Hawk, just keep an eye out for him.* Sweat was now rolling down his face and neck. Not just from the heat of the day, but the condition that his condition was in. Fearful! *Don't let him reach the road,* he reminded himself. *Pick up the pace a little.* Hawk heard himself talking and uttering little popcorn prayers up to God as he carefully walked forward. Still no sign or sounds of the FBI Chopper. *Where the hell are they?* Hawk repeated to himself again. He began to worry more.

I am as good a tracker as any of my grandpa hunting dogs. He taught me how to track bears, mountain lions, deer, coon, skunks (I don't know why) down to the smallest worm, lizard, or snake. This guy would be easy, especially with shoe and blood prints. Maybe he will run out of blood, and my job will be made easier. No chance; he isn't bleeding that much.

At the edge of the stream, Hawk saw where Blood had washed his wounds and drank a little water, because it was all over the ground. He started to look around on the other side of the stream to see where the perp might have crossed. *He picked this spot because of the narrows and the boulders on either side of the water. Not sure how bad his leg was injured, but jumping around on rocks can't be good for it.* Hawk's eyes hardly left the other side of the stream and the trees beyond. Somewhere in the thicket ahead of him was the meanest bastard alive. A very cold killer. A murderer. Someone that the FBI wanted real bad. Someone with a long, long list of kills.

Hawk got lower to the ground after thinking about it. At 6'7 ½" and 245 lbs., Hawk was a big target. How could he hide under a small three-foot boulder? Directly behind him was a small twenty-foot Monterey pine tree and a cluster of larger boulders. A good advantage point to look for anything out of place—a branch moving, a glimmer of metal, a movement of any kind, shadows, or sounds of steps. Hawk was carefully walking backward up to the rocks and the pine tree when his foot slid on a half-buried flat rock next to the boulder he was trying to duck behind for cover.

The next series of events happened almost simultaneously. Within a fraction of a second, Hawk's legs came out from under him, causing him to fall on his back. Then his head hit the ground and onto another small boulder. Hawk was semi-conscious. His eyes were blurred, his head hurt. Then he heard a very insidious sound. A sound no one wants to hear this close—a rattlesnake coming from behind the rock where his head was now laying. Hawk heard the rattlesnake shaking its tail at him and felt blood oozing out of the cut and large bump on his head. He also heard the sounds of footsteps. Blood had come out of hiding from across the stream bed and was going through the water, limping his way over to the direction where Hawk was down.

As Hawk fell to the ground, the shotgun came loose from his right hand, falling away from him. He started to raise his head toward the sounds of the footsteps—still only semi-conscious, having hit his head so hard on the rocks. His eyes would not focus and just as well.

The rattlesnake was tired of rattling and struck forward at Hawk's throat as he was attempting to get up. The force of the strike slammed his head back down to the ground, and then all he felt was a tugging and pulling and twisting of the rattlesnake. It must have been a granddaddy of a rattler because Hawk was being turned right then left with every twisting movement of the thing. It seemed to have taken Hawk a few seconds to realize that the rattlesnake had missed its intended target—his neck and bulging veins. Instead, both fangs went through his shirt collar, and the snake was hung-up and unable to break free; barely scratching the surface of Hawk's neck with each twist and turn. This snake was big, ugly, and very strong. With every twist of the snake's body, Hawk could feel a little hot liquid run down his neck. *My own blood or poison venom?* Hawk didn't know and couldn't take the time to find out.

Blood was now walking more casually toward Hawk about twenty-five yards away. Hawk heard him laughing at what he must have thought was the luckiest day of his life. He had to have been thinking that the gods of the universes were on his side. The rattlesnake was still twisting to get loose. Again, within seconds, Blood didn't realize that Hawk's right hand had attached itself to his pistol grip. Hawk managed to unsnap the hammer guard strap with his forefinger and was trying to lift the big six-inch 357 S&W revolver out of the holster. Then he realized that the gun was partially stuck in the holster by a rock and his right leg. Meanwhile, his left hand was busy groping for the rattlesnake. Hawk finally caught the snake just below the neck and squeezed as hard as he possibly could. Hawk has very large hands that can grip a basketball and hold it in mid-air, but this rattlesnake took all of his hands' grip and strength to just hold on to it.

Blood was still laughing when Hawk felt lots of pain on his left side. Then he heard the sound of his semi-automatic handgun recoil. A bullet from his gun had ripped through Hawk's flesh. Hawk's left hand was holding the rattlesnake and having a real tug-of-war, as the rattler was trying to dislodge itself from Hawk's shirt collar to strike again and again. Hawk still could not see Larry Blood, his intended target, because of his head concussion. He pulled the trigger of his 357 six times, emptying the revolver in the direction of the laughing and Blood's weapon firing. Hawk never pulled his pistol; he just fired through the bottom hole of his holster. The laughing stopped. In fact, all sounds stopped except the rattlesnake still trying to free itself. Hawk's grip tightened more.

Fortunately, Hawk had practiced what is called Point Shooting for years. One simply points in the direction of the sounds in front or at one's side. Shooting even when blindfolded. Years of practice and concentration was paying off big dividends today, even though Hawk was semi-conscious. All this before the perp could squeeze off a second round! His bullet hit Hawk in the left side, and he felt the deep pain where the bullet had gone through his body. Not knowing and not caring about the rattlesnake still squeezed in his left hand, Hawk raised himself up slightly and saw that his aim had been true. Blood was down and not moving. His chest cavity was pumping out spurts of dark red blood where his heart would have been.

Hawk's choice of bullets had mostly been 357 Magnum, silver-jacketed and hollow copper points. When they hit a target with any resistance, the hole going in is small, and then the bullet opens up, expanding, cutting and churning all meat and bones into mush. *Job accomplished,* Hawk thought. Blood was down and not getting back up. He laughed one too many times and caught the silver bullets in his chest, which he should have received years before all his killings and carnage started.

Still holding a not-so-aggressive rattlesnake, Hawk just laid there in a semi-coma, watching the clouds above him as if he were looking through a vail. He felt the rattle-snake still shaking his left hand and arm around a little, attempting to gain its freedom to strike again. Hawk wasn't sure where his buddies were, and he didn't care. He felt strangely at peace with himself and the world for the moment. It was quiet. Very quiet. Watching the clouds and their formations reminded him of being a kid again, sitting up in the tamarisk pine trees on his grandparents' ranch. It was there that he would watch the same clouds roll by, looking for animal faces and cartoon characters. Those were difficult times in Hawk's life, yet probably the best of times too. God was always close to him.

Hawk casually noticed that his left arm was not being pulled around so much. The rattlesnake was dying because of his death grip behind its head. Hawk still wasn't going to let go of it. If it were possible, his grip only tightened around the snake's throat.

Finally, Hawk heard the sounds of a rotary blade chopper coming down toward the clearing across from the area that Blood had been hiding in. Next, he heard sounds of several voices yelling words he couldn't really make out or understand.

Two people approached Hawk with caution, seeing his left hand full of problems. They didn't quite know what to do, but the rattlesnake stopped moving around. All Hawk could think to say was, "Welcome to our state's park, gentlemen. Can I introduce you to one of our most, deadliest residents?" Laughter and "hell no" was the last thing Hawk could remember hearing before he passed out, leaving all his troubles and the rattlesnake to the visitors.

Waking up after surgery left Hawk with a cotton mouth sensation and a tremendous headache and sounds of many voices. In the room with him, surrounding his bed was Sheriff Lamb, FBI Agent Kevin King, his friend and sometimes partner Red, and several other FBI agents. The press with all their cameras and lights were on the other side of the glass window of Hawk's hospital room. It was a circus of sounds, and the doctors were trying to keep everyone quiet while the doctor tried to take some vitals with his stethoscope.

Out of panic and auto responses, Hawk tried to raise his head and pull his left arm up to check the rattlesnake. It was gone. *Where was it? Had I dropped it?* Panic began to set in, and the doctor and one of the FBI agents were holding Hawk down, knowing what he was thinking. *Snake,* Hawk uttered.

"Snake? It's OK, Hawk, we had to pry it out of your hand. But it is gone. You managed to choke the son-of-a-bitch to death. We took it from you and were thinking of getting it stuffed along with Blood."

"Good job, Deputy," Agent King said to Hawk. "You brought down one of the ten most wanted killers on our list. How you managed to draw your weapon and empty it into the bastard and re-holster that cannon is beyond me. I didn't say anything but just let him think what he wanted. You managed, Deputy, to put six bullets into Blood's chest, killing him. He died on the ground in seconds. Good Job! Good job, Hawk."

I guess I am now some kind of a celebrity. "Just did my job, sir," I said.

"Yes, Hawk, you did good," Agent King replied.

Sheriff Lamb let Hawk know all was well and reassured him that everything was going to be alright. The wound in Hawk's left side was clean through and through, and the doctors said he would be up real soon. They were more concerned with Hawk's head injury where he hit the back of his head on the rocks behind him when he fell. Then there was the matter of the rattlesnake choke hold. Hawk's left hand was still rolled into a fist. The doctor and nurses were injecting something into his hand to make his fingers relax. *I guess I really did choke the damn snake out and held on, even though I was unconscious at that time,* Hawk thought. It was only then that he was able to quietly close his eyes and give God all the praise and glory for his life. "Thank you, Father," he said.

As one could see, God always answers Yes, No, or Wait a little longer. Nevertheless, today He was there the entire time. Hawk asked Sheriff Lamb if his wife was there and he said yes.

"Wait just a few more minutes, and I will clear the crowd from your room and get Annie in here," Sheriff Lamb said.

"Thanks," Hawk said.

"No, Hawk, thank you," the Sheriff replied.

"God is good," Hawk replied, "isn't He?"

"I reckon so, Hawk. I reckon so!" the Sheriff said.

CHAPTER 2

A NEW SERGEANT IN TOWN

Three months had now passed since the Larry Blood shooting and the accident on Refugio road.

Phone ringing: "Hello," Hawk answered.

"Hi, Hawk, it's Under Sheriff Williams."

"Yes, sir, I know your voice. How may I serve you today, sir?"

"Stop brown nosing. You can't do anything for me today, but I can do something for you. When can you get down here?"

"Will, I have been working on the patio, so after a shower, I guess. In about one hour tops?"

"OK, good. Put your Class A's on please and don't be late."

"Yes, sir."

"What the hell is this all about?" Hawk asked the phone that was already hung up. "What is going on?" The phone was silent as if to be goading Hawk on to somehow ask it more questions. Hawk kept looking down at the instrument on the cradle, wondering why his best friend, the Under Sheriff, was calling him down to the station in Class A's.

Hawk began reviewing his last few weeks and especially the last two days at the Airport:

I wonder if I have to make a public apology or something for all the bullet holes in the hangers over there. Maybe we hit a few other buildings or the tower? Oh No, that couldn't have happened. The tower was too far to the right of the hangers. However, with my 38-cal. copper jacketed hollow points, one might... No, that would not be possible. The first time one of those suckers hit a metal wall, it would have most likely flattened out and dropped to the floor. Now if I had left the steel pointed armor piercing bullets in my S&W, they might still be flying. Most likely on their way over to Hawaii. None of that is the problem, is it?

Oh God, could the Cartels have made a complaint about us winning the battle the other night? The war is not over, but we did cripple them a little. I doubt it, so I guess I had better jump in the shower and get down there. What the hell; it's only my day off today. No rest for the wicked! Was I wicked? Is that what this is all about. Being too hard on Misty about her pregnancy or something?

Hawk just could not stop asking himself questions as to why he was being called downtown.

"Hey, Annie."

"Yes, I am out front, planting some flowers by the porch!" she yelled.

"OK, coming."

Opening the front door, Hawk leaned out. "Hey, babe, the Under Sheriff just called me in to the office in my Class A uniform. I am going to jump in the shower right now and get down there. He gave me one hour to meet him in his office. Something is up, but he wouldn't tell me what."

"OK, but don't worry, I am sure it is nothing. Can I fix you anything to eat on the way?"

"No, no, honey, thank you. I will call you after whatever it is, and we can make plans for something."

"Don't forget, Hawk, I already made a roast, which is cooking with carrots, onions, and potatoes. It's in the oven and just about finished."

"No, I won't forget, honey. Thank you. That is my favorite. Got to hurry. I thought I smelled something really, really good in the house. Dinner in the oven is always a good smell. Ummmm!"

In the shower, getting dressed, and driving downtown, Hawk just could not answer his own puzzling question. *What the hell is going on?*

After driving around the block a few times, Hawk finally found a parking spot a half of a block from the office. He walked in and saw

Red, Carlos, Robert, Misty, Billy, and a few others standing in the squad room.

"Hey, guys, what is going on? Why have we all been called in here today? What the hell is going on? Why is everyone dressed in Class A's? Are the Cartel Lords here trying to get us to drop the charges or something on their crew?"

"I don't think so, Hawk," Red and Misty said at the same time. But it must be important, that's for sure," Misty muttered.

"OK, guys, if it's not about the Cartels, then why the hell is the news camera crews here from the TV station? Is the airport commissioner here complaining?"

"As a matter of fact, he is, Hawk," Red said. "Look over there," he said, indicating another windowed office.

"Oh, crap, did we hit a lot of other aircraft out there or something and someone is complaining or threating to sue us?"

"Could be," Red attested. "At least we are not alone. We are all in it together. You did a good job, Hawk. You got it done, and we all got back safe, Hawk, with no rigor mortis bodies to write up. Ha ha. Your words, remember?"

"Yeah, I remember." Hawk looked over the crew who were all avoiding his gaze. Just then, Hawk's eyes turned to a glare. "OK, what the hell is going on here?"

"Put the face away," Hawk. Misty had to remind him that Lt. Joel had said they did a good job and were all in it together.

"In what?" Hawk pursued.

Before Misty could answer, the Under Sheriff stepped out of his office and met everyone in the squad room. He asked for everyone to take a seat and be quiet. The news teams moved into the back of the room. When they were had finished setting up, the anchor news person nodded to the Under Sheriff that they were ready.

"Ladies and gentlemen, you have been called down here today on a special occasion. Our department, the City of Santa Barbara—" (The mayor just walked in behind the news crew and walked forward and stood next to the Under Sheriff. Next, the Airport Commissioner came forward, standing next to the mayor, followed by Sheriff Adams.)

Under Sheriff Williams continued, "This team of dedicated deputies carried out a very important mission the other night involving a major shipment of drugs designated for our local streets and population. Our department, the Mayor of Santa Barbara, the Airport Commissioner want to personally thank each one of you directly and indirectly involved in the mission ..."

Is that all it is, Hawk was thinking. *They interrupted my day off for a lame thank you? It's our job, good grief. Where in Heaven's name is Williams going with this?*

"… The Cartels had a bad day, and we had a good one. Would Red, Carlos, Robert, and Misty please come forward and stand on my right? At that moment, FBI Jack Renton and Kevin King came through the door and walked up to the front.

"Next, would Sergeant Hawk Barton please step forward?"

What? All Hawk heard was yelling, whistles and laughter coming from every direction, and then he saw the smiles on everyone's faces. *But did I hear that right? Sergeant Hawk Barton? Could it be true? Oh God, I can't walk up there. I am stuck to the seat. No, this isn't right. I don't want to do this right now. Why couldn't the Under Sheriff just tell me in his office or somewhere private?*

Red came over and helped Hawk up and threw his big arms around him in a congratulatory thank you. "You made it, man. You did good for a cowboy, Hawk!"

Some members of the team had tears in their eyes, including Hawk's good friend Under Sheriff Williams. Hawk walked up, looking straight at him with a big smile on his face and met his outstretched hand with his. "Thank you, sir."

"No, Hawk. The department thanks you, as well as everyone here, and a great many more who are not. Because of you, Hawk, your actions and directions the other night, and all the hullabaloo causing the department to go on high alert and putting extra patrol cars on the streets." Everyone split up laughing. "Please Hawk, say something for the folks in the back," Under Sheriff Williams said.

"All I can say is thank you. Thanks to everyone who worked so hard, trained so long and are the best law enforcement officers around. Around here, I mean. In the Courthouse, only!" Again, there was laughter. "Sheriff, thank you for trusting me with the new rank of Sergeant. I am honored beyond belief. If this department can continue to work alongside the teams of FBI, CIA, and all the other local agencies, we can make a big difference in the war on drugs. Our communities and families will have a safer place to live. Thank you again. To all of you, thank you. Now … all of you, back to work," Hawk said

(Everyone walking up to Hawk in the room had big smiles on their faces, saying congrats.)

Under Sheriff Williams walked up to Hawk and asked him to go with him into his office for just another moment.

"Close the door, Hawk. First, my personal congratulations, Hawk. The moment I met you, when you were just sixteen, I knew you had something special. You had special qualities of a born leader and not a follower like Sam had said. Hawk, you have done well and deserve this promotion for all your service to this department and our community. And on that note, you must take care of Annie and your kids. Intel has it that more garbage is being distributed out there by the Cartels. You and your family are at risk. Nothing eminent but keeping your eyes open and being aware is essential. They (the Cartels) have your number on their call list. A bounty is being offered as we speak. As a department, we will continue to monitor the situation and will be working with the other agencies until a safety net is in place around the families of your team."

"Thank you, sir. Can I ask how much this time?"

"How much what?"

"How much the bounty is for?"

"Unknown. Very few facts are known at this time. You, your team, Jack, and Kevin over at the FBI are on the list, though, as Cartel property. Your whole team is being spied on, Hawk. Where and when anything more goes down, if at all, is unknown. Just keep sharp and don't for one moment forget who you are. Please, advise your teams to stay alert and keep their eyes open."

"How is Misty doing?"

"I can't tell you yet, sir. It has only been two days, and she was pretty shaken up. Having a crazy dope fiend ready to shoot your brains out while all the time choking you, then your partner missing your head by an inch or two with a bullet is a little disconcerting. Personally, I would order her to take a couple of days off to regroup."

"I agree, Hawk. Go ahead and give her the order. It's your team. Just write it up and give it back to me."

"Yes, sir. And thank you again for the stripes, sir."

"Hawk, I want you to know something. You should be supporting bars right now. I want you to finish up your Post Certificate and management classes at the college and who knows, maybe this time next year we can have another promotional department meeting."

"Thank you, sir. I will get it on. I can think of only one other thing better, and that would be if you ran for Sheriff, sir."

"Maybe?"

Hawk opened the door and walked back into the briefing room and asked Misty to take a walk with him outside.

"What's up, Hawk?"

"Just take a walk with me, please."

* * *

As Hawk and Misty walked outside the big wooden side door of the courthouse, they were met with a wonderful fragrance. The smell of violet, pink, and white Wisteria flowers. They had grown up and over the big doors and reached up at least fifteen to twenty more feet. The Courthouse and these doors were hung over a hundred years ago. But that smell was overpowering and melted visitors and deputies alike, every day. Once the smell hit their noses with such pungency, it nearly took their breath away. Someone more than fifty years ago planted the beautiful Wisteria plants around most of the entrance doors surrounding the Courthouse. It was like putting honey up to one's nose and breathing in deep. Hawk could imagine himself lying down in a field of such flowers and another time being a child again.

Hawk looked up at the blue December sky and saw a very familiar and pleasant sight. Little bellowing puffer clouds making animal faces at him again. It took Hawk back to his grandparent's farm in Ventura when he would sit at the top of the tamarisk pine trees for hours at a time looking up at the clouds and watching the animal faces blow by.

Such an innocent and important time it was. Such good times. It just blew by too fast. All of it. Rex Allen and his accidental death in the rock yard. Then grandpa's subsequent heart attacks and strokes, and ultimately his death eight years later. Finally, Nana—harassed and threatened by Sam in her final years and dying in a nursing home. First, Sam, and then mom shortly after that. Now all had passed away. All of the older generations of my family were gone. It didn't seem fair at this moment that no one was left to say, "Well done, son. You made us proud."

Misty cut in on Hawk's momentary departure from reality. "Hawk, what's going on?"

"Oh, not much. Just want you to consider taking a couple of days off to relax and get your breath. You had a very traumatic experience the other night, and I need you all in one piece."

"Why? What's going on, Sergeant Hawk?"

"Just told you. Take some time off starting now."

"What if I say no?"

"Then I will put you on the desk for a couple of weeks for disobeying an order."

"Just two days off if I follow orders?"

"Yes. Or three if you like."

"No, two days would be fine. It will take me that long to find the vacuum to clean the house with."

"OK, it's done. Have a great time cleaning! Just fit some rest and relaxation in too."

"Yes, sir Sarg. Congratulations on your promotion."

Misty turned around to walk back into the office. As she did, she mentioned in a low voice that she was no longer pregnant. Hawk said from behind her, "Thank you, Misty, for being here today. And you did a great job the other night. Glad to have you on my team. Uh—what? I am sorry for your loss," he said as the big wooden door closed behind her.

She smiled and walked back into the office and joined the other deputies.

Red then walked out and put his hand on Hawk's shoulder just as Hawk tilted his head back up to the sky.

"Thank you, Red. You know that I could not be standing here today if it was not for you always watching my six and standing shoulder-to-shoulder in all the scraps we have had."

"Cowboy, it would only be for you. Don't forget you have saved my ass more times than I can count. That's only because I am a better shot than you. Faster too."

"Ha ha ha!" Red exclaimed. "In your dreams."

"Meet you at the OK Corral tomorrow morning, son, for a shootout. You're on, cowboy."

Hawk then turned to Red and asked him a question: "In all seriousness, Red, the other night when I was walking up the Lear's ramp and reloading, I thought of something that I would like you and I to do as a team."

"What's that, Sarg?"

"We need to switch over to Glocks and start practicing seriously again. Quick drawing from a different holster setup and accuracy. I have a feeling that in the coming months and years, we will need more firepower and speed. You know that each clip can hold between twelve and seventeen bullets to our six now and we can carry six additional clips?"

"You kidding me? Hell no. My Python stays right where it is."

"OK then, will you consider carrying a backup Glock instead of that little 22-cal. in your boot?

"Maybe."

"Good. Consider it now, and I will see you on the range tomorrow morning before work. We have a lot to do and talk about. I will bring the weaponry and my new Glock."

"See you at ten on the range."

"Thank you, Red. And know that sometime very soon I am going to be recommending you for strips."

Red was heard laughing all the way back inside the squad room. Hawk didn't want to break the festive attitude and party atmosphere today with what the Under Sheriff had told him about the Cartel's new wanted posters. Hawk knew that anyone associated with him or that night at the airport was in danger of being caught up in the same chance of execution style examples that the Cartel used over and over again.

Hawk reminded himself that what he said before was true. *The fingers of the Cartel are long and don't have an expiration date.* Sergio's father was on the vengeance trail now, and he wouldn't stop until Hawk was dead.

But then, the Cartel didn't know Hawk that well either. Hawk was going to be ready as would every member of his team. The promotion was not going to be in vain. Annie would have to get over Hawk not being home that much, because it would be even less now. Too much work and training had to be done. Not only because of his new promotion but having created the Special Ops Team required so much more of Hawk's time.

Maybe it would serve more than one purpose to pay a visit to Sergio who was still in the jail division awaiting trial for the drug bust and murder of four FBI agents at the airport. Time for a little advice on prison life without his cronies around to protect him. Time to maybe call in a few favors for cigarettes with some of the inmates that Hawk put there. A good word from Hawk to parole officers never hurt a possible early release date. Some of the petty criminals that wanted to be part of a tough crew would help out in matters of freedom. Never underestimate the price of freedom. A pack of cigarettes for a black eye was easy. Two packs for two black eyes and so on. *It's that, or I get on my knees and pray for my enemies. That's what the good Book says.* Hawk felt a long way away from the Book right now. Probably because he was so tired and in need of rest himself. He gave out an order for Misty a little while ago, and now he needed to comply with the same order for himself. A few more simple but true antidotes popped into his mind. H.A.L.T. Don't get too Hungry, too Angry, too Lonely or too Tired. Another bothersome antidote was K.I.S.S. Keep It Simple Stupid. *Go home and rest,* Hawk thought. *Just go home and rest. Take your own advice. Annie has dinner waiting.*

When Hawk got home, Annie was so excited and ran to him and jumped into his arms.

"I love you, baby. I love you. Congratulations on your promotion, Hawk."

"What! You mean you knew about this all the time?"

"Yes. Sorry, but Williams told me not to tell you why he wanted you downtown in class A's today. Please, forgive me."

"Not a problem, babe. Thank you, and I love you too. Would it be possible to take a little nap before dinner?"

"Sure. By all means. Can I get you a blanket or anything?"

"No, I will be fine. Just need to get this uniform off and get comfortable."

As soon as Hawk's head it the pillow he was out. Annie put his dinner away until the following night because he didn't wake up until 0700 hrs. the next morning. When he got up, he was visibly shaken and a little lost. He woke Annie up and asked her what had happened. She related to him that after the promotion party downtown at the department, when he got home, all he wanted to do was lay down and rest for a while.

"Wow, I didn't think I was that tired. Sorry, honey. Thank you for everything. Can we have your roast dinner tonight?"

"Of course, we can. Not to worry. How about some eggs and bacon for breakfast?" Annie suggested.

"Didn't I tell you last night that I was going to the range this morning?"

"No, but I understand. You must eat something, though. What can I fix? How about some Oatmeal?"

"That sounds good and fast. I will take another shower, shave, eat, and get to the range. Should be home around noon. Is that alright with your schedule, babe?"

"Yes, of course," Annie replied.

"When I get back at noon, maybe we can talk. OK?"

"What about? Did something happen yesterday, Hawk, that you failed to mention?" Annie asked.

"Yes, and you are going to be busy sewing on stripes. Seriously, though, we need to talk a little."

"OK! Have a good time at the range. Be careful!"

"Thank you; I will. It is going to be a new chapter for me because I am switching over to a semi-automatic weapon. Red and I are going to try it out today.

"Wow, when did you think of this?" Annie asked.

"I will tell you later, honey."

"Hawk, would you mind taking the Lincoln to the range and let me take the Vette shopping? I miss not having the wind blowing through my hair," Annie said.

"Why, you sexy thing! Who you showing off for today?"

"Oh, there are a bunch of cons down at the market waiting to see momma jugs strutting her stuff," Annie joked.

"Not today then. No way, no how. That car is off limits to you from now on."

"Stop, stop. Ha. I am just kidding you, Hawk."

"Remember you told me to make an appointment to get the Vette cleaned up and checked out? You told me to get it done this week, so I did."

"OK, but without the con thing," Hawk jibbed.

"Love you. See you later, honey."

I almost forgot how this car floats down the road. What a dream car. Even though it is five years old, it still has the looks and the feel, of a brand new Lincoln. A good choice! I like the Corvette convertible, but with the moon roof of the Lincoln, it just makes all the difference with such a smooth ride. Best of all the world's, Hawk thought.

"Hey, Hawk, you got the big tank today. How come?" Red asked as Hawk pulled into the parking lot of the Sheriff's shooting range.

"It's time to blow the dust off, that's all," replied Hawk.

"OK? What's going on, Hawk? You seem really edgy. What? Did you stick the needle in your finger while sewing on strips or something?"

"Yeah, funny dude. We have some serious things to talk about."

"Did you bring your new Glock?"

"Yes, and a brick of ammo and they aren't wad cutters either. The real thing is, so we can see what this baby can really do at high speed."

"Let's do it, cowboy. Although, it's going to be hard calling you Sarg because you don't really look like a cowboy anymore. With that sissy high belt holster, you look different."

"Maybe I will call you Cowgirl?"

"Just one time, try it. I swear, I will kick your ass and then rearrange your brains by shoving them up your butt."

"Sorry, Sarg, but you and your horse posse couldn't do it in a weeks' time."

"Ha, watch me, Red boy. I will put more center nines and tens in the mule target down there than you can all day on your targets."

"Want some coffee, Red? I brought a thermos."

"Sounds good. Thanks. Now tell me, what was getting you so riled up yesterday afternoon and today?" Red asked.

"Just wanting to prove my point and kick your ass here on the range. No, not true, my friend. We have problems, Son. Big problems. I received Intel that the Cartel(s), with emphasis on the plural, are organizing a new wanted poster. Don't know the amount being offered, but the Intel is real, and so our team and our families are in real danger. We can't treat this lightly, Red. It's a real threat, and we need to prepare for it."

"Yeah, and we expected this. We even talked about the possible retaliation," Red answered.

"Yes. We did, but none of us were thinking about the extent of the circumstances. I thought it would be just me like before, but now the problem extends beyond me, Red. It goes to our families and who knows how much further."

"They touch my kids or my family, I will eliminate Mexico as a country," Red retorted. "It will look like a wasteland of cactus, sand, and sidewinders."

"I hear you, Red, and I would drive the tank, but we must make a better plan that will not compromise our families or the team. Whatever it takes, we must plan and work harder than anyone else. I will not let the Cartel get the best of us or our families. I just don't know where to start yet. Any ideas?"

"Is this why you are changing over to that sissy looking automatic?" Red asked.

"Yes. I feel the real need for more rapid fire and the firepower. Red, the other night, I emptied the canon in seconds, squeezing off each round and could not hit all the targets without reloading. I lost time, balance, and realized I was not just putting myself in danger but the team. If I could have put twelve to seventeen rounds into that bird, no one would have walked out and maybe Misty would have been safe. Maybe this poster would not even be on the menu."

"Horseshit, Hawk. I get it with the additional shots, and the faster reloads, but the poster would be just as real. Dead or alive, the familia was crippled, and we are all responsible, along with the FBI, for the results."

"Thanks for reminding me, Red."

"Cannons or no cannons, I won't let you down, cowgirl."

Hawk and Red were standing shoulder-to-shoulder on the range with the bullseye target standing off about thirty-five yards. The next sounds heard were frightening.

"Draw, Red, and then count my holes."

Both men drew their weapons with lightning strike speed. The Glock in Hawk's hand told the story in four times the holes and in fractions of seconds to Red's big Python. Red was exhausted by the time he was finished reloading and shooting while Hawk was already cleaning his weapon.

"See what I mean, son? That big ass cannon of yours cannot compete with the Glock. This is the new wave in our future. While I am killing the outlaws, Red, you will be hiding somewhere and trying to reload as the perps walk upon you. Times have changed, my friend, and so do we. The Glock is a necessary tool that we need to learn to use with as much speed and accuracy as our big guns. Only now we need to push to draw faster and shoot smarter."

CHAPTER 3

FORMULA NOT FOR BABIES

*I*nformation only:

What does the formula and the glass labs have to do with one another? Peru, FedEx, no X-Ray machines. Glass Lab chemical cookers for pure Heroin, Chrystal Meth, Yellow Clay, Tia Stix, Coke, White Clay, and now Black Clay. How many cuts before everyone is dead? From Peru in 50lb bags. Unstoppable. Neither X-Ray machines or drug sniffing dogs have been invented yet—everything was dependent on Intel in the 1970's and 1980's.

Eastside and Westside gangs were being supplied by the various Cartels and Mafias from Mexico, Central and South America, and then came China. *Our border personnel, graft, political empires are being built on the backs of people struggling to survive. Our young and our old and all in between being subject to fallen morals and twisted greed. Where do we go from here? How do we stop this evil monster from destroying our World?*

April rains had just stopped at four-thirty in the afternoon. When Hawk rolled down the side window of the Corvette, it smelled so fresh and clean outside. The taste of the air was perfumed partially because of the wild blooming jasmine along the roadside. That and the smell of fresh cut rosemary. *The spice of life*, he thought. Such an enthralling moment, experiencing the taste and smell of things after a spring shower. Actually, the weather station reported almost a half and inch today. Pretty good for the central coast of California. *Normally we don't see more than five or seven inches all year. This year is not starting off so well, though. Not sure who to blame it on. Maybe the politicians who, on a regular basis, blame us. Or it is because we drive muscle cars, have heavy smoke industries, our waste, or even El Nino? Take your pick.*

Who really knows what the problem is? Unless you make it your life's work studying the ongoing effects of our long-term weather. Industry and of course our muscle cars must be the reason. If it could happen to the dinosaurs, why not us? I don't think the dinosaurs had muscle cars or industry unless you count their constant routines of eat, sleep, and poop day in and day out. Through the history of our planet, governments have tried to collect taxes on everything we own. So, they would rather I just give them my corvette and my home. Of course, they would. I could see a politician expropriating my home, my Corvette, and then asking me to pay double the taxes and charge me a walking tax for using their streets. Hell, they just stole everything. All the while they are driving my car and their moving vans are backed up to the front door of my home. I am ticked off because I just dropped off my property tax bill at the auditor's office. Nothing has changed since last December. No new assessments, nothing. Selah.

Hawk wanted to put the top down, but saw more clouds up ahead and thought better of it. It was only then that he settled down and listened to the beautiful hum of the engine. He imagined the hoof beats of three hundred and fifty horses galloping in time to the piston firing. Deep and throaty it was. Then he coaxed it with a little more pedal. Deep throat became a monster at 5000 RPM. Still a long way from the red line and he was already exceeding the speed limit by forty miles per hour. *Sweet,* he thought. Just for that brief moment, Hawk reflected back to his racing days in Europe. *My 1958 Porsche or this 1967 Corvette?* That was the question because they each had a talent for different reasons. The Corvette was best on straightaways. The Porsche was best in 'S' curves and short narrow tracks. Even the smell of the engine today was intoxicating. Time to back it down and coast into the department. *Cool her off, Hawk. Let her go back to the hum.* Hawk noticed the rain clouds again. They really came in fast when going at that speed. On the radio was a new song playing that was no coincidence. "Slow down; you move too fast, got to make the morning last now." It was called "Feeling Groovy," or something like that. As Hawk's gaze moved heavenward, he muttered a little prayer to God, and got the message! He let go of the tax bill for the moment and made a decision to just enjoy the rest of the day. Hawk was hoping the biggest decision he would need to make today was whether to put the car cover on or leave it off. He decided the cover-up option. *Wish all things were that easy.*

Hawk looked over a couple of cars and saw Misty kind of rocking out to some faint Beatle song. Both of her arms and hands were snapping to the beat. She was totally lost in the moment. There was such beauty in that innocent of moments.

Misty had changed a little after the freeway Cartel bust at Rincon. Anyone would have, given the same circumstances—having been kidnapped by the Cartel in Laguna Beach and beaten for information on Hawk. She was stripped of her clothes and tied up like a wild beast for the Cartel's inspection. Misty hasn't quite recovered to the 100% she was. She is receiving weekly therapy help and light duty for now. Time will tell if she can even make a full recovery. But for now, she is best suited in dispatch. Hawk really prayed that she would back away from the team for at least six months. She needed a long rest and confidence building time. Slowly. However, that wasn't Misty's style. She wanted everything right now. Not tomorrow or next week; she wanted it right now. She was ready to get even right now.

What a beautiful day this was starting out to be. Hawk was determined to keep it that way. Smile all the day long, laugh out loud, and be one with the universe. *Thank You, Lord, for such a wonderful day. Help me to keep it that way.*

It was time for the evening briefing. "OK, guys; everyone take a seat, please. Today's briefing is going to be short. We have current Intel that crime is over for the day, so we can all go home." That was Hawk's answer for keeping it simple and staying happy the rest of the day. Cheers from everyone erupted in the squad room.

"Vacation time, Sarg?"

"No, I just don't feel like kicking ass today. How about all of you? Do you think you can make it all shift long without hurting anyone, stopping anyone and just look the other way at some perp's silly, stupid look?"

"No, sir!"

"OK, OK, it was just a nice thought. I know you got to do what you got to do. A wild bunch of tough looking rogues you all are."

"What isn't such a nice thought is the following information. But first, here is a question for all of you. The first to solve the puzzle gets off early. Maybe. Free coffee at the least."

"It's always free, Sarg," someone said out loud.

"Well, maybe, but I am talking about free coffee at the Big Yellow House or something similar."

"What does FedEx, fifty-pound boxes, and our department have in common? You have thirty seconds to answer."

"The second question is a little easier: What does the letters PC, GW, TS, GLC, YC, ML, CM stand for? Anyone? Come on, people. You should be studying this stuff daily."

"It could be my initials," Misty exclaimed. "Misty Lane on the ML?"

"NO, it is not. That isn't what I am looking for. Someone else, please?"

"FedEx and fifty-pound boxes could be drugs?" answered Carlos.

"Yes. It has come to our attention that the Peruvians are shipping Coke via FedEx air to Los Angeles International Airport in fifty-pound bricks. Real stuff people. Heavy duty and ready for cutting. That fifty pound is pure 100% Crack in yellow clay bricks. Surprisingly, it is fairly cheap in that wrap, but after cutting it with diluents such as simple sugars, or baking soda or worse things like levamisole, which some of you may know is a cow dewormer, translates into millions of dollars plus sick and dead people."

"With that information, who can now tell me what the initials stand for and what else is coming into our area?"

Looking down at Misty, Hawk noticed something in her face change. A flashback perhaps, or seething anger being swallowed down her throat, forcing a look of contempt. Whatever it was, it wasn't pretty. A look back at that horrible, wretched night—and now new discussions surfacing—could not be easy for Misty. Immediately, he felt bad for her and just wanted to hold her and let her know she was going to be alright, but that would not be appropriate. After the briefing, Hawk needed to talk with her, though, and reinforce the positive.

"OK, someone tell me what the initials stand for?" Hawk said.

Carlos stood up and gave the correct information to everyone's nod. "PC-pure coke, TS-Thai STX, GLC-glass lab cookers, YC-yellow clay bricks (pure cocaine), ML-meth labs."

"Thank you, Carlos. Remember this, people. When you know it; you are more likely to hear more, see more, and be better equipped to handle the situations that usually accompany the lingo. You want to be on top of your game? Then learn the game. When you make a stop, look diligently around the back seat and if you have probable cause, pop the trunks. Get with your street people and filter down some information. Be looking for the old chemistry glass lab cookers because that is a sure sign the powder is around somewhere close," Hawk said.

"Yes, sir!" was heard throughout the briefing room.

"Next, be careful out there today and know that with this new Intel comes more traffic. The Eastside gangs and the Westside gangs are for now acting as one with the Cartels and Mafias leading the charge. Dismissed. Misty, please hang back a few minutes," Hawk said.

"Yes, sir," Misty replied.

"Sarg will do, or even Hawk," Hawk said.

"Yes, sir," Misty again replied with a stone face look.

"Be right with you," Hawk said.

After closing the doors, Hawk came back to where Misty was sitting and scooted a chair across from her.

"OK, kiddo, what is going on? What is your pretty little head telling you? And please don't placate me by saying nothing," Hawk said.

"Nothing that you need to know about, sir," Misty said.

"Misty, I warned you. Don't shrug this off. I can see the writing all over your face. Listen, I need you with me and not sitting on the dispatch desk. How are you doing in therapy?" Hawk said.

"Alright, I guess. It just keeps coming back to me. You know … what they did to me and how easy it was for them to trap me," Misty said. Her face held tight the stress and ugliness of that night on the Freeway.

"Have you told the doctors everything?" Hawk asked.

"Not entirely. Why do you care? Do you really think they can put me back together again the way I was? No," Misty said.

"Maybe, Misty. Maybe they could if you would give them a chance to learn more about that twenty-four-hour period. That is why they are there. The doctors want to help you, Misty, and get you back to where you belong," Hawk said.

"And just where do I really belong now, Hawk? I was violated. Violated, drugged, and beaten. Who am I now? Nothing. Just a dirty piece of garbage. Just like the day my stepfather sold me into prostitution. I am nothing, Hawk," Misty said.

"Misty, that isn't going to work. Yes, it happened; yes, it hurts, but you must rise above this. You are not garbage, and you are worth everything to me and this department. You now have a purpose, Misty. A purpose that I will personally help you vindicate. Misty, you are so much better than all of it. Your inner strength is begging to get back out and follow your dreams," Hawk said.

"I know, I know, Hawk. It's just that I feel so dirty, so embarrassed, so worthless. I don't even know why I am here anymore. To be violated in that way has destroyed me. I want to quit and just take a very long vacation and maybe scrub up on my teaching credentials. I just don't think I can do this anymore, Hawk," Misty said.

"I hear you, Misty. I hear your heart is hurting, and I hear how broken you are, but if you quit now, I would not only be losing one of my best deputy's I have but a real friend and someone who can watch my six. I don't know what I would do without you. I also know that whatever you chose to do, you would probably fail at it. If you don't take care of business and be an overcomer on this, it will affect your entire life. Don't carry that unfortunate night's tragedy with you for the rest of your life. Do you hear me, Misty?" Hawk asked.

"Yes. I don't want to, but I do. Will you do me a favor, Hawk?" Misty asked.

"Of course, anything," Hawk said.

"Hold me. Please, just hold me. Nobody will even shake my hand or touch me," Misty said.

"Come here a moment." Hawk stood up and helped Misty to her feet and held her tight. It may have been unorthodox and written somewhere in the playbook that this was wrong, but he determined, after what he heard, that it was mandatory. *We all need to be hugged and touched to feel human and part of the pack at some point,* Hawk thought.

When Hawk brought Misty in close to himself and her body touched his, she let loose with big sobs of regret, bitterness, pain both physical and mental. He let her cry and cry until there was nothing left. She almost dropped to the floor, spent of all energy.

Hawk gently helped her back down into her chair and held her hands, and she wouldn't let go. It was probably the first time he really looked at her hands so close. They were on the small side, a little rougher than normal, probably because of all her karate training and range work. Beyond that, they were very strong and somewhat freckled like her face and neck and chest. Misty was very cute and more than capable of tracking and taking down a grizzly bear if she had too. That was even on her list of things to do in life one day; she later told Hawk.

Hawk gained a lot of respect for Misty for the strength she had in telling him the little she did. Her face had softened for the moment, and her body was limp and not so rigid as earlier.

"Misty, how about taking some more time off. You don't have to spend it alone either. You can stay with Annie and me in our guest room. You are family and will be treated like family. What do you say?" Hawk asked.

"Thanks, Hawk, but let me think about it. I appreciate the gesture, and maybe I could use a little more time off," Misty said.

Hawk almost knew what she was thinking and where she wanted to go and he couldn't let her do it. She was too submissive and afraid what circumstances might deliver.

"Look, Misty, here is the deal: I will authorize your time off if you let me help you pack your bags and lead you out of town so you can regain your strength. Do you understand what I am saying, Misty?" Hawk asked.

"Hawk, I need to do this. I need to avenge myself and shoot their balls off," Misty said.

"I get it, and I will help you do it. However, you are not going that far south just yet. No need. I tell you what, sweetheart, get your game face back on, your body in top strength form, your head tried and true and I will personally make the appointments for you. We will go together. I promise," Hawk said.

"How would you do that?" Misty asked.

"As you know, I have connections, and I will use them and set up those bastards and help you shoot the hell out of them," Hawk said.

"No, that part is all mine. You can shoot their asses off, but the other part is mine," Misty said.

"We have a deal then?" Hawk asked.

"Yes, Hawk, we have a deal," Misty replied.

"Why don't you at least come over after our shift tomorrow morning and spend a couple of days and we can start on our plan?" Hawk asked.

"Are you sure Annie won't mind?" Misty asked.

"I am sure, as long as you don't talk about our plan in front of her. This is between you and me only. Agreed? And one more thing. No sex. Even if I want to," Hawk said.

"Thank you, Sarg. I hesitate to say this, but it's true, I love you for wanting to help me, for holding me and encouraging me. You are like the big, big brother I never had. You have saved my life now more than once. And, don't worry and don't flatter yourself. I wouldn't have sex with my brother if I had one. I know my place," Misty said.

"You're welcome. And I would save anyone's life if given the opportunity too. That's my job, Misty, and you are part of a bigger family here. We all have a responsibility to save lives and help those less fortunate than ourselves and each other. You have already proven you are an overcomer. Work smart now and get yourself back to form. Now get up on the platform and start dispatching. Your contribution is that you dispatch and make it the most important thing you do right now. OK?" Hawk asked.

"Yes, sir," Misty replied.

Hawk's thoughts were a mixed bag of confusion regarding Misty. He didn't know if the Santa Barbara Airport Cartel incident was maybe part of a deeper emotional problem or the fact that she was kidnapped from her mother's home or the showdown on 101 Freeway at Rincon. One or all of those incidents could have put an average untrained person into a heart attack mode, the least atrial fibrillation.

Hawk just knew something was different, but he could not put his finger on it. *Watch, look, listen, and protect her for the moment. I guess I had better call Annie and give her a heads up on our new dinner and house guest.*

"Hi, honey, it's me," Hawk greeted.

"Hi, me. How are you?" Annie replied.

"I'm fine. Just wanted to let you know that I invited Misty over for a couple of days. She needs some restoration and people close to her. She has no family up here, and I think we could be a help to her. Is that alright with you?" Hawk asked.

"It's a little late for my input, isn't it? I mean, you already asked her over, right?" Annie asked.

"Yes, but I believe it is very important. I would do it for any of my team members, not just her. But it is only right to ask you. I didn't mean to invite her without first telling you. I tried! Sorry if I have offended you," Hawk said.

"No, Hawk. It is alright. Please just ask me first next time, so I can think about what to make, how to act, etc.," Annie said.

"Again, I am sorry. Must get back to work now. Love you and thank you," Hawk said.

"Love, you too," Annie replied.

Hawk hung up because he had no further comments, just frustration over a simple request. He understood where Annie was coming from, but she didn't seem to understand where he was coming from and now was not the time to really go into it. *Oh, well. I will put that on the someday-to-talk-about list.*

Before leaving the station, Hawk told Misty, "After work, go home and pack a suitcase and come on over. Plan on a couple of days to just hang out and rest, eat and lounge around the pool and spa."

Now it was time for Hawk to get out and join his team in the village. Before going down into the basement to check out his patrol car, Capt. Joel asked for Hawk to meet him in his office.

"Capt. Joel, you wanted to see me, sir?" Hawk asked.

"Yes, Hawk, come on in. Take a seat. Capt. Gee and I have been discussing your last firefight. You were lucky you didn't get your butt shot off. We also recognize just how much time and effort you have been putting into your teams and the Hit Squad," Capt. Joel replied.

"Thank you, sir," Hawk said.

"I am not saying this to comb your mane, but to tell you to take some time off. You have earned it. Capt. Gee told me he had to have you taken home because you were so exhausted after the fight. I am not asking; I am telling you. Submit to me tonight a time off request for a week," Capt. Joel said.

"Yes, sir. I appreciate that. I am doing the same for Misty. The therapist called me yesterday and advised that she might not make it back to 100% without some time away," Hawk said.

"I agree, Hawk. Get it done."

"Thank you, sir. See you after the shift in the morning. By the way, how is the Sheriff doing? I know he made it through his heart surgery, but what are the doctors telling him now?" Hawk asked.

"They are advising an early retirement. It would be a loss, but his life is more important than this job. It will kill him. Probably kill us all," Capt. Joel said.

"Thank you, Captain," Hawk said.

* * *

After checking out the patrol unit, Hawk radioed Red to meet him at the Chili Factory Restaurant in Goleta.

Hawk: "Unit 4, this is Unit 7."

Red: "Unit 7, go ahead."

Hawk: "Unit 4, meet me at Chili's in fifteen."

Red: "10-4 Unit 7."

* * *

"Hey, Red, thanks for meeting me. I have been told to take a week off, and I told Misty the same. How are you doing?" Hawk asked.

"I am good, Sarg. Very good," Red replied

"Can you continue training both teams and the new dogs as well?" Hawk asked.

"Not a problem, Hawk. Just give me your to-do list, and I will get it done. Are you and Misty going somewhere together? Ha ha," Red said and laughed.

"Get your mind out of the gutter. She has no one up here, so Annie and I want to help her try and bridge the gap," Hawk said.

"Got it. Didn't really mean anything. Sorry. Can you laugh, Sarg? A little maybe, like you used to?" Red asked.

"Sorry, Red, not much to laugh at anymore. Things have gotten out of hand, and I need to bring it all down a few bars. Which reminds me, do you still have that old nag at your place?" Hawk asked.

"Yeah, I do. Need her for a ride?" Red asked.

"Yes, maybe. Just thought of it. Maybe Misty would enjoy some saddle time?" Hawk asked.

"All yours, cowboy. Anytime, you know that," Red replied.

"Thanks, Red. I will try to keep the smile on. Just for you. See you on the range. By the way, amigo, what I was talking about earlier regarding the Intel, it is coming in hot and heavy. Expect a little more business at the hospitals and corner cases. These kids don't know 100% pure coke. I would expect many overdoses in the weeks ahead. This crap formula is not for babies, Red. It's death in powder form," Hawk said.

"You know, I was thinking about that earlier, Sarg. Wouldn't it be a trip to somehow build a handheld X-Ray machine that could look into packages and cartons to reveal drugs? Can you imagine how rich we would be?" Red asked.

"Maybe someday we will have such a tool. For now, how about training Lulu, your Shepard, to sniff out the stuff?" Hawk asked.

"Could be. Could be," Red said as he was walking back to his car, scratching his head. Obviously in deep, ponderous thought over the possibilities of what the future might bring.

* * *

At 0300 hours in the morning, Hawk's nice quiet day was shattered by one of their patrol units stumbling onto a strong-armed robbery. It seemed that a couple of perps wanted in a donut store before opening.

Not that this was a police headquarters of some kind, but the owner did make a nice old fashioned donut and had good coffee every morning for our troops.

Red joined the cleanup crew and asked Hawk what had happened, and what he could do to help. Hawk related in some detail what the perps' mission was and that Bill took a hit in the gut. Henry was alright; just shaken up.

"How did they get into the store at three in the morning anyway? What's up with Henry? Was he hung over, or drunk or something?" Red asked.

"Good old Henry used to have a drinking problem years ago, Red, which landed him in jail a few times for drunk and disorderly. After arresting him one time, I got to talking with him. He seemed like a nice guy that was taken under by alcohol addiction. He had lost his job at one of our local think tanks and about to lose his wife and home. After our conversation, I asked Henry what he would like to do for the rest of his life if it were fun and free. He told me that if he could only stay sober, he would like to become a baker and own a coffee specialty store and have different bread and donuts. So, I made a deal with him. I told him that alcoholism was a family disease and I wanted to talk with both he and his wife, Millie, before he got out of jail. He agreed, and ten days later, he called me from the jail and asked to see me. We agreed that I would take him home and meet his wife and we would just take it one day at a time from there. That was six years ago, Red. Henry went to work at a local donut shop in town and went to AA meetings every single day for a minimum of one year," Hawk said.

"Why so many meetings in a year?" Red asked.

"Because Henry didn't have a part time drinking problem. He had a full-time, everyday drinking problem. If he could drink every day, he could go to a meeting every day until the daily craving was somewhat out of his system. That is the only way, Red. It is like learning a new habit, and that takes repetition and time. Then Annie and I helped organize, a small business loan for Henry and Millie to get them started and the rest is history.

"So, every time you come in here, remember that. This is only one of Henry's ways of giving back and saying thank you to all Law Enforcement. They are very grateful for a new start in life.

"Red, Bill cannot talk much with that gut shot, but what I could understand and putting that with one perp's statement, Bill was looking around the back of the store when these two guys pulled up in the front, demanding to be let in. Bill was accustomed to walking straight in the back door which Henry always left open for us. So, the perps had no clue we were even there. Henry, being the good guy he was, went to the front door and yelled through the glass that the store was still closed and that they should come back in two hours and he would be open. I guess these guys were famished or something because one of them pulled a gun and pointed it at Bill's head. Henry was looking on but didn't know what to do. He said that Bill started to pull his weapon when the perp shot him through the door.

"The perp then opened the broken glass door and immediately began shouting for Henry to open his cash register and put his personal wallet on the counter. Bill, hearing all this, stayed down until the perps were ready to walk out. Bill, then pulled his gun yelling, for the perps to drop their guns and lay them on the floor. They must not have heard very well because instead of dropping their guns, they raised them and started firing in Bills direction. Meanwhile, Henry ducked down behind the counter, grabbing the telephone on the way down. Thanks to his quick action, patrol cars were soon there on all sides of the building. The problem was, Bill got hit a second time in the fracas as did one of the perps. The other was trying to scoot out the front door but was stopped before he could leave the sidewalk. That's all I know at this time. Take it from here, Red. Maybe get someone out front and make sure this area is secured. I need to brief the medics on what we know.

"Will do," Red replied.

I realized that by driving into the scene, his quiet, serene day was over and he had a serious situation that could have been a maze of dead or dying bodies on my hands.

* * *

Hawk: "Dispatch, this is Unit 7. We have an officer down, but alive. Gun shots. One perp down with gun shots."

Dispatch: "Need additional back-up."

Hawk: "Negative, Dispatch, I will be in touch."

Hawk went to Bill to see how he was doing. The medics and Carlos had already started first aid by administering compresses on the stomach wound to help slow down the bleeding. Bill did not look too good and had lost a lot of blood, but Hawk didn't think he was in any critical danger. The bullet didn't exit, and that wasn't good, but he was being cared for.

The one perp that was shot was just hanging on. Linda and Robert both were taking turns doing CPR and chest compressions to keep the man alive. As soon as the ambulance arrived, they pronounced the victim dead. The second perp was cuffed and given his Miranda rights and placed in the back of Robert's patrol unit.

An early morning coffee and donut run ended in tragedy and one of Hawk's team members shot. Hawk felt ripped from reality at that moment. He was doing everything by rote and non-feeling. It kind of felt like he was standing on the outside of his body once again and looking at the entire scene at one blink of the eye. Sounds and energy were muted, only the color was actual. Surreal was the red blood of Bill and the perp laying on the floor. Pools of blood that reminded Hawk of his own head wound when he shot it out with Mr. Blood in the Valley a few months back. *Oh, yeah, the rattlesnake too. Now I remember.*

Red came over next to Hawk and asked if he was alright.

"Yes, of course, I am. Why?" Hawk asked.

"Because you haven't moved in several minutes and you were staring off into space like you were some kind of statue or something. What's going on, cowboy?" Red asked.

"I am OK, Red. Just a little tired of all the fracases, I guess. Thinking about that shootout with Larry Blood up on the mountain," Hawk said.

"Look, partner, you need to go. I will take over here, and you get that vacation slip off to Capt. Joel this morning. OK? I got this handled. Thanks for all the information," Red said.

"Thanks, Red. I appreciated your help," Hawk said.

"Get some rest, cowboy, and come anytime to the ranch when you want to ride that old gray mare," Red said.

Hawk gave Henry a hug and made sure he was alright before leaving the scene, and then got back into his patrol unit and radioed dispatch he was en route.

Hawk: "Dispatch, Unit 7 leaving scene en route your 20."

Dispatch: "10-4 Unit 7. Are you alright? Your voice sounds weird?"

It was Misty's voice in dispatch coming over the radio, which sounded so concerned.

Hawk: "Negative, dispatch. Please advise the captain that I am returning and parking the unit in the garage for now."

Dispatch: "10-4. Be careful!"

CHAPTER 4

DUMPED BY MISTAKE

"Hey, Hawk how're you doing tonight, man?" Red asked.

"Not bad, Red, not bad. Anything new with you?" Hawk replied.

"Not too much. Had to go over to the valley earlier today and pick up some hay for the horses. When are we going riding again?" Red asked.

"Soon, I hope. Shadow seems to be getting a little antsy. He keeps begging me to take him out," Hawk said.

"Yeah, I bet. That was a great ride last month with the Rancheros," Red said.

"Yes, it was. Until whatchamacallit politician tripped over the fire rocks and landed on his hip. That was all we needed," Hawk said.

"Too bad he had to break it," Red replied.

"How'd you do with his horse and pack getting back?" Hawk asked.

"Ah, no big thing, Hawk, just messed up my time with the rest of you," Red replied.

"Good of you to take Roxy back home with you, though. He's a good horse," Hawk said.

Sergeant Cole just walked in from the Lt. Joel's office.

"OK, people, grab a chair and listen up," Sergeant Cole said.

"Hey, Sarg, any word yet on taking off a little early tonight?" Red asked.

"Not yet, let's wait and see how the night progresses. We have some business out at the airport that I will need you and Hawk to secure first. Hawk, take Misty, and Red, you take Carlos. You are team one, Hawk, and Red, you are team two," Sergeant Cole said.

"OK!" Hawk replied.

"Yes, sir," Red replied.

"The four of you, see me after the briefing for more information," Sergeant Cole said.

"Yes, sir," they all replied.

"John I need you south tonight with Jacob, and I need Richard and Larry north. Larry, take Randy with you. Richard, you will be floating, and keep alert in case Hawk or Red needs you for back-up," Sergeant Cole said.

"Got it, Sarg," John said with a big smile on his face. It looked like he just ate a Cheshire cat for dinner.

"OK, keep a lookout for the list of kids on the bulletin board and again, stay off the freeway. Let the CHP handle the roads with the exception of our areas. By the way, I have more complaints of taggers on the overpass at Fairview still at it and throwing the empties down at the cars going in both north and southbound lanes," Sergeant Cole said.

"If anyone catches them tonight, throw them over the guard rail and make them clean up their mess!" Red yelled.

"Yeah, right, Red. We might have another way," Robert advised.

"Well, if you need help, give a call. Be happy to dangle a couple over the edge. Guaranteed they won't tag again. At least not on the overpass," Sergeant Cole said.

Laughter erupted from everyone in the squad room at the thought of how that might look to passer buyers.

"OK, guys, be safe, watch yourselves. No heroics out there. Stay in touch at all times and see you all back here for debriefing in the morning. Team one and two, up here," Sergeant Cole said.

"Yes, sir," they replied.

"Hawk, you and Red, as you know, were selected because of your experience and knowledge of the perps flying in tonight. They are well armed and very dangerous. Don't take any chances that you don't have to. Misty and Carlos, follow their lead. I want you all back in one piece. You will arrive at the back of hanger twenty-three at eleven thirty. Your contact is FBI agent Jack Spartz and Kevin King. Hawk, you know him, right?" Sergeant Cole asked.

"Yes, sir. Unless he has changed his looks again. Last time he looked more like a homeless addict, and I was ready to arrest him for panhandling. Then I realized he was giving me Intel on a couple of the perps in the alley behind us dealing dope. Clever guy when he's dirty," Hawk replied.

"Well, tonight he should be in battle gear with his troops. You four are providing back-up only to the FBI. Is that clearly understood?" Sergeant Cole said.

"Yeah, Sarg. Back-up only," Hawk replied.

"OK, get on the road, guys, and hook up with Jack for up to date Intel," Sergeant Cole said.

"Red, I will see you in the garage. Got something for you," Hawk said.

"OK! See you there in a few," Red said.

Misty approached Hawk and asked, "Hawk, what's going on with back-up only on this ops?"

Misty was a five-year veteran of the Sheriff's Department and had spent several years in the detective bureau working narcotics. So many more women were now involved with dealing and using drugs in the community, and the department was and always has been short of good female officer candidates. Besides Red and Carlos, Misty seemed to be Hawk's regular patrol partner of late.

"Not our collar, Misty. This is FBI all the way. Their intel dates back more than three years with perps who rolled over with Intel on this landing tonight. This is an FBI thumbprint. I need you to stay alert, Misty, and ready for anything. If drug deals can go wrong, which they usually do, you have to be ready to move. You are experienced and know this. Do not let the plane get out of the hanger. If I am not available to stop it; you stop it. Got it?" Hawk asked.

"OK, but I wish I had more information on who these guys are. Do you know what is being brought in?" Misty asked.

"No. Don't worry about it, Misty. Just keep your eyes on everything and anyone that moves wrong or looks suspicious within the meeting. We do not know who is on the list or is an agent, or who is part of the end run. Consider all of them the Banditos. Jack should be able to tell us what his team is comprised of. Just get yourself at peace inside, alright? Breath deep and steady. You seem overly excited tonight," Hawk said.

"Hawk, I just failed a test today that I didn't want to fail," Misty said by accident.

"What kind of test, Misty?" Hawk asked.

"A stick test," Misty answered.

"What the hell is that? You're good with your baton." Hawk was clearly thinking all police work tonight.

"Hawk, I think I am pregnant," Misty said.

"What! What? Why didn't you tell the Sarg earlier and get off of this detail? Why are you telling me this now anyway?" Hawk asked.

"No. I need to keep up and not let this get in the way, Hawk," Misty said.

"Damn it, Misty, do you realize the position you are putting us all in?" Hawk asked.

"I guess not. Sorry, Hawk. I will calm down and be ready. Don't worry about me. I am fine," Misty said.

"Just a little late for that, Misty. Crap! How can I keep my eyes on this ops and on you too? What the hell are you thinking?" Hawk asked.

"Hawk, don't worry. I will have it under control. The moment I get into this patrol car, I will be good," Misty said.

"Have you told Hank yet?" Hawk asked.

"No. Not sure it's his," Misty replied.

"What? Are you kidding me? Your mind is too warped out on this, Misty. You need to go tell the Sarg right now. Is there anything else you want to talk about before I leave?" Hawk asked.

"No, Hawk. Please, I am trusting you not to share anything with anyone. I told you because I trust you. Hell, if I can trust you with my life every day on the streets, I can trust you with this Intel," Misty said.

"Yes. You know you can, but that is not the point here. This is too important of a detail tonight and sharing this in the last minutes before a drug bust that has the potential of going wrong could spell disaster for everyone," Hawk said.

Hawk was visibly upset, and this operation just had its first unexpected curve ball thrown at it. Clearly, this was not a good start to the evening. Hawk knew more about all the details on this mission than anyone else present, and tonight was a big night. The entire operation required complete teamwork and trust. Being alert and on point. Too much depended on everyone's mental and physical toughness. *Are we ready?* Hawk thought. *Not with this current Intel.*

"Not to worry, Hawk, I will be ready. You just watch yourself. I am sorry. Sorry for not saying anything earlier," Misty said.

* * *

The ride from downtown to Goleta was very quiet. Hawk didn't know what else to say or do with Misty. His mind was speeding on events that led up to this moment and Misty's predicament. It was Hawk's experience that deputies that chewed on unchecked personal problems were bad and a formula for disaster. Hawk knew that he would have to keep an eye on Misty and the rest of the teams. More now than at any other time. His question was, could he safely do it?

One of the events that kept repeating itself in his mind was the night that he and Red came across a couple of young kids on the outside of a liquor store in downtown Goleta. He and Red were watching the kids from a local bank parking lot across the street from the store. Red, looking through the binoculars, related to Hawk that they looked as if they were getting ready to run into the store and rob it. The kids were just too hyper looking. Every few seconds, one or both would look around as if to see who was walking up to the store. Or looking for cops driving down the street. Red noticed the taller of the two had something sticking out of his back pants area. Just barely hidden by the kid's sweater.

"I think he is armed, Hawk," Red said.

"OK, let's wait until they enter. You go right, and I will go left. On my signal, I will enter first and assess and disarm the taller one if I can," Hawk said. "Dispatch, Unit 7 at 7348 Hollister, Mandy's liquor store. Watching two suspects. Well, advise."

Dispatch: "10-4 Unit 7. OK, let's go." It looks like they are headed in. Hawk turned off the dome lights. (That way, while opening and closing the car doors, no interior lights would be glowing, which otherwise would reveal not only the team's position but who they were.)

After crossing the street, Hawk and Red took their positions on either side of the front door of the store. Looking through the glass windows on either side of the door, both Red and Hawk could see both boys. The taller of the two kids, the one possibly with a weapon, was closer to Red, but Hawk saw the shorter of the two boys with a pistol already in his hand, standing behind a rack of potato chips closest to the register on the left. Hawk signaled to Red what he saw, and Red signed that both boys had weapons visible.

As a custom, when one sees drawn weapons in the hands of perps, it is not the time to casually walk into a building and show off one's quick draw skills and techniques. Both deputies knew what the possible outcome could be and their first concern was the safety of all patrons and employees of the store—locate the perps and protect everyone else.

Hawk gave the hand signal to go in with guns drawn. As they did, Hawk yelled out to both perps to drop their weapons. "Drop them now!" Red demanded. At the sight of the deputies and their guns, the cashier and the only patron in the store dropped down to the ground. The shorter of the two kids swung around as if to fire his pistol at Hawk. Not waiting to see the whites of his teeth, Hawk opened fire, wounding the kid in the right shoulder. He dropped to the floor screaming, and the gun lay a couple of feet from his head. The kid on Red's side froze. Red yelled at him again to drop the weapon. He bent down, placing his pistol on the floor as if it was made of glass; Red's black steel Colt Python Magnum following the kid down and back up again. The kid was visibly shaken, and his pants were showing signs of wetness in the crotch area. Both deputies walked slow and precisely up toward both boys. Hawk told Red to stay on point. "Something is wrong here. I feel that there are more or someone we missed," Hawk said. Red looked around and saw a young teenage girl crouched in a corner in the back of the store near the cold freezers. Red's perp was looking toward her direction as well.

Meanwhile, Hawk picked up the wounded kid's weapon and stuck the revolver in his belt. He told the screaming kid to put his other hand on the wound; then he handcuffed the kid to the potato chip rack with the arm he was shot in. Running away would be impossible dragging that chip rack. Weapon redrawn, Hawk walked over toward the girl while Red handcuffed his perp. As Hawk walked toward the girl, the taller handcuffed kid yelled out in Spanish (*ocultar el pistol*) for the girl to hide her gun.

"Watch out, Hawk, she is armed," Red warned.

"Understood!" Hawk replied. With his big Smith & Wesson Magnum 357 held out in front of him aimed directly at the young girl's head, Hawk drew down on the girl and told her both in English and Spanish to stand up (*lavantese lentamente e no pistol e las manos vacias*) slowly with hands empty. She did as he said all the while, hypnotized at the cannon in her face. The gun she had was on the floor close to her feet.

Hawk noticed that she could not have been older than fifteen or sixteen. All three of the kids were, in fact, about the same age, and all three looked to be of Mexican descent. *What the hell were they thinking?* Hawk wondered.

Red walked over to the cashier and made sure he was alright along with the only other girl in the store. Red asked to use the store's phone to call in the situation and to have dispatch send an ambulance.

The team made sure that the only other patron in the store was safe, took her statement and that of the cashier. They finished taking pictures, measurements—all of which was the start of their report. The smaller of the two perps said his name was Sergi; the taller boy said his name was Steve, and the girl was Macy. None of the kids had Identification, so the team had to take their word for it until their parents could be notified. Sergi, the one with the hole in his right arm, was treated and released to Hawk's team's custody for transportation over to juvenile hall. All three kids were booked into the hall after the team had taken written, signed, and recorded statements. The three kids basically had the same story of wanting to run away from home and dominating parents. They got the guns from their fathers' offices in San Diego, stole one of the family cars and made it as far as Santa Barbara and got hungry. They forgot to steal any money from their parents and thought robbing a liquor store would be the answer. Of course, they had no intention of shooting anyone—just scare people and grab the money—until Red and Hawk walked in.

That night in the liquor store was the beginning of a three-year investigation that led to this night's FBI sting. When the FBI got involved, Hawk didn't know, but they did, and Hawk and his teams then learned that all three kids were part of a family of drug lords out of Mexico that was trying to lay claim to the Santa Barbara Valley area. Those three kids were transplants in our community and trying it on for size. As beautiful as Santa Barbara is, this little town had a long history of drug penning by Cartels out of Mexico, Central and South America. Heroin and pot being the boxed cache. It was true, gangs, assaults, burglaries, murder and drugs were all on the rise in this little sleepy Spanish village known as Santa Barbara.

When Hawk and the team arrived at the back of Hanger twenty-three, the atmosphere inside the patrol car was all business as Misty radioed in their 10-20: "Dispatch, unit teams are standing by at The House." The House was the designated call sign for the airport hangar where team one and two would be meeting with the FBI team. For the first time in a long time, Hawk didn't want to be on this mission. He just didn't feel like it was going to be a good night for the good guys. Partially because of Misty's personal news prior to leaving the station, but also because of the weight of the Cartel and its long fingered, retaliation ability. That arrest of the three kids three years earlier was only the beginning of Hawk's troubles and his feelings tonight, but he and the team were ready, present, and in position. Jack sauntered up to the side of Hawk's patrol unit, half-scaring Misty to death. She was almost at the point of yelling out, which would not have been a good thing. Even though the plane was not down yet, other ears were sure to be close at hand and watching and listening. A drug drop about the expected size as the one planned for tonight was not going to an unknown trip. Many in the community's savory would be expecting it in the morning.

"Hey, Hawk, how are you doing?" Jack asked.

"Good, Jack. How about you?" Hawk asked.

"Doing well, thanks. Who you got with you?" Jack asked.

"Jack, this is Misty, and you know Red and Carlos, right?" Hawk asked.

"Yes, of course," Jack replied.

"Good. I need your teams at both ends of the hanger and you to stop any enclave of traffic that tries to break free from inside the hanger. One back door on the west where you will be positioned." Hawk nodded and then asked Jack if he was sure he didn't need the Calvary inside to assist the boys in black. Jack half-laughed and replied, "Not this time, Hawk. I know your background in the case and your abilities to handle the situation, but my guys are ready for this one. Everyone in the know had been waiting a long time to put the Los Zetas Cartel away. You are best helping us by securing our six. We have everything in control." Hawk acknowledged Robert with a quick nod of the head and an audible 'you got it, Captain.' At the same time, Hawk knew better. This night was only getting started.

Hawk gave last minute instruction checks to the team members and asked Misty one more time if she was with the program.

"I am here, Hawk. All here," she said.

"OK then. Engines off, keys left in the ignition, and shotgun racks unlocked and ready. Dome lights off and radios turned down to mute. Please, don't forget to turn the volume up if you need to use the radio in an emergency. Red, you take your team and cover the West corner of the house and the exit door and Misty, and I will take the East corner. The bird should be landing in about fifteen minutes. Stay down, but make sure you have the right bird. Bravo-Charlie-Eco, one Niner, two, two, Niner. A San Diego-based Lear. Check. One last thing, kids; make sure you keep your heads down. I won't be doing any rigor mortis reports tonight. Got that?" Hawk said.

Both teams took their positions on each corner of the hanger and were ready. Hawk looked down at Misty and could not help but wonder how her life got so messed up lately. She and Hank were not married yet, and Misty said she didn't want children for a while. She said she was on the pill. So how did her pregnancy happen? Inside, Hawk knew to keep an eye on her and the rest of the team. Let the FBI handle the assault and capture one of Mexico's largest drug Cartels, The Los Zetas Cartel, with active Mexican Military bounties on the Lord himself, Raul Hernandez Lechuga. His capture or death was carrying a hefty bounty of fifteen million pesos or one million US dollars. His young illegitimate son of one of his teenage captors, Sergio Pens Solis, could possibly be with Raul tonight. It was Sergio that Hawk had shot in the liquor store three years prior with Red. All three of the teenage kids involved in the attempted robbery of the liquor store were runaway teens from two different Cartels. Sergio was part of the Los Zetas, and Maria Arellano's father was the Lord of the low life Tijuana Cartel. Same bounty payment, either Mexican or American, but there was bad blood between the two Cartels. Not just the turf war, which is the most common place, but because Maria and Sergio were betrothed to each other. Raul and Fernando were two of the unhappiest fathers in Mexico sworn to kill one another. The problem was, Sergio and Maria had a child between them, which muddied the waters. The Rio Grande was cleaner than they were.

* * *

The sound of a small jet making a pass over the airport was heard. It must have been the one Hawk and his team were waiting for, and he prayed that their cars were well out of sight and unseen by the jet. Even though they had parked between hangers, it was not perfect. The jet passed overhead at a low angle as if to realign itself with the runway. Jack was listening to the tower giving the pilots landing instructions for runway number 036 which would have put them in a north heading when landing. They would have to taxi back to the drop zone hanger if they wanted to unload. Everything was going just fine after the landing. The jet reverse thrusters came on, and the brakes were slowing the sleek

Lear down. It looked like one of the newest models out. Why not? The Cartels were rich. *Maybe I could put together a syndicate and buy the thing at the government auction real cheap?* Hawk thought. He drew his weapon and flipped open the cylinder to check one more time. Misty heard him and looked up from her prone position on the tarmac. Yes, Hawk was worried because it was at this juncture that almost anything could happen. Surprisingly, nobody saw their patrol units or anything shiny laying on the ground. Hawk's thoughts were that they were too high and the lights on the Lear were pointed straight ahead of the nose about one hundred yards, not down where they could have picked up a nice shiny pair of handcuffs or shiny badges.

The Lear was slowing down even more on its approach to the hanger and Hawk felt himself tensing a little. He quietly told Misty to take the safety off and be alert.

"What's the problem, Hawk?" she whispered. "Are you expecting too?"

"Shut up, kiddo," Hawk hissed back. "I expect you to follow directions."

As the Lear got closer, Hawk noticed the loading door open on the left side of the bird. He figured they might just throw the bricks down and jet off in a hurry if they saw any sign of trouble. His other thoughts were on the tower. Hawk forgot to ask Jack who was up there that evening. *Could he have checked them all out?* Hawk thought. It would not be the first time, though, that an overworked, underpaid radar jock took a bribe for a quick landing and takeoff. Almost like a touch and go scenario, and he earned himself a quick ten thousand. A couple of heads were peeping out of the doorway of the Lear, and they didn't appear to be Susie Steward of the mile-high club. It looked more like Sergio's friend and Sergio himself. Wonderment of wonderments.

"They have come back to serve the time they both missed because their respective parents had big money in Santa Barbara and surely paid for their release and exodus from our community with a promise not to return. But here the little rodents were. Come on, Jack, we have got to do this tonight and make it right," Hawk said.

Hawk's mind was racing in retro gear when he thought most of his problems of attacks on his family and himself were coming from the Panthers up north, not the Cartels down south ever since Red and he, by chance, that one cold night in Goleta, happened upon a couple of kids looking and acting strangely at the liquor store and subsequent wounding of Sergio and the arrest of three Cartel family members.

Chance or no chance, it came down to this night and this time and the outcome of the Lear Jet that was about to pull into the hanger. *Would justice prevail or death on the streets of our community?* Hawk thought.

Inside the hanger, Jack and his team were positioned behind boxes and inside a waiting van with the Mexican restaurant manager's right arm handcuffed to the steering wheel. He was there because the Cartel needed him and he just drove into the arms of the FBI. He was told to use his left arm to jester hello and was told that if he did anything to warn the Cartel, he would be the first to be shot.

"Your kids will grow up with goats, essay. Comprendo?" One of Jack's agents held the gun to the drivers back.

The Lear came into the circle between hangers twenty on one side and twenty-three. The pilot's intent was to turn into the hanger once he got straightened out. The turn was slow and purposeful. *I am sure that the pilots are overly cautious this night with more than ten million in heroin gold and pot ready to be dropped off,* Hawk thought. The party market and addicts were huge, and the demand was enormous. The distribution would be completed within the week up and down the coast.

Several Mexican looking and speaking agents resembling the county's local dealers and pushers were standing by the van and some closer to the hanger door. They wanted clear shots through the doorway of the Lear if it came to that point. As the Lear was making its final turn toward the open hangar door, it lurched a little, dropping a few bricks of pot. It spilled on the tarmac, confusing the agents. They froze; they were not prepared for the incident. The Cartel expected help and bodies running over to pick the pot up, but no one moved a muscle. The Lear engines were so loud the ground could not hear what was being said, but Jack yelled out, "Ole Senoir! Coma Estas." The driver of the van kept waving his arm like a prom queen debunked by the master of arms. It was too cheesy for Hawk, and he thought Sergio noticed it too. He yelled something and the Lear engines started back up to a roar again. The hombres in the jet's doorway started shooting into the open hangar door instantly. Then they tried to reach up and close the jet's door, which could not be closed fast enough, thus staying up. Anyone standing up to grab it would have been shot. The FBI agents inside the van jumped out and shot the nose gear tires out and one of the main tires, crippling the jet from moving more than at a snail's pace.

As soon as Hawk and his team heard the shots being fired, they moved up to the front of the hanger and stood by, just watching the exchange of gunfire from the open Lear's door and the hanger. Some grunt peon from inside the jet tried to reach up and grab the door latch and was shot before he even touched the swinging leather tether. Everyone on the ground fighting the fight lost sight of what the pilots were up to. Hawk saw the pilot's window open and a semi-automatic machine gun come out and let loose a rapid volley of bullets which rained down on the FBI agents in the hanger doorway. He saw an opportunity to nail the pilot and further cripple the Lear from moving any further, allowing him and his team to end the hail of bullets coming from both ends of the jet. He then took aim and shot into the window of the semi-auto weapon, and it dropped to the ground below the jet's window. The pilot slumped over partially in the window.

Hawk gave orders for Misty to follow behind him and stay close. They both ran around the opposite side of the jet and grabbed a pair of wheel locks and shoved them in place between both mid-ship wheels. The Lear stopped, even though the engines were screaming. Bullets continued to flash toward the hanger from inside the jet. Suddenly, Hawk's team pummeled the jet's doorway with more bullets than their local armory. Hawk's guys were prepared, that's for sure, by stopping any further activity from the inside of the jet. As soon as the gunfire from inside the jet stopped, Jack gave the command over the traditional pompous bullhorn for all of the crew and passengers, one at a time (*Venido salir el avion. No pistolas*), to come out of the jet without weapons. Both in English and Spanish, several times and at intervals, the same command was repeated. Finally, one at a time, six people came to the doorway, hands up and each walked down the stairs, one behind the other like a family of ducks. All but two who were still missing. Hawk hadn't seen Sergio or Flavio walking down the plank. That meant they were either dead inside the Lear or waiting.

Hawk motioned to Jack, who was now standing in front of the driver, and related in sign language that he was ready to extract the remaining occupants. Misty was standing to Hawk's right rear under the fuselage, and he was directly under the doorway. He could hear sounds of talking inside, but not very clearly. Getting the go-ahead from Jack, Hawk engineered himself, so his gun was sticking into the doorway, and he began firing. First toward the pilot's cockpit and then center and tail section. Screams emitted calling for a truce. (*No mas disparar.*) Soon, a white flag or shirt was swinging outside of the door radically, back and forth. Hawk recognized Sergio as the flag bearer and ordered him to walk down the stairs very slowly. He did as ordered but not quietly. He was looking directly at Hawk, cussing and swearing in such a low brow Catelyn dialect that Hawk was getting embarrassed: "You, Pendejo. Screw you, man (Carajo joderse. El Pendejo)." Hawk grabbed his left leg and pulled him down off the stairs and put him face-down on the ground. Handcuffed, Hawk was ready to put his white shirt into his mouth when he got another order. No one had Hawk's six. He yelled for Misty but no answer. Misty was silent. Not wanting to avert his eyes from the jet's doorway, Hawk heard a second order from behind him. It was a man's voice.

Team two was still in place, and four FBI agents were down, firing from the open hanger doorway, and nobody saw the missing tall kid from the liquor store, Flavio Santiago, who had jumped down from the starboard side of the co-pilot's window. With all the noise and the tilted wing of the Lear nearly on the ground, he managed to sneak up on Misty and put a nine millimeter to her head. She dropped her rifle and stood there with teeth grinding and waiting for the silencing of a bullet. Flavio had her around the neck and was nearly choking her out. Misty's eyes were obviously scared, waiting in anticipation of Flavio's next demand or action. (After the incidence, she told Hawk that she knew she was going to die and didn't know what to do.) Flavio yelled at

Hawk, "Pendejo, drop your gun, or I kill her (Lo Hare Matar a Sus)!" Misty saw Hawk's face contort and his eyes narrow, which could cause a wild boar to take heed and run in the opposite direction. Misty had seen that look one time before, and it scared her to death. Misty knew what was coming and closed her eyes not wanting to see anymore. Death was nearer to her than her next breath.

"Poncho, I don't drop my gun for you or anyone else," Hawk replied and started walking toward him, and Misty with his magnum pointed at Flavio's head—his eyes got wider and wider than the night in the liquor store. His skin lost its color, and he was yelling at Hawk to stop, or he was going to shoot. Before he could chant for the third time, Hawk pulled the trigger and shot Flavio between the eyes. He dropped like a lead balloon straight down to the tarmac, letting loose of Misty in the process. Misty dropped to her knees, knowing that Hawk's shot was mere inches from her head. Tears began streaming down to the ground as the realization of how close a call to death she just had. Her shaking was uncontrollable as was the flood of her emotions. She was choking and trying to breathe at the same time.

In seconds after watching the drama unfold, Sergio began screaming more vulgar words at Hawk for killing his best friend and Captain in the Los Zetas. He swore vengeance for Flavio's murder and Hawk's head on a bull's horn. He yelled at the top of his lungs, "I am going to kill you, birdie (Lo hara se pajaro. Lo hara el pendejo. Se hijo de puta)."

After picking Misty up and holding her for a second, Hawk looked down and asked if she was alright.

"Thank you, Hawk. I owe you one."

"I will make sure to collect someday. Stay here and keep your gun at that doorway. Can you do it?"

"Yes, I think so," she said.

"Lean against the stairwell."

"OK," she mutely said, and Hawk turned to go up the stairs to see who else was inside.

The rest of Hawk's team and what was left of Jack's team came closer to the open jet door as Hawk walked up after reloading. Apparently, Hawk loved his S&W canon, but could clearly see the need for additional firepower such as a Glock or Sig Saur and what they could provoke. Each clip can hold twelve bullets of hard firepower, especially with the copper jacketed hollow points. *I could easily carry six additional clips on my belt for any war. Guess I will look into it tomorrow,* he thought.

Hawk hesitated in the doorway of the jet with the flashlight of his kills in his left hand and stuck it in the doorway, illuminating the interior of the jet and his right hand firmly holding his six-inch magnum. Peering inside the left quickly, then to the right, the only thing he saw was stacks of dope and a couple of dead bloody bodies, including the co-pilot sprawled out between the cockpit and the kitchen area. The one and only woman present and dead was an unfortunate stewardess. The show-and-tell half-naked women providing alcohol, joints, and no doubt a little sex to the gun-toting dead roaches on the floor was now a memory. Surprising how stupid some of the warlords are. To allow their army to get drunk and stoned in the middle of a very costly job. Having a party before the work. Hawk looked back at Sergio who was now face down on the tarmac still screaming his head off and his hand securely handcuffed behind him. Each lobo was hooked by plastic ties to each other to prevent runners. *It would be all run, not just one. Heaven forbid! If one lost his pants or shoes, they would all go down in a heap. Ha!* Hawk actually laughed at the imagined sight of it.

Red, meanwhile, came up while Hawk was surveying the damage on the interior of the Lear. Red went straight for Misty to make sure she was alright. Carlos came up and followed Hawk into the jet.

"Ally-ally auction free!" Carlos jibbed.

"Come out! Come out, whoever you are."

"Sorry, Hawk, it looks like we wasted all of them. No one left to play." It was a nervous laugh, but they both managed to smile.

"Looks that way, doesn't, Carlos? Another win for the good guys."

"Amen! Amen!" Carlos chanted twice. The next new passenger inside was Jack. "Whew," he gutted out. "This is what we have been waiting for. Look at all that shit. Bales of pot, bricks of heroin, and freshly cooked cocaine. Wowa!"

"From your vantage point, which one of the perps kicked out the bricks that started all of this party?" Hawk asked Jack.

"The pilot was trying to slow the jet down and gave too much brake, which caused the bird to jolt and hiccup that lost the merchandise out the door," Jack replied.

"You mean to tell me that pile was dumped by mistake?"

"Yeah. I guess the crew had started stacking the shit in the doorway to get it out faster. They didn't expect the bird to buck like that."

"I would really like to see Sergio's father right about now!" Hawk exclaimed. "He must know by now that the entire shipment was a bust, including his son, the captain, and his soldiers."

"All lost or going deep into the penal system to never be seen again. You got that right, Hawk," Jack said.

"Listen, Jack, do you mind finishing up on your operation so I can get Misty back to the office? I can leave Red and Carlos and even bring in one other deputy. I can fax you all our reports and tomorrow we can collaborate if you need to."

"No, not at all. Go ahead, Hawk, and thank you very much for all you and your teams did. How is Misty?"

"She will be alright with a little time. You are welcome, Jack, and I am very sorry for your losses. Red and Carlos will hang with you awhile to help with the coroner's reports and pictures. I just know to get Misty back. She went through a lot today."

"Yeah, man. Go, go, Hawk. I should have known, Hawk, that you would clean up and save our asses today." Hawk winked and flashed a thumb's up and walked back down the jet's stairway. As he reached the end of the stairway, he turned around to take one last look at the Lear jet. The jet was full of holes and blown out windows. *Don't think it would be worth very much at the Government Auction. I am going to pass on this one*, he thought with a smile.

More units arrived along with a couple of vans to transport all the dope and the perps back to the FBI offices. Meanwhile, Hawk's two teams picked up all their gear and loaded everything back into their patrol cars for the slow ride back to the courthouse office.

Misty kept thanking Hawk between choking back tears and then went silent for more than half of the trip back. It was just like they had started out with the mission. Silent.

In his report, Hawk noted the following additional facts on the Cartels they encountered:

Los Zetas just lost two pilots and a brand new Lear Jet. Millions of dollars shot up. Millions in dope that would never hit the streets. Six total dead on the Los Zetas side and six more, including Raul's son Sergio going down for a long, long time in our prison system.

Many years later, Hawk learned that Raul was killed in December of 2009. A second Lt. Raymundo Morales was captured in 2009. Flavio Santiago was killed that night at the airport. Sergio served his time, got out, and was recaptured for more bad drug deals in 2009 and will probably be very old when or if ever he gets free. The business has made him an old, old man before his time.

The Los Zetas suffered many losses over the years as having many other Cartels, but somehow, like living cancer, they keep on percolating. It was obvious to Hawk that Los Zetas had lost a great deal of money, drugs, sons, daughters, and pride that night at the Santa Barbara Airport. Their standing in the drug world slipped a little.

Hawk's talons clawed deep into the Los Zetas chest that night, and even today, they are still bleeding at their losses.

There is but one problem. Sergio and Maria, had a couple of children as did Flavio. The war is not over. All of their sons and daughters have vowed vengeance. Venganza!

CHAPTER 5

GLOCK TIME

For the next month, both teams met every day before their shift duties for practice. In the beginning, it was all shouting, screaming, and scolding in trainees' ears. It was crucial that the teams started out right and gain confidence in themselves, the weapon, and each other. "You are out of kindergarten, people!" was Hawk's favorite disclaimer, which he yelled at the top of his voice.

The Glock was the choice of every member of the team, including Red. Eventually, he got the message and took the matter very seriously. Red, in fact, became the second most proficient with the Glock. Not unexpected. Hawk remained number one. Again, not unexpected. As the team captain, he had to show the way into the light. Semi-auto firepower would make the difference one day to each member of the teams.

Like any combat team, Hawk's special sniper squads were becoming renown for being the Glock Time Deputies. Every extra moment beyond studying was spent on the firing range becoming the fastest, experienced Glock shooters in the industry. Hawk's rationale for this emphasis was to let the Cartels know in advance that no one would be better than his team and any thought of retaliation on the Airport ops the previous year would be sheer suicide—as the popular saying goes, "Don't step on the snake and try to cut its head off or you will die trying." So far, the intimidation was working. The Glock time team was becoming known statewide. The word was getting out, and so were the scores, the proficiency marks, and the trophies.

Hawk even demanded that the entire families, especially the wives or husbands be safely trained on how to use the Glock semi-auto gun. No surprises, no mistakes, and they had one hundred percent success. Even some of the older teenagers understood the importance of what it means to be a law enforcement family.

"Alright, teams. Today is show and tell. I hope you are all prepared for an all-day session on the importance of our work. Each one of you has undergone extensive training, and throughout the day, you are going to get a chance to recall everything you have learned and show me your work skills. This is it, guys—your final test. All my yelling, and telling chilling remarks can be turned in after today. If you have learned anything, it will be to save your own lives and the lives of others.

"You must be skilled in every weapon in your arsenal down to the safety pin holding your badge on. It could save your life one day.

"Today you will have a chance to use everything you have been issued and more. Water is available to all of you in limited supply. This training session is going to be in real time. As if you were in the field all day doing battle. If you have to pee, hold it. I will be polite and give you all ten minutes, starting now. When you hear the whistle, come running. When you have completed your marks at all stations, then you may take a breath but no more. Your duties will continue until the last whistle is heard by both teams.

"Your first target is maximum seven rounds in seven straight line targets at twenty-five yards. Then holster. You will be allowed two misses beyond the eight.

"Station two: seven rounds, seven pop-ups at thirty-five yards. When finished, holster and walk over to the table. On the pop-ups, you cannot miss. If you hit a civilian or cop, you will finish the course, but you will not qualify until you repeat the entire course today. If you can't, then you will be disqualified until such time as you can complete the course in time.

"Station three: remove the clip and dislodge the chambered round. Break down your weapon into eight parts. Hands up when finished. You will be inspected and authorized to reassemble but not before you have answered a series of questions on your Glock. If you have answered correctly, you can proceed to the next station. The questions are no different than what you have studied all along. Weight, size, ammo description, magazine capacities, trigger pull pounds, etc. Why are we carrying Glocks?

"New whistle. Move to station four: Seven targets in semi-round position. Empty clip. Reload and complete firing. When finished, holster.

"Proceed to your final destination, station five: Complete the perp and civilian course without mistakes. When your Glock is empty, holster. Proceed to hand to hand course. You must down your opponent in less than thirty seconds and move to the next target where you have a choice of baton strike or knife thrust. You must deliver a death blow to the dummy. No perp must regain consciousness to hurt us from behind. There is no option. As long as you have active fire in front of you, there is no time to stop restrain.

"Is everything understood?"

"Yes, sir!" both teams yelled back.

"One last thing. A new real-time wrinkle. The opposite team will referee for the active online team. When finished, reverse roles. No breaks. You must ALL hit your targets with an eight or better. We will score from behind in the tower. No civilian casualties on the pop ups and your hand-to-hand opponents are real Karate trained athletes. You must down your opponent within thirty seconds or less. Beware, they will be moving and don't want to be put down. You must be decisive and quick. Who is better? If you are downed, get back up and finish the course.

"When you have finished, get back into formation and reverse roles on my whistle only.

"Are we clear? Each team has a total of ten people. You ARE the best."

"Yes, sir," came the shouts.

"Alright."

Each team was lined up to run to the first target station. No one knew who was going to be called to the line first. Team A or Team B?

"Time starts now: Team B, advance to the white line."

Off went the whistle. "Start. The clock is running."

Everything was quiet on the western front so to speak. Santa Barbara drug trade was down. The narcotic officers under the tutelage of Lt. Gee were making good long strides in the cleanup and getting drugs off the street. For a short time, Hawk and his teams were winning the war on the drug trade.

The only people getting high were the base jumpers in the foothills behind Santa Barbara known as the Ceilos.

A few school kids were still determined to experiment with pot, but the county's education was stepping up on all fronts.

All was good, and Red received his sergeant stripes and was the official commander of strike team two. Misty was promoted to Sergeant along with Carlos on Red's team, and both Misty and Carlos were the official team medics. So, along with monthly proficiency qualifications with the Glocks, they had to be up on the latest first aid methods and carry a split kit in their backpacks for emergency patches.

"Something new this week, people. Back to the range in full gear. Compliments of LAPD; we now have a new light weight bullet proof vest." Getting used to wearing it was very challenging and the ones to complain the most were the girls. Misty told Hawk one day that she was cutting holes in front of her vest. He laughed at her until one day at the range two of her top buttons popped open, and he saw two black points of a bra that should not have been there.

"What the hell have you done?" Hawk asked. "Did you cut holes out of the vest for your breast? Is that your bra I am looking at?"

"I told you what I was going to do. If you don't like it, Hawk, try growing some tits and wearing this stupid heavy flak jacket over them."

"But your lungs and heart are now exposed. The vest can't protect you."

Then Misty came up with an idea: "Call the manufacturer and tell them to custom make a vest for women. We need them in B, C, D, and Double D cups for me. I will be the first to buy one. Then I will sew the tit patches back into this old one. But until then, my tits are out. Period."

"You got it, Missy. As soon as we get back to the office, I will be calling," Hawk said.

"And by the way, Hawk, why are you looking down the front of my blouse at my breasts? What would Annie think?"

"Why aren't you buttoning up your shirt? Come on, Misty. Any man would be looking. All the crew does. When you walk by, everyone is looking at your bum. Misty, you are beautiful, and you have a... Never mind. You're one of the boys, but it stops at your neck. Everything else is exciting and refreshingly beautiful compared to those targets out there that we shoot up every day."

"Oh, thanks, Sarg, for comparing me to a flat front still target. Real nice," Misty chirped.

"Come on, Misty. Give me a break here. Besides, it is getting hot out here, and it's December."

"Why should I? This is more fun getting your spurs up."

"OK, I got it. Now let's get back to the office. Need you and Red for a patrol meeting. New Intel chatter coming in finally. We have more work to do, kiddo."

* * *

It was 2100 hours, Friday night on December 5th and Hawk had both teams in the squad room for a briefing.

"New Intel we are getting is for real. The Mexican Cartels are on the move. We need to be mentally ready as well as physically. I am very pleased with all of your weapons qualifications and your stamina to finish the physical training courses. Congratulation! You have all passed.

"OK, you are ready. Now stay ready. Don't let down for a moment, people. Believe me when I say that the Cartels are not letting down and their patience is wearing thin. They want revenge, and they wanted it yesterday. Watch each other's backs out there and treat every call with respect and just as important as why you have trained so hard.

"Now that we have the Intel that the Cartels are on the move, be vigilant at work and in your leisure times as well. If you have children, be mindful of where they are at all times. I cannot emphasize enough; do not let your guards down. Not for one second.

"OK, let's get out there and keep the community safe."

Lt. Joel had been promoted this year, along with Red, Misty, and Carlos. Hawk felt it was good to have him as their watch commander. Capt. Gee made it too, and he just walked in to talk to them.

"Glad you're still here, Hawk. I need to talk with you and Joel. Can we use your office, Joel?"

"Sure. Would you like some coffee or soda?"

"No, thanks," Capt. Gee replied. He closed the office door behind him and took a seat next to Hawk.

"Guys, we have a serious problem heading our way. More Intel from San Diego and Los Angeles. A large shipment of hard stuff is coming into our area sometime within the next two or three days.

"The shipment will not be alone. Two large semi-trucks are expected. One filled with the dope and a few soldiers; the other with an army that will be heavily armed. I was told that this was going to be the turning point for the Cartels."

"As in who wins?"

"Yes," Gee said.

"Now we can get the bodies from Los Angeles, Ventura, and San Luis Obispo Counties. I am sure we can match armies but we need to discuss options, and we don't have much time to do it."

"How much is known throughout the office?" Capt. Joel asked.

"Only high ranking on a need to know. We don't want chatter anywhere," Capt. Gee related.

"Good," Hawk said. "Because there is one who is chattering out there."

"Stop, Hawk. We know your concern. Don't go there. Your concern is being kept silent to those ears."

"Thank you," Hawk said.

"Can this convoy be stopped outside of our county to avoid injuring life and property?" Capt. Joel asked Gee.

"No. The drop zone is here in Santa Barbara, and we don't know yet where the army is boarding. They might wait to board until they get closer to the end zone," Capt. Gee said.

"I am afraid this operation is all in our lap—with outside assistance only."

"Gentlemen, know that our two teams are ready, but obviously, we are not enough. So, when can we call for additional Calvary?" Hawk asked.

"We, the Sheriff's Department, have watched your teams, Hawk, and they look good. You have done a good job with them. However, we recognize that you are going to need more help. Much more to quail this war. As soon as we get the Intel, we will pass it on to you, and make the calls," Capt. Gee responded.

"Yeah, I realized it last year at the airport. Sergio yelled it in my face. Vengeance was his. So how do you suggest we handle this?"

"Hawk," Capt. Gee replied, "I will have four detective units taking turns following the tractor trailers and two jumping ahead, if need be, to the on-ramps. As they pass the ramp, we will follow for a short time, then either turn off or pass off to shoot down the freeway. They will never figure out if anyone or anything is following them. We further need to keep these trucks out of the residential areas if at all possible.

Once we know that they are for real, the stop needs to be effected in the Carpentaria area. Off of the freeway somewhere near the cemetery or high school."

"And if you can't lead them, then what?" Hawk asked.

"I think we can if we stage an accident on 101 and detour everyone off 101 and down El Camino Rd. From there, we can re-route them where we want," Capt. Gee said, pointing to the county maps.

"Do you have an alternate plan should that one fail? Capt. Joel asked.

"No," Capt. Gee replied. "It won't fail unless they want to make it an all-out war on the freeway."

"You know it might be easier to keep them on the freeway and save more lives."

"What do you mean, Hawk? Where are you talking about?" Capt. Gee inquired.

"Well, I was just thinking. What if one of the detective cars uses a silencer and flame resister and blows out one of those big trailer tires. You see gators all over the freeways anyway because these guys run retreads that just won't hold under loads. So, we blow the tire a half-mile after the top of the Rincon grade. The trucks won't be able to see down the bottom of the grade, so the CHP can hold traffic down there and a mile north on 101. I don't think they would realize any problem until it is too late. We will come out of the ditches and over the fences, swarming them like bees. No one could get out of the back of the trucks fast enough. Even if they had dropped down hatches underneath or hatches up top, we would have tagged them. No escape from any opening. Plus, there are open fields to the west and industry to the East."

"Hmm!" Capt. Gee was deep in thought. "That sounds like a logical plan that we could control with minimum civilian casualties and without alerting them. Like you said, Hawk, flat tires occur all the time, and we could control all civilian traffic in both directions without them even realizing it until it is too late."

Capt. Joel jumped into the mix. "Wouldn't that depend on the time of day the trucks are rolling?"

"Yes of course, but our Intel says they would be rolling at night. Even if it was daylight, they still could not see behind them on the downgrade or around the turn in front," Capt. Gee reminded them.

"Well, I have a big if," Hawk said. "What if these guys have a tail behind them that we are not aware of? They could be stopped in our traffic control a half mile behind, down the grade, with a radio that would tip our hand. What do we do then? How do we ferret out a tail?"

"Good question, Hawk," Capt. Gee responded. "The only thing I can think of is having one or two of our detective units hanging back a couple of miles, and make their way up with wireless set-ups and ping for radio and cell traffic. We would start as far back in the valley prior to the grade."

"That might work," Hawk said. "As long as they didn't keep radio silence. Crap, this isn't going to be easy, but we have very little time to plan and be more creative. Any night flyers available? Something black, kinda hawkish and armed to the teeth with rotary blades sharp enough to cut off the top of the trailers?"

"I can call the base in the morning and find out. Again, the CHP has both a fixed wing and rotary they might lend to the task. I will make the calls," Capt. Gee said.

"Any more questions, tonight?" Capt. Joel queried. "If not, then we should let Hawk get out to his patrol units. Hawk, you probably should brief them in the morning after shift."

"I agree. See you both tomorrow, and we can put the finishing touches on the program," Hawk said.

"One more thing, Hawk, keep your teams ready. We might be called on to help all the way down the line. We are not the only city involved. Over the course of the next few months, this shit will be coming in by boat, plane, and trucks. I know that Art at LAPD will need your teams work there."

"Have a good and safe night, Hawk."

"Amen."

Why did I say that I wondered? Amen? OK, Lord, I am listening. Please give me directions, Father. We need to protect a lot of people here, Hawk thought.

The early morning shift came very fast. A few citations issued, one barking dog complaint, two burglaries in progress that were false, and two drunk drivers arrested. Quiet evening for sure. What kept Hawk busy were mission questions and the mission itself. *What If he made the wrong decisions? What If our casualties were heavy? What If?* Hawk thought.

This was the most difficult time for Hawk because he arrived at work as the sun was setting and was ready to go home at sunrise. 0600 hours was not the time for more coffee, but time to cuddle up with Annie in bed. Today, however, more meetings were scheduled and a briefing with both crews as to the new plan and the Cartels.

Back in the squad room, Team A and Team B were back to their raucous behavior, and Hawk had to raise his voice a couple of octaves to be heard.

"Alright, people, listen up. Misty, would you please smack a few heads to shut the troops up?"

At that, everyone stopped talking and stared at Misty, hoping she would walk by. Everyone knew she had the best bum on the force. So did she.

"OK, people, we have a new situation. All of you are going to be working tomorrow afternoon. This is important, so take notes, please.

"Intel has it that the Cartel is on the move, heading north to Santa Barbara with two (2) tractor trailers filled with dope and soldiers. They will be heavily armed, and their mission is more to hurt us than the dope, I think. Although the quantities that I have heard are staggering, sales and distribution are in the millions.

"A plan is in place to stop, arrest, and terminate their mission. You will be told tomorrow at our final briefing scheduled at fourteen hundred hours. I will need everyone to go home now, rest, and prepare yourselves for all that you have been training for. I would suggest you eat lightly, drink lots of fluid, and get your gear in order. Strip, clean, and oil your Glocks.

"This is for real, guys, and the mission that needs to be accomplished must be done with precision and accuracy. If you are inclined to pray, I would be doing it tonight."

On the drive home Hawk, was very much aware of his need for God's help. He felt way over his head. The Cartel was much larger than he is and had no problem killing anyone. They were callous and bloodthirsty demons as far as he was concerned. Was he really able to do this? Certainly, not without God's blessings. He was hoping that Annie was home and could just listen to his insecurities tonight. He needed her strength for a change. He also needed sleep.

Hawk was tired; that was for sure. It had been a long couple of weeks with the training and team qualifiers. Then the long planning meetings for the best way to take out the Cartel. Now Hawk was second-analyzing everything. Had he thought of all the wrinkles and shortfalls that possibly could happen. He wouldn't know until the fight unfolded. Maybe if he got online tonight, he could learn more. Worth a try.

As Hawk drove up the driveway at home, it was a little past 1100 hours. He noticed four young girl scouts at the front door. Annie was apparently buying cookies again this year. *Silly, but I hope she got the lemon cookies for me. Love those high cholesterol buggers,* he thought. Then he instinctively began looking around for the mothers of the girl scouts. *Where's the cars? Nothing. They must have walked from within the neighborhood.*

Annie waited at the door for Hawk and saw in his eyes and his walk just how tired he really was. She was glad he was home. Hawk had called earlier and related the ops that was in progress and approximate time frames. All things being equal, this day should be a nice quiet time at home. Annie already had the fireplace going, and breakfast was on the table. Maybe they could take a shower together again and conserve water. At least that used to be what they told the kids—when all they wanted was to get close. Finding time in a busy household of kids, meals, work, and chores made it almost impossible. Annie felt that sex was just as much a part of everything else that the attempt was well worth the extra effort. If we could do everything else, we could make time for us.

Annie knew how tired Hawk was, but her idea was to make sure that after making love, Hawk would want to sleep and not wake up for at least ten to twelve hours. At least not until his next shift.

It worked. After the shower and lovemaking in the oversized natural stone shower with the new rain head in the ceiling and dual station adjustable seven-foot shower heads, Hawk was now in bed and sound to sleep. Nothing would wake him up. He was so tired that eating was not an option. Annie felt just a little bad about that.

Hawk was totally spent. There was nothing left but tired, weary bones. Annie was looking down on him and loving her man very much. Sweet, loving, kind, affectionate, a good provider, handsome, and strong. What woman would not want Hawk as a husband? She stroked his forehead while he was asleep. He never even moved or twitched a muscle. "I love you, Hawk, very much," she whispered. "Please take better care of yourself." Selfishly she admitted in a quiet breath, "I need you forever."

Annie got up from the side of the bed and went back into the bathroom to clean up. In doing so, she affectionately looked over at the custom-made elongated shower bench where she and Hawk had just made love. She felt like she tricked him into making love. Hawk was so tired he couldn't finish. She did and felt closer to him than ever.

When Hawk went to sleep after the shower, it was 1 p.m. Why was the phone ringing at 6 p.m.? Who in the hell was calling at this time? Annie answered the phone on her side of the bed.

"Oh, hi, Capt. Gee. What? Oh, no, no. Capt. Gee, he is exhausted. Hold on, sir; I will try and wake him. Hawk. Hawk wake up, honey, it's Capt. Gee."

"A new emergency, Hawk."

He was drowsy but rolled over and took the phone from Annie. "What? What the hell, Captain? What happened? Better yet, how and who leaked the information? I am telling you; Numb-nuts is in this somehow. Yes, sir. I will get ready and be there in thirty minutes. I will call the teams on my way in. Take the phone Annie and start calling the teams."

"What is going on, Hawk?"

"The Cartel is on their way days early."

"Oh no. What are you going to do?"

"Annie, I need you to start calling the teams. Start with Red while I am getting dressed, please."

"OK. I am so sorry, honey."

"Yeah, please just call, babe."

Hawk ran into the walk-in closet and grabbed a pair of walking shorts and tee shirt. He slipped them on, grabbed some athletic socks and put them on. Next, he put his fatigues on and laced up his military boots. On his way out of the closet, he grabbed a couple of handkerchiefs shifts and stuffed them in his rear pockets. He then grabbed his holster gear and put it on. He walked over to the locked top dresser drawer and took out his Glock and six ammo clips. Annie handed him his favorite red, white and blue Corvette racing baseball hat and gave him a big kiss.

"Hawk, please be careful. Come back in one piece. Call me when you can, please."

"Annie, I didn't tell you every detail of this mission, but I want you to listen now. Lock every window and door in our home. Do not leave. Put your shoulder holster on and cover it up with a shirt or jacket. Give Geri a call next door and ask her to come over. Smitty should be there too. Tell them to get armed. This is not a drill, Annie. It's for real."

"OK. But you are scaring me."

"Do not allow yourself the pleasure of fear. Take control now. You have practiced over and over, and you are very proficient at this. You can do it, honey. Keep the TV on but low enough to be able to hear noises outside. If you hear anything suspicious, call at 911 at once. There will be a unit in the area all night. Love you!"

As Hawk was driving, he grabbed the handle of the bag phone and began dialing Red.

"I'm assembling my team as we speak," Red answered

"OK, good. See you soon at the barn."

He then dialed Misty's number. It rang and rang, but there was no answer.

"Come on, Misty, pick up! Dam it!" Hawk exclaimed!

He tried again. Nothing. His mind was racing and trying to figure out where in the hell she could be after yesterday's long training and work. She has to be dead out. Hawk wondered if he should take the time to swing by her home. *No, get to the barn,* he thought. He then dialed the non-emergency phone number for dispatch and asked Carla if Misty was in the office.

"No, Hawk, she has not shown up yet."

"OK, do me a favor, Carla, and keep trying her number."

"Yes, sir."

Hawk drove into the detective's parking lot across the street from the office. He opened his trunk and pulled out his flak jacket, one thirty-round Uzi like 9mm clip, and his second Glock—which he stuck into his flat back empty belt holster. Gloves and baton, and he was ready.

Hawk was more than half way to the office door when he realized that he had forgotten his tactical hat. *Oh well, I will get it later,* he thought.

He fast walked into the squad room where he met Capt. Gee and Capt. Joel. "Red just came in and is in the locker room," Capt. Joel said.

Hawk opened the conversation with "What the hell happened tonight, sir?"

"Our Intel was a partial ruse. Someone decided to move the schedule up and get the trucks moving a day early. We agree, Hawk, it sure is smelly, and I am ordering an investigation into the matter to make sure it is not on our end," Capt. Gee said.

"Good," Hawk replied. "Anyone see Misty yet?"

"No!"

"Red, get everyone assembled in the squad room and come back in here. OK?"

"You got it," Red replied.

"Capt. Gee, I don't think we can improve on our plan, and I don't see how we can make our plan work on such short notice," Hawk said.

"We don't have a choice, Hawk. We got to make it work."

"What about the Intel units lagging behind for chatter?" Hawk asked.

"They were dispatched one hour ago to the valley," Capt. Joel replied.

"Has anyone contacted the CHP for air support?" Hawk asked.

"We have one small rotary spotter available, and that's all," Capt. Gee said.

"OK, I guess we will have to go with what we have then. All the teams are assembled. We should probably get them up to speed," Hawk said.

All three men walked into the briefing room, one behind the other. Hawk entered first and brought the attendees to attention.

"Sit, please. OK, people, you are here because our mission has been stepped up a couple of days according to our Intel. I am sorry that the rest is something you will only dream of until we get through this night. Capt. Gee is going to relate the Intel that we have up to this time, and I need all of you to pay specific attention to the designated stop location. Capt. Gee, sir," Hawk said.

"Everyone, we have two semi-tractor trailers en route from San Diego. The first purportedly is crammed full of the hard stuff. The second, if our Intel is correct, has an army of Cartel soldiers heavily armed. Expect both trailers to be armed to the teeth.

"Once the convoy and any trailing cars or trucks are up over the Rincon grade at least one-half mile, one of our unmarked units will do a drive by and blow out a couple of trailer tires and in effect, stop them pretty much in their tracks.

"In case you might ask, the shooter will have a silencer, and fire suppressor on the muzzle to keep us unknown should anyone be watching or spotting for the trucks, which you can count on.

"All of your training comes down to this night, guys. Expect a lot of return fire from paramilitary Cartel on the roof of the tractor trailers, underneath on the ground, and they may even have drop-down metal protection shields. So, bring some armor piercing ammo in your bags. I cannot stress enough that this is a must stop operation. If we have to light up the block, I will do it. Is that understood?"

"Yes, sir," the room echoed. The chalkboard vibrated for a moment afterward.

"Any questions?"

"Sir, do we havta wait for fire on the ground to melt these guys?" Cpl. Carlos asked.

"Yes. Intel is Intel but never concrete enough to kill innocent people. This entire ops could be nothing more than a fishing expedition to see how awake we are. But neither can we risk hard junk hitting the street in such quantities. So be where you are with eye and ears on the targets.

"Sergeant Hawk, it is all yours. God speed, people," Capt. Gee proclaimed.

"OK, gang. Any more questions? None? Then I have one. Has anyone seen Misty, anywhere?" Hawk asked.

"Yeah, Sarg. Misty told me the other day that she was thinking of going to see her mom in Laguna while on her next break."

"Thanks, Linda. Do you have her mom's phone number?"

"No, Sarg."

"OK, thank you."

Even though Hawk would not have Misty on this operation, he still needed a specialist in putting band aids on.

"Carlos, do you have anyone in the ranks that can assist in medical?" Hawk asked.

"Yes, sir. I think Richard is current on all apps," Carlos replied.

"OK, would you contact him and get him down here, please? Do not share anything other than uniform requirements, weapon, and flak jacket," Hawk said.

"Yes, sir," Carlos replied.

"Oh, one more thing, Carlos. Make sure you check his kit out and see that he is up to date with everything.," Hawk said.

"Will do, Sarg," Carlos replied.

"Those of you so inclined, stick around for our prayer. Those who are not, you are dismissed," Hawk said.

To Hawk's surprise, nobody got up to leave. Silently, Hawk gave a look up and a thank you to God for all who stayed.

"Father, please keep special watch over each and every member of this operation tonight. Keep them all from harm as well as their respective families. We claim victory now, Lord, over our adversary and Your blessing over each and every one of us. Thank You, Father God. Amen," Hawk prayed.

Hawk's prayer was short and to the point as usual. He was pleased down in his heart to have heard the resonated Amen from nearly all who were there in the squad room this night.

"Capt. Gee, what is our timetable?" Hawk asked,

"As far as the Intel coming in," Capt. Gee related, "the convoy should be packing up the Rincon grade in about two hours. We have enough time to get set. Nothing yet from the scramblers waiting in the valley."

"OK people, Off and On," Hawk said. "Let's move'em out. We are going signal file, normal spacing to our target area of the industrial park buildings off Carpentaria Ave. In case you have forgotten, they would be on the east side of the freeway—where the mountains meet the sea," Hawk said.

"Yes, sirrr!" most of the troops shouted.

Capt. Gee was in direct contact with the CHP both north and south of the Rincon grade. They each had three units standing by to first slow traffic down, then stop traffic in either direction for as long as it would take. They were prepared to detour civilians back to Ventura and reroute to interstate five. No one knew how long this ops would take.

Hawk tried to swallow a yawn, but it still half closed his eyes. He was obviously tired, but the adrenaline was finally beginning to pump through his veins, waking him up in degrees because of the mission awaiting him.

The teams arrived at the designated target location and unloaded all the equipment. Trunk lids were open in all vehicles as each deputy took his or her readied gear out and began the tasks of hooking belts, snapping snaps, and adjusting gear. In mostly a straight line, each deputy would check the rear flaps and snaps of the front deputy's backpack and so on until all was completed. They took their places on the ground behind the fence next to the 101 Freeway. Hawk looked down the line from his vantage point on the other side of the freeway with his team. The only thing protecting them was their firepower. No fences, no culverts, no bushes or rocks. A normal guard rail was all they had. A small diversion above our heads. If a bullet hit the metal rail, it would shatter the nerves, for sure, of everyone in the line. Behind them came the sounds of the ocean waves. Hawk thought he could smell the night ocean air, but the creosote post in front of him was too overpowering.

The deadline was nearing, and the traffic chatter was suggesting the load would be in their approximate within five minutes.

"Red, are you ready?" Hawk asked.

"Ready, cowboy," Red replied.

"Capt. Gee, both teams in place and ready, sir," Hawk said.

"Good. We are ready here as well. Good Luck, Hawk," Capt. Gee said from his tactical vehicle located in the IHOP parking lot in Carpentaria.

"Thank you, sir." Hawk had a funny thought come over him all of a sudden. *Why am I calling Gee and Joel sir all the time? Who the hell do they think they are? Both are almost the same age as me. I might even be older. They should be calling me, sir. Tiredness brings blindness sometimes,* Hawk thought. *Just disregard that stupid thought!* Hawk was military oriented, and he liked it that way. Give respect where respect is due.

It was just a little past eleven when Hawk saw the first truck rolling ever so slowly up and over the grade. Then number two. Next were two cars slowly following in the fast lane slightly behind the trucks which were in the slow truck lanes. The two cars waited and finally picked up their speed a little and began their pass. Hawk and his teams could barely hear the "pop pop" sound of the gun. The blowouts were a bit more substantial. The cars kept their speed the same and continued northbound on 101 as if nothing happened. The two truck drivers, on the other hand, were struggling to keep the rigs from jack-knifing. They jumped on their brakes and came to a stop just as predicted. Both drivers exited the trucks, looking to see what the problem was. When they realized that both trucks had duplicate blown trailer tires, they began to run back to their respective units. While running, Hawk and his teams could hear them shouting in Spanish at the top of their lungs, "Emboscada, emboscada (Ambush, ambush)." Within a moment or two after that, all hell broke loose. Cartel thugs came from every direction out of the truck cabs and both trailers. Guns were firing in every direction with little or no target in mind or sight. Then I gave the order: "Fire at will!"

The sky truly did look like it was lit up just like the 4th of July only in December. Tracers from the armor piercing heads were flying at warp speed across the median, striking wheels, tires, metal, windows, and bodies. Then, over the bull horn, another command, "Stop shooting! Stop shooting!" in broken English was heard. All firing stopped in and around the two tractor trailers. After that, an announcement was heard over a bullhorn, "Stop your firing. Stop your firing. We want Deputy Hawk to come forward."

"Deputy Hawk is not here. He is at our Headquarters!" Red yelled back from behind the trailer.

"Then bring him here. Now."

Red replied, asking everyone in the trucks and trailers to lay down their arms and walk to the center of the freeway, with hands in the air.

"I think not amigo. Bring me Hawk!"

Within a second or two, the side of the first trailer opened up, revealing a woman tied to a chair with ropes around her neck, middle, legs and ankles. She was half naked, with no shoes, or clothes on other than panties and bra. Her head was facing down, and her hair was curly and tangled and down in her face.

Hawk was watching the scene unfold from behind the guard rail. This girl looked too familiar.

"My God! It's Misty. How in the hell?" Hawk quietly spoke.

The guard standing beside the woman grabbed the girl's hair and yanked her head back revealing a bloody face and neck. Yes, it was Misty, and she had been severely beaten. In the guard's other hand was a can of gas. The guard kept repeating "Bring me Hawk!" as he slowly dripped the gas from the can onto Misty's head and shoulders. She wasn't making a sound. Misty must have been drugged out or beaten unconscious or was already dead—maybe all three for all Hawk knew at this point.

"What are we going to do, Sergeant? We can't just let her stay like that."

"Shut up and let me think," Hawk snapped. His teeth were barred nearly shut as he snapped out orders and his eyes were again slits like a lion ready to attack his already wounded prey. The kill—that is all Hawk wanted.

Hawk began to take his uniform off to the surprise of his team members that were looking at him and waiting for the next order.

He got off his boots and socks, pants, and shirt, leaving only his tan walking shorts and white tee O'Neal surfboard shirt. He took that off and began smearing dirt and road oil, whatever he could find on the ground near him. The wooden post holding up the metal barrier had been soaked with creosol and aided in making his clothes look filthy dirty. He then rubbed as much of the creosol oil as he could over his face, bare chest, and stomach. He asked for Billy to come up beside him from down the line twenty yards or so. Billy did a low crawl over to Hawk's position and asked what he could do.

"Billy, did you bring Big Bertha?" Hawk asked.

"Yes, sir, I did. Right here, sir."

"OK, see that guard holding Misty's head up? That is your target. Take the son-of-a-bitch out the moment he tries to light any kind of incendiary device. Shoot him between the eyes. Got it?"

"Yes, sir."

"I want him to fall backward into Red's lap. You tell everyone to kill every last son-of-a-bitch there and let no one near or point anything at Misty. Keep her alive, Billy. If I go down prior to any glitch, shoot'em anyway."

"Yes, sir."

Hawk was putting all of his confidence into Billy, who was by far the best sniper his team had. Then he radioed Red.

"Red," Hawk whispered over the radio. "Get your team ready. I am going in after Misty. Billy has orders to take the guard out, and I want you to take everyone else out."

"You got it. How are you going to play this?" Red asked.

"Just watch me," Hawk replied. "However, if these bastards get on to me, start shooting. Don't wait. Just get Misty safely out of that damn truck trailer."

"Roger that, cowboy," Red said.

Red's words somehow invigorated Hawk. Cowboy! That was a handle he put on Hawk a long time ago while riding at his ranch in Goleta. They had been roping calves for branding and castrating. Red had liked my moves and accuracy, and thus he never stopped calling Hawk that. Now was the time to show such stupid brilliance. *OK, Cowboy, do it!* Hawk said to himself.

Hawk motioned for Billy to reach behind himself and grab the brown empty beer bottle on the ground. He crawled backward a few feet, grabbed it, crawled back, and gave it to Hawk. Hawk took the beer bottle and then put his now dirty, filthy tee shirt over his hair draped down his back and then his baseball cap which he had totally forgotten to replace with his tactical hat. He never made it back to his car at the office.

Hawk looked up at the sky and said, "OK, Lord, I really need Your help on this to get Misty out alive. I am asking You for Angels of mercy around Misty and shields around us both. I am putting on Your full armor, Lord, from Ephesians 6:10. Amen."

Hawk raised up and climbed over the guard rail, yelling, "Go to hell, man!" He was yelling at the police and staggering like a drunk man, holding an empty beer bottle. He even fell down a couple of times on his face, not allowing his two Glocks to show in his pocket. He got up a third time and started cussing out the police for waking him up and telling him he couldn't cross the street. "Who the f**** do you think you are, man? Screw you pigs." Hawk was more than half way to the parked trucks with all eyes on him. The Cartel idiots were half laughing and baiting Hawk on. No one had recognized him yet. Not even Red or any of the good guys. Hawk kept shouting at the top of his lungs, and when he got close enough to the open trailer door, he dropped his beer bottle in front of himself. Then he acted like he was crying over the spilled beer, and reached behind his back, pulling out both Glock's. With the precision of a surgeon and the swiftness of a snake strike, Hawk fluidly swung the Glock's forward and began spitting out bullets as fast as he could pull the trigger. From behind him, Billy was doing his job as was the rest of the team—cutting down every standing, sitting, or laying eggs soldier. The only two people left in any of the vehicles were Misty and Hawk—who had now reached the open doorway of the trailer. He looked right and left for any movement and sent one more round into the guard with the canister. Right between the eyes. Behind him and filled from floor to ceiling were bales of dope. That's not what Hawk was concerned about. He ran over to Misty and slowly brought her head up. He felt for a pulse and found a very faint one in her neck.

As Hawk was taking his hat and tee shirt off, he began Thanking the Lord. "You are our Mighty Lord and Savior. You are the most high God. Thank You, Father."

Hawk found a corner of his tee shirt that was still white and began cleaning the blood and dirt around Misty's eyes, lips, and mouth. Hawk, kept repeating his thanks to God. With his knife, he started cutting the ropes away from Misty's body. The ropes had cut deep into her skin and cut off a lot of the blood flow from her wrist and feet. She was in a great deal of pain and made little noises each time a rope was cut, and the painful removal occurred. Finally, every fiber was removed, and Hawk picked her up from the chair and handed her to Red who was waiting on the ground by the doorway. All the while this was going on, the teams were cleaning up the weapons and doing a quick inventory of the trucks. Last but not least, they checked for life itself.

In all, ten thousand pounds of dope were removed from both trucks and forty dead Cartel bodies. There was no one left in the Cartel to give an account of the night's activities. It would be up to Misty, when she recovers, to fill in all the blanks and open questions: What happened and how did it happen? When was she kidnapped?

Red, handed Misty off to a waiting ambulance team that was called in by Red's team when the shooting was over. Hawk yelled after her, "God's speed, Misty. Hang in there, girl. Do not give up." Hawk was clearly stricken by the entire operation. All the training, long hours, seeing Misty tied and doused with gas, and the threat of being burned alive. The gun fight and Annie. Annie? Hawk had to call home right away and make sure she was alright. He asked Red for his radio to call Capt. Gee and ask if he would call Annie. Hawk soon learned that Annie was fine and that Smitty and Geri would be staying in the house until he got back home.

The time was early morning, and the darkness was only marginalized by all the TV cameras and flashing bulbs from every direction. What was, a few hours ago, a serious battlefield seemed now like a three-ring circus—two trucks and trailers surrounded by a sea of humanity gawking at the horror show that had occurred here earlier. Hawk had to leave. He had to get cleaned up. He had to change clothes. He had to just cry aloud to God. Hawk needed God to just hold him close. He was totally spent.

Capt. Gee ordered another deputy to take Hawk home after seeing him and hearing from Red's debriefing what occurred. No detail was left out. Capt. Gee knew he had a very delicate situation on his hands with Hawk. Hawk had no more change left in his pockets.

CHAPTER 6

SECRETS CAN KILL

It seemed like the vacation would never end. Hawk's mind and body were eager to get back to work. The time off, however, did allow him the time to finish a few projects like painting the back door, deep cleaning the pool and filter; of course, there was spring pruning and leaf raking and just general work from sun up till sun down. Oh, where did the time go and where was the restful vacation? Or did Capt. Joel say resist pollination? The bees were hard at work right about the time, making sure Hawk and his family had the sweetest oranges, pears, grapes, apples, plums, and roses. *Yes! Go, bees. Doesn't matter; it's all fun and part of the good life that only ten percent of us in this world can attest to,* Hawk thought. He bent his head next to the grape vine where Annie and he would play like Adam and Eve in the garden of Eden. Hawk, with his tee shirt off, and Annie, with her bikini shoulder strap off, would take pictures, holding the bounty of green clusters of little tart wine grapes. Even though they didn't drink wine, the tart little devils were good.

While in the garden, a thought occurred to Hawk: *Lord, please give someone the courage and abundance to help feed the poor and sick around our world.* Then he heard, "What are you doing, Hawk, with the dollar in your pocket? Pick up the phone and join Billy Graham's charity work. Is that so hard?" Hawk was convicted right there in his little garden of Eden to share with Annie what his newest revelation was for them to follow-up on.

For the first couple of days that Misty was staying with them, Annie and Hawk got a chance to know her better and learn of her childhood growing up years in South Laguna Beach, California. That was one of Annie's favorite haunts growing up as a kid herself. They found out she was a surfer chick, so they had a lot more in common with Misty than they had thought. No end to all the big wave and wipe out stories. It was fun just taking a little time to share and pray and get to know her better. After all, she was one of Hawk's partners. Annie was a little concerned when she felt that something else was wrong but couldn't put her finger on it. She felt like Misty was hiding something that really was bothering her. Wednesday morning came, and Misty told them that she was headed back down to her mom's in Laguna Beach to just relax and spend a little time in the sand and water. After talking about surfing, she thought it might do her good to jump back into the waves and feel the old acceleration thrill of looking down the face of an overhead wave and cutting into a tube ride. Whipping the board around from the bottom of the wave to the wave crest is a real killer. Nothing can get your heart pumping faster than looking down into the abyss of Davey Jones Locker and then taking control of your destiny by pure strength, agility, experience, and guts. Either you make the turns and maneuvers, or you are face-down and shoved to the bottom of the ocean very quickly. Just the thought of dropping down in a wave made Hawk's mind jump in automatic spasms of joy and fear all at the same time. Somehow, he was on his old ten foot Yater surfboard taking the drop. And then, not a fraction later, He was thinking of Misty paddling out for the big set. As a man dreameth of such things, Hawk would have wished for that moment to be her surfboard as she lay down on it. Just feeling her breast and thighs rhythmically moving while paddling out for the set waves. It was true, Misty could really fill out a bikini, but Hawk had his own darling. Annie could fill out a bikini too, very well. But alas, sanity and reality crept back into Hawk's mind as he was harnessing the energy of an extension cord and plugging in a power tool to re-hinge a garden gate. However, he would, for the rest of his natural life, be cursed with thoughts (not actions) of loving other women. It was a curse because he loved Annie so much and was devoted to her for life. There would never be another woman in his life than Annie. His one and only prayer was to love her to the end and be the last to go. *That! And please take the stupid daydreams away,* Hawk thought. He learned that was the key. If he gave those thoughts to God, immediately when the thoughts occurred, He would take them. The bondage and slavery of the thought were broken for that moment. Never could Hawk let those thoughts take control and make a nest as it were in his churned up flaky mind. *Concentrate, Hawk, you have work to do. Everyone else can play, but not you. You made your choice to be a married man, with kids, a mortgage, nice cars, and responsibilities. You have a job, so just think about that for a while. Oh hell, why did I ever have to grow up anyway? Concentrate, Hawk, those screws won't get put back in right if you don't. Do you really want a crooked gate? God help me!* Hawk thought.

This was the ironic side of his thoughts: True he was trained in pilfering glance(s), or straight looks at people to see hair color, clothes, marks, scars, and tattoos. It was part of his business and survival as a cop. In three seconds or less, they were trained to see the entirety of a person, top to bottom. *Especially front to bottom? No, Hawk, get back to the gate. You don't have to make a case for yourself here. Or do you?* he thought.

Annie and Hawk had a fantastic BBQ the previous night at home prior to returning to work. Their time together had flown by and in truth, he wished that moment would last forever. Time for love seems to always be stolen by the need to fix, be an adult, employment, children, things, and more things. *Why does life seem to be going by so fast the older we get? Puzzling and a little frightening all at the same time,* Hawk thought. But this afternoon and evening were left for just them. Cozied together, a brush of their lips, a melting of hands that lingered together. It had been too long that they actually took the time to look at one another in an embracing attitude. *Maybe we could put the BBQ off for an hour and just take that needed time now?* Hawk thought. Looking down at the BBQ, the Tri-Tip steaks were sizzling, and tin foil wrapped Idaho baked potatoes cooking in butter. Annie had already prepared a green salad and homemade blue cheese dressing. Hawk's mouth was watering at this point and could hardly wait to cut into the steak. *Our moment would come after dinner maybe?* he thought.

Both of them were sitting in their double lounge chair when they heard an explosion of some magnitude not too far away. Annie and Hawk looked at one another and then Hawk started to climb out of their chair. As he began to move forward, it was time enough for Annie to grab his hand and pull him back down to her.

"Hawk, don't. You don't have to go."

"Wow, Annie, I am still a cop. Maybe on vacation but still sworn to uphold the law and protect and serve 24/7. You know that."

"Hawk. You needed a vacation for a reason, and this is part of it. You need to calm down. You don't want to be put on an administrative, leave do you?"

"For what, doing my job? Come on, honey, I am just going to make sure we are all safe in our little abode—see what the problem is and check for any injuries. You're welcome to come."

"No."

"OK, I will be right back. Please watch the steaks for me. They are almost done."

As Hawk was walking out to the front yard, he kept looking for smoke, something that might have been associated with the explosion he heard. Nothing. His next thought was a vehicle accident somewhere in the neighborhood. He opened the garage door to get the Corvette out, and another explosion went off. This time, he heard the direction and approximate distance.

The explosion noise came from a Northeast direction about a mile or less away. Between his home and the explosion was a few homes and then open fields until the Yardley Ranch. Hawk ran back into the house, grabbed his gun, handcuffs, and car keys. In the vet backing out, a third explosion occurred, and this time it was even louder and more profound. The vet came out a little faster than Hawk wanted but was careful not to back into any traffic. A couple of neighbors came out to see what was going on after the third explosion. Hawk waved to Jerry across the street and gave the signal to call the department. He acknowledged and was running back into his house when Hawk took off down the street in the direction of the noise. He didn't mean for the rear tires to smoke, but they did. He thought to himself, *I need to put a red light and siren on this rocket ship. Then I could smoke the tires all day long. The top is down; my baseball hat was on, so let the wind blow.* Hawk was feeling reborn, renewed, and ready to get back to work.

The closer he got to the Yardley Ranch, the more distinguished a familiar smell whiffed in his nostrils. As he was driving toward the smell, his thoughts were racing a hundred miles an hour. *How in the hell could Ryan Yardley be involved with cooking meth? No way. We have ridden our steeds together, and I helped Ryan to get into the Sheriff's reserve and …* he thought. Hawk was pulling up to the long driveway off the frontage road when he saw fire trucks coming fast behind him. He pulled in and drove up the drive, looking straight at the hay barn totally engulfed in flames and an old gray single-wide trailer next to it. *Oh, Lord, please don't let there be any people or animals in there,* he thought. After looking out of his rear-view mirror, Hawk estimated that the Fire truck was less than a hundred yards behind him. He turned the Corvette left through a recently mowed grass area fifty yards from the house.

Outside, even over the roar of the Corvette engine, Hawk could see and hear Melody yelling for help. When he pulled up, she screamed that Ryan had just run after their son Jimmy and a girlfriend who were in the barn. The fire trucks were pulling into place in front of the burning buildings and prepping water hoses and other gear to extinguish the out-of-control blaze.

"Where was the lab, Melody? Where were they working?" Hawk asked. She gave him a kind of a dumb look. Hawk thought they were working in the far back corner of the barn. "OK, stay here. Don't move," he said. The fire chief was on his way over to them, and Hawk met him part way and related the information to him. He left to give the information to his battalion to concentrate the water on the back right corner of the barn and trailer.

Hawk ran around to the rear of the barn to see if there might be anyway Ryan or anyone may have gotten out before the explosion. He found Ryan laying on the ground approximately twenty feet from the barn back door. Inside the barn was a horror show of red, yellow, blue, black flames and smoke so thick that it would have been easier to walk through a block of ice or a concrete wall.

Ryan was partially awake but apparently convicted of smoke inhalation and slight burns on his hands and arms. He was pleading for Hawk to look for his son Jimmy and his girlfriend Barbara. "The horses? Hawk, the horses?" he asked.

"I don't know, Ryan. I will check," Hawk replied. He tried to gain entry through the open door of flames and heat. It was just too intense and unyielding. The fire was a bully of such a magnitude Hawk wondered if an armored tank would have survived entry.

As the water was pouring into the barn, the black smoke was relenting to white, but Hawk could not see any further into the thick cloud. He was afraid of what his upcoming autopsy of the fire might reveal.

Within the next twenty minutes, they would know something. Hawk just was not looking forward to what he already knew.

Capt. Snicker came running around the side of the barn and saw Hawk holding Ryan in his lap. He radioed to his crew to call for an ambulance with one burn victim thus far. All they could do was watch the burn until it was put out completely.

After the ambulance team had arrived, Hawk let them take over Ryan's needs. He left him in good hands and walked back around to the front, and then walked over to Melody who was wringing her dress in fear of the worst. Hawk related to her that Ryan was alright and not to worry.

"If you want to go with him in the ambulance, I will take you over to him," Hawk said.

"Oh, yes, please, Hawk. Please. Thank you. What about Jimmy and Barbara? They are alright, aren't they?" she asked.

"We don't know anything yet, Melody. What were the kids doing in the barn?" Hawk asked.

"Jimmy and Barbara were working on some kind of a science project together. We even gave them some money to buy things for the project," Melody told Hawk.

After hearing that, Hawk winced.

"Come on, I will help you over to the ambulance," Hawk said. All Melody could do was cry in anguish, knowing more grief was in store. She was completely devastated by the current ordeal.

As Ryan and Melody left in the ambulance, Hawk walked over to Capt. Snickers and advised him of the little bit of information he got from Melody. She was privy of Jimmy and Barbara working on a chemistry project in the back of the barn next to the trailer.

"Hawk, you really think the parents didn't know what was going on here?"

"I know they didn't. Melody was in shock and not capable of lying or hiding any such knowledge from me. Neither was Ryan. He is one of our own reservists and is a man on target."

"OK, I will put that in the report. Are you ready to see the carnage, Hawk?"

"No, never but it must be done. Let's do it."

Everywhere they looked, there were burning embers smoldering and smoke still prevalent in what was once an old barn. The trailer was worse. Nothing left but melted rubber tires and melted plastics, a burned up suitcase, a computer, and burned up boxes of glass bowl tubes. The same every chemist or meth cooker would use. In the barn was the anatomy of the meth lab itself that two very young inexperienced kids were attempting to make. They didn't have a clue what could and did happen today. The lure of big money, the thrill, and addiction were the culprit's here.

One of Capt. Snicker's men found two human bodies, one male and one female, tucked away in the corner of the lab where the first explosion had occurred. Capt. Snickers found two dead horses partially burned up across the aisle from where the kids had been. The Mare was one of Ryan's favorite Arabians. A mother and her little filly. The filly could not have been more than one month old and still nursing. Dead—all of them. They had no chance of getting out of the barn. Sad. All of it was just too sad. Hawk's next thought was: *How am I going to tell Ryan and Melody that their son was gone and Barbara as well as the livestock?* This was always the most difficult part of Hawk's job—the death notifications. It was never easy to tell the grieving families that they had just lost a loved one, especially when their children were the victims. People always think that as parents, they should go first. Not our kids.

Hawk asked Capt. Snickers to tell his men inside the barn to look for any paper, anything with names, addresses on it for trace evidence; he had to get out of the barn and get fresh air. Not so much because of the smoke, but the sadness and the smell of burned or burning flesh and dead things and parts strewn everywhere. The explosion did its job in mingling all the inhabitants in the barn and the barn itself together in a murky, watery and smoke-filled propane mess. *Oh God, help me find the right words to use in breaking the news to the family,* he thought. He was ready to cry over the utter loss and devastating destruction. Hawk wished that Jimmy and Barbara were still alive so he could shake them into reality and tell them, "You see … you see how secrets can kill? Using drugs is not cool. Look at this. Do you see how dangerous and stupid it was?" *But who am I to judge? I have done a lot of stupid things in my lifetime too, and could be and probably should be lying right next to them right now,* he thought.

Hawk let Capt. Snickers know that he would be leaving to go to the hospital and tell the parents. He needed to ask Ryan or Melody who and where Barbara's parents were.

Two patrol cars had driven up to the property at some point while the Captain and Hawk were in the back. Hawk gave an update and said he would meet them later at the office to complete his report. One of those patrol officers was Robert. Hawk related to him what he had asked Capt. Snickers to do regarding any kind of evidence to link Jimmy and Barbara to any other people. Robert understood and would take it from there.

Hawk then slowly drove home. He was no longer in any hurry to go anywhere.

After sharing the sadness with Annie and letting her know what he had left to do, she wanted to come with him to the hospital. Sadly, he let her know what a painful responsibility that was to do.

Annie had already taken the steaks and potatoes off the BBQ and turned it off, hours ago. After hearing Hawk's immediate report of what happened, she was thankful that he was a cop and on duty 24/7. Especially knowing that Ryan and Melody were friends.

If it didn't get too cold, Hawk thought it would be a good night to drive the Corvette to the hospital. He could use a good blowing out—by the wind going in one ear and out the other. Just knowing the pain from years of experience in telling families they have just lost a loved one is hard enough, but when it's friends and co-workers, it seems to be doubly tough. Hawk just wanted to get it over with. Talking with Annie on the way to the hospital helped him to focus on the task at hand and not to get too far ahead of himself.

Before going into the hospital, they both prayed for God's will and healing for Ryan and Melody. *And Lord, please help me to stay strong and focused. Amen!* Hawk thought.

At the front desk, they asked the attendant where Ryan Yardley was.

"What floor and room number?" Hawk asked.

"I am sorry, sir, but visiting hours are over," the attendant replied.

"Which floor and room number?" Hawk asked the attendant in a stronger voice while flipping open his wallet badge and identification card. He professed the need for urgency and stared at the girl, waiting for her answer.

"Sorry, sir, I didn't know. Mr. Yardley has not been assigned a room yet because he is still in surgery."

"Surgery? I didn't think his burns were that bad."

"Oh, I don't think it is for burns, sir, because Dr. Kilmer is our best heart surgeon."

"OK, Mary, is it?" Annie asked, looking at her name tag. "What floor can I find his wife, Melody, and what floor will the doctor be seeing her?"

"Yes, sir, that would be CCU on the third floor. If you take the elevator, the door will open right into the CCU head nurses' station."

"Thank you, Mary. Has anyone else been here to see Mr. Yardley?"

"No, sir."

"OK, thanks."

"Why did you ask that, Hawk?" Annie inquired on the ride up in the elevator.

"Honey, there are things that I have not told you yet regarding the origin of the fire, the why of the fire, and last but not least, who else might be involved and looking for answers, money, or drugs."

"Hawk, don't you think you should tell me first before we see Melody?"

"No, I don't. Not yet anyway. I will tell you when we have a moment alone. Maybe in the Chapel."

"OK," Annie said, knowing not to question Hawk any further.

Walking off the elevator, Annie and Hawk could see Melody sitting in a chair across from the Nurses' station wringing her hands. Her face was red and swollen from crying and worry. As soon as she saw them, she got up very slowly and began crying again while holding both Annie and Hawk with her arms outstretched around their shoulders. She was barely tall enough to reach their shoulders, but she at least got her hands there.

"We are so sorry, Melody. What happened after you and Ryan left the ranch in the ambulance?"

"Halfway to the hospital, Ryan suffered an apparent heart attack. It was just all too much for him" Melody said.

"How are you doing, honey?" Hawk asked Melody as he positioned her to sit back down in the chair.

"Thank you. I am OK. Where is Jimmy and Barbara?"

"Melody, I am sorry, but Jimmy and Barbara are gone. They didn't make it through the fire. We tried to get in, but the flames and heat were too much. Ryan tried and was blown back outside. I am so very, very sorry."

Melody looked up at Annie and Hawk and asked one little question: "Do you know if they suffered any?"

"No, Melody, they didn't suffer at all. I firmly believe they didn't even know what happened after the explosion." Before Hawk finished his sentence, Melody had fainted. He called one of the nurses over and told her what was going on. "Can you get a blanket and some water, please? She will need it."

"And you are?" the nurse inquired.

"A good friend and a cop in charge of the investigation of the incident."

"Sorry, sir, we are trying to ensure the safety of the patients and family members here."

"It's alright. Please get her a blanket and water."

The nurse checked Melody's pulse and for any fever, and then got up to secure the blanket and glass of water. Melody was beginning to stir a little, and Hawk picked her up in his arms and laid her on the couch next to where she had been sitting. Internally, Hawk made a note of how light Melody was. She was barely there. If she were even a hundred pounds, Hawk would have been surprised. He didn't remember Melody being so small.

"Oh, Hawk. What happened?"

Hawk could see in her eyes that she recognized a little memory tucked away in a cove of her brain, but the shock of the fire had numbed her thinking process. Her eyes got wild momentarily, and then uncontrolled sobs and tears of the remembrance of what Hawk had related to her came plunging out.

Annie came closer to help console her as they both just held her tight and let cry her eyes out.

Nurse Merissa returned with the blanket and a glass of water. Annie thanked her. The nurse motioned for Annie to follow her back to her desk. The nurse began to update Annie on Ryan's condition and the surgery success. Then Annie explained the additional loss of Melody and Ryan's son Jimmy.

"Oh, no, I am so sorry," Merissa said. She asked if she should tell the doctor to wait a few minutes before coming out.

"No," Annie said. "Melody needs good news right now, which will help her to refocus on what she has left, not what she just lost. The loss will still come and have to be dealt with, but not now."

Melody was almost fearless; however, her little body still shook like a small earthquake inside her. Annie came in close to Melody and relayed to her that the doctor would soon be out and had good news about Ryan. "He is OK, Melody. Ryan is alright. Can you hear me?"

Annie and Hawk both heard a very faint yes. *Thank God*, Hawk thought. Then she physically and emotionally let go and fell into a slump. She just fainted again. This time, Hawk kept his fingers on her neck pulse and made sure it was nothing else.

Annie motioned to Hawk that Merissa was returning with the doctor in tow.

"Hawk, I am Doctor Bayne, the cardiologist that operated on Ryan Yardley. Is this Mrs. Yardley?"

"Yes, it is, doctor. And this is my wife, Annie."

"Hello!" was his only reply.

Dr. Bayne checked Melody's pulse and listened to her heart while Merissa checked Melody's temperature and put a cuff on her left arm.

"You know, Hawk, I think it might be a good idea if we checked her in here and kept an eye on her situation. Without further tests, I think she is a stroke candidate."

Hawk replied that he agreed and related to the doctor all that was going on with the fire, the loss of their son and his girlfriend.

Hawk felt like he should post guards outside of Ryan and Melody's rooms in the event someone came looking for retribution on money returns or drugs owed from Jimmy's and Barbara attempt to set up and cook meth in their makeshift barn lab. He had a gut feeling on this that something more was required of the Yardley's before the investigation could be stamped 'case closed.'

A couple of orderlies came with a gurney and with Hawk's help, they got Melody comfortable on it and into a room. Annie and Hawk stayed with her for a few minutes longer to ensure there was nothing else they could do if she came too.

Hawk decided now was a good time to give Annie all the information and details to the cause of the fire and the total loss of lives and animals. After hearing about the botched meth-lab cooking and consequent explosions, Annie nearly collapsed in shock herself. Her knees definitely got weak, and she could not stand up for several minutes.

"Oh, Hawk, what are you going to do? That is horrible news. My God! They all could have been killed."

"Yes, it was close. I just can't believe the kids were doing that, but I guess Jimmy was a little more adventuresome than I thought. Why he got involved with drugs and manufacturing of them will be under investigation for a while, but I will get to the bottom of it. I owe it to Ryan and Melody. I think I need to put armed guards in their rooms until they can leave the hospital. How would you like to go home and eat or would you like to go somewhere else?"

"Honey, I don't really know. This is all such a shock. How do you do it, Hawk? Or maybe you don't?"

Annie took a long hard look at Hawk with tears of her own melting in her eyes.

They stayed on the couch a little longer amongst the hustle and bustle of the hospital. Hawk was really hoping to check in with Ryan prior to leaving, but they heard from Merissa that his recovery could be a few hours longer.

Helping Annie up from the couch, Hawk put his right arm around her waist and lifted. They went down the elevator and walked that way out to the car. Annie said she felt very cold and asked if Hawk would mind putting the top up on the Corvette.

While putting the top up, Hawk was running the motor and the heater so she could at least start to get warmer.

They decided to grab a couple of hamburgers and fries to take home and just cuddle up together in bed and have their long overdue dinner.

The next morning, Hawk gave Captain Snickers a call at the fire station and inquired as to any further information on the Yardley barn fire.

"Nothing yet, Hawk, other than what we both already know. It might take a few more weeks to get all of the toxicology reports in and so on."

"Not a problem. If you would please give me a call when you have something, I would really appreciate it."

"You bet, Hawk. Thank you for your help out there."

Over the next few weeks, Annie and Hawk visited Ryan and Melody at the hospital. After three days of rest, Melody was ready for hospital release and getting back home to the ranch. They also assisted in the funeral arrangements for Jimmy. Robert took care of notification for Barbara's family, so Hawk's job was made a little easier. Only one thing remained: find out what the parents knew about Barbara's involvement in the drug lab.

Hawk used Ryan's John Deer tractor to dig a ten-foot-long and six-foot-wide and ten-foot-deep hole in his bean field for the Arabian Mare and her filly. Melody asked that Hawk leave everything else for a while longer and maybe use the destruction factor as a school learning project. She wanted Jimmy's friends and the entire school student body to know that drugs and secrets kill. Her statement was very potent and accepted by several schools as a field trip to the legacy of anyone messing with drugs.

Whether or not the message got through to any of the kids would be bought out in time. Hawk prayed to God that any child at the end of the needle received the message loud and clear with sober thoughts of dousing any idea of cooking or using drugs.

After two weeks had passed, Hawk again used Ryan's tractor in the fields preparing the fields for planting—adjacent to the frontage road—when he noticed a car about a quarter mile from the property line. It wasn't right. It was facing away from the gas station and food service and now facing north on the road with no exit. Wouldn't hurt to check it out, so he kept the tractor headed in the direction of the lone car. The closer he got, the more he realized his intuition was right. This car was typical of a Mafia tank. Older Lincoln, four doors, dressed out in all black. As Hawk approached, it began to back-up very slowly, making reading the license plate impossible. Hawk counted four, maybe five people inside the semi-darkened windows. He slowed the tractor down and reached behind his back for his Beretta. In his head, he was planning on a shootout, and the tractor was his shield. Just for a moment, Hawk felt naked with no armor vest—armed only with his little eight shot Beretta and not his Glock. Hawk was very much alone out here in the field. Alone and worried going up against a world of people clothed in drugs, fires, guns and the horror of the fights that happen each day in our world on death by drugs and their association. Just as he was about to jump off the tractor, the front passenger door of the Lincoln flew open and a dark haired man swung out with a sub-machine. From behind Hawk's left shoulder, he only heard the echoing thunder of a single shot that must have broken the sound barrier. It was a bullet tumbling past him and through the opened

REX BARTON

door window, shattering the glass and hushing the tractor's humming engine. Momentarily, Hawk was confused as to how he could fight on two opposing fronts and no real protection. *Where could I hide to protect my back and still be shielded on my front,* Hawk thought. Then he asked himself aloud, "How did they get behind me?" As he remembered from his service days in Berlin, Germany, and the Bravo Check Point canal shooting: *When you can hear and feel the flight of a bullet passing by your head, you know you are too close by fractions of an inch.* It was time to duck and take cover.

Hawk's focus was still forward on the man with the sub-machine gun who was slowly disappearing behind the car door. His weapon pointed up firing bursts of bullet missiles at Hawk's make believe animal clouds. It seemed like a minute passed before Hawk could turn his head around and see who was shooting at him from behind. When he finally managed to turn his head to survey the landscape, he saw Ryan. Hawk saw a long rifle in his hands, and it was going back up to his shoulder. The next sounds were the sounds of four individual tires screeching in the opposite direction Hawk was facing. The Lincoln swiftly sped backward down the road. It did a full one-eighty degree turn and was now putting down a slick black trail of smoke and rubber on the asphalt as it gained speed in its attempt to escape the pestilence of bullets. Hawk was unclear for a fraction of a second in his mind in which direction to fire the Beretta. He kept telling himself, *Make sure you have a clear shot because you only have eight bullets. That isn't enough for war.* Hawk chased the Lincoln because he saw Ryan drop to one knee. He could imagine that after only a couple of weeks after heart surgery, he was exhausted just leaving his bed and walking outside. *He could have killed me,* Hawk thought at the same time spinning around and firing on the rear tail lights of the Lincoln. Miss or hit, the occupants received the message.

Hawk looked back again toward Ryan, and he was still on one knee, and now the rifle was on the ground. Slowly Hawk moved forward in the direction of the body on the ground where the Lincoln once rested on the side of the road. Hawk jumped over the fence with the Beretta still his right hand, ready for the kill shot, and then to the ground. He knelt down to make himself a smaller target should the perp in front of him still be alive and able to turn and fire the sub-machine gun held in his left hand. Hawk was intently focused on his fingers and hands. His eyes and lips were turned away from Hawk, so no indicators of life seen there. His hands were motionless, so Hawk allowed his body to proceed forward, but the Beretta was pointed directly at the back of the perp's head. The closer Hawk got, the more sweat was forming on his forehead. When he was within three feet of his hand holding the gun, Hawk saw a slight movement and immediately enlarged his stride and stepped on his left forearm. He let out a groan and limped out. Hawk bent down and physically relieved the perp of his machine gun.

Holding the gun in his left hand, Hawk used his foot to flip this idiot over onto his back. More groans and a slight scream forced its way out of his mouth. His eyes opened slightly, meeting the blue hue of the sky. Hawk's next words were ridiculed. "You bastard! You shot my animal friends in the sky." Only Hawk would ever know what he meant. A second joint meeting of their eyes turned to glare, and a faint grin came over the perp's face.

"Pendejo Hawk? Good to see you again too." He was choking as he muttered, his words. Ryan's shot hit just off center of the perp's chest. Hawk could hear the sounds of sirens in the distance and knew help would soon be here. He now could breathe a little easier. Other than the noise of passing cars on the freeway, one could also hear a gurgling noise of blood accumulation in Poncho's chest.

"Pendejo, today I collect a debt and disparar se (shoot you)."

"Not today, Poncho. Today you are a dead man dying again. You just don't seem to have any luck lately, butt head. Poncho, your crew has left you to die, man. What do you think? You are all alone with me now. Any last prayers? Anything you want to tell me before you go to hell?"

Poncho tried to say something. Hawk thought it was just another derogatory word or two, but the sounds were familiar.

"Amigo? Dinero?" One could hardly make out the sputtering sounds.

"Come on, Poncho, give it to me, man. What the hell are you saying?"

There were no further words coming from the perp on the ground. He wasn't dead. Not yet anyway, but damn close to it. Hawk attempted to pick him up by his shoulders and shake him. As He was about to do it, another shot rang out and instinctively, he dove down into the culvert in front of Poncho. Ryan was still on his knees, but the rifle was back in his hand and pointing up in the air. *A warning shot, maybe, or a miss?* Hawk thought. Then he looked back up the road and saw the patrol car coming. Looking across to the other side of the Freeway, the black Lincoln was back and slowing down. Hawk had no way of warning the unit that they were heading into a firestorm of bullets. He crawled up the culvert toward Poncho's head in an attempt to drag him into the ditch when the hail of bullets began to rain down all around him. He kept his head down and forgot all about Poncho. He heard the bullets hitting the ground just above his head, then a twang as part of the fencing he had jumped over was cut in two by a bullet. Most of the bullets just flew overhead. But a few found their way into Poncho. He was not moving any longer. The Lincoln, once again, was taking flight southbound on 101. *His own men had just shot him to death in an attempt to kill me,* Hawk thought. Standing up in the culvert and looking down on Poncho, Hawk lost count of the blood holes in his body after ten. "Dios sea con ustedes Poncho (God be with you)," Hawk said but couldn't really see how.

Guess the target is still on my back, Hawk thought as the Lincoln was speeding off. He wondered for a fraction of a second if Ryan's shot was a lucky one or a miss.

What the hell am I thinking? Ryan just saved my life. He's my partner and neighbor, Hawk thought. Still, it gnawed at him a little in the days to come.

The patrol car was coming up to a stop on the other side of the fence Hawk had just recently jumped over. "Linda!" he yelled, "Keep down. Call dispatch and advise them to put out a BOLO for a late model black Lincoln Town Car with three, maybe four people in it, then go up the driveway to your right and see if Ryan needs any help. Get him back inside the house. Be careful because he is weak and handling a loaded gun. Not sure which way it might fall."

"Are you OK, Hawk?"

"Yes. Go."

Linda had called for another unit, and now John and his newbie partner just rolled up.

"John, call for a corner unit; we have another SBA (shot by accident) victim here," Hawk said. Of course, the newbie had no clue what SBA meant, and that was on purpose.

"What the hell happened?" John asked. Hawk briefed him about the incident and told him to stay there and photograph and measure the crime scene.

"I need to get up to Ryan's and make sure everything is alright," Hawk said.

He jumped back over the fence and climbed aboard the tractor and headed for the house. All of a sudden, the day seemed to get a little warmer. Then Hawk felt real heat on his back and neck. Looking around he saw flames crawling up his back. His shirt was on fire because of the fuel spilling out of the gas tank. He jumped off the machine and rolled around in the dirt for a minute until all the flames were out and assessed the fire. He then saw the reason for the fire. Someone put a big bullet hole in the fuel tank and as he was driving too fast in the field. The bumping of the tractor caused the fuel to slosh out and onto a very hot wiring. Throwing dirt on the flames extinguished the fire and Hawk ended up walking the last seventy-five yards to the house. All he had left on his upper body was a burnt rag of a shirt and a sunburn. It crossed his mind that he had more lives than a cat.

Stepping inside the front door, Hawk asked Linda how Ryan was.

"I think he is alright, Hawk. Just a little tired."

"Hawk," Ryan said, "I am just fine after hearing my question for Linda. Going to rest for a moment. Did you get them?"

"Poncho didn't make it. After you shot him, his own men finished the job."

"You alright, Hawk?" he asked.

"Yeah, not a problem, Ryan. I am sure glad Melody wasn't here, though."

"You got that right. I would have had my ass whooped. I was watching you tilling the field and saw the black Lincoln driving up real slow. You didn't see it."

"You are right; I didn't. But how did you know it was the Mexican Mafia? It could have been a tourist, anyone."

"Hawk, remember last month when we were driving down Milpas Street? You pointed out that very car to me with the darkened windows. You said to watch out for it."

"Yes, I vaguely remember." *But something just isn't fitting,* Hawk thought.

"Ryan, I need to get home. I am sure Annie is beginning to worry. If she calls, keep your mouth shut, you hear?"

"OK, Hawk. I won't say anything. Thank you."

"Not a problem, Ryan. You just get better and say hi to Melody when she gets home. Linda, would you do the report honors for me?"

"Will do, Hawk. You don't think they will return tonight, do you?"

"No. I doubt it. Think they have had enough for one day. We will get back on it tomorrow. Thanks, guys. See you later."

Hawk knew in the back of his mind that something was not quite right, but tossed it off to his time off being cut short. Annie was right again. *Shoulda', coulda' stayed home and rested.*

After a cooling shower and putting clean clothes on, Hawk sat down and explained to Annie what had happened. She got up and went outside, and Hawk knew she was out back in their garden of Eden, silently crying her eyes out. Surely, she was wondering how many more incidents they could all survive.

"Captain Gee, you called for me?"

"Yes, Hawk, I did. Please come into my office."

On the way to Gee's office, Hawk looked up at the few detectives in the room, nodded his head, and uttered a few comments. He received return waves and nods from all except Prince. He kept his head down, attempting to type a report without paper in the typewriter.

Funny, Hawk thought.

"Hawk, sit down, please. I would like to talk with you a minute."

"Yes, sir. What's up?"

"Hawk, you have sort of been working independently of the narcotic detail. You and your teams I know handle more than just drug deals, but your fingers are now crossing over into some of our secret affairs. Do you realize that?"

"I am sure, Captain, that from time to time my contacts would intermingle with your cases and vice versa. I thought that you were pleased with the Intel that my team has accumulated and provided."

"Don't get me wrong, Hawk, and don't jump ahead. I am not here to deflate all of your efforts and good work. You have done an excellent job out there; we just need to redraw our boundaries."

"How's that, sir? Hawk asked.

"I want you and a few members of your team to join my bureau. What do you say, Hawk?"

"I say wow, horse. Who, how many, when, and do I have to wear a tie?"

Capt. Gee laughed. "No tie, Hawk. Your wings have to be free. I understand that. As to whom, we would like Misty, Robert, and yourself, Detective Sergeant."

"I don't know what to say, sir. Thank you I guess would be appropriate. What about my teams?"

"What I understand is that Red will lead his team as number one and Carlos will inherit number two, which would be your old team. I think Capt. Joel wants to beef up both teams with two or three more members. Of course, we would like your input and knowledge of the personnel and qualifications."

"No disrespect, sir, but may I have until tomorrow to give you my yes answer? I would like to just give Annie heads up."

"Not a problem. Wouldn't have your yes answer any other way, Hawk."

"Thank you, sir. Thank you very much."

"You are welcome. Now please stay in here for a few minutes longer. We have other business to discuss that will blow your mind, I think. I have Ryan and Melody Yardley coming in."

"But Captain, I am still investigating that case."

"Yes, I know. Just hold on. Prince, can you come in now?"

"Yep. Be right there, Cap."

Yep? Cap? No respect for rank over here in this division? Hawk thought to himself. *Yep?*

"Come on in, Mr. and Mrs. Yardley. Please sit down." Melody was crying and had a hand full of Kleenex, dabbing her eyes. Ryan's head was down, looking at the floor, and behind him was an old Attorney friend then came Yep following behind the procession of people. "Sit down, everyone. Please."

"Hawk, Ryan and Melody have something they would like to say to you, and their attorney is here as an advisor."

"Advisor for what?" Hawk asked, somewhat bewildered.

Ryan started out, and Melody just cried a little harder. "Hawk, this is really hard for me, but I first wanted to say thank you for all that you and Annie have done for us. You have been good friends and—"

"Wait, Ryan, no need to thank us," Hawk interrupted. Capt. Gee asked that Hawk withhold any further address.

Ryan went on. "Hawk, we got hooked up with the Cartel. They contacted Jimmy and Barbara first and when they said no, they kidnapped them and shot them both up full of dope. Every day someone would come and pump heroin into them. When I found out, they threatened to kill the kids and us.

"Melody was the go-between and took care of all the necessities for acquiring the lab material, and they came and showed us how to start our little enterprise.

"We were told that we could pay off our indebtedness on the ranch and have enough money for the rest of our lives by cooking for them. If we didn't, they would find and kill all of us. You know them, Hawk. We believed them."

Hawk was staring at Ryan in disbelief. Yes, he knew the ways of the Cartel. But his partner?

"Then the money started to flow in a little bit, and it was unbelievable how much money and how easy it was. No one would have ever found out. But the kids were kept in a state of under the influence and barely able to go to school. They were to acquire more users. It became hideous, Hawk. Melody and I just didn't know what to do any longer.

"The last thing was you, Hawk. We were never told you were the reason. Melody was to poison you when I got home from the hospital.

When she couldn't do it, I was told to kill you. Remember the Black Lincoln? They asked me to shoot you, or they were coming in to kill all of us. I didn't know what to do, Hawk. So, I just shot the one gunman and prayed to God you could finish them off."

Melody broke out in loud sobbing and tried to spit out "I'm so sorry, Hawk," and then she went back to speaking intelligible language. "Excuse me, please," Hawk said. He got up and walked out of the meeting, his face horror-stricken and his emotions completely canceled. Hawk felt sick and just wanted to regurgitate all that he had heard. Prince followed him out of Capt. Gee's office.

"Sorry, Hawk. I know this is a real blow to you. Ryan was your neighbor and a decent ride-a-long reservist cop. Ryan came in the other day after the shootout and told Capt. Gee that he was responsible for all of it. The Captain advised him to call an attorney and told him to bring Melody in to collaborate the story. The Cartel really wants you dead, man. They really want you dead."

Hawk just stared at Prince, not knowing what to say or how to respond. He was stunned and speechless. He walked back across the street to the patrol office, and Numb-nuts was sitting at the desk.

"What do you want, Hawk? This isn't your shift."

Hawk could have sworn he said it wasn't his shit and he was ready to knock him off the desk and out of the second-floor window. Thank

God Robert and Billy were there to hold Hawk back. Destruction was on his mind and destroying Numb-nuts would have been just fine.

Hawk told them both he would be in the squad room on the phone and not to let anyone in for a few minutes. Hawk glared back at Numb-nuts as he walked back to the squad room.

"Not a problem, Sarg," Robert replied.

Hawk shut the door to the room, picked up the telephone, and gave Annie a call. When she answered the phone, he told her not to say anything but just listen.

"Capt. Gee has asked me to join him in the Detective Bureau and bring Misty and Robert with me. The teams will be restocked, and I will still have time to train with them and help guide Red and Carlos who will be replacing me. I need to do this, Annie."

"What's wrong, Hawk? The betrayal?" Annie had heard the anger and helplessness in Hawk's voice.

Hawk wanted to scream, but not at Annie; wasn't sure who or how he was going to vent his feelings, but someone was going to pay a big price.

Secrets. More damn secrets! Hawk blamed. *The next person dead from all this is going to be from the Mafia Cartel. I will not stop until they are either dead or in prison. My streets will be clean again one day,* he thought.

Hawk decided to go to the range and take out all his anger, frustration, sadness, fear, and loneliness out on a few helpless targets. At least they couldn't shoot back.

After his shooting spree, Hawk took one last glance back at his thoughts and how secrets can kill. Yes, secrets can kill, and Hawk had one big secret in his heart, growing, which needed to be fed. Just like a piranha fish, Hawk was making a secret commitment that the Cartel was going to pay and pay dearly for coming to his house.

CHAPTER 7

CONTEMPT

Annie told Hawk that he had to let go of the Yardley calamity. Such disappointment and sadness and probably a lot more feelings than he cared to even think about. Contempt mostly. One day, the emotions he chose to tuck away in the recesses of his mind for the moment will eventually come out and bite him in the butt. *I pray that it bites just me alone*, Hawk thought.

Meanwhile, one activity that usually took Hawk's mind off things was riding. He missed the time he used to spend with his horse, but work comes first. After weeks of studying manuals, files, and pictures of drug-involved perps to get up to speed with the rest of the Narc Detectives, Hawk managed to craft a long weekend off.

Annie agreed that a ride into the sunset might be good for Hawk's solvent attitude. When he called Red and asked how his horses were, Hawk knew he would ask if he wanted to ride. Little did he know it might just take a few days to get it out of Hawk's system.

"You know something, Red? I don't think there is anything better than sitting on a horse and riding the trails. Perhaps sex, but riding is second best."

"Yeah, I know what you mean, cowboy. Kinda like being in a groove that is numbing to the ass yet massaging to the soul."

"Never heard it explained like that, but you're right. Massaging to the soul. How come we don't do this more often, Red?"

"Too busy these days, I guess. Hell, you are never free for anything anymore. Ever since your caboose to the Bureau, we don't see hide nor hair of you. What the hell you doing over there these days?"

"Too much, my friend. Can't really talk about it anyway. Let's ride and bend grass. Branding new trails is all I want to do today. Smell the pines, kick up some dust. Where exactly is the fishing hole we are going to? Never been up this way before, Red."

"Can't tell you, cowboy. In fact, I will have to put the old hood on your pretty head real soon so you can't ever find it again. This is a Top Secret fishing hole. Ha."

"Are we digging for worms or fly fishing only?"

"Worms, son. Worms. Got to get your hands dirty."

"There had better be some big trout in this little sickly pond of yours, Red.""

"Bigger Rainbows than you ever did see. Just a couple more miles ahead and we will be there. This is God's own fishing hole, Hawk, so take your boots off when we get there because you will be on the hallowed ground."

"What do you know of hallowed ground, Red? I am sure you haven't been to Church lately."

"Hawk, the Church is now my second home. The wife and I go every week. Sometimes twice a week. See what you miss when you're working all the time?"

"Yes. I am surprised, buddy. Did you bring your Bible with you by chance?"

"Yes, sirie. Dolores gave me a little NIV New Testament to carry around. I even take it to work with me now. Why? You figure on saying a blessing over the giant rainbows tonight and need to find the appropriate words or something?"

"Actually, now that you've mentioned it, Red, why don't we have a little starlight Bible study around the campfire tonight? You see, I carry my Bible too."

"Hawk, I can't think of anything better. In fact, why don't we pick up the pace a little so we can get started earlier?"

"Red, thanks for sharing that with me. I am excited to know that you and Delores are attending Church and even more excited that you gave your life to Christ. When was that actually?"

"Remember that night on the freeway after we shot the hell out of those Cartel dudes and Misty was all tied up and almost dead?"

"Of course, I do. Was that when?"

"Hawk, after seeing all the dead bodies scattered everywhere and then seeing Misty almost dead, I took a quick glance at my own life and how long Dolores has been after me to join her and the kids. She really told me how important it was that we all had Eternity together. After seeing all that death on the road, I realized how short life can be and how I would have missed out. I was only one bullet away from losing it all."

"Praise God, Red. That day my prayers were answered. I prayed that someone would find Jesus and that someone was my best friend. Thanks for sharing, Red. We are blessed, my man," Hawk said.

"Isn't that the truth, cowboy?" Red said.

Somehow, Hawk thought that their horses were as excited as we were. Probably because they both were just about ready to start a downhill descent. They had been climbing for hours. Red's horse of many years was Nelly. A beautiful golden Palomino mare who had had several fillies over the years. She was as sure footed on mountain terrain as any mule, Hawk knew. His steed was Dolores' Appaloosa named Shadow for all the brown and white spots. He was almost a Leopard Appaloosa. Another good trail horse that could get one where they wanted to go and back. Nice and easy on the butt and the back. Hawk and Red rounded a curtain of rocks and trees and there below

REX BARTON

them was a valley with a spring fed lake surrounded by trees. Beautiful setting against the blue sky. Plenty of time in the day to set their camp up, dig a fire pit, gather wood and get set for fishing.

On the way down to the valley floor, Hawk took note of all the possible exits. Just a normal thing he always did. Being trapped is no fun, so being prepared is advantageous.

From the top of the Vista, prior to their descent to the lake, Hawk saw yet another little lake and valley set in a clandestine shadow of trees where he presumed the headwaters of the stream feeding into Red's famous rainbow trout came from. He made a mental note to ride over to the other valley in the morning. Maybe do some hunting with the camera.

The closer Red and Hawk got to the valley floor and the lake, the more pungent the smell of cedar trees and north facing trees and rocks which skirted mossy contingents of green flora was pleasing to Hawk's senses. He could even smell the clean freshness of the lake water and soaking cattails in the shallows like Centurion fortifications, undoubtedly protecting Red's Rainbow Trout.

Red found his old camping spot where he had enjoyed fishing-filled days away from all the rigors of law enforcement, and it was obvious to Hawk the necessity of such tranquil spots in their lives. He needed to find this moment and soak it all in.

They dismounted and unsaddled the steeds and fixed a rope line to their halters. Red put down a flake of good looking alfalfa hay for each and centralized water bucket. They were about as happy at this moment as two horses could be. Just to rid their bodies of two heavyweight Cowboys probably would have been good enough, but green alfalfa? Yes, they would say, if they could talk. Judging by their nods, they were saying plenty.

Red and Hawk both gathered rocks and broken pieces of wood for the campfire to be. Next, they laid out their sleeping bags, fishing gear, and rifles.

"Red, are we on Hallowed ground yet?" Hawk jibbed.

"Pretty close, cowboy. Just a little yonder nearer the water's edge and you gotta tiptoe in barefoot."

"Will, my friend, I think it is worm time. I'll see what I can dig up for us." Pulling his boots and socks off and rolling up his pant legs, Hawk literally jumped up and ran to the lakeshores edge. He had to use his hunting knife to get far enough down in the wet dirt to find enough big honker worms to satisfy the waiting hungry trout. Red joined him, and together they hooked the critters to the line and cast away.

As the minutes ticked away, Red and Hawk drifted toward a small outcropping of rocks to sit on while the sun continued its migration from the East to the West.

"Thank you, Red, for bringing me here. This is just outright spectacular. God is truly here in this place."

"Hey, Hawk, I am glad to share it. Get ready, though. As the shadows grow longer over the lake, the fish will take the challenge of our bait real soon."

Red just said it, and then Hawk got the first strike.

"Woaa. Look at my pole bend. There must be a five pounder on the hook Red!" Hawk couldn't see it yet, but she was a fighter. After several minutes of playing tug-a-war, he was able to land one of the prettiest rainbow Trout's he had ever seen. It was a shame that he would have to clean it and cook it for dinner. But then that was why they were there, and he wasn't bear enough to just eat leaves and berries.

Red had an entirely different way of catching Trout. One won't believe this, but it is absolutely true. Red had devised a split hook fishing technique. Two separate lines about fifteen inches in length, two smaller hooks to hold the bait and two small cork bobbers to keep the two baited lines separate. All Hawk could figure was, Red was either bored about fishing and didn't want to wait and enjoy the moment, or he was just plain hungry and figured an easy way of quickly catching and eating. Whatever the reason, it turned out to be ingenious. To Hawk's laughing surprise, five minutes after his catch, Red caught two large trouts simultaneously. If Hawk hadn't been there to see it himself, he would never have believed it.

"Well, cowboy, should we get to cleaning these critters and start the BBQ?"

"You bet, Red. I can do the cleaning and prep work while you get the fire going and set up the spinner." Everything they needed was within easy reach. The spinners were two three-foot limbs from tree branches that had a 'Y' configuration at the top, and they carved the bottom to a point and stuck it in the ground. Another branch was used to skewer the fish on and then it was just a matter of spinning the fish to cook on both sides. That many fish was about four minutes per side. The pork and beans were already in a sauce pan cooking up just fine. Within ten minutes, thy were chowing down.

"Gosh, Red, this is about the best fish dinner I have had in one very long time. Thank you again for this, my friend. What do you say we get the Bibles out and start a cowboy study?"

"You're welcome again and let's do it."

After dinner, and the study, Red and Hawk talked a little while about coming events until Hawk could not keep his eyes open any longer.

"Think I will call it good day, Red, and get some shut-eye. Thought I might take a little ride up that splinter deer trail in the morning to see what the other little lake is like. Want to come?"

No, I don't think so. Need to just relax and sip coffee. When you get back later in the morning, I will have some bacon and eggs ready for you."

"Sounds good. See you in the morning then after a good night's sleep."

In the wild, the sun comes up early, and it's best to get up with the sun when it's shining and not wait for bugs and other critters to gnaw at you, Hawk thought. So, he was up and saddled and ready to go. After putting a couple of logs on the fire for Red, Hawk swung up into the saddle like the good old days and rode off down a deer path toward the other lake which he figured was a couple two or three miles away. As he got closer, he saw smoke from a small campfire. *Guess we're not alone, after all,* Hawk thought. Being upwind from the camp helped in hiding any sounds or smells of Hawk's presence. All he had to do was remain unseen and quiet as possible. Something told him to approach with extreme caution, so he tied Appy up to a tree branch, took the rifle out of its scabbard, and the camera, and then proceeded on foot. Hawk's approach was silent as an Indian. What he saw was short of amazing—four Mexican males in their twenty's, maybe thirty's, and four younger girls between fifteen and twenty. Hawk observed them for about a half hour, watching their interaction and destinations to and from the adjacent fields. Fields of pot, which must have been several acres of stream fed pot plants. From Hawk's upwind vantage point, the plants all seemed very healthy. The girls were there to serve the men, and the men each had side arms and rifles slung over their shoulders. The only time they took the rifles off was when they were sitting down to eat or play with one of the girls, i.e., sexually harassing them—grabbing at their butts or trying to disrobe them, exposing and squeezing their breast. The men would laugh and joke while the girls would scream, trying to get away. Clearly, they were victims of kidnapping and forced labor at this pot camp. Hawk took all the pictures he could snap.

Having seen enough, Hawk very quietly backed out of his Vista and went down to where he had tied Appy up. He decided to whittle off a few leafy tree branches and tie them all together to drag away any trace of his coming—he didn't want any company dropping in by accident like he just did. Hawk dragged the limbs a good mile or at least until all the leaves were stripped from the branches.

On the ride back to camp, Hawk kept thinking to himself, *Isn't there any safe places for us to go anymore without coming in contact with the drug trade crap? This was supposed to be a nice quiet three days off with no work and no gun play. Maybe I could just forget about what I saw and not tell anyone, including Red whom I know will want to ride back down here and shoot the hell out of the place. It's just in his DNA. And this is a long way away for any back-up or medical help. Better think twice, Hawk. Lord, please give me wisdom.*

REX BARTON

Hawk rode very slow back to camp thinking of what to do. Clearly, something must be done. He just didn't know what yet. As he rode up, Red was cooking up the bacon and eggs and sported a big smile when he saw Hawk riding in.

"Hey, cowboy, how was the ride?" Hawk's hesitation was a dead giveaway. He didn't know what to say yet, but clearly saying nothing and not answering his question was the reason for his frown.

"Well, friend, we have a problem. I got up this fine sunny morning and took a nice little ride a few miles away and what do you think I found? A stupid pot farm and four armed men and four young maidens keeping guard. So, what do you think?"

"What the hell, Hawk? Where and how far away?"

"About two and a half or three miles away. Hard to gage because of having to ride around trees and back switches. I did cover my trail so we wouldn't have any visitors. Other than that, I saw three makeshift lean-tos, his and hers maybe, and then kitchen in-between. Lots of buckets and tools for digging trenches and field maintenance. They have it all set-up nicely. What they are doing is trenching from the stream that is feeding the lake and piping over to the field trenches. All of which is sloping away from the camp."

"Hey, that might be our way in, through the pot field?"

"No, Red. I feel this is one operation that will require a lot more help than what we can manage on our own. We need to get back home and set up a meeting with Capt. Gee and get some input."

"Why don't we eat first and then break camp and get back home? Do you think they can see our camp from there?"

"No. We are way out of their line of vision. Don't think they could even see our smoke unless they climbed a tall tree. Even then, it would be hard for them to see us. We need to get back and report this to the Bureau. The only way I think we can attack this is to repel from a chopper a canyon over and walk in. Come at them with a small contingency of officers from two sides. I think it would be over pretty quick with only a few shots."

"Hawk, I want to be there with you guys. Tell Capt. Gee, I know the area better than anyone."

"Not to worry, Red. I will let the Captain know we need you."

"Thanks, man. So, let's break camp and get back."

"Yeah. We need to make sure that this camp is clean and not ever used in case the Cartel stumble on it."

After breakfast, Red and Hawk packed everything up and broke camp after cleaning everything up. Hawk don't believe a dog could have ever smelled their presence, let alone humans.

They made excellent time climbing to the ridge and the long descent back down to the trailhead. From that point, it was another hour to

Red's ranch. Once they arrived at the ranch, they unsaddled, stowed all their gear and went into the house to make some calls. First, to Annie, telling her what was up and to set another plate for dinner tonight.

Hawk called Capt. Gee and related to him what they had found and that he had pictures. He just needed to go to the one-hour photo stop at Newberry's 5 & 10 and be in with pictures and a report. Capt. Gee was delighted in learning what Red and Hawk had found. A validated pot farm that would test the skills and training of the narc team. Capt. Gee agreed with using a chopper and walking in. The only difference was sending only two men around behind to crossfire rather than five or six. That way, it would be less likely anyone could get hurt. Red and Hawk would be the two cut off men, should the perps choose to try and escape out what they perceived might be a back door. Plus, Red and Hawk could pick them off one by one, should the front team have any problems.

"OK, my friend, you are in, and we need to get home and get some sleep. Tomorrow will be a busy day. Capt. Gee will set-up the chopper and details. Ready?"

"You bet," Red replied. "Can't wait."

When Hawk got home, Annie was curious about what had happened while on a planned three-day trail ride that ended in one and a half. Hawk explained everything over a tuna noodle casserole dinner. Annie just sat there quietly while Hawk explained what a wonderful time Red and he had until his early morning exploratory ride.

"Honey, I wasn't looking for anything but taking pictures of what I thought was one of the most beautiful spots on earth. The Rainbow Trouts were amazing and how Red caught his dinner was even more amazing."

Annie wasn't so amazed at all. She was, in fact, disappointed that Red and Hawk didn't have the full three days off. And now another dangerous detail in the mix in the morning.

"Babe, you need time off. Can you ask for it after the detail?"

"No, I don't think so, but I will try. Maybe Capt. Gee can give me next weekend off, and you and I can go to Disneyland?"

"Hell No!" That was the first time in a long time that Hawk heard any kind of swearing come out of Annie's mouth. She was always careful not to swear and slow to anger. But her thunderous 'Hell No!' told me I had better find another alternative and fast. So, I asked about a possible beach vacation down in Laguna Beach.

"Hell no! Isn't that where Misty is?"

"Honey, I don't think so. She is at the Bureau, working. But I have not seen her since I left Friday."

"Sorry, I am a little on edge. Why don't we stay closer to home and go up to Pismo Beach if you can get the time off?"

"Whatever you want, dear. I will ask Capt. Gee after tomorrow's detail."

"Do you think we can take a nice Jacuzzi together now and then early to bed?"

"Sure, go ahead and get in while I do dishes."

"OK. Thanks, babe. Great dinner. And please don't be worried about tomorrow. Everything will go as planned. No big thing. Really."

"Hawk, every detail, raid, bust, ops is dangerous. Stop trying to soft-pedal it. I am just trying to catch up with all the changes myself. But nothing is easy and safe unless you are behind a desk. I wish now that you would have said no to the Bureau."

"Annie, come here, honey. Let me hold you. This isn't going to be forever. You know that I really want to retire to a small town like Cambria or something and sit and stare at the ocean."

"Yeah, right. I don't think so. You are too ambitious, and I happen to know that you would like to be Sheriff someday. Right?"

"Well, this is our home, and this is my town. But let's put it out there anyway. What do you say? Put the dream on a list and attach it to the refrigerator. OK?

"Sure, why not?"

"The sun went down pretty fast tonight, and you sure look good in that bikini. Kind of hard to see it under water, though. How about I take it off you and look at it a little closer?"

"You are a horny old man, aren't you?"

"Horny, yes; old, no. Do I look that old? Hey, am I getting gray on top or bald?"

"Settle down, Hawk, just kidding. You are just fine, and the rest is in your dreams."

"What happened to spontaneous fun?"

"Nothing. You just don't deserve it tonight."

"Don't deserve it? What?"

"Just kidding. Come here, big man."

As he moved closer to her, she handed him her polka-dot bikini top and the rest is now history.

Four a.m. came early on Monday morning. After another wake-up shower and shave, Hawk dressed and kissed Annie goodbye.

"Be careful, honey. I want you home tonight and in one piece. I have some more desert planned like last night."

"I will give you a call once I have landed back at the office. Not to worry. Love you."

"Love you more. Sorry for being edgy last night."

"You mean those luscious curves I am staring down at?"

"Kiss me again, and I will show you."

"Aw... I think I had better go. I am late already. Bye. But thank you. Tonight!"

As Hawk waved goodbye, Annie flipped off the covers and revealed her naked body. Those curves almost made Hawk turn around and go back to her.

"You are not playing fair. You are a big tease."

Giggling, she blew wind kisses at him. Hawk smiled as he left, knowing what he had when he returned.

* * *

When Hawk arrived at the detective office, everyone was already there and ready to go. Capt. Gee had given all the details and photo information to the troops on their mission today. Misty was there, including Prince, Red, Little G. (not related to Capt. Gee), Bob, Billy (their sniper), and Larry.

Capt. Gee spoke through an air horn, "Alright, guys, in the bus to the airport. Make sure you have all your gear bagged and last minute weapons check. Hawk, maybe you can go over more of the topography and what to expect."

"Yes, sir. The main thing is, I don't know about our landing spot at all. Was never in the other canyon. However, our drop zone is about one mile from the first Pot field. We will enter there and neutralize any perps we find. Quiet, surprise, and early morning darkness are our advantage. When we reach the fields, Red and I will take off and hike to the opposite side to seal the back door shut. I know nothing of the eastern area other than what we all saw on the overhead. West (Red looked up at Hawk and motioned with his finger to his lips not to reveal their fishing hole location) is an open canyon, trees, and another little lake. No significance. Red and I can cover that exit if it becomes an issue. The east door is yours, Billy. If they try to run that way, put them down.

"These guys are heavily armed and ready to defend. Real bastards, I guess, just by the way they were drinking and screwing with the women. So be alert and don't wait for them to take the first shot. If any of you see a muzzle coming up, shoot first and ask questions later.

"Again, having never been in the drop zone before, be ready for anything. Your pilots are Cam and Kevin. They are your Eagle eyes, but that doesn't mean you can go to sleep up there. Stay vigilant. Hell, we might land in another pot farm, I don't know. If Cam can't find a clearing to put us down, we will repel. So, again, be ready for anything and make it quick. The more downtime for the chopper, the more possibility of exposure to the perps.

"Alright, let's roll."

Seated to Hawk's left furthest from the jump door was Misty. Hawk asked her if everything was alright.

"Are you ready to take back a part of your life?"

"Yes."

"I believe the women you will see are innocent of any crime here. Watch them closely and spare whom you can. From what I saw, they were all being held as prisoners by these perps. If it is like other farms, the women cook, clean, are forced to do sexual favors, bear the children for legacies, and so forth. But trust no one until this is over."

"Got it, Hawk. I got it."

Misty was grinding her teeth, and her jaw was set hard under her helmet chin strap. Hawk felt he had a stick of dynamite lit and ready to go off. All he could do at this stage was watch and correct if he could.

I need to talk with Capt. Gee, when this ops mission is over, about what I feel is going on inside of Misty, Hawk thought.

Lt. Cam Donovan (pilot) just announced over the radio that they are now five minutes from the Red Zone. "Get ready!" was heard over the loudspeakers.

Capt. Gee and Hawk looked one last time at the mission crew and waited for a nod of ready from each. Prince had a big smile on his face in anticipation of the coming action. This was his cup of tea, having come from the 82nd Air Born Division before joining the Sheriff's Department more than eight years ago. Hawk and he both shared the sergeant's job in the Bureau and had the same goals—get the Cartel out of their county. It was finally made apparent that Los Angeles, Ventura, San Luis Obispo, and Santa Barbara Counties had the same goals and worked together in a law enforcement community effort with manpower and Intel. The Cartels were being squeezed tightly around their throats and had suffered many losses in the recent years. Today would be yet another loss on a grand scale. *No import of drugs growing on our land,* Hawk thought. As he was thinking, something occurred to him, which might help Misty over the long run: give her the company camera and make her responsible for all the movie taking and recording, which would get her out of the frontline action, yet keep her in the mix.

Hawk made a mental note to come back on this idea when this mission is over.

Lt. Cam again announced, "One minute to Red Zone."

"Alright, guys. Off and on," Hawk yelled at the top of his voice.

All of a sudden, they experienced their first of several hic-ups. The chopper engine sputtered like it was out of gas or something. It jolted to the left and then Lt. Cam over corrected the right and down. The jolt didn't happen from air turbulence or any incoming gunfire. It was an engine or some other malfunction. Hawk told everyone to hook up and repel the last twenty-five feet to the ground.

Billy, Hawk's one and only sniper, was closest to the door. When the second jolt occurred, he was in the process of hooking his lanyard to the exit hook when he tumbled out and landed on the ground below. Hawk yelled for Red and Prince to get down there to help Billy. They both repelled down in seconds. Next was Misty with all the group's first aid gear, Bob, and Capt. Gee. Larry was next when a third sputter happened, and the entire group was wondering if they were going down on top of the crew. Hawk looked toward the cockpit and Lt. Cam was struggling to keep the bird up.

"OK, go Larry. Little G, you're next." Hawk was last out and signaled to Lt. Cam to move away. Hawk's drop was a little higher, and he was dragged while still in the air toward a tree. Rather than hitting the tree, Hawk let go of his rope and free-fell the last fifteen feet. Slightly shaken and a twisted ankle, Hawk looked up and gave thumbs-up to the chopper. "Damn it. How in the hell are we going to make it to the pot fields in this condition!" Hawk yelled up toward heaven. He centered his sights on Prince to find out how Billy was doing. Prince signaled that Billy was not good and would not be going any further. When Hawk reached the group, everyone was in a ready posture, surrounding Billy and Prince, pointing weapons outwardly.

Hawk joined Prince inside the circle and looked down at Billy and Capt. Gee. Capt. Gee and Misty said that it looked like Billy may have broken his back, shoulder, and one leg. Capt. Gee radioed Lt. Cam to find out what was going on and if he could make it back to Evac Billy. Lt. Cam replied that he would try and sit down next to them between the trees, but it was risky.

"Do it. Do it now!" Capt. Gee yelled.

Within minutes the chopper was back and landing. Bob ran and got the flat board to carry Billy on. Once secured, he was moved to the chopper and taken out of the area. Lt. Cam said he would be waiting for the group's call to return. "Sorry, guys. I don't know what happened." Hawk gave him the signal to lift off and gave Billy a thumbs-up, unsure if he even could see through all the pain of broken bones.

Capt. Gee yelled into Hawk's ear, "We are now short one, and our mission might have been compromised by the delays. Hawk, I need you and Red to proceed at point and radio back any suspicious movements in the camp. I need to know what these perps may have heard if anything."

"Yes, sir. Let's go, Red."

Red then saw Hawk limp and asked if he was alright.

"Not a problem, man. We need to get up there on that knoll." Hawk's ankle was swollen and hurt like hell, but his determination was stronger.

"Red, keep a sharp eye." In all honesty, Hawk's focus was twinge with pain.

"Do your best to keep up, cowboy. Control your breathing, Hawk. Slow it down and refocus that pain to gain."

"You remember your training will, Red. Thanks. Lost sight for a few minutes there." Hawk did what he was trained to do when injured—slowed his breathing, distributed the pain in all parts of his body to actually calm the nerve endings and pump additional serotonin into his brain. In minutes, there was no pain. Hawk juiced up the hill like a sprinter behind Red. He kept repeating to himself, *Focus! Focus! Don't let down. There is no pain.*

* * *

It took them thirty-eight minutes to go two miles uphill around trees and boulders before they came to a place between rocks to look down on the pot fields and the encampment. They watched for ten minutes six men in the fields and two women cooking something in a pot over a fire pit inside the three-sided middle tent. Something told Hawk that there were more people sleeping in the other two tents; they just could not see into them. So far, nothing really seemed out of place or a worry to the field workers. They did not hear Hawk's group coming or the faulty chopper engine. *Thank God,* Hawk thought.

Hawk half-slid and half hoofed down the hill about thirty yards and radioed Capt. Gee. "It looks like we have more people here. Could be eight to ten men and five or more women. Can't see into the tents. All six are armed and working in field number one. Over."

"10-4," Capt. Gee replied. "Can we safely get into the fields without notice, Hawk?"

"No, sir. We will have to wait until they leave the field or it is siesta time. It looks like breakfast is nearly ready. Coffee on the fire."

"10-4," Capt. Gee acknowledged. "We are on our way. See you both soon."

"10-4," Hawk replied. "FYI. Noticed a few rattle snakes part way up around the big boulder field. Be careful. No shooting or screaming. If someone gets bitten, tell them to bite back."

"10-4, and thanks for that information. They scare the hell out of me," Capt. Gee replied.

By the time the team reached Hawk and his group, it was five-thirty. The camp was stirring. They weren't going by OCHA and Union rules out here. Everyone settled down in a hole around rocks and bushes with their field glasses on. All eyes were on the targets and counting. Checking movement, checking the perps' guns for firepower and their ammo belts. Most of the rifles looked like the newer M-14's the military used.

Hawk and his group heard a scream down in the cook's tent. One shirtless and shoeless man walked out of the tent left of the cook's tent and grabbed a young girl tending the pot over the fire. He had grabbed her from the back, flipped her dress over her head and was trying to bend her over a large rock and sexually assault her. The girl stopped screaming and squirming while he did his thing. It was vulgar and

REX BARTON

sadistic. Hawk was mentally making this guy one of his first targets. He hoped he didn't just give up and fall to the ground. Hawk wanted to see a rifle muzzle pointed toward him so he wouldn't have any excuses not to waste him. *Count your minutes to live in this life butt head,* Hawk thought and believed every deputy present felt the same when they saw what happened to the young girl. This was what was happening every day at this camp and no hiding it or any pretense of privacy. Animals are all they were.

One of the perps in the pot field looked up at the oncoming sunrise and motioned to the others it was time to eat and drink. Work would wait a few hours. As they were walking into the camp, the rapist was zipping up his pants and then kicked the half-naked girl in the butt with his foot, knocking her to the ground. He was yelling at her, but Hawk and his group were too far away to make out what it was.

As soon as everyone was sitting around the makeshift table and rocks or overturned buckets as seats to eat, Capt. Gee gave the hand signal to crawl down the slope and into to the pot field. It was about a seventy-five-yard crawl on dangerous ground, knowing that this was snake country—through bushes where they like to hide, over rocks, and by snake holes. This was not going to be fun.

Red was in the lead and first to happen upon a big rattler. The group all found a useful tool by way of Red's chewing tobacco. Apparently, rattlesnakes do not like the taste or smell of chewing tobacco because no sooner had Red spat it at the snake, it backed up really quick and ducked into a hole like a crevice below a big rock.

"Red, spit again around the hole to make sure nothing dared to come back out," Hawk said, though not wanting to promote chewing tobacco, but he was glad Red was chewing and leading them.

Misty shimmied up close to Red and entered the pot field first. For all Hawk knew, she had a motive for passing Red, and it had something to do with the perp that raped the young girl. Hawk could not go any faster and just watched as she inched ahead of Red. He reached out and grabbed one of her ankles and held her fast. When she looked back, Red signaled to her right and made a sign of a snake with his hand. Very slowly, Misty turned her head in the opposite direction and nearly came face to face with a rattlesnake that was shaking his tail in displeasure of the group's visit to his green acres. Misty froze and just stared at the rattlesnake, wondering what would be next. Fortunately, Red got up on both elbows and spat a big blob of tobacco over Misty's back and right arm, hitting her elbow closest to the rattlesnake. Lucky for Misty, enough of the chewing tobacco splattered onto the rattlesnake that it backed up slowly and far enough away to let them all pass. When Red went by, he waved at the snake and spat again, backing the snake up even more.

Red and Hawk split from the group and headed off toward pot field number two to outflank the perps and close their back door of escape. No further rattlesnake encounters, and in twenty minutes, Red and Hawk were in place.

Capt. Gee gave the order to move in. Misty and Prince were up and moving forward at a good clip, shouting in Spanish, "Police, drop your guns (Policia, Carer Sus Amoss)."

As predicted, the men jumped up with rifles in hand and started shooting in the direction of the team. Red and Hawk jumped up and started firing, dropping three of six perps. Six more came running out of the tents, firing in all directions. Hawk saw Red grab his arm, and he point-shot the perp that had fired on Red. Misty hit one perp, and Prince another. Together, they hit two more, blowing them off their feet. Four were left. Guess who one of them was?

The girls all ran into the cooking tent, screaming and yelling for help. They shouted over and over, "Don't shoot. Don't shoot (No disparar. No disparar)." Misty got to the rapist, perhaps first, and rifle-butted him in the head, sending him backward head over heels. He didn't get up again. His forehead was crushed in the blow. Three more were standing with their hands in the air. Hawk advanced into the camp, yelling for the three remaining perps to get down on their knees with hands on their heads. "Don't move (No te muevas. De rodillas. Manos en la cabeza)," he ordered.

Little G took pride in cuffing the three perps very securely. Misty came next yelling in their ears, "Bastards (Hijo de puta)," then kicking them in the back, forcing each face down in the dirt. It was evident that Misty sought and received a little justice for having been raped and beaten like the young girls huddled in a corner of the cook's tent, crying and shaking in fear.

Little G stood guard over the three perps as Misty and Capt. Gee searched the tents for any other perps. When finished, Misty went into the cook's tent. She took off her helmet and goggles, revealing her short strawberry blond hair and trying to console the women. "Girls, I am your friend (Chicas, me amigo). It's OK now (Esta bien ahora)."

All four girls walked out of the tent in a daze. They were not sure what to expect. Hawk was sure they all thought of deportation and family exile because of what these perps had done to them. Misty was grabbing shoulders and hugging them one at a time. Eventually, they clung to Misty for assurance and safety. But there was one task left to do. Misty had each girl hold the other's hand while she led her team of girls toward all four perps on the ground. The girls started to resist, not knowing what Misty was showing them. They were now visibly frightened of these men, even though they were rendered harmless. Misty started to show the girls what they needed to do. She spat on each perp and then kicked dirt in their faces. One by one, each girl caught on and did the same. Spitting in the faces of their captors and kicking dirt on them in a semblance of burying them alive. There was no other cymbal as degrading to any Cartel soldier than that. Only then did the girls jump with joy and praised God for their newfound freedom from their captivities. A couple of the younger girls went a second and third time to spit, curse and kick dirt on each rapist and horror mongers. Misty even spit one more time on the perp that she watched rape and beat the youngest little girl. Hawk wasn't sure if she was still crying out of fear or crying for joy or pain or all three. It didn't matter at this point. They were free as long as they could give a full report of where, how, and who all the attendees were and the Cartel names elsewhere. It was believed that the Cartels were operating locally because they had homes in Santa Barbara. The young Mexican girls were told that their captives would never see freedom again. Prison for life was all that they had to look forward to.

Capt. Gee got on the radio and advised Lt. Cam to come back and take the team home and bring fresh bodies to mop up the scene and start cutting down the pot plants and burning them. They needed a second chopper for the perps to ride in. Preferably one without doors. The four young girls would ride with Hawk and his group.

Misty took a look at Red's arm and bandaged him up for the moment, but told him that the bullet went clean through and stitches were needed and cleaning inside to keep infection away. Bob got a ricochet shot to his left calf muscle and was bandaged and given a crutch stick from a tree limb.

In total, the bad guys' tally was nine dead perps, three in custody but a little dirty, and four hostages freed. The pot plants were being cut and safely burned so not to prevent a major forest fire.

For the good guys, unfortunately, Billy was hurt real bad, having fallen out of the chopper; Red was wounded in the right arm and Bob in the left calve. *So, the good guys won,* Hawk guessed.

"Capt. Gee, if you don't mind, I would like to run background checks and serial numbers on all the weapons in the morning. Would like to work with ATF, CIA, and FBI to see any of those weapons were stolen from armories or what."

"That will be fine, Hawk," Capt. Gee said. "And good job today too. In spite of the injuries, this mission was a success."

"Thank you, sir."

The group didn't get back to the office until after three in the afternoon when Hawk called Annie to let her know they were all back and safe. He revealed little to Annie of the day's business because he knew it would only serve to worry her more.

As Misty was coming out of the office, Hawk called over to her and asked how she was doing. She actually smiled and reported she was fine and Hawk believed her for the moment, after having seen what she did with the four young girls at the pot camp. Misty, too, had buried her trials from the freeway Cartel shootout.

Before going home, Hawk stopped by the hospital to check on Red and Billy, and both were busy jousting with one another and telling the nurses all about how brave they were on the day's mission.

"Let me give you two guys a hug. You both did good, and thank you, Red, for taking care of the rattlesnakes. I guess you won't hear it from me, but don't quit chewing. Especially when we ride or have to crawl again in this country," Hawk said.

"Always got your back, cowboy. Thanks for having me with you, Hawk," Red replied.

"You got it, partner. Take care of yourself. See you in a few days," Hawk said.

Hawk took a few minutes to reflect on himself to see if he still had as much contempt for the Yardley's now as he did in the wee morning hours at the start of their mission. *Contempt—funny poison if left unattended for very long in our minds,* Hawk thought. It had melted away a little today and Hawk expected it to be gone completely one day soon. Perhaps another mission might help.

CHAPTER 8

VENGENCE IS MINE

Misty was so excited after the group's meeting with Capt. Gee regarding the consorted efforts of various law enforcement agencies to put a real short circuit wrench into the Mexican Cartels operating in San Diego. ATF and the Border Patrol discovered by accident a long one-and-a-half-mile underground tunnel leaving Tijuana and ending up in the flatland fields North of the border. Perfect unpatrolled area for night time extractions of drugs and people.

Several pick-up trucks would not even be noticed because so much of the areas were for off road motorcycles and dune buggies. Any vehicle painted in camouflage would be dismissed automatically as military and not even given a second glance. That is what was regularly occurring at least once per week. These tunnels are dug two and three at a time and about a half-mile to a mile apart. That way, if one tunnel is discovered, the others are still in operation. This is all part of the drug Cartel business. The excavation (tunnels) for transporting material, people, and drugs by the truckloads to the United States.

Misty was beside herself, with excitement, because this was part of her father's Cartel the group was scheduled to hassle. Misty knew that she could conceivably come face-to-face with her father and brothers, plus many other Cartel banditos who had at one time or another molested her. She tasted it in her mouth the blood of vengeance like an expensive bottle of red wine trickling down her dry throat.

Misty now felt that she was getting the help she always needed to stop at least one or more Cartel families for decades to come—her father, the Sinaloas, and the Los Zetas. If the Gulf Cartel were there, it would be frosting on the cake.

Misty confided in Hawk that she was both excited and scared, which was a good formula mix. One feeling can level out the other, keeping an individual at maximum alert status internally, and still exercise caution and safety. Not uncommon when working in a death-defying operation. And entering the enemy's basket would qualify for both. Crawling into dark tunnels that could collapse on anyone at any moment or be blown up by the enemy or discovered and shot is always a real possibility.

Sound devices like speakers were installed every fifty yards or so to help detect unwanted intrusion. On the Mexican side of the tunnel, the tunnel builders would install air vents along with manhole covers, which the Cartel could pop in and start shooting, or grenade tossing to kill anyone attempting to use their tunnel for anything other than their drug use. The tunnels were never crude in origin, but very sophisticated in their support beam construction. If on the return escape back into Tijuana, any soldier was being chased, they could simply kick one specially marked beam, which would collapse only one chamber behind them, thus eliminating the pursuing threat.

Very clever and dangerous missions. That was why Hawk's group's Intel had to be spot on and done only when the tunnel was not going to be used. Deputy Tab was the group's appointed lead officer who would be dressed in a similar jumpsuit, only no backpack other than the equipment necessary to muffle the speakers. That was his whole job on this mission—muffle the speakers and get to the opposite end of the tunnel quickly.

Silence was the group's only advocate in sending ten to fifteen people half standing and crawling for a mile-and-a-half in these tunnels. Added to that, the heat of the tunnels and each group member's weapons and gear in a sixty-pound plus backpack. Even with all the gear they would carry, one important part had to be left behind—their flack vest. It could mean the difference in being killed or just wounded. Oh well...

Everything, including weapons, jackets, food and additional ammo had to be placed in a backpack so nothing could be dragged on the ground. Special boots with sponge-like soles were used to minimize sound. Every zipper was made to open silently for commando jumpsuits. Black on black, head to toe, one after the other the group practiced with sound meters overhead to determine if this operation could even be accomplished at all in silent mode. They were unable to train in actual tunnels, but used every method they could find, including but not limited to crawling in ten-foot conduit pipe to get used to confined spaces.

Meanwhile, Capt. Gee was brokering a deal with an old friend of his, Miguel de la Madrid, who was the current president of Mexico. Madrid came to power through the governing party called the Institutional Revolutionary Party.

Madrid had received his Master's Degree from the Harvard Kennedy School of Government, where he met a very young George Gee. When President Madrid came to power, he inherited a very bad economy. Fortunately for him, he won the election and quickly turned things around until the 1981 8.1 Magnitude Earthquake which killed more than ten-thousand people. For some reason, President Madrid was not present for two days after the earthquake, and it was said he initially refused to accept International Aid help.

At the time, President Madrid's brother was reported to have amassed a fortune in a very short period, which was linked to the Cartels. The Cartel drug trade was on the move and needed to stay close to the International Banking system and the President, so making arrangements with the Mexican government for Hawk's group's small contingency force to be allowed inside the borders of Mexico was necessary and a joke all at the same time.

The question always was: Why would the Mexican Government allow any interference from the United States to mess with the breadwinner (the Drug Cartels)? Mexico's second producer, the Oil Lords, assisted the government and police, preventing the Cartels from shipping drugs across the U.S. borders. In spite of the Drug Cartel's combined wealth and ruling party strengths, the United States was still needed from time to time. Many trade embargoes were on the line and assistance in the form of Aid would always be required. Losing a few pounds of pot or heroin and pharmaceutical products was a very small drop in the bucket compared to the overall picture. Even a few tunnels mattered little. Lives meant nothing because people were always replaceable.

Even the United States was part and parcel of the money changers and the hands that collected bribes and favors from the Cartels' long arms stretching half way around the World. A lot of people should be in jail but then, some of them even working in the detention divisions were corrupt.

* * *

After a month of training exercises and gear changes plus physical strength training, Hawk and his group were ready. All they needed was a starting time. In the event of any miscue or bogus Intel, their special ops group might have to stay in the tunnel for two or even three days with minimal food and water. They just could not afford to be overly burdened by accessories like C-Ration cans, tools other than their all-purpose knives. They could only take protein bars already opened and held in soft plastic containers that could be untied quietly. The ammo was the heaviest, followed by the water. Remaining hydrated was probably more important than the food itself. It was a fine balance.

Too bad that Hawk and his group could not just cut the speaker wires, but the tunnel builders had installed professional monitors and alarms, should that be tried. The Mexicans based in Tijuana had pretty much thought of everything.

The group had a plan B, which included an insertion expert to locate and render inoperable the tunnel guards monitoring the group's operation. Eliminate the guards and the tunnel was the groups'. The only problem with that plan was having good enough Intel to locate and destroy the guarded monitors. The Cartel usually used normal, hard-working everyday laborers. Possibly the same families that help dig the tunnels. These people were expendable and constantly under threat of death. If word ever got out, as to the tunnel locations, then most of the little shacks, which hid many monitors, would be blown up.

Scared families with little to live for but hard work and constant threats of killings. It was not the typical local monitoring or radio station that the group could just walk into and shut down. Out of the thousands of the shack-like dwellings, which one was the right one in the village? No one was talking. Not yet anyway.

Other than living under the threat of death, these poor families had to deal with their own daughters and sons of all ages being molested and/or mutilated. The Cartel needed mules (people) to carry drugs, ingest drugs, and often surgery to remove them once in the United States. The only future most of these people would ever know was death, and it couldn't come soon enough. God, they thought, had forgotten them because this has gone on for such a long, long time.

Hawk's group had sent several people over to Tijuana to the villages close to the border to investigate and thus far had nothing. Were the monitors bogus? Maybe, but the group could not take that chance. With or without the Intel, they had to make a decision to jump into the tunnel because their delivery date, and their green light, would soon be arriving.

When the call came, the group was ready. Backpacks filled with extra ammo, weapons with silencers, and minimal food. Masks, personal first aid kit, including sutures, mouth held thirty-minute breathing devices in the event of a cave-in or an attack of confinement issues. This type of operation involves breathing in and out very slowly for fifteen or twenty minutes to calm one's nerves, busy yourself by exercising while lying on your back—anything to shut down the claustrophobia feelings. The other thing about this type of operation that can be very unnerving is that the only light was in the hands of the two lead coyotes and Hawk trailing second from last. First was Tab, and then Sargent Prince. That light was a kind of black light, not a normal flashlight. The entire group would be required to crawl a lot on their stomachs, keeping within an arm's length of the person in front of them in those tight areas. Otherwise, they were all bent over, walking and side stepping the support beams to proceed forward within arm's length of the person in front. If one wanted to know where they were, they just needed to reach out and touch somebody. Hopefully, it would be a deputy and not a big desert dragon lizard or something worse. Hawk had read some place that the famous and most poisonous dragon lizard loved living in dark tunnels.

Night blindness had to be the group's friend, not their enemy. Often in their training, they would all wear blindfolds to get accustomed to the lack of sight. Everything learned was by their sixth sense and touch. When all else failed, hey needed to listen with ears that can hear in silence and then touch if they must. Sitting in a dark room blindfolded with only one's self brings in-depth confidence. One learns to hear things that they didn't even know made sounds. Bugs, files, electricity, the earth shifting, the wind, birds outside that individuals normally learned to ignore. When one can see, why bother to listen? People just become lazy because some things are just not that important until they are.

The difference in being courageous or stupid is being well-trained, and Hawk believed he and his team were just that. In Hawk's estimation, his team was the best trained, the best athletes, and the best guerilla fighters in the world, bar none. All members of the teams were expert marksmen, intelligent thinking soldiers, team players, confident, and focused. Plus, every team personnel had dual language abilities. They were trained in every discipline required to enter into an operation like the present, succeed, and return alive. Even if wounded, they can set-up a makeshift operating table and attend to most any wounds. They were prepared to do operations on themselves. Being experienced, Hawk also knew that mistakes happen, usually when they are not expected.

Very few people could ever qualify for such detail and selection is hard, and training is harder. Time and patience is a valuable tool, but only if one were a capable team player. The team members had no star quarterbacks, yet they all were able to lead at any moment. Being a team member meant being able to interchange in any position at any called upon time.

Finally, they received the Intel that the Cartel was moving people and drugs through tunnel 'numeri dos' (#2) early the following morning. The team was called in on a Tuesday night in December, which is usually a warm time of year in San Diego.

Ten team members assembled at the Santa Barbara Airport, loaded into a special bird with seats for twenty plus cargo, and took off for San Diego. Their secret destination was a small airport outside of the grid with just enough room to land their Lear on a dirt runway with one old metal mechanics building to one side of the landing zone.

"Alright! Listen up, people! You are seated in numbered seats, which you will memorize, and you will maintain that number in the tunnel throughout the mission. You have been positioned according to your required discipline and strengths. When we get up topside again, you will be digging foxholes and remain spaced every eight to ten feet apart in two arrow formations on opposite sides of the tunnel opening. You will bury yourselves and remain hidden until our targets are ready to embark into the tunnel. Watch out for the unarmed male civilians. Do not fire on them unless you are sure they are holding weapons. Does everyone understand?"

"Yes, sir," the team responded.

"Are there any questions?" Hawk asked.

"No, sir," the team responded.

"Good. Enjoy your flight, and I hope that you use this time to rehearse your roles. Those who want prayer, listen up. Those who don't, then don't listen.

"Heavenly Father, I pray for safety for all our team members and the success of our team's mission. God Bless us tonight, Lord, and that of the innocent people we might encounter. For those who do not know You yet, I pray for their souls, Lord, and a new way of thinking. In Jesus name. Amen.

"If there is anyone needing to see me alone or personally, I will be in the back." There were no takers, which saddened Hawk. *Am I even making a difference anywhere?* Hawk asked himself. No answer came. He spent the rest of the short flight time praying in silence.

* * *

ATF, FBI, BP, and SDSO were all standing by with back-up for the mission.

Looking at the team, prior to disembarking the bird, Hawk could see on each camouflaged face a somber attitude. Some faces expressed open fear which would settle once boots were on the ground. Some expressions were that of regret or the lack of saying anything to a loved one left behind. And other faces reflected the grayness of death pockmarked on the eyebrows or around the mouth. Hawk was hoping that whatever the reason for the worry, each attendee was rehearsing his or her own capabilities and duties for the night. *They are ready,* Hawk kept telling himself. *We will not fail. That's not even a word in our vocabulary any longer.*

Hawk looked over at Misty who was their mission's Spanish Linguist, EMT, and Cartel face recognizer. No one knew who Misty was other than Misty and Hawk. Sargent Prince was trying and striking out. Misty did not want to get melted into any relationship yet. Hawk knew only a little bit of what she had shown him and told him in the women's restroom a couple of months back, plus a couple of years training with her and having her as his partner. This mission might be her defining moment, where Hawk would, possibly, learn more than he wanted to about her. He was sure to see more blood than he could wipe away. He had a vision of blood strewn streets and buildings after the last bullet was fired. The desert floor being turned from tan colored sand to red molten blood. It would not be pretty. If President Madrid even suspected for one minute that this mission had a twinge of family hate and vengeance mixed in, and not about illegal drugs being transported into the United States, then this mission would have been scrubbed long ago.

Misty was special. A hard-working, well-trained killer. A woman that no one wanted to mess with. She was as deadly on her feet as she was with a sub-machine or a knife in her hands. On her medical equipment bag was a symbol of a snake climbing a staff which reads, 'Don't Tread

On Me.' That personified Misty completely. Tough, confident, angry, and ready to strike.

Enough said about Misty, except for the creepy feeling hovering around in the back of Hawk's mind. If all went as planned in the early morning hours following, many of her family members would be dead. Cris-crossed emotions had to be going through her mind. Hawk knew she would not be distracted by the family death toll. These were animals that had mutilated her body and tried to destroy her mind and spirit. She would not be daunted any longer. She told Hawk in a quiet moment the previous day that she was ready for justice and retribution of past sins against her by her family. She was a willing executioner. That coldness scared the hell out of Hawk. He reminded her that death was no substitute for forgiveness. "If God could still forgive us after what humanity did to Him, then how could we not forgive our enemies? To accept Jesus means no more personal vendettas," Hawk said. Misty agreed and told him she would reconsider after the mission. Hawk told Misty that he held her to it.

"Alright, people. 'Off and On.' Load up with all your gear in the deuce and a half by the tin building over on your left. Double check everything. The ride to the tunnels is only fifteen minutes away," Hawk said. He asked the pilots to call his department and let Capt. Gee know they had landed and were ready to go.

"Acknowledged, and God speed," Capt. Gee answered.

Capt. Gee had a debilitating health issue, and he knew he would be a danger and a liability to the mission, so he stayed by the phone at their office.

Disembarking the deuce and a half, Hawk reminded everyone to remain in single file as numbered on the Lear. This was their order and would not change unless commanded to. They had about a two-mile walk to the hidden latch which had a big sage bush covering the metal locked lid.

When they arrived at the steel lid, Terry cut the lock off, and they descended the stairs down a good fifteen feet plus into a staging area which measured about ten feet in diameter. It was big enough for several people still on the ladder and a couple in the tunnel. Tab was their lead speaker man who would cover every speaker throughout the tunnel with a foam rubber pad. He had only a small backpack which held as many covers as needed and his 9mm. Dressed only in a jumpsuit and tennis shoes to reduce drag and noise, Tab was on his way, with his dimmed headlight on his head. Silence was the message to everyone. The mission was green.

Sargent Prince was second, and Misty was third. Typically, half-crawling and half-walking a mile and a half slowly and quietly takes two hours. Waiting for Tab to cover and muffle the speakers slowed the team more than expected and they didn't make it to the

Mexican border until three and a half hours from their start point. Unfortunately, not all things went as planned. The heat was more intolerant than anything they could have imagined. They had trained for everything but this kind of December heat. It was nearly as hot below ground as it was on the surface. It took its toll on all of them. Their new jumpsuits were of little help being this drenched. The jumpsuits were, in fact, a liability. Their bodies began to slip and slide inside of the suits and that made noise and a lot of discomfort. When this mission was completed, Hawk would be registering a complaint with the manufacturer. They lied regarding the suits capability of absorption and wicking the body sweat away from the skin. If they had been wearing the suit like a space suit, they would have all drowned.

At the half way mark of their tunnel journey, Hawk heard a slight noise behind him. It was Jason. Jason was their second to last in line, number 8. He was a new recruit to the team and physically capable and well-trained for this operation. The only problem other than the heat and saturated wetness was the night blindness and the feeling of claustrophobia. Hawk turned around and grabbed Tony and quietly told him to grab Jason by the arm and hold him to let him know it would soon be over. Hawk then told the person in front of him to do the same up the chain. It took another ten minutes for Jason to regain control of his nerves and the feeling of wanting to run and scream right

REX BARTON

into a supporting beam possibly killing all of them. When Jason was quiet again, Hawk moved him up ahead of him so he could continually pat him on the shoulder, letting him know all was well. The occasional black light gave them a little bit of hope that they were not totally blind.

Tab was close to the end of the tunnel—about fifty yards ahead of the pack. He stopped dead when he saw around a slight bend in the tunnel a dim lantern and two guards. Both guards appeared to be asleep. Hawk and his team were no longer alone. Prince's black light was on Tab, and he saw that he had stopped and was motioning the news of the two intruders. Tab took his backpack off and took his 9mm out with the silencer attached. Now he was on his belly crawling, even though he could have stood up. Slowly, he crawled to within twenty yards of the two guards and shot them both. Then all team members laid down and waited to see if anyone heard or had monitored the noise. Nerves were tested to the max during this down time, not knowing if a full combat Army was waiting to flush them out or not. They all felt trapped in their positions. Tab, Sargent Prince, and Misty were in view of the tunnel's end. All members waited a good ten minutes, and Prince finally motioned for the go ahead. Misty stopped to look at the two dead bodies to see if she recognized them. No.

The steel lid was superseded by a galvanized water pipe four feet wide and ten feet long and supported by big wood beams. From the top, it would be covered with dirt to hide its location and then the steel latch door would be locked from the outside to prevent anyone from using the tunnel to do exactly what Hawk and his team were about to do. Their next task was to start digging upwards to the surface and make a new escape route short of the galvanized pipe. Cutting the lock off the steel lid from the inside position in the tunnel was impossible for the team. The only problem they were faced with now was dispersing the excess dirt. One at a time, each team member spread the dirt on each side of themselves and forwarded the excess dirt toward the staging area, which was the same as their entry room on the U.S. side. One by one, the gallon cloth bags were passed back and forth. Once all the dirt had been repacked, the order was given to dislodge the last twelve inches of their new exit hole. Ketch was their climber up the shaft—by digging hand and foot holes to the top. His off-duty fun time was rock climbing without safety ropes. Once outside, he would either tie the knotted rope ladder to a tree if they were lucky enough to find one close or dig in and brace himself like an anchor and hold until everyone was out of the tunnel hole. The team members had little cover on the mostly barren ground, but the night was as dark as the tunnel was. This was one night Hawk was grateful for the lack of a full moon.

Ketch was their best climber, that's why he was chosen. He was not chosen because he was the strongest team member as they learned. With each person going up the knotted rope for balance along with the carved in foot holds, Ketch would lose ground on his anchorage. Hawk nearly fell fifteen feet back into the tunnel had it not been for Prince. He caught Ketch and the rope in the last second and got Hawk up topside.

It was good to be out of the hole and into the fresh air, even though the open sewers and stink of Tijuana drifted on the wind toward the team's downwind position. The wind blew a warm, stinky air at about six miles per hour. Hawk told the team to start digging foxholes to hide themselves when the Cartel vehicles arrived. They were supposed to arrive at four in the morning—one hour from now. There were no guards posted anywhere near the team's outside position, which made Hawk a little uneasy. *Was our information contact in Mexico, correct in telling us the tunnel being used was number two?* Hawk thought *There should have been guards posted out here, if anywhere.*

It only took fifteen minutes each for the team to dig a two-foot by seven-foot hole, slide in with their backpacks in front of them and their weapons at the ready. Next, they had to recover themselves with dirt, much like a sea turtle would do, by using only their arms and hands. Their night time field glasses were the only thing left showing on the surface.

When the last team member was out of the tunnel, Tab took a small five-foot black tarp from his backpack and covered the opening; then he spread dirt and some brush over all of it. The rope acted like an anchor holding the tarp down securely in the event of wind. This time of year, wind was always a factor and so was the possibility of dust and dirt foiling the team's efforts. It might have even given their position away. Thank God they were in their foxholes and covered. Each team member knew individually what to do. When the vehicles arrived, they were to carefully pick their targets and precision-fire with silencers attached— quiet perfection like a surgical procedure—and then confiscate all the drugs. If possible, the team could reload all the contraband into the cars or trucks and speed their way back to the border and climb over the wall. Ladders were already in place. So was the Calvary. If that were not possible, they would burn all contraband, jump back into the tunnel, and return the way they came.

The team's arrow formation foxholes were complete, and everyone was dug in. Then thirty minutes from touchdown, they all heard a muted scream coming from the inside of the tunnel. Hawk thought Misty had checked to see if either of the guards that Tab shot were still alive and if so, finish them. Ketch was closest to the entry hole and tried climbing down by the footholds that were dug, and ended up falling to the bottom of the tunnel floor. The Mexican guard screaming saw Ketch falling and raised his rifle and fired. Then Ketch was dead, but not without getting off a shot, which was more reflex than marksmanship. Nothing more was heard from the guard or Ketch. Nothing but sadness and regret. Before leaving, the team would go back down into the tunnel and bring Ketch out and take him back with them. Like any good ops unit, the motto was: leave no man behind. To the last man or woman, they would fight and die, if necessary, to bring their team home.

* * *

At a few minutes before 0400 hours in the morning, Hawk and his team heard, and then saw five vehicles, each with one headlight on. Hawk supposed the one headlight was to let the unknown enemy across the border get confused, thinking the lights were motorcycles or just flashlights in the desert night.

As the vehicles approached, Hawk held his breath, praying that God would give them victory.

All five vehicles came to a stop in a semicircle around the regular tunnel hatch opening. Each vehicle or truck was ten feet from the lid, with the headlights still on. It was obvious they had some hesitancy in leaving the safety of their vehicles until they were positive no one else was here. Someone must have said they heard a noise coming from or around the tunnel opening. But these guys were holding for too long, and their suspicion was obvious. Then Hawk heard another two vehicles approaching. It looked like two one-ton trucks loaded with Cartel soldiers. They were pulling up behind the cars and jumping out. Each truck had eight to ten rifle-carrying men ready to protect and defend their cargos. Someone in the first truck was pointing in the team's direction.

Misty couldn't wait any longer and broke ranks in front of Sargent Prince. She began shooting at the soldiers, dropping them one by two as she spread her AK-47 rounds in front of her. The rest of the team did the same from their respective foxholes as more soldiers were preparing to jump out of the vehicles. Then came the surprise. Three more vehicles were speeding up to the team's embattled location, filled with well-armed soldiers. To the team's fortune, none of the arriving vehicles, including over half of the original fleet of cars and soldiers, knew where to shoot.

Misty and Sargent Prince were cleaning house on the soldiers. They were the only team members fully exposed to the war, yet more people were dying than they could have shot. Even though this was all business, Hawk could not help but be pleased with their surprise cover. The enemy couldn't find them or see them, other than the dust billowing up from the ground every time the round left a mussel chamber.

The action was loud and fearful and so intense that Hawk wondered if anyone would be left alive. He really had no ability to determine who was still firing from the foxholes and who might have been shot or killed. It was still too dark, even with the vehicle headlights on—at least one vehicle light was on. The rest were shot out. Noticing that,

Hawk took aim and shot the only remaining headlight. Now they were all plunged into darkness once again.

Fortunately, Hawk's team had enough ammo to continue the fight. The Cartel Soldiers were mostly dead and unable to use their weapons, so Hawk's team just had to escape their holes and take up the enemy's guns to continue. Bullets were flying all around Hawk from the ensuing three trucks bearing down on his team's positions. Misty and Sargent Prince moved up to the two trucks and did, in fact, pick-up weapons and began firing on the approaching vehicles. Hawk saw headlights veering off in different directions as the trucks either drifted off into buildings or just drove off course and rolled over. One truck slowly kept going into the flat desert area; location destination unknown. The driver and occupants most likely dead, but the accelerator stuck to the floor.

The fight was over. Silence was once again returned to the team's battlefield front.

Hawk jumped up and got the team out of the holes. At least all but one. Jason was dead. He scarcely had shot through a magazine when he was shot in the head. Hawk checked his pulse to make sure.

"Prince, where are the drugs?" Hawk asked. Tab joined Misty and Prince and lent a hand.

"Watch yourselves. Make sure the perps are dead before reaching in," Hawk said.

"Misty, come with me," Prince yelled. "Check for lives and look for the gifts."

Misty was already inside the vehicles and turning over bodies, looking for family and friends. Those moaning or pleading for life had their throats cut. Ammo was now a precious commodity.

"Charlie, Larry, start checking ammo for matches and fill us up. Hurry, people, we don't have a lot of time here before daylight and more company," Hawk was yelling.

Everyone on the team was busy with their duties as Hawk was watching for unwanted visitors.

Prince, Tab, and Misty were piling up the drug presents in a large pile next to one of the lead vehicles. The pile grew to more than seven feet high and ten feet wide. Millions of dollars were invested into this shipment that the Cartel had put together, and in a few minutes, it would be burned into dust.

"Misty, do you have a count yet?" Hawk asked.

"Yes. Five of six," she said, motioning with her hand while slitting another throat. "One brother missing."

Hawk gave her the thumbs up.

Prince was busy putting gasoline on the pile of drugs and then weapons on top of all that. Everything would be burned and unusable this night. The bonfire was ready to light.

"Charlie, are any of these trucks useable? Hawk asked.

"Not finished checking, sir. Give me a moment," Charlie replied

"Hurry up, people. Time is running out. The Sun will be rising soon, and we will have visitors. Prince, wait until we are ready to go before lighting the fireworks," Hawk said.

"You got it, man. This was a good night," Prince replied.

"Not really. Two of our own are dead," Hawk said.

"Who?" Prince asked.

"Jason and Ketch," Hawk replied.

"Oh, crap. I am sorry, Hawk. I thought we all made it, OK?" Prince said.

"Charlie, how are you doing with the transportation. Give me a report?" Hawk asked.

"We have problems, Sarg. Can't find anything usable. We did a good job destroying these old beasts," Charlie replied.

"OK, everyone, look for a couple of tarps or ponchos and get back into the tunnel. We are out of time. Move, move," Hawk said.

Off in the distance Hawk could hear, not see, more vehicles coming their way. They would soon be out of the laborers' villages and on the flat toward Hawk and his team. Most likely, it would be the Mexican Army ready to defend their Country against who they didn't know. But they outnumbered the team and Hawk didn't want any part of it.

He grabbed Jason and lifted him to his right shoulder and carried him back to the tunnel entrance. With Larry's help, they lowered him into the tunnel floor on top of Ketch.

"OK, one by one, guys. Jump in the tunnel. Now," Hawk ordered.

Misty was first, Larry, Charlie, Prince, and Sam—who was slightly wounded in the left hip.

"Can you make the climb back, Sam?" Hawk asked.

"Yes, sir. No problem, Sarg. This is nothing. Just a scratch," Sam replied.

"When you get inside the tunnel, have Misty check your wound, soldier," Hawk said.

Last in the tunnel was Daniel. "You OK, Daniel?" Hawk asked.

"Yes, sir. Just a little dust in my eyes," Daniel replied.

"When you get down there, tell Prince to take charge. Tell him to wrap the boys up and start dragging them to our side of the border. Do it quickly. Flashlights on. Just move. Tell Prince that I will be covering our exit," Hawk said.

"Yes, sir," Daniel answered.

The lights of the oncoming trucks were quickly racing to the team's location. Hawk took three flares, lit them, and tossed them on the pile of drugs and weapons. It exploded into flames, and before the trucks could skid to a stop, the flames were white hot and burning out of control. Hawk began laying down a spread of bullets from his AK-47 and eliminating the threat of any soldiers trying to put the fire out or getting too close. So far, it worked, but ammo was getting low. Then Hawk felt someone crawl up next to him. It was Misty.

"Funny thing meeting you here? Want some ammo?" she asked.

"Thank you, dear. Now get back into the tunnel," Hawk replied, but she couldn't hear him over the pop, pop, pop of her AK-47 spreading the good news of their relentless barrage of thundering death. More soldiers by the dozens were dying this drug lit night, and it wasn't going to stop anytime soon.

The last truck started to back away from the team's location, and Hawk smacked Misty on the back and motioned her to hit the tunnel. This time, she complied.

The fire was out of control and spreading to the vehicles, and one by one, the leaking gas from the cars exploded. Before Hawk jumped back into the tunnel, He let loose one more burst of automatic fire and then jumped down to the tunnel floor. Everyone but Misty was well on their way in the tunnel. Hawk told Misty to hold up and help him do one more thing. While explaining to Misty what was next, he asked her why she broke cover and charged the Cartel firing away.

"Because I heard them say, 'I see something over there,' and they were pointing toward our team arrow," she replied.

"Thought so. I believe I saw them motioning toward us too. Thank you," Hawk said.

Then they half-ran, and half-walked to the first formal bracing poles and Hawk told Misty to hold his rifle for him and then to keep going forward. After she was at least twenty feet ahead of him, Hawk kicked the supporting beam down and the entire back of the tunnel collapsed. *The builders did a good job. Only have thirty more sections to go,* Hawk said.

Misty was waiting for Hawk to catch-up when she saw him wave. She was climbing the ladder toward the top and handed Prince their weapons. After that, she slid back down to where Hawk was ready to climb.

"I just wanted to say thank you, Hawk. The head of the snake was cut off tonight along with its young serpents, except for one, and thrown into the fire. Thank you, Hawk, for helping me right a wrong," Misty said.

She grabbed hold of Hawk and hugged as tight as she could. It felt good, and now Hawk was hoping to see Misty lighten up and give God a chance to heal her completely.

That was Hawk's prayer. Then he looked up the ladder and beyond the smiling faces and cheers to the starlit sky above all. "Thank You, God, and bless the two souls that gave their lives for so many others," Hawk prayed. He momentarily wept and felt the weight of the mission and the loss of lives hold him down fast to the ground. "Give me a minute," he yelled.

After a couple of minutes, Hawk regained enough strength to climb the last fifteen feet to the top and into the fresh air.

Many welcomed handshakes addressed him on top and a few hugs.

"OK, people, enough celebration. We have a plane to catch. 'Off and On!'" Hawk said.

Hoops, hollers, and singing could be heard on the way to the makeshift airport where the Lear was waiting. As the team approached, the sound of the engines could be heard over the drum of their deuce and a half. *It will be good to leave this place thinking to myself,* Hawk thought. He was getting tired and wondered when the pain in his stomach would stop. "Soon," he prayed.

Then Hawk's thoughts turned to the two dead deputies in the back. *Two dead. That's all I could think of? Come on, Hawk, they had names, and they have families. Jason and Ketch. You will have to see their wives and family today. You had better pull it together.*

Maybe Annie was right; I need to find another line of work. My guts are falling out, constantly spitting up blood. I am beyond tired and have trouble sleeping at night and just generally feel like nothing. What is going on, Father? Who am I becoming? Bloody missions. Carrying dead team members home. Sparing with higher ranking department members and getting a little help. Pressures at home. Politics of the job in general. The rigors of constant training. What do I do, Lord? Who or what am I becoming? I need rescuing right now, Lord. Please help! Hawk thought.

CHAPTER 9

THE ABC'S

The Lear landed at the Santa Barbara Airport and taxied over to the SBSO hanger. Everyone disembarked the bird tired and a little forlorn over the loss of two friends and two brothers in arms. Not everyone knew what had happened until they started back through the tunnel from the Mexican side. Prince and Larry were carrying the two tarped bodies, one over each shoulder, all the way back to the team's staging area. It was then that the team recognized the full potential of the loss of Ketch and Jason.

During the short flight home, Hawk went up front to the pilot's cockpit and radioed Capt. Gee of their successes and losses. Capt. Gee reminded Hawk that this could occur every day, not just during special operations. He gave himself to assist Hawk in contacting the wives and parents.

Hawk made a last request of Capt. Gee to have the department posthumously award their Service Medal for the families of Jason and

Ketch. They needed to ask PERS to arrange for ongoing benefits to the survivor's wives and children.

"Not to worry, Hawk, I will send two deputies over to Jason's wife now and then over to Ketch's parent's home," Capt. Gee volunteered.

"No, sir. Please let me take care of it myself. This was my squad and mission, and I need to finish my work. I will go as I am. They will understand; I am sure," Hawk said.

"OK, Hawk," Capt. Gee said. "Go and finish your detail and I will wait here to hear from you."

"One more favor, sir. Would you mind calling Annie and let her know that I have landed, but duty still calls? After notifications, I will give her a call from the office. Need to start my report this afternoon," Hawk said.

"Your six is covered, Hawk. See you here later. God be with you," Capt. Gee said.

"Thank you, sir," Hawk replied.

On the drive out to Goleta, Hawk stopped on the side of the freeway and prayed for God's help. This was one of the hardest tasks for any deputy to do. There are books on 'Notifications of Next of Kin.' The book's method was too cerebral. *Screw the books. There is no easy formula. Each case is different and just as hard as the first,* Hawk thought. He remembered his first death notification. Hawk was only fourteen, and he was at the St. Francis Hospital visiting with his grandfather. After three heart attacks and four strokes one of which cost him is left leg to infection, he passed away in front of Hawk—from Pneumonia. Hawk's mother, grandmother, and aunt Arden were still at the house in Goleta getting ready for dinner. After signing all the death documents, Hawk took the bus home and walked into the house. He asked everyone to join him in the living room. It was there that he related the information and death of his Grandpa. He could remember his mom sitting down in a chair, and his grandma and aunt Arden rushing to his side.

"Hey, it's OK. I am glad that I was there for Grandpa," Hawk said. Tears flowed from everyone but Sam, who was sure he was going to get a few bucks out of the deal. Hawk's Grandma would be selling the ranch soon and scaling down. Sam was rubbing his hand together like a dishonest shrew capitalizing on others' sadness.

Hawk and his mother had taken care of his grandpa's day in and day out care. He lived in the guest room next to Hawk's—where he could hear anything his grandpa may have needed during the night. For eight long years, Hawk's mother suffered for his grandpa's care. Daily bathing, cleaning, laundry, and three meals a day plus snacks. It was no wonder she just sat there in a chair in disbelief of what those eight years took out of her. Everyone told her she was wrong for doing it, but that was her dad, and no one else volunteered. The only other solution, according to family, was a bad choice of nursing homes. The suffering of Hawk's mother's care of his grandpa eventually turned to cancer.

Ultimately, it killed her. She joined the many victims of breast cancer in the mid-nineties after many years of personal sufferings. However, Sam may have been the greatest cause—due to his child molestation crimes.

* * *

Hawk went first to Jason's little condo in Goleta and knocked on the door. Sheila answered the door and stared at me. She knew but wasn't a hundred percent convinced until she saw the tear in my eye.

"Sheila, I am so sorry, honey. We lost Jason this morning in a firefight. He didn't suffer, though, not even for a second. I just wanted you to know that. His body was taken down to the morgue, and I will call you when you can go and see him. I will help you in any way I can. You need only ask. OK?"

Sheila, just looked at me with an unbelieving blank stare.

"This can't be," she uttered at last. "We just had a baby. What about the baby?" Low continuous moans expelled through her open lips. The physical pain had not committed yet, but the numbness in her mind was already trying to deal with Jason's death. Twisting, turning anguish was collapsing the arteries in her head, choking off the blood supply to her brain; fear of the unknown wrenching her from side to side.

"May I come in, Sheila? I would like to share some thoughts with you," Hawk asked.

"No," Sheila said. "No, not now. I have to get the baby ready. Oh, no. No!" she screamed, "This can't be."

Sheila threw her hands up in the air and then gently touched each cheek as if remembering Jason's last goodbye kiss.

"Sheila, is there anyone I can call to come and be with you? Sheila?" Hawk asked.

She was attempting unconsciously to close the door but didn't have the strength nor the ability to do so. Instead, she held the door partially open and fell through it and into Hawk's arms. He caught her and carried her into the living room and laid her on the couch with a pillow under her head. Across the living room was a rocking chair where either Sheila or Jason would sit with the baby to feed or to rock her to sleep. On the back of the chair was a small knitted quilt. Hawk grabbed it and gently put it across her and then went to the kitchen, looking for a glass to fill with water.

Hawk heard her crying when he returned to the couch. She was trying to understand, but the shock was clouding every avenue of reason.

After a few minutes, Hawk asked her again for a phone number.

"A name or phone number, something of any relatives," Hawk said. She motioned to the dining room table and a black book resting next to the phone. Hawk grabbed it and brought it to her. Sheila opened the book to what Hawk presumed was her sister's name and number in town. He asked to make sure, and she nodded her head yes. He then made the call and explained the situation and asked if she would please come and be with Sheila and the baby who was getting a little restless in the bedroom crib.

Sheila tried to get up and could not stand yet, so Hawk went into the bedroom and gathered up the baby in a blanket and handed her over to Sheila.

Sheila's sister was on her way over, and Hawk stayed with Sheila and the baby for almost an hour before Rhonda, Sheila's sister, arrived.

"Thank you, Rhonda. I appreciate you helping out at this time," Hawk said. He gave a brief explanation of the mission and what happened to Jason. He then related what to do to make arrangements to see Jason later at the morgue.

There could not have been anything as sad as the news that Hawk brought Sheila and her sister this day. The pain and loss of a loved one is more than what most people at such a young family age can bear. Hawk felt so sad for them, especially knowing the baby daughter will never have a chance of seeing her daddy again. He knew that feeling himself, having never seen his own father. Just emptiness. A never-healing, empty hole in one's heart.

Before leaving, Hawk tried to give Sheila a hug and say one more time how sorry he was that Jason was gone from them. She could not accept Hawk's touch, which was totally understandable, and he didn't force the issue. Hawk just said goodbye and gave Rhonda his card and phone number if she needed to contact him. He told Rhonda that at some point, he would need to talk with her and Sheila about coming arrangements for the funeral and personal things she just needed to know about.

Rhonda thanked Hawk and said she would call, and he left. The harder of the two commitments was over. Hawk now had to return to town and notify Ketch's parents of their loss.

Ketch's parents took the news as well as anyone could expect.

"There is no right way or rule of saying thank you for not protecting our son. What were you doing out there if not protecting him?" Ketch's mother left the dining room and went into Ketch's bedroom and cried. Probably all night. His dad was understanding and appreciative of his son's contribution as a Deputy Sheriff, which was his longtime dream. He was proud of Ketch and all that he had accomplished in the short time of his life. Hawk shook his hand and left through the back door and circled the driveway, walking back to his car. The drive to the office was one of intermittent tears of today's events and losses.

Hawk's official notification duties were concluded but not over. He still had Annie to tell, and that may be the most difficult yet to do. His stomach was killing him, so he stopped at the five and dime store to get some Tums. Hawk couldn't remember the last time he ate, so he ordered a hot dog to go. Once that was inhaled, his stomach just got worse. Hawk was confused, but couldn't stop for anymore disruption from his body, so he pushed on to the Bureau office. Annie would surely know from the tone of Hawk's voice that he was in physical trouble of some kind. She always did. He never knew how she could tell. Some weird sixth sense or just a wife thing, he couldn't just say.

Capt. Gee was waiting for Hawk when he got in; he stood up from behind his desk and grabbed Hawk's hand and held on. It was a little strange for a person who never liked getting very close to anyone, but then Hawk wasn't just anyone. They had both gone through many death notifications over the years and shared a mutual respect for this part of the job. Their faith was all that permitted them the strength to handle the darkest and saddest side of the job. Watching and enduring grief-stricken families' loss and horror of the circumstance was never made easier with time or experience. The last notification was as bad as the very first. *Pain is pain, and gut-wrenching no matter the way. Pain.*

"Have a seat, Hawk," Capt. Gee asked. "I know this has been a very hard couple of days. You deserve a long rest, and I am going to order it. I am so very sorry for the losses, and I am sure you did everything within your power to bring everyone back safely. Please don't let the losses prevent you from going forward. We both have a job to do, and from all the early reports, you did one hell of a good job today in Mexico. Not that your job can ever be reported that way. As you know, regardless of the political posturing, Mexico is off limits, even in a pursuit. However, President Madrid called to inform me to keep you out of Mexico. He said for you never to return. He was pissed that so many of his men were killed and so much dope burned. 'Why did you have to burn it all up?' He asked me. 'It could have been redistributed.' Realizing what he had said, he then stopped talking.

"I re-informed him of our agreement and the ABC's of the Cartel's work here. I told him we were not going to have the Cartels running amuck here in Santa Barbara. Not anymore, and that he was damn lucky you didn't march all the way to Mexico City and take it over. Needless to say, we probably won't get any further cooperation from Madrid. Oh, well, you Abolished the Bully Cartels today in Tijuana. I was told that a total of five tunnels was dynamited by ATF and the Border Patrol. It will be a good long time before that method will be used again," he said.

Hawk laughed at his call information and then asked to be excused to write the report. Capt. Gee made one last comment, "Annie is aware, but you had better call home."

"Thanks, Capt. Gee. I will call her first," Hawk said.

"Hi, honey, it's me."

"Hi, me! Annie replied."

"I know that Capt. Gee called you already, but I wanted to touch base and let you know that I need about two more hours here at the office to write the reports out on the mission."

"Hawk, Gee did tell me what happened. I am so sorry about Jason and Ketch. Was anyone else hurt? Are you alright?" Annie asked.

"Everyone else is fine. Nothing more than a few minor flesh wounds, bumps, and bruises. The norm.

"Yes, I am fine. Just tired, babe. Can't wait to get home and get some sleep," Hawk said. Annie's calmness surprised him. He didn't indicate any fear or trepidation. "Thank You, Lord," Hawk mused.

"I have your favorite stir fry and salad waiting. Come home as soon as you can, OK?" Annie said.

"I will, honey. Don't worry. See you in a couple of hours. Don't think I can eat much, though."

"Why? What's wrong? Is it your stomach again?" Annie asked.

Oh, no, here it comes. I just gave birth to her worry, Hawk thought. "Nothing, dear!"

Trying to recount all that happened from start to finish of the mission took much longer than Hawk thought it would. Capt. Gee left a good half hour before Hawk, and Hawk told him he would lock up. The longer Hawk gave of himself to remember the tunnel experience, the near panic feelings of such a dark and tight place for that many hours was enough to start the panic and stomach pain all over again.

Then the two Mexican guards that Tab shot and no one checked to see if they were dead, which gave way to Jason being killed. How could Hawk put that in his report? The truth was, he should have checked to make sure himself. *God knows we were down there long enough, sifting dirt around from the new opening that anyone could have checked. Why was I watching a hole and not checking the guards? It was all my fault, and I must write it down that way,* Hawk thought. Even though he had assigned the duty to someone else, it was still his call to make, and he screwed up, plain and simple.

Hawk's report reads the thus: *The two Mexican guards that were overtaken and shot were thought to be dead. Their pulses were checked, and none was detected. I did not check them myself; therefore, I am unable to determine life in either guard. When Jason returned into the tunnel upon hearing screams, he slipped on the rope and fell to the tunnel floor in the dark. The Mexican guard that was screaming fired once into the darken shadow of Deputy Jason Howling as Jason himself fired in the dark at the guard. Both expired from their wounds. Deputy Jason Howling was shot in the head and expired immediately. I take full responsibility for the life of a very good Deputy Sheriff Jason Howling and my lack of better actions.*

The foxhole incident was different. Any one of us could have been shot and killed.

Losing Ketch was just a mistake of bad luck. It was a stray bullet that killed him while defending our position, lying in a shallow foxhole.

Providence, I supposed. God needed Jason and Ketch home with Him for reasons I won't understand until the day when I can ask Him myself.

Somewhere and at some point, the last line of Hawk's report regarding his responsibility in the death of Deputy Howling was scrubbed. He didn't find out until the last five minutes before the hearing. Capt. Gee told Hawk and said not to worry about it. That was all Hawk did, though—worry about it for months until he was asked at the inquest if his report was true and accurate. *Do I tell the truth and say no, that my report is missing a line of responsibility? Or just let it go so as not to embarrass the department?* Hawk thought. Politically, he was being postured, and he didn't like it, nor did he have all the answers why. Hawk agreed with the attorney's question in part by saying that his report was as accurate as he could recall. No one asked if Hawk could recall anything different, or if he had anything else to add. So, the incident, as it was so lightly called, was concluded and Sheila and the baby were awarded full retirement with benefits, the accommodation medal worth about a nickel and a wonderful write up in the county's local news press paper.

When Hawk returned to the office, he gave Capt. Gee a disturbing look, and he just smiled and nodded his head in agreement. One day soon Hawk would ask him what happened and why. Hawk guessed the department got away with not paying out more money. To stay in the ranks and continue on, Hawk, unfortunately, kept his mouth shut on the issue—as shut as he could, because the stomach ulcer was playing hell with his body and throwing up blood was a regular thing now. Eating was impossible, and something had to give.

* * *

Hawk closed the office up and started toward the Vette. Another car was parked next to his. It was Misty.

"What's up, kid?" Hawk asked.

"I have been watching you for the last hour writing your report. Are you OK?" You look very tired and in some kind of pain. Are you hurt?" Misty asked.

"No, I am alright. Someday when you are in command and writing reports and notifying families of their losses, you will understand," Hawk said.

"I am so sorry about that guard that killed Jason. I did give a cursory check and felt no pulse. Really, Hawk. I didn't feel anything," Misty said.

"I know, Misty. That is something easy to overlook, and his breathing was probably so shallow we all would have missed it. Not a problem anyway. I took the heat and said it like it was. Just missed feeling any heartbeat. Something easy to overlook when adrenaline is running high, our own heartbeats are elevated, and most of us were in a quiet panic from the tunnel experience in itself. Not to worry OK?" Hawk said.

"Thank you for all you have done for me, Hawk. Your word was true. I still don't know what I feel yet, but I am sure that will change soon. Without you, Hawk, this would never have happened. Some vindication and respect was returned to me tonight, and the Jefe's head was cut off. Women all over Mexico will soon know that freedom is being exercised in ways they are not yet aware," Misty proclaimed.

"Good, Misty. My only prayer is that you come to terms with God. He is patiently waiting for you, and He loves you so much. You promised me that when vengeance was exacted, you would listen to me. Are you willing now?" For some reason, Hawk started coughing, as if choking on something.

"Hawk, what's wrong? You are coughing up blood?" Misty inquired.

"Nothing. Just bit the inside of my mouth. I need to get home," Hawk said. (More coughing.)

"Hawk, that is too much blood. Are you shot or something? Tell me what is going on with you," Misty inquired.

"Nothing, Misty. I just need to get home. Annie is waiting," Hawk said.

Hawk got into his Vette before Misty could stop him or ask any more questions. There was just too much pain in his gut to stand around, jawing. The enemy (the devil) was taking advantage of an opportune time. Misty didn't really want to hear anything more about God and was more concerned that she let the team down by her vendetta actions, and not checking the guards closer. Hawk opened the car door and spat up a little more blood before leaving the parking lot and said, "The day is done, Misty. Gone the sun from the land, from the sea, and from the sky. Rest now, God is nigh." He pointed to his cheek to avert any further questions and drove home. How was Hawk going to avert the choking red pain from Annie? She was far too wise for his games.

In the days to come, Hawk found out how to cope with the pain of his stomach. The doctors ordered a wonderful white milky, horrible-tasting medicine for Hawk to drink, and a new diet. "Lay off of all the tacos and fast food items for a while and avoid all spicy foods!" was the advice given. Luckily, Hawk could still eat bananas and a little milk. No coffee or orange juice. No steaks and nothing he liked. Banana diet is good if one wanted to gain weight, which Hawk didn't need to do. Ironically, the gross blood spitting was not over. Next stop exploratory surgery was performed, and the doctors found cancer in Hawk's stomach, and a whole new diet ensued—one with hanging bottles on stainless steel stands fed through Hawk's veins for the next few weeks to come.

The time off gave Hawk reason to pause and get his priorities straight and keep the Bible open. Every time Annie and Hawk read the Word or had friends over for a Home Bible study, his stomach was calm, and he felt better. Especially after prayer. That was a clue for Hawk to change his life sooner than later if that were even possible.

It took several months for Hawk to get back on his feet, and he was not physically ready for any strength training. Just slow track, walking a lap at a time per week. It took longer than Hawk had expected to put everything behind him and let the Bureau run on its own without much of his input. He felt worthless as far as any missions were concerned as Prince and Red who transferred over to the Bureau took over that arena. It was good to have Red to talk to again on a daily basis. Often during the day's duties, Hawk and Red would take the time to pray and keep their priorities straight. When they saw Misty standing around, they would invite her into their standing prayer meeting. She agreed to learn more and listen to the Word of God when read. If anyone began to try and explain what a passage said, she would balk and stop them in mid-sentence. "If it is not from God's Word, then I don't want to hear it," she would say. Hawk agreed, and that was why God left the Holy Spirit for them as a teacher and guide. Misty was learning, and Hawk gave God the praise.

Capt. Gee called Hawk into his office just before Christmas and asked what his priorities were for the coming year. So far, Hawk's only contribution to the Bureau since his stomach cancer was riding a desk and working on missing gun reports. He wanted to find the common thread between the military thefts and the sloppy evidence rooms. He never could quite make the connections, but it never stopped him from trying.

Hawk didn't have anything in mind other than making cases for tighter gun controls when evidenced, and proper disposal once cases are completed.

Capt. Gee said he had thought that maybe Hawk could devote some time to cold case files.

"We have far too many unsolved cases that need results. Just look at all the rape cases never solved and the cold murder cases that need trials and felons imprisoned," Capt. Gee said.

"I think that would work. I could do that and feel I am really contributing to the overall justice program. Thank you. Yes, I would like that very much," Hawk said.

"Good," Capt. Gee commented and then announced that he was officially putting Hawk in charge of the cold case unit.

"You can start by going down into the evidence room and sorting through the overdue murder cases. If you have any questions, call me. There is more to do than you realize. We have cases going back thirty years or more. With all the new links in fingerprints at the local, FBI, CID, and national NCIS units, you might make a real dent in that city," Capt. Gee said.

"Thank you. I will get started today, if that is alright?" Hawk asked.

"It is all yours, Hawk," Capt. Gee replied.

After having time to think a little, Hawk realized that maybe he was being led to pasture for a long rest. Was this the answer to Jason's death and Hawk's report scrubbed lines? Hawk didn't want that to be on his epithet nor was he going to let that report become a cold file itself. He vowed to keep it open at least in his mind until he could find all the answers and lay it to rest properly. *Or does it have something to do with the Cartels? Had someone like President Madrid come through the back door of our politics office to side track me from any further missions or attacks? Did Maria get to someone that I didn't know as yet and put a halt on the 'Dragon Slayer'? Something to think about,* Hawk thought. He had more questions than answers at this point and would take his time in acquiring those answers. That was for sure.

In the weeks that followed after Christmas, Hawk's eye kept coming up on a strange word in a couple of the cold case murder mysteries. *Panga? Panga boats? Who and what are they?* Hawk thought. In his research, Hawk found that in each incident he studied, a very fast twenty-two-foot shallow bottom boat was being used to carry people and drugs into the California Coastal Cities. Santa Barbara and San Luis Obispo, just to name a couple. The crafts were being sold by Yamaha of Mexico and a U.S. manufacturer with hidden shell names of the principals. *Game time!* Hawk thought, for they all knew that the

Cartels were operating big fishing boats in deep water channels, but this was a new effort. A new green twist in money and pot. A way to quickly put drugs and people into the county's areas at night and avoid all detection. Coast guard vessels could not keep up with the Pangas, not just because they were fast but being a shallow bottom boat, they could skirt the shoreline barely detected and travel for a couple of hundred miles at a time. Once the drop zone was determined, they would run the craft up onto the beaches and unload into waiting trucks. Not unusual for trucks to be in or near the county's local beaches during certain fishing seasons. Not unusual for Pangas to drop off their cargo on privately owned beach front ranches either. The new green was fast becoming the answer to a new front in drugs. The problem was, some of the passengers who were flipped out of the boats were on their own and most drowned. Thus they either ended up in Hawk's Cold Case office because of the lack of identification or just listed as accidental drownings if a name or mementos were found in pockets indicating local families.

Hawk could feel his blood pumping again, and he shared some of his investigations reports with Capt. Gee. Hawk's answers were slow in coming and literally ignored for the most part. Strange, he thought, but it was suggested that he look into the many other cold case murders that needed clearing before tackling the boat theories.

Hawk went home with a little burden in his stomach that night for the first time in a while. *Could be another clue as to which direction I should go in the future!* he thought!

Panga—a mysterious name that really meant flat blade or machete. Probably for the thin flat bottom. *Interesting*, Hawk thought, and the following day, in spite of what Capt. Gee had to say about it; Hawk was going to investigate further. *Maybe start with a dinner at the Wharf Restaurant with Annie again?* he thought. Hawk was sure that Antonio might have more clues.

CHAPTER 10

THE GUN RUNNERS

"Hey, guys, how is everyone doing today? Prince, did you know that your gas tank has a rag sticking out of it? Not sure what that is all about?" Hawk asked.

"What? You messing with me again, Hawk?" Prince replied.

"Why would I be messing with you, Man? Because of the mud smeared all over my car windows? Or the flat tire? Or the sugar in the gas tank?" Hawk inquired.

"Bull shit! I only pu—"

"Oh, but you did do the rest. Right?" Hawk interrupted.

Everyone laughed for a few minutes. It was kind of funny how easy it was to trap Mr. Yep. Prince always liked to play jokes on people, and threaten beautiful young women with a traffic citations or arrest on a bogus charge and then offer to take them to coffee instead. That was just his dating style. *If I were a woman, I would challenge him. Then I would report him to the Sheriff,* Hawk thought. Somehow, that never happened. To Prince, why give up a good entry into a relationship or a bed party?

"What do you say, Prince, are we even until next time?" Hawk asked.

"Yeah, OK," Prince agreed.

"Capt. Gee, good morning, sir. Thought I would start in on the weapons list for any matches of missing or stolen guns," Hawk said.

"Hi, Hawk. Got the list right here. If you need help, grab one of the girls," Capt. Gee said.

"OK, will do. Any word from the hospital on Billy's injuries from the fall yesterday?" Hawk asked.

"Yes. In fact, I talked with him this morning. His back is fractured between L-4 and L-5. Shoulder popped out of place and went back in, so that was a relief. His leg was definitely broken, but doctors expect a quick recovery. His spirits are good, and doesn't really remember that much. When he hit the ground, he was definitely in shock," Capt. Gee said.

"How about Red and Larry?" Hawk asked.

"Both good and both minor wounds. I expect both back to work on the desks next week," Capt. Gee said.

"That's great, sir. It will be good to get everyone back again. Maybe I can get started on that list then? Need to find out where the holes are in the system. The Cartels are getting them from somewhere. I think, first, I might talk with Tania and see how many stolen weapons from our own tri-counties area," Hawk said.

"Good idea, Hawk. Maybe we can take a few off the street along with some crime families," Capt. Gee said.

Hawk walked upstairs and over to Tania's desk.

"Hi, Tania, how are you doing today?"

"Good, how about you, Hawk? To what do I owe the pleasure?"

"How about a date?"

Tania looked at Hawk with arrows in her eyes ready to shoot him down.

"Drop dead, Hawk."

"No, I am serious, dear. Need a date to discuss any and all things you can share with me regarding stolen weapons and calibers within the last two years. If you're not too busy of course?"

"Oh, that kind of date. A data date. Too bad, because I was going to give you a second thought right after cleaning up the horse shit on the floor."

"OK, I am sorry. Can you help me out, though?"

"Why are you asking?"

"So we can spend more time together, of course."

"More horse shit on the floor to clean up, Hawk. This time, you clean it up."

"Here's the deal. In the last operation, the perps we fought with were using AR-15 semi-auto's and a couple of M-1's and ten 45 autos. It seems that every single operation is filled with military grade weapons and I would like to know where they are coming from and how the perps are getting their hands on them."

"Alright. A date it is. Come on with me over to the Intel office, and we can acquire a lot of data on the fax machine recall lists. I can type in all Military bases and then lost or stolen weapons. Along with police departments and deep sea disposals."

"Oh, that would be great, Tania. Big help and a lot of homework."

"Yeah. Well, that is your problem. I could help but you or someone else might miss-construe that as a date."

"I promise, Tania, I would never call that guidance a date. My lips are sealed."

"Come on, Mr. Hawk, let's get started."

Tania was always fun to tease because she was quick and witty. She wouldn't take any guff from anyone besides her husband, Capt. Gee, who was right downstairs. Hawk loved them both.

For the next couple of hours, Tania presented Hawk with a virtual book of data on every known weapon stolen from military bases in California, Nevada, New Mexico, Texas, and Arizona. Many stolen guns from police department evidence rooms and deep sea disposals. Weapons on manifests to have been disposed of and showed back up in use on the streets in new crimes. *According to the records, more than 200,000 guns reported stolen, and many showed back in use today. Dumping the guns in the ocean is clearly not the answer—too easy to track and fish up. Melting the weapons down would be a better answer.*

After several hours of work—tracking down missing weapons from police evidence inventory rooms and that of the ATF, FBI, and many military armories—Hawk was exhausted and confused. *How could so many weapons be missing and nobody really cares? Who's looking for them? Where are all the reports? Most police departments made small, insignificant incident theft reports that were all but hidden in the daily activity logs. Where is the call to arms? No pun intended. Why wasn't there a big deal being made? Someone, some organization, or political party is clearly acting out as arms dealers and getting rich,* he thought.

"Hey, Tania, can you explain to me why this local report from our own evidence room is listed as a daily log activity and not a full blown report on missing or stolen weapons?"

"Yes, I can, but you need to call Capt. Gee up here first."

"Why? Am I just not understanding how things are done around here?"

"Hawk, everything has a logical reason. All those reports you are digging up from the ATF, FBI, Military, and Police Departments are the tip of the iceberg. Please get Capt. Gee up here. It may save a lot of time."

"OK. I need a break anyway, so I am going down stairs for a few."

Hawk went outside to get a breath of fresh air and stood behind a rather large Bougainvillea bush. It was at the rear corner of the detective bureau, and he didn't realize it at the time, but this beautiful red, purple, and pink flowering bush was hiding Hawk in captivity of its sheer magnificence. He was not only camouflaged by its colors, but by the density of the bush as well.

It was nice to stand braced by one foot up on the building, leaning back and looking up at the mountains above the city of Santa Barbara. The bell tower of the courthouse just resounded four bongs. It was so peaceful until Hawk heard two very familiar voices around the corner from where he was standing. The voices were clear and meaningful of orders and directions. Hawk didn't dare breath or move for fear of embarrassment and being found out just on the other side of the Boggy—until he heard what was being discussed.

The male voice was proclaiming victory one day soon, one way or the other. He kept saying over and over: "Get the guns tonight Victoria (Esta noche tenemos las armas Victoria)?" "I could not understand about a small bird or something like that (Es un pequeno halcon, pajaro)?" "Only that he will die (El va a morir)." "Again, something about a Victoria fast (Victoria pronto, Victoria pronto)?"

Hawk didn't know any Victoria, but he did know the female voice. He knew it well and didn't have to see her to confirm her identity. It was surprising to hear the female voice speak such perfect Spanish and so fluently. Hawk's heart was breaking, and he could tell no one what he just heard. Who would he tell? This brief meeting was so far out of space that Hawk was not sure afterward if he really heard what he heard.

When they left, Hawk was in a daze. Completely crushed by the chance meeting at the Bougainvillea bush. He stayed in his position for more than an hour. He didn't dare move. Detectives and cars came and went yet Hawk remained a steadfast pillar, frozen at his post.

Hawk had to tell someone but who? Who could he trust well enough not to get killed? Capt. Gee? Hawk felt something wrong with his investigation of the missing weapons—as if it was no big thing to Capt. Gee. *What is wrong, Hawk? What is it that's wrong?* Hawk kept asking himself. *Commander Williams? He is getting ready to retire, and I know he is tired of the hole kit and caboodle. But I could trust him. I don't think that I could trust any of his recommendations. I just need to think. Go home, Hawk, and think.* "What about the night guns (Esta noche armas)?" *Is that what I even heard? That means night guns or guns with night vision? God, I don't know. Too tired myself right now. Go home, Hawk. Go home and get some dinner,* Hawk told himself.

* * *

"Annie, I am home. Annie? Where are you?" Her car was in the garage, so she had to be there somewhere. Hawk went outside and looked in the pool and spa. Nothing. "Annie," he called with a little more stress in his voice. "Annie! Where are you?" Hawk began to panic in light of all that he heard this afternoon.

"Hawk, I am over here at Donna's," Annie said. Hawk momentarily exhaled a sigh of relief. *Donna's? Thank God she has more guns, and she knows how to use them all very proficiently,* Hawk thought. In all of Hawk's neighbors, except Casey and Loraine, Donna was good for Annie's safety. Now Casey was in the Israel Military and a well-trained guerilla fighter. Hawk would stand shoulder to shoulder with him all day long. The problem was, they were going back and forth to Israel all the time. Casey's family was still there working the land, but lately, their father had an illness. *Get back, Casey and Loraine, real soon, please. I may need you,* Hawk thought to himself. He knew, from many talks with Casey, that Casey's home was a virtual fortress full of automatic weapons, handguns right down to grenades and low-grade rockets. To say they were ready for war was an understatement and none of the weapons were stolen, neither were they registered—at least, not in Hawk's country. They may have been registered in the homeland of Israel. Who really cared? All the weapons were legally mailed. Hawk knew because Casey told him. They came in lightweight plastic boxes, all wrapped up in tin foil so as not to get dusty. Hawk wondered for a brief moment how that happened. *Let it go, Hawk,* he thought. *Who cares anyway.*

Hawk walked over to Donna's, expecting she and Annie to be in the pool but they weren't. They were both sitting in the patio chairs, talking about the neighborhood and him! *What else is there to talk about?* Hawk thought. Walking up, he gave Annie a kiss on her cheek, and not to leave Donna out, he gave her one too.

"So, my two favorite ladies, what's going on this afternoon?" Hawk asked. Donna was still blushing, so Hawk looked down at Annie who was about to speak when another neighbor came walking around the corner of the house. Now they had a crowd and Hawk didn't really feel like talking, so he politely said hello and then bade goodbye and told Annie he would be working in the garage.

"OK, honey, I will be right home," Annie said.

"No hurry, babe. Enjoy. I need to finish a small project on the work bench. How're you doing, Harry?" Hawk asked.

"Good, good. Need any help?" Harry asked.

"No, just need to putter. See you all later," Hawk said.

Hawk heard OK's faintly behind him as he was walking off. He just was not ready for small talk, and especially with nosey neighbors. He walked back over to his home and into the garage and took one look at his messy work bench and thought, *To hell with it. Not today. I have cleaned enough crap up today.* Hawk's head was still trying to figure out what and who he was going to talk with regarding all the missing weapons in his department. *Think, Hawk, who is benefiting from all the missing guns? Who is driving a new car or just purchased a newer, bigger home? Who just came back from a big vacation or who just lost big in Vegas?*

Hawk started thinking of each member of the evidence room deputies and clerks. Then he expanded his criteria to the people in the offices near the evidence room. At that point, he couldn't think anymore. He just sat down in his easy chair by the fireplace and picked up a new Sunset Magazine with tempting articles on camping out in California—*Who has the best hamburgers and freshest salads?* The camping was interesting the rest put Hawk to sleep. He was uneasy, tired, and just wanted to take a break. Looking up at a picture hanging on the living room wall of Desiderata and re-reading the words, "Go placidly amid the noise and haste and remember what peace there may be in silence. As far as possible without surrender, be on good terms with all persons." The words just threw Hawk deeper into the hole he was already digging for myself. Then he heard the front door opening and Annie calling out, "Hawk, where are you, honey?"

"In here; in the living room."

"Why? I thought you were going to work in the garage and doing some cleaning up?"

"I was, then I said not today when tomorrow will come soon enough."

"What? What are you talking about, Hawk? That is laziness."

"Annie, I need some rest. I wish I could talk with you but I can't. Heavy police matter's that I need to just work through, you know? Details which I hate."

"Oh, yes. The details. Would you like something before dinner? Maybe a V-8 or lemon-aid or something?"

"No, honey, nothing really. Just tired. Think I will close my eyes for a few."

"OK, I will be in the kitchen working on dinner. I think Tommy and Rainey will be over a little later. You all right with that?"

"No. Tell them I have chicken pox or some other horrible disease. I don't want to see anyone tonight. I am just too tired."

Annie came back around the corner from the kitchen, looking straight at Hawk and asking, "What is really wrong? What is it, Hawk? What is going on downtown?"

"Nothing, dear. Nothing I can discuss. Police business, don't you know?"

She walked over to where Hawk was sitting and sat in his lap, making an escape impossible.

"Look, mister, I don't want to hear your excuses or all about secret police business or any of that crap. What is going on inside your head?"

As Annie was pointing her index finger at Hawk's head and thumping him with it, he was trying to come up with an excuse not to talk about any of the day's problems.

"Ah, just police business, honey. I heard from Capt. Gee today that Billy will be alright. So will Red and Larry. It was just difficult re-thinking all that happened, you know? The operation itself. Very stressful."

"OK. Do I really believe you or is that just a smoke screen? Come on, Hawk baby, give me the truth, please."

"Can't, honey. Top secret, you know? Sorrrry! And If I did tell you, then I would have to take you into the bedroom and make love to you, and then we would both miss dinner and …"

"OK, that's it. Give it to me, mister. Tell me the truth, and what is bothering you so much or I am going to start pulling some hairs out of your head."

"Wish I could, honey, but I really can't."

Telling Annie would be the worst thing of all. She didn't need to be worrying about all the missing guns and problems with Billy, Red, or Larry. Even though she didn't particularly like Larry, being fired on or shot was one of Annie's worst nightmares. Every time Hawk left home with guns on was a potential day from hell for her. She would always worry if he would come back in one piece, if at all.

"OK, but your dinner might get burnt tonight. And no desert either. Know what I mean?" Annie said.

Hawk smiled up at her and kissed her on the lips. That should have been enough but it wasn't, so he bent his head down slightly and kissed one of her breasts. She was wearing a new bra that she purchased at Sack's Fifth Ave. It not only held her beautiful breasts but lifted and created a very nice cleavage look with the low neckline blouse she had on. That didn't work either. Annie was five steps ahead of Hawk. She put both hands on her breasts and lifted them even higher and rearranged her blouse.

As she got off his lap, she half turned back to him, saying with a devilish smile, "OK burnt it is, and hands off the goods. No dessert for you until you tell me."

* * *

The nap did Hawk good physically but mentally, he was still running the conversation over and over in his mind and then writing it down in order to see the actual words. *Did I really hear what I heard? Something about a Victoria going faster and killing a small bird? Didn't make any sense. And then what was all that stuff about guns and night vision? Was it really who I thought it was? No. No, I had to be wrong,* he thought, but who could he talk to? There was nothing he could do but leave it until the next day.

Morning came too soon, and Hawk was awake early, showered, dressed, and kissing Annie goodbye when she reached up and gave him a big hug. She was still mostly asleep and wanted Hawk to know how much she loved him.

"Love you too, honey. Talk later," Hawk said.

"Ummm," she sighed.

* * *

When Hawk arrived at the detective office, Capt. Gee called him in to his office right away.

"Hawk, we have a problem. Our evidence room was hit last night, and a few more automatic weapons are missing along with a few bricks of heroin that was evidence in the Moreno trial. In light of your investigation, this is not going to be written up on the daily log sheet. I ordered a full investigation, and the FBI is here to help us. Your friend Kevin from the Bureau is here and wanted to see you as soon as you got in. I told him what you were working on," Capt. Gee.

"OK, thanks, Captain. Talk with you later," Hawk said.

Hawk took his time walking up the stairs and stopped by to see Tania.

"Have you found out anything new? I don't mean the break-in, but from our conversation yesterday," Hawk said.

"No, Hawk. Nothing yet. Will let you know, though, when I do," she replied.

"Thanks. I may have something. It will wait until later, though," Hawk said.

Walking back down the stairs, Hawk ran into Kevin who was coming up the stairs looking for him.

"Hawk, my man. How are doing?" Kevin greeted.

Hawk shook his hand and put his other hand on his shoulder. "Doing just fine, Kevin. Got any more gigs coming up like the one at the airport?" Hawk asked.

"Ha, no not today," Kevin replied. Something bigger that we need to sit down and discuss. Need a private office or room where we cannot be overheard. Follow me down the hall," Kevin said.

"Extra support room on the right up here," Hawk said.

"That will work, Hawk. How do you like it over here in the detective bureau?" Kevin asked.

"Oh, it has its advantages, but I sometimes do miss the street action. We had a good team out there," Hawk said.

"Yes, you did," Kevin replied. "A great team and you trained them well, Hawk. Have a seat; let me close the door," Kevin said.

"Agent King, what's going on?" Hawk asked.

"Capt. Gee told me you were working on missing evidence room weapons and why we are all running into them back on the streets.

Well, I thought we could collaborate and do the investigation together jointly because I am running a similar one in the FBI's missing weapons cases," Kevin shared.

"Sounds fair. But first, let me ask you a couple of questions. In looking through all the evidence logs yesterday and reviewing the data sheets for the six western states, my biggest problem is with the Monterey Presidio Intel Battalion, and then Edwards Air Force Base. These guys are hanging out their dirty laundry every month; it seems like. The Presidio has four downstairs floors accessible only by elevators. On the street, no one knows about the lower floors and what is taken up with weapons and munitions. It is regularly being broken into, which leads me to think it's all inside maneuvering and not just run of the mill thieves. This points to all inside dealing. It seems to me that the Cartel is finding new friends all the time," Hawk said.

"You're right, Hawk," Kevin said. It is inside, and we are working with Intel there to find out who and why."

"Can you trust their Intel" Hawk asked.

"Have to, for now, Hawk. That's why I need you to stay on this investigation. I need names, dates, amounts, everything," Kevin shared.

"Alright, Kevin, let me share something or someone else with you. (Hawk figured out that Kevin was his safest bet to unload what he had heard the previous day while taking a break behind the Bougainvillea bush.)

"It breaks my heart but I was taking a little time yesterday outside and around the corner of our building, and I overheard a discussion between two deputies," Hawk said.

"Who and what did you hear, Hawk?" Kevin inquired.

"Sir, I really don't want to say anything, but I know it could be crucial to what happened last night and the missing weapons. So here it is: I heard Misty and Capt. Rodriguez discussing, in Spanish, plans to get guns. I couldn't believe my ears and how well Misty speaks Spanish," Hawk said.

"What did you hear, Hawk?" Kevin asked.

"Oh, crap. Now I understand something that I didn't understand until just now. I could have probably prevented the break-in of our own evidence room last night," Hawk said.

"Wait, Hawk, let me get Capt. Gee in here. He needs to hear this," Kevin said.

"Are you sure, Kevin? I am just not so trusting of anyone right now," Hawk said.

"Hawk, you're a good cop, and I am here to tell you to slow down and not to worry just yet. Alright?" Kevin said.

"What do you mean don't worry just yet?" Hawk asked.

"Call Capt. Gee up here first, Hawk. We need him," Kevin said.

"OK, it's your party," Hawk said. He got up from the table and opened the door. He walked down the hall and past Tania's desk. He asked her to call Capt. Gee and get him up there to the support office.

"OK, hon," Tania answered.

Hawk sat back down across from Kevin and just stared at him, trying to figure out what he was writing down. Usually, Hawk could read writing upside down, but his handwriting was very small.

Capt. Gee walked in: "Hey, fellas, what's going on?"

"Captain," Kevin said, "Hawk has some interesting intel that you need to hear. It seems that Hawk overheard a conversation yesterday afternoon that he wasn't supposed to hear. It involves two known officers and leads into your missing evidence room weapons. It also involves one of mine," Kevin said.

"What did you overhear, Hawk?" Capt. Gee asked.

"One of your what, Kevin? Hawk asked.

"First, tell us what you heard," Kevin responded.

"OK, two people talking in Spanish by the corner of the building. Capt. Rodriguez and Detective Misty speaking in Spanish only about guns and killing small birds. I couldn't hear that clearly, but all the words spoken ... I know now more of what they were saying and what it meant," Hawk said.

"What was that, Hawk?" Kevin was trying to spur Hawk on to the revelation.

"Well, they started off with 'Esta noche las armas Victoria.' It means 'get the guns tonight, Victoria.' I had not put that together until now. But Victoria is unknown to me. The only word that comes close is victory. Then I heard: 'Es un pequeno halcon, pajaro.' Then I remembered the Airport shootout; the Zeta boys calling me a small birdie. But Halcon means a big bird. A Hawk. Then something like 'El va a morir,' which means 'He will die.' The last thing was that name again. 'Victoria, go fast.' Rodriguez was telling Misty to go fast. I don't think there is a Victoria but victory. 'Go fast; victory is ours,'" Hawk said.

"Hawk, you heard right, and the only problem is your safety. Traps are being set, and there is only one person that can hopefully cover your back, if possible, without breaking cover herself," Kevin said.

"Who?" Hawk asked.

"It's Misty, Hawk," Capt. Gee said in a lower voice.

"What? What the hell do you mean? What are you telling me?" Hawk asked.

"Hawk, Misty is one of our own," Kevin quietly uttered. "She is FBI and has been working as a double agent for years. Let me tell you a story and then you will understand a little, and it must not go any further than this room. Understood?" Kevin said.

"Yes, sir. But this is getting a little weird, guys. Misty a double agent?" Hawk asked.

Capt. Gee just sat there nodding his head up and down in silence.

"Hawk, we have suspected Rodriguez for many years of being one of the principals in the drug Cartels locally. He has his fingers in just about everything. He and a few others in the community. Misty was recruited about four years ago because she basically grew up in Mexico. Her mother is full Irish, and her father, Mexican. Her father decided at some point to join the Cartels, and he worked his way up to the rank of Lieutenant. Misty's mother made the decision to leave the husband, Misty's step-father, and bring her back to the United States where she continued to grow and went to College at UC Irvine. You know the rest which is in her personnel files that you have read through to build the right team. Isn't that right?" Kevin asked.

"Yes. But what now? What is she really doing here and why me?" Hawk asked.

Capt. Gee started by saying, "Misty is on our side but has to walk a tightrope to stay hidden this long. You have been right about Rodriguez all along, but we need you to bail on this entire weapon's investigation. Frankly, Hawk, I didn't think you would ever really find out much meaningful information about the thefts. And stupid us, we forgot your knowledge of Spanish and always being in the wrong place at the right time. It's uncanny or just being a damn good detective.

"Hawk, we are ordering you to let us now take the information you have accumulated and back out of the entire thing. We can't afford Misty to be compromised in any way. She is bringing us valuable information that will, at some point, end the Cartel fronts here in town and all the members associated with them (including Rodriguez) in the near future."

"I understand. Do you still want me to include her in our various operations and special ops?" Hawk asked.

"Yes, by all means. She is your best deputy. Just don't give her up or put her in any compromising situations that could possibly blow her cover or get her and you killed," Capt. Gee reiterated.

"I understand. One more question: Will you tell her that I now know her mission so I can advise her to be more careful in the future?" Hawk asked.

"I don't see why not," Kevin answered. "Capt. Gee, do you agree?"

Capt. Gee acknowledged and said, "I agree. I think if Misty knows that Hawk has her intel, then she can continue with more ease, knowing Hawk is front line helping to protect her."

"What is her father doing now?" Hawk asked.

"He is still active and crossing the borders as well. He thinks Misty is working for him and supplying valuable intel to the Cartel. In turn, Misty is giving us times and dates for raids, drugs, names of rival gangs that are new targets. Her intel to the Cartel has been flawless, and they are happy to have her. Just like Rodriguez. And Hawk, you don't have to worry anymore about him. We will take care of him soon enough.

Again, Misty is our first concern and making sure she has a safety net at all times. And that means you too, Hawk," Capt. Gee said.

"I got it. Thank you for sharing what was in the bag, so to speak," Hawk said.

"Hawk, like Misty, you are our main focus, cowboy," Kevin said. "Now I would like some of the information you found out on the Presidio up north. What have you found out?"

"Still trying to get a handle on it. If I can give you a call in a few days, I should be able to give you enough to do something with. Names and possibly how they are getting in," Hawk said. "By the way, who else knows about Misty's situation?"

Kevin immediately responded, "No One. No one at all, and we want to keep it that way. You are number three, and no more people will ever find out," Kevin said.

"Hawk, if you have any intel or questions or anything, just let me know," Capt. Gee related. "Like Misty and several other FBI doubles, we need to keep the lines open both ways."

"Understood, sir," Hawk said. "Thank you again for trusting me."

"Did you give us any choice?" Capt. Gee asked. "Like I said earlier, you're too good at your job, Hawk, and I need you to stay that way."

"Yes, sir. Little chance of me changing. At least I know who to go to now. Thank you for bringing me in," Hawk said.

"Hawk," Capt. Gee stated, "you have no idea how thankful we are that you didn't understand all of the conversation between Misty and Rodriguez. Had you acted on it, we would have lost a very valuable agent and a lot more."

"Amen to that," Kevin responded. "Years of tough investigations would have been thrown down the toilet."

"I don't want to think about it at all. In fact, I might just go back to the old fishing hole and spend a few days feeding the bears big rainbow trout," Hawk said.

Capt. Gee nearly jumped out of his chair. "What fishing hole? What trout?"

"Well, Capt. Gee, you see, that is my secret. Ha. Think I will get back to work and getting as much intel as I can for you, Kevin, on the military bases. Then if you don't mind, Capt. Gee, I would like to leave early and see Billy at the Hospital and then over to Red's," Hawk said.

"Not a problem, Hawk. You have done good. Just need intel on the fishing hole when you get a chance," Capt. Gee said.

"Thank you. Talk with you both tomorrow then. Bye," Hawk said.

* * *

Hawk left the office without seeing anyone or wanting to talk with anyone. He just had nothing to say. He was still in shock and had more questions than answers with Misty. The biggest question being:

"Why did she allow the Cartel to beat her and rape her on the freeway shootout?" *Or had they? Was it all just a ruse? It sure seemed real to me. I know that a lot of people put their life on the line for her just for some intelligence reports. The airport? What was that all about and fluff head (Flavio) threatening to kill her?*

For a moment, Hawk just didn't know what to do. How could he act normal around Misty and the crew knowing that someone might die one day because of the trust someone has in someone that is working both sides of the street? *God, what if I slipped and said something stupid without thinking first. Maybe I don't want to be an agent. Maybe I just need to go and see how Billy is doing,* He thought.

At the hospital, Hawk saw little Mary at the front desk who smiled when he walked in.

"I remember you," Mary said.

"Yes, I remember you too, Mary. How are you today?" Hawk asked.

"I am fine, thank you. How may I help you?" Mary asked.

"Mary, I need to see one of my deputies. Billy Wagner. Can you tell me what floor and room he is in?" Hawk asked.

"Yes, sir. He is on the fourth floor, room 431," Mary said.

"Thanks, Mary. See you later," Hawk said.

As Hawk walked into room 431, he yelled out, "Billy, my man, how're you doing, soldier?"

"Pretty good actually," Billy said with a big smile. "Can't wait to get out of this place, though. You know that you can't get any sleep here. Constant noise day and night. Then they give you sleeping pills and pain pills and wake you up every two hours to take blood or something and ask how you are sleeping or if you have any pain. What a bunch of crap. No one can get well here."

"I know what you mean, Billy. It's ridiculous but necessary, I guess. I have been on your side of the bed too many times myself. Speaking of pain, are you having much pain, Billy?" Hawk asked.

"No, not really, unless I try and move. The fun part is coming up later this week when I start physical therapy. Won't be going anywhere but they said that I need to slowly start rebuilding some stomach muscles and my good leg and arm exercises," Billy said.

"It sounds like a lot of fun, my man. I don't envy you at all. So very sorry for what happened. Just wanted to find out if I can bring you anything or if you need something, Billy. Maybe one of those blow-up dolls? You know they can ease certain pains?" Hawk said.

"Don't make me laugh, Hawk. It hurts to bad. No, all bases are covered. Besides, there are some mighty fine looking nurses here. Did you know that?" Billy asked.

"Yes, I remember some of them. Very fine looking nurses," Hawk commented.

"But thank you, Hawk. Appreciate your visit and coming in to check on me. It means a lot," Billy said.

"That's what I do, my boy. Besides, you are my best shooter, and I need you back," Hawk said. "Going to see Red and Larry now too. I will say goodbye for now, Billy, but I will be back. If for no other reason but to make sure you are letting the good nurses do their jobs. No grab ass, alright? Take your medicine like a good boy," Hawk said.

"Yeah, yeah, all right. See you later, Sarg," Billy said.

After leaving the hospital, Hawk started driving down the main drag in town with the top down on the Vette. At one of the stoplights, a big Lincoln pulled up next to Hawk. He had seen it in his rear view mirror a block or two back. He was casually watching it. Very similar to the one that he had had a shootout with at the Yardly Ranch. Hawk only saw one person in the vehicle, but one person with a gun is all anyone really needed.

Then Hawk heard: "Hey, you. Aren't you the local Sheriff in this town? Can you give me directions to a good restaurant, Sheriff?"

"Well, good-looking lady, I actually have a little time on my hands. Why don't I take you to a dark place that serves good Pizza?" Hawk replied.

"No, I was thinking about fish; a big fish. Maybe chips too," the lady said as she intentionally licked her lips.

"OK then. Fish it is, Ma'am. Follow me, sweet thing, back down the street and out onto the pier. Nice place down there called The Big Fish," Hawk said.

"You mean the Harbor Restaurant?" the lady chided.

"If you like. Follow me around the corner and back onto State Street," Hawk replied.

They both parked at the restaurant's valet parking lot and walked in. This was one of Hawk's family's favorite restaurants, and the owner and managers knew them all too well. This was, in fact, the place Annie and Hawk had their wedding dinner and reception so many years ago. No prettier place in the world to be to watch the sunsets or the boats coming and going from the harbor. It was always fun and always good food.

"Alright, my dear wife. How can I make this serious, secret police life up to you? How about a nice charbroiled halibut?" Hawk asked.

"Umm, that sounds good," Annie replied. "What are you ordering, Sheriff?"

"Same thing, I think. Sounds easy on the stomach this evening," Hawk said. *Oh no! Why did I have to say that? Now Annie is going to start asking questions. Damn, Hawk, just keep your mouth shut!*

"What's wrong with your stomach, Hawk?" Annie asked in a very serious tone.

"Oh, nothing really. Just felt a little squeeze earlier today. Not sure why but it will be fine. Probably because I forgot to eat breakfast," Hawk said.

"You know better than to skip breakfast. I offered to make you something. Or, is it something else like what you couldn't tell me yesterday?" Annie asked.

"Ah, no. I think it was just not eating and being in a hurry all day. Hey, look at that sailboat coming out of the harbor. Beautiful forty-footer. Look, I think that is your doctor. Yes. That's Dr. Secord's boat, isn't it?" Hawk asked.

"Hawk, you're doing it again. Avoiding the real issue," Annie said as she poked a finger at Hawk's ribs.

"Babe, I really cannot tell you all that is going on in the Bureau. More for your own good and safety. I honestly can't," Hawk said.

"Hawk darling, if these things are so upsetting to you, then maybe you need to look for another job, because this affects me too," Annie said.

"Annie, again I am very sorry for how my career affects you. It isn't easy, I know. Sorry. But like an attorney or doctor, there are many things that you can never, ever know about concerning certain people and operations. I just can't share everything with you, honey" Hawk said.

"I know that, Hawk, but I hate to see you suffer alone and getting sick more often. Not to mention how dangerous the job is," Annie said, fighting back the tears.

"Then think on this, my dear. In a few years, we can sell everything and move somewhere that crime can't find us. Somewhere sunny and warm, with mountains, islands, trees, and with clean, clear blue water," Hawk said.

"Sounds nice, honey. All except a couple of years from now. Can we make it that long? Will you last that long?" Annie asked.

"Yes. We will. Let's keep that dream up front in our minds and make it happen. Where the dream takes us, I don't know, but we can pray that all the kids and family will follow. Like buying our own island and building a home for each and—"

"Hawk," Annie interrupted, "you are such a dreamer. You've got to stop. That is not going to happen, and you know it. The reality is, you are a cop. A dam good one that goes beyond the limits every day. You have a thirst that is unquenchable. You make life-changing choices every day that affect a lot of people and not just our family. I respect that; I just don't like what it is doing to you—to us, for that matter. You are dealing with bad people, honey, that want to hurt anyone that gets in their way. You cannot be the only dragon slayer in the kingdom. You don't have to sacrifice all of us for the monsters running around out there. One day, a bullet or knife or something will find its way to your heart. Please don't let that happen. Volunteer for court duty, or warrants, or even civil," Annie pleaded.

"That's a unique way of saying it, and I assure you I am not the only dragon slayer in the kingdom. There are many of us out there. Again, Annie, I am sorry for the threats and secrets, and I promise you I will look into another way. Don't forget … all my years of training and to end up in Civil or the Courts? Please. I am serious about retiring one day soon and going in a different direction. Can we order that Halibut now, please?" Hawk said. "Dragon slayer! That's funny. I love you, Annie."

"Good evening, folks. May I take your order now?" Wanda asked.

Pop – pop – pop.

"Annie, get down. Wanda, get down and put the chairs in front of my wife and yourself. Get down, everybody," Hawk shouted.

Hawk drew his Glock after hearing three shots up front at the cash register. He used as much of the tables and chairs as protection as possible, running in a low bent position toward the register. *What the hell is going on?* Hawk asked himself just in time to see two men wearing black hoodies running out of the front door. Just before the last perp moved through the door, he turned around and shot the owner/manager, Antonio, one more time. Hawk, while running, fired at the perp and was sure he hit him. Hawk stopped to help Antonio who then told him to get them, that he was alright. Hawk did a cursory look around the restaurant to see if anyone else had been hit. One waitress was face up, bleeding from a bullet in her head. Her eyes were open. It was obvious she was dead. Hawk pushed open the door very slowly from his crouched position to check and get a visual of the scene outside. He couldn't see anything, and as he opened the door wider, he saw both men holding one of the Valet boys hostage while the other perp was looking for the right car to the keys he had in his hand. When he saw Hawk, he yelled for Hawk to drop his gun or he would kill the young boy he was holding in his arms, and his gun pointed at the boy's head. Hawk kept walking toward him without saying anything. The other kid yelled back and said he couldn't find the right car. Then he looked at Hawk and yelled to his friend, "Juno, that's that cop!" He dropped the car keys he had and jumped over the railing and took the long plunge into the ocean water twenty feet below.

Juno, on the other hand, thought for a moment he could become a hero and kill "the cop" that the other perp was talking about. He was shaking like a leaf and approximately some thirty yards away from Hawk. He fired one shot, which went wide, and then let go of the boy he was holding. He must have figured he would have a better chance of hitting Hawk if he used both hands on the gun. At least the shaking might stop.

When he let go of the valet boy, the kid dropped like a sack of potatoes—straight to the ground. Before the perp could fire another round, Hawk fired one shot, and his shot rang true to its course and dropped the punk where he stood. The Valet stayed on the ground and didn't move. Everyone else stayed down as well. Hawk ran over to the railing and looked over to see the jumper franticly trying to swim a long way. It would be a good three hundred yards to shore using the pier as his shield.

Hawk didn't want to get wet, and he didn't feel like running all the way to the beach just to handcuff the kid and get wet anyway, so he did the only realistic thing he could think of—he took aim and put a bullet into the punk's right leg above the knee. The perp dropped the gun he was trying to hold onto and swim with and screamed for help. Yelling back at him, Hawk said, "Just hold onto the pier pilings. I will get a boat and come and get you. Hopefully, I can reach you before the sharks do." Hawk took a deep breath and slowly walked back to the valet boy and the dead perp in the parking lot. The perp in the water was screaming even louder, "Help me, help me, sharks." That was OK with Hawk because his screaming and frantic behavior would probably save the taxpayers a lot of money in the long run. *The Sharks might just have a tasty morsel tonight.* As far as Hawk was concerned, the two shooters just ruined the dinner Annie, and he had planned for the evening.

The perp in the parking lot was not familiar to Hawk, but his tattoos were. He was part of the Westside gangs trying to extort money from business owners, making the business owners pay for their safety and supply help in the way of prostitutes and cheap laborers. Drugs were always available at less cost for any employee and of course whatever the patrons would like. Nice scheme if it worked, but it never did. Hawk told the valet not to touch anything and just wait for the police to get there; he could hear sirens off in the distance coming down State St. Back inside, Hawk knelt down next to Antonio and asked how he was doing.

"OK, Hawk. Thank you. He shot me in the leg and shoulder and then shot Doreen. I think it was one of those punks' girlfriend," Antonio said.

"What did he want here today, Antonio. No bull shit; give it to me straight," Hawk demanded.

Antonio related to Hawk that they came for payment for services rendered. "Doreen was a plant, I think, and she was getting familiar with some of our bar customers and trying to enlist some of the other waitresses too. Then he wanted more protection money."

"OK, thank you, Antonio. I get it. The punk that shot you is dead, and the other is shark bait in the water. Police are on the way. I need to check on Annie and Wanda.," Hawk said.

"Thank you, Hawk. I will be alright. Order anything you want, OK, Hawk? On the house," Antonio said.

"Hey, you," Hawk said, pointing to one of the bartenders standing there in the bar doorway. "Get a couple of towels and bring them here. OK, put one of the towels right here on Antonio's shoulder and apply pressure. Do not let go." Hawk then told one of the waitresses watching to tie the other towel and make a tourniquet on Antonio's leg. Hawk patted him on his cheek and got up to check on his girl.

Annie and Wanda were trying to help many of the patrons get up off the floor and back into their chairs. "Good job," Hawk told them. Then he yelled out to everyone, "The bad guys are gone, and the police are there. Not to worry, and don't go anywhere. Just stay at your tables until the police come to you. Thank you." As Hawk was talking to everyone, he held up his wallet with his badge and ID card that reads "Sheriff" in bold green letters.

"Annie, are you alright, babe?"

"Yes. I think. Shaking a lot. What happened? Did you know that the floor is filthy under the tables? I need to talk to Antonio about that. Where is he, Hawk?" Annie asked.

"Not now, Annie. Antonio has been shot, but he is OK. Another waitress was killed, and the police are arriving now, so I have to get back up front," Hawk said. Annie was visibly shaken, and so Hawk sat her down at the table. "Wanda, do me a favor; bring fresh water to Annie and a piece of bread, please. You might do the same for some of the other tables as well," Hawk said.

"Yes, sir. Right away," Wanda said.

"I will be back as soon as I can, Annie. Do you hear me?" Hawk said.

"Yes. I will stay here," she said.

"Wanda is bringing you some new water and something to eat to help your nerves," Hawk said. He gave Annie a kiss on the head and headed back up front to see who had arrived from the police department.

Bill was on his knees attending to Antonio, and a couple of medics were checking out the dead girl. A few more police officers came in and asked if Hawk had been there when the incident happened.

"Yes. My wife and I were just about to order dinner when two perps came in with guns. Now, may I suggest we clear the bar and use it as a staging area for taking statements and starting the investigation?" Hawk asked.

The lead officer looked at Hawk and asked, "Just who the hell do you think you are giving orders to?"

Hawk heard his name called out behind him and turned around. "Hawk, you son-of-a-gun. What did you do this time? Doesn't the county have any good restaurants for you to shoot up?"

"Well, well, if it isn't my retarded brother-in-law. Tommy, why are you working the streets again. Can't find a chair comfortable enough for your ass at a desk?" Hawk asked. Both police officers turned to look at Hawk with very puzzled looks in their eyes.

"Ha, that's funny. What happened here, Hawk?" Tommy asked.

"I was just telling your officer here to make a staging area in the bar for witnesses and for taking statements from everyone. I don't think he believed me or heard me," Hawk said.

"Do it, Bill. You heard the man. Have you ever met Hawk?" Tommy asked.

"No, Sarg. Hi, Hawk. Good to meet you. Sorry about that. Why do they call you Hawk anyway?" Bill asked.

"Not now, Bill. It would take Hawk all night to tell you, and he gets mad when he's asked. Hawk, I take it that you are the one that popped the perp outside?" Tommy asked.

"Yes. You know that I get upset when I go somewhere to eat, and people start making a lot of noise and playing with guns. I hate that, so I politely as possible got up from our table and shot them both, and then gave them a stern warning not to do that again," Hawk said.

Both officers were visibly stunned with what they heard coming out of Hawk's mouth. One could see from their expression: *Who the hell is this guy?* The first officer, Bill, turned around to see if Hawk was for real or not. Tommy and Hawk just laughed.

Tommy then let Bill in on the news: "Bill, this is Sargent Hawk of the Special Units Division of the Sheriff's Department. Hawk is the man, and one you don't want to ever mess with if you are a bad guy."

Hawk then began telling the story of his dinner date with Annie and the perps that walked in: "The dead one in the parking lot is the perp that gunned down Antonio and the girl. When I got outside, he was the one holding a young valet with a gun to his head, while his partner was looking for a get-away car. Oh, by the way, if you look over the side railing behind the restaurant, you will find the other one hanging onto the pilings. That is, if the Sharks haven't already eaten him," Hawk said.

"Oh, shit! Are you kidding me?" Tommy asked. "There's one in the water out there?"

"Yes, and you better get to him fast. I saw some black tips hanging around down there earlier. If you hear him screaming for help, he is probably OK, but if he is quiet, take your time. It means that they already ate him. Oh yeah, he is bleeding a little in one leg. He tried to shoot me, so I shot first. His gun is at the bottom of the pier," Hawk said. Bill was listening to Hawk's story and shaking his head in disbelief. How the hell could Hawk have managed to rip so much flesh in such a short time and walk away joking? Bill just couldn't quite make it all fit in his brain.

"Now, if you don't mind, brother, I am going to gather up my belongings and my wife and go somewhere to eat a nice quiet dinner. We will see you later to tie up all the loose ends. OK?" Hawk said.

"Yeah, that's fine, Hawk. Thanks for swatting the flies for us. You're a one-man wrecking crew," Tommy said. Hawk looked at Bill and saw his head going up and down in agreement after Tommy's statement.

"Well, hear this: I was just recently called the Dragon Slayer of the county today. So, there you have it. Two small dragons you don't have to worry about. You can thank your sister-in-law for my new title. See you later, man," Hawk said.

CHAPTER 11

THE DRAGON SLAYER

Originally, the name was meant to be cute and a slight slam on Hawk's way of doing business—Shoot first and ask questions after—on some of the toughest ops of his career. That wasn't exactly the case, but many shootouts came with guns blazing on both sides simultaneously. Now one might ask, "How can you give someone a chance to prove their innocence if you shoot first?"

Well, Hawk would say 'simultaneously' is a good read on the situation, and excellent recognition and response time of seeing real life weapons in the hands of the dragons, or the bad guys, as it were.

Hawk never quite understood, in all his days of law enforcement, how the media people could put such spins on saving lives—his included— or judge cops by doing their job and putting a good light on the bad guys. Should each killing or shooting be investigated? Absolutely, each and every time. But to apply such pressure on the law enforcement community is prehensile in Hawk's eyes. Case in point: *The Wharf*

Restaurant back in the eighties when two perps from the Westside Gang, who were jacking the owner/manager for protection money, prostitutes posing as waitresses, and a host of other crimes. They came in and shot the owner three times and killed a waitress with a bullet to the head. The perps ran out of the restaurant, looking to steal a car from the valet parking lot, holding a hostage and then firing a shot at the lone policemen walking into the line of fire, giving the frightened hostage a chance to get away. The perp fired one time at me, dropped the hostage, thus giving me a clear shot to kill. The other gang member jumped over the side of the pier railing and into the ocean in an attempt to escape. He still had a gun in his hand and was able and ready to shoot me in the head as I leaned over the railing when I put a bullet in his leg, causing the perp to drop his gun into Davey Jones Locker. I gave orders to him to hold onto the pier pilings until I could return with a boat to haul his ass out of the water.

The Daily News reporter decided to make it her personal business plan to venomously attack Hawk and the Sheriff's Department with words like "Murdering our poor brothers and sisters in cold blood who were defenseless and unable to protect themselves. Innocent people like Sergio, Flavio, Juno, and other numerous Cartel and gang members who were well-known to the task force."

Who the hell did Maria Espinoza think she was. Hawk knew, from investigating her after her front page stories, that she was fresh out of college in Texas and was hired to keep her stories on the front page to incite anger in the citizens in the community. Proving it was harder. The editor was nearly out of a job for his lackluster editing career and was looking for one last chance to retire with some sort of pension. He brought a timely person by the name of Maria into the newspaper locker room to sell more papers. It didn't matter what the slant was or really if truth prevailed or not. It was all about greed and selling papers. The Daily News was going to be cleaning house in order to be sold if something didn't happen soon to pick up the paper sales. Money is always the bottom line.

When Maria heard the name 'Dragon Slayer,' she immediately started investigating all the police-involved shootings in the area over the last ten years. Hawk's name was in the lead. Hawk this and Hawk that, and then Dragon Slayer caught her eye; she exploded into a feeding paper sale frenzy. A front page writing diva.

Yeah, it was real cute, and Hawk thought that he should have nailed that lid shut when he first heard it. But he didn't, and now he was busy trying to defend himself and the department. Hawk preferred the advantage, not sucking the hind tit of a bore, but that was where Maria was posturing him.

He thought that Maria might learn something if he suggested she ride along with him as a 'Citizen on Patrol' to investigate firsthand what police officers deal with every day in the streets.

Maria said yes far too quickly, and Hawk should have been a little more suspicious, but a little something got in the way. Specifically, a little five foot four, dark brown hair, big brown eyes and lips that suggested the words 'kiss me' if you can. Her skin was beautiful and slightly tanned, with no bra straps, which would have indicated a tanning salon rather than hanging out by a pool. Her golden skin color was for real. No, she was nearly perfect in every way and wore burgundy nail polish and matching lipstick. She dressed very well and knew what looked good on her with enough reveal but not too much. Just enough low cut blouse to excite and cause one's eyes to dance with anticipation of more. The height of her skirts was more than appropriate and professional until she bent over, usually on purpose, to reveal gorgeous legs all the way up. All of the above were very obvious clues, but once one began talking with Maria, she dispelled any vulgar thoughts of what the news publishing enemy writer may do. She was always interested in who and what was said, with eager eyes and lustful remarks keeping you plugged into her at all times. Many times, when she felt she was losing her angle, she made it a point to come in close, touching Hawk on the arm or shoulder and would leave a scent of White Diamonds wafting in his nose. More times than not, she could steal one's mind back from any wayward suspicious thinking. White Diamonds were for sophisticated women, and she played the game very good, even though she wasn't that sophisticated in Hawk's views. Something was missing!

Maria was more than smart. College graduate and a dictionary for a mind, yet she possessed a real sense of humor. One might say she was a total package wrapped up in near perfection. Her body contour was not exaggerated or out of proportion in any way. Just a nice and comfortable hold on to Hawk. 36-22-36.

All of this Hawk took in on his first three-second glance. His police training in identification of people/recognition was in full play. It might have been, in all truth, a little longer glance than the normal three-second rule, and Hawk may have stayed at the water cooler taking more in, but she was delivering. *So why not enjoy?* Hawk thought.

At any rate, another thing Hawk suspected was more curiosity than expected into his life and routines. *Why the detailed need to know?* These were the type of questions from Maria that would make one want to ask, "Why do you want to know that?" Questions like, "What happened in your life that put you on this path?" "Where were you when you were seven and eight?" "What difference did it make?" "What was your growing up years like and who was your real father?" Questions that Hawk hardly knew himself and didn't want to waste time looking into. But, why was she? The red flags slowly began to sway in a slight breeze always masked by pretty perfumes, a touch on the arm or leg, and complements like "You are such a great guy; your wife is very lucky to have you." It was almost too obvious until she leaned over to give a sneak peak of her breast in a see thru bra that hid nothing. Or, when she somehow knew her questions were going beyond reporter necessary, she would find an excuse to bend over, revealing those perfect legs again. It was like being in a mind control experiment. Take a little here, little there, and repackage the opportunities for tonight. It left Hawk guessing many times.

The one thing that Maria could never figure out was Hawk's wedding ring and how important that ridged symbol was in his life. When all else failed, a glance at his wedding ring always brought Hawk's wayward eye or heated breath back to a neutral zone very fast. He just wouldn't play with her that long or allow his senses to feel anything but for Annie. Hawk truly believed that the circle of gold was a symbol of "Our unending love." This was a puzzle to Maria and one she obviously wanted to conquer quickly if she could.

They both did a few ride along with patrol gigs, and nothing really happened that was too much out of the realm of normal. No shoot'em up days or nights to speak of. Mostly checking on the troops, a few traffic stops, and open door call. One domestic disturbance that kind of left Maria in a strange mood. It was as if she had really been there or experienced such combativeness in her own personal life. Hawk tried to extract those feelings from her, but she was equally tight-lipped as he.

Nothing ever settles down much in a Detective Bureau. There is always work to do daily. It's either a follow-up or going back to cold case files because a new lead may have surfaced. That was until one day when The Daily News started reporting on the lack of trained law enforcement personnel. Law Enforcement as a whole body was being attacked for its credibility and a smeared tarnish was being wiped over its members to unveil the vulgarity of gun carrying, untrained men and women killing the citizens' babies, brothers, sisters, and parents—articles that put a lot of people at a simmering unrest, and that was what Maria had intended doing. She was going to start a campaign of smear on everyone she could find and attach a name too.

She wanted the public to have a more exaggerated view of the enemy in their midst:

Warning: Mr. and Mrs. Public, look up because the Hawks are circling and ready to swoop down and grab your babies and take them away. They are called and identified by different names, but you can always find them if you look. And by the way, Hawk, as he is known, lives at 2424 Sherwin Ave. Drop by his home and leave a note or something to let him know you were there and we are watching. No more killings in the fields or blood-soaked trenches of our lives and families as if they don't exist. We are humans with certain rights and privileges, and the eye of the tiger is now watching. Stay alert, carry a camera, and write what you see if a patrol car is in your neighborhood.

* * *

It was time to pay Maria a little visit and set the record straight. It was also time to leave a mark on her ass. Hawk began a long process of investigation into who Maria really was and why this vendetta of hers was spinning out of control.

She was keeping the public on edge from two different and opposing sides. Crime did not stop nor did the need for law enforcement, but the jobs of law enforcement were made more difficult by all the nosy people standing around crime scenes. Loitering at a crime scene and getting in the way or breaking a police line could land good people in a jail cell overnight. Unless invited into a crime scene, one stayed out. Anything that might hinder the investigations of law enforcement could get arrested. One shouldn't even think about filing complaints of police harassment or brutality charges. Most of this behavior was carried out, as one might expect, in the lower income neighborhoods and areas of known gang activities. Suspicion was raging on both sides now, and Hawk's investigation was taking center stage in all departments. He was told outright to get the lowdown on this broad and put her away.

Starting with her growing up years—blank. Re-checking her names or possible names—blank. Known relatives and friends—blank. College in Texas and her journalism experience was about the only information available. It became very clear that Maria was a plant, but that was not sufficient enough to eliminate the pest. Hawk would need more than insecticide spray or a fly swatter to engage this prey. Every single turn or twist came up empty or was just blind maneuvering until one day when Misty came into Hawk's office, having just come back from a two-week vacation. Misty and Hawk hadn't really talked since she was told that he now knew she was a double agent for the FBI and the Cartels deep into Mexico and Central and South America.

She walked into Hawk's office after a slight knock on the window. She entered and sat down opposite him.

"Sorry, Hawk, for not telling you what was going on," Misty said.

Hawk nodded his head in her direction without saying anything, forcing her to continue with her explanation of events.

"I am very sorry to have not entrusted you with my connections and what I was doing and for how long. You are a good friend that has saved my life more than once, and you deserved better from me. I just could not involve anyone in my business, or more lives would have been lost. You have been a target for a long time, and I hated to see it, but I had to slip bits and pieces of information out to keep my contacts happy. The bureau wants names, addresses, and pictures of every known Cartel member below the border. It's not easy, Hawk, living two separate lives like this, but I did sign up for it. Anyway, I am here to help you any way I can, if you will have me back?" Misty said.

"I don't know what to say, Misty. You left a hole in my heart that afternoon outside our bureau office when you and Numb-nuts talked about lifting more guns from our evidence rooms. Calling me names and working with that slime ball made me sick," Hawk said.

"I know, Hawk, and I am sorry. Truly sorry for that, but please believe me when I say I can help put Maria away. Away for good. And don't worry; that slime ball Numb-nuts, as you call him, is going down one day soon as well.

"Hawk, I need to show you something. I don't want to, because it is so embarrassing, but I feel it necessary to show you my honesty and why I have done what I have done. It was never to you personally, but for the greater good of our Country and your department. Yes, I am with the FBI, and I am a double agent. You must believe me when I say none of this was to hurt you purposefully. I have a very good reason, and I need to show you, and you only, but it is my secret and never to be discussed again. Agreed?

"Remember this: after I show you why, I want you to always know that I love you and will always have your back. Don't ever think I am not watching out for you," Misty said.

"Thank you. Appreciate your candace, Misty. You don't need to show me anything that is going to jeopardize your position. I believe you. Whatever you are asking me to do, it really isn't necessary now. It will just take me time to put it all back into some semblance of order in my mind. This hasn't been easy, girl," Hawk said.

"But I can tell," Misty said, "that you still don't believe me all the way. It is very important to me that you trust me again, Hawk. Please follow me. I need to show you something," Misty said.

"OK, but where are we going? This is still a work day, and I am in the middle of some work here," Hawk told Misty. "You don't have to show me anything."

"Just do as I ask," Misty requested in a very firm voice. "I am the one risking it all here, not you." She grabbed Hawk's hand and led him into the woman's restroom down the hall from his office. Over all Hawk's objections, Misty pulled him inside and then checked the bathroom stalls to make sure the room was empty and then locked the door. Misty just stood there looking at Hawk for a very long awkward moment. She was searching for some recognition in his eyes, trying to find the lost trust, something, and Hawk didn't get it. Nor did he understand why he was standing in the middle of the women's restroom.

Tears began to stream down her face, but she kept choking them back as best she could. Whatever she was looking for in Hawk's eyes, she must not have found it. He really didn't know. Then Misty took a step backward, took a deep breath, and started to undress, the entire time looking straight into Hawk's eyes.

"What the hell are you doing, Misty? Stop taking your clothes off, right now. This isn't necessary. Stop, please. That's an order, Misty!"

Hawk said. He was totally taken back and not expecting what was happening right there in the women's restroom in the Detective Bureau.

"Misty, I am telling you to stop right now. We are not making love, and that's that," Hawk said.

"Shut up, Hawk, and let me show you the truth. You must understand who I am and why. This is the only way," Misty said.

She continued to take all of her clothes off and revealing the beautiful body Hawk always almost saw so many times. She was beautiful, but Hawk didn't understand what was going on until she said very sternly, "Look, Hawk! Look here and here and here. Look at me, Hawk!" She was pointing to different parts of her body while talking and challenging him to look carefully at her. At that moment, Hawk saw beyond her nakedness and into her bloodied past. Her hurt and angry soul and early life with the Cartels. Misty's body had been beaten and scarred by many unfathomable crimes that had left the unbelievable on her body.

"Hawk, my own father, did this," Misty said, pointing to a ten-inch scar just above her pubic hair. "He raped me at age ten. The bastard never stopped raping me. Anytime he and my brothers or uncles or just their friends got drunk, I was raped. And at age fourteen, I became pregnant. My father and my uncle, who was a supposed field doctor with no training; they took a knife and cut my baby out of me after getting me drunk enough, to not feel the pain. Hawk, I felt the pain.

It hurts to this day, Hawk. The horror of it hurts beyond today, and I hope it always will, to rekindle my hate of them. I hate them all, Hawk," Misty said.

At this point, Misty's tears turned to sobbing and Hawk could see her breast heaving up and down, even though he didn't want to look at them until she told him and directed his attention to her left nipple, or at least where one used to be.

"Look, Hawk, do you see where my left nipple used to be? It, too, was cut off by some drunken Cartel bastard and his son as a memento and trophy to hang off their damn belts. I am a souvenir of some lowly Cartel bastard today, Hawk. You got that? Many women have had this done along with genital mutilation. They don't care. If you can't or are too old or passed around property or not making money, they mutilated you just for the fun of it. Every time I screamed for help or tried to run, someone would hurt me, and this would happen.

"Some time, Hawk, if you ever get the chance again, look at the skin tags on the belts of these sick bastards, and you will see how many women they have tortured and carved up. Some women are missing both nipples as a sign of disfiguring dominance. Women who are put into prostitution for the greater cause of the Cartel revolution; too old to have suckling babies, then they cut off their nipples. They so emboss the drug trade that they will do anything for one another to show their power over any human being. Young boys not excluded. These people are twisted evil son-of-a-bitch devils, Hawk. They belong dead. All of them.

Look at me, Hawk. Look at me. Look at the back of my thighs, look at my butt, look at my back. What do you see Hawk?

Scars like knife cuts I uttered in shame barely able to look at her any longer.

Yes, knife carvings and whip marks. Slashes from long leather whips that cut into every woman just for the fun of it. Do you get it yet, Hawk?" Misty asked. Now Misty's tears could not be held back. She all but collapsed onto the bathroom floor. Embarrassed, exhausted, filled with hurt, pain, and humiliation beyond rational reason. No one, even Hawk, could have truly understood what he saw or believed such things could be done to women. This was the most despicable thing Hawk had ever seen. *How could such evilness in man do this to young women and boys for any reason?*

Hawk knew what Misty was showing and telling him was true. He just had a horrible time putting it all into a fathomable form, even though Misty showed him. He picked Misty up off the floor and just held her close to himself. Her sobbing attracted the attention of others outside, but he assured them everything was under control. It mattered little if they understood or not, though at that moment, anyway.

Through her tears, sobbing, and labored breathing, Misty asked Hawk, "Do you see now, Hawk, what I mean? Can you see why I hate them and have to do what I am doing? I am going to kill them all, Hawk. Make no mistake about it."

"Yes, Misty, I do. I am so sorry. I never knew any of this. Let me tell you something very important, though. It matters little how many scars or burns or tortuous things that the Cartel did to you, Misty, because you are still so very, very beautiful. I am envious of any man that marries you," Hawk said.

"Hawk, what you have seen means more to me than all the scars. I think that you understand at least a little—what I must do and why. The endless pain in my heart and how a father and other relatives could have done this to me. I can never have a baby. I can never have a baby suck on my tit for milk. Damn it, Hawk, these Cartel BASTARDS, from Mexico clear down to Central and South America, must go to hell and I intend to put them there. Alone, if I have to. What they did to me on the way up to Santa Barbara that day at Rincon was the last straw. They beat me for information about you, which they didn't get and then raped me just for the fun of it. Three or four of them held me down, and others watched and took turns. Hawk, I am going to kill them," Misty said. More tears could not be stopped. "They intended to kill me afterward, Hawk, because I was Cartel property turned COP. It mattered little whose daughter I was. In fact, my father put the hit out on me. I cannot forgive him. I can't forgive any of them. I can't understand why a loving God would allow such barbarism and pain. If pain alone could kill, I would have died many times over."

"Again, Misty, I am so sorry. I wish I didn't have to see such pain and molestation in your life. It hurts me to know what these bastards did to you and are still doing to so many other women. It must stop. This goes beyond borders and drugs. Here, Misty, let me help you get dressed," Hawk said. He reached down for an article of clothing, handed it to her, and then thought better of helping her. He chose to give her her dignity and respect back—by turning around and letting her dress herself. He didn't need to see anything more; he had seen the horror of years of abuse. It saddened Hawk beyond belief. He was not sure how he was going to respond to that. It was so shocking, so horrible, and painful to have just witnessed it, let alone felt Misty's pain.

Hawk was not a man that would avert his eyes to any women willing to openly expose herself. But this time was different and a big exception required. It was Misty being totally honest, totally vulnerable, completely devastated over all the years of Cartel dominance, bondage, and cruelty in her life. This was freedom, and liberating humiliation of sorts all rolled into one. She was disgraced and needed reaffirming and rebuilding. She thanked Hawk but didn't need to say anything more.

As she was putting the rest of her clothes back on, she told him more of her story: "One night, after one of my father's and brother's drunken celebrations of a successful delivery of pot into the United

States in big quantities, my mother took my little sister and me across the Texas-Mexico border. She carried us across the Rio Grande on her back and into the United States. Momma worked hard every day, Hawk, cleaning and caring for others, caring for an American woman. Cooking, laundry, cleaning, anything she could do, to provide food, clothing, and education for us. We lived in one room made over the garage, with one queen bed. We shared everything for two years while my sister and I went to school. I graduated high school and started city college. Having excelled in all my classes, I earned a scholarship to go to a four-year university and then I was recruited by the FBI. When they found out I was an illegal and yet so valuable, they granted me, my sister, and mother citizenship in the United States. My father never knew who or where we were. Our names were changed to reflect my mother's maiden Irish name. But the Cartel was not done with me yet. My father did, in fact, find us and under the threat of death for all three, he told me to utilize my position to spy for the Cartel. If I refused, we would all die. I told my superiors, and the plan was set into motion. That brings us up to Rincon. My father knew that I was lying and telling the FBI everything, so he gave orders to Lt. Sanchez that after beating me, he could rape me first, then kill me when the delivery was completed. All the drugs in that shipment were to be offloaded up at a boys and girls club on APS in Santa Barbara. Somewhere near the old mission. It was Sanchez's idea to burn me like a whore of no further value.

"Now you know it all, Hawk. Please forgive me, but I had no choice. I moved my mother and little sister up to Laguna Beach two years ago and thought they were safe. They are now here in Santa Barbara living with me," Misty said.

"You are a very brave woman, Misty. I don't know how you even lived through this entire thing. You, your mother, and sister are probably the bravest three human beings I know. Praise God, Misty. Do you realize that in your darkest hour, God was protecting you and your mother and sister? Even with all the pain and humiliation and suffering that you had to endure, God still had a plan to lift you up and out of that Hell. You got to know that, Misty. God could have stopped it but chose to bring strength to your hurt body and soul. He created you, Misty, to love and to forgive others. Just remember what our Lord went through as he was hanging on the cross. He lifted his head in the last moments of his life and asked the Father to Forgive us for we didn't know what we were doing. That was for all humanity, Misty. Not just back then. It wasn't just the Romans or the Jews that killed Jesus. It was ALL of humanity, because none are righteous except Him. I know it is hard to understand, but—"

"No, Hawk," Misty interrupted, "I can't forgive them yet. Here is the deal; I need your help. I want to kill these bastards, and I won't stop until I do or my life has been taken from me. Will you help me?"

"I don't know how, Misty, but I will do everything in my power that I can," Hawk said. Her answer was not the one he was hoping for, but he wasn't through asking or trying to share the truth with her. Hawk knew it was only a matter of time that his prayer would be answered. *God's hand is upon Misty right now,* he thought.

Hawk's head was hurting just knowing what he now knew and what his eyes had just witnessed in Misty's reveal. It sickened him and angered him at the same time. He was sure Misty did so with the intent of reclaiming her life back and enlisting him in her personal war with the Cartels, which was fine because now he knew they were on the same side. He also knew that Misty now had his back and would once again champion their fight to at least make it harder for gangs and Cartel members to rule in their county. Yes, together they could make a difference. But first, Hawk needed to eliminate one pretty reporter.

Misty said she would help bury Maria and Hawk was counting on that, but then he wondered if Maria had been treated the same as Misty. Had she been used and abused by her family or others? Hawk would not have an answer to that question for some time, but the Dragon Slayer was about to slay yet another Cartel martyr.

It is well documented that if you cut off the head of a poisonous snake and that of its young, then it cannot rise again to hurt you. Throw the head into the fire, and you have done a good thing. That was the new mission of Hawk and Misty—cut the heads off the Cartels business ties to their area and burn every bale of pot, sack of drugs, and anything else they could find, and burn it. Burn it all.

Command gave Capt. Gee and Hawk full approval to kick their mission statement up a notch to put a harness on the gangs and Cartel members floating around in their community. The War on Drugs was on.

After a couple of months, Misty came into the office early one morning to give Hawk new Intel on Maria Espinoza, the Daily News reporter attempting to destroy by ink what their department had and was doing to the local gang members and the new Cartel citizens of Santa Barbara. The campaign was fierce, the battle lines documented. Success was still colorless, but that was alright for the mean time; Hawk and his team were not going to give up.

"Maria's last name, Hawk, is Beltran-Leyva," Misty announced. "Her father was Arturo Beltran-Leyva or better known as Jefe de Jefes. El Barbas. He is a butcher and likened to the main boss of bosses. There is now a thirty-million-peso reward for his head. El Barbas' father is

Edgar, and he was recently killed in a raid by another Cartel from the Gulf area.

"So now you have it, and you can start on the offensive. She will either go somewhere else a little friendlier or back to her roots," Misty said.

"It's going back to her roots that worries me, Misty. She can ruin a good cover or blow the endgame because of other leaks in and around our departments. We shall see. I will tell Capt. Gee the good news, and we can plan our attack.

"Meanwhile, I have Intel, Misty, that a consortium of Cartel members is massaging the Tijuana border areas. Apparently, they have dug numerous tunnels which are being used to bring Coke, Heroin, Pot and Illegal Pharmaceuticals into the United States. We are working on a plan to join the ATF, SDSO, FBI, and BP to intercept a new shipment being extradited here. The transfer is huge and worth millions in the US, and we need to stop it. Let's get together later and start working on a plan. I need your Intel to combine with what we know and fit the puzzle together. OK?" Hawk asked.

"Yes, sir Sarg. Yes, indeed. I will bring any fresh Intel with me later," Misty apprized.

"Thanks, Misty. You have saved a lot of stress for me by helping me eliminate Maria. At least I think we can. If nothing else, reassign her to the cooking column on the back page of the newspaper," Hawk said.

It was past time to install a failsafe plan to remove Maria and Hawk thought no better time than now to invite her to dinner. *A little wine, soft music, nice lobster dinner, and then wham. No after dinner sex; just hit her with our discovery and what and where I want her to go,* he thought. Maria had become far too dangerous, and it was time to say good-bye. Hawk called her up to ask her out and received a very loud and cold NO.

"I am far too busy for you," Maria said. "My deadlines are due this week."

"El Asesino de Dragon (The Dragon Slayer) is coming out of hiding. Wouldn't you like to interview him?" Hawk asked.

"What! Hawk, are you actually threatening me with something?" Maria asked.

"No, just giving you an opportunity on some first-hand information. But that is alright. Nancy over at the Sun would be happy to run with it if you are too busy," Hawk said.

"Wait just a minute... Yes, I can change some things around and join you later; let's say at seven-thirty tonight? But why me, Hawk?" Maria asked.

"Because we rode the streets together a few times Maria. I think we have somewhat of a bond. You now know how it is out there on the streets," Hawk said.

"Meet you at the usual place (The Whales Tale)?" Maria asked.

"Good. See you later then, at seven," Hawk replied.

Hawk knew that any mention of the Dragon Slayer would perk Maria's ears and a new story would be great for the Cartel and public information. It felt like Hawk was on a soap opera every time one of Maria's articles was printed. So this night, he had great hopes it would end. At least in their area.

Hawk related his Intel from Misty to Capt. Gee, and let him know what was for dinner. He needed a wire and got set-up for it after work.

By seven o'clock, Hawk's wire was on, and he jumped into the Vette and headed down to the Wharf. After parking his car, he entered the restaurant and asked the hostess for a nice quiet corner window table. She obliged him, and seating was immediate at the last window table facing the Marina.

Maria was fashionably late, which was just fine. It gave Hawk more time to rehearse in his mind how he was going to break the news to her. He didn't think she was going to like what he had to say. Nor did he like what she had been saying for months.

Hawk stood up and waited for her to slide into the booth seating. Offering her a glass of Chardonnay Wine surprised her a little from the raised eyebrow movement. The waitress offered Maria a menu and suggested the Prime Rib with garlic mashed potato, a green leafy special salad, and choice of dressing, spring mix vegetables, and then she asked if she would like anything else to drink.

Maria seemed satisfied with her choice of dinner and Hawk gave the waitress his order for Lobster tail with rice pilaf.

"Well, this is nice enough," Maria acknowledged. "Why the wine and dinner, Hawk? Are you also planning to take me home and get into my pants? I thought you were happily married and all that crap?" Maria asked.

"No sex, Maria. Not on our first real date anyway. I am kind of old fashion that way. And yes, I am happily married, but I do from time to time enjoy the company of a beautiful and intelligent woman. Can we agree on that?" Hawk asked.

"Of course! So, tell me about the Asesino de Dragon. That's you, right?" Maria asked.

"No, not yet, please. I would like to enjoy looking at you, thinking of what might come, and sipping the wine. I like eating a fine meal before a serious discussion. And by the way, you might want to take notes tonight," Hawk said.

"Oh, good, because my tablet is on and running. Is yours?" She lifted her recorder out of her purse and showed me that the green light indicator was on and that the recorder was, in fact, pre-recording our meeting.

"Sorry, Maria, I don't carry a purse from which to hide a recorder. And I would be disappointed if you hadn't recorded this. Let's at least have our wine first," Hawk said. Then he opened his shirt part way to reveal his chest. The microphone wire set-up was attached to Hawk's right breast, below his shirt opening. He did it fast to confuse her a little and then patted his jacket pockets. "Nothing, dear. You are welcome to touch and feel your way around, though," Hawk said.

"Wow, I thought for sure you would be wearing a wire or something. Should I be suspicious or disappointed?" Maria asked.

"Disappointed, maybe. You can look under the table if you like, or in my pants pockets. I don't think that would bother me too much. On second thought, unless we both agreed to touch various parts of our bodies together, maybe we should wait until after dinner.

"Maria, can we just have a nice dinner and enjoy each other's company for once? Forget the Newspaper and Law Enforcement for a while. It is just too nice of an evening to waste it on grudges and let go of all the old baked suspicions and hate. I am offering you a toast. Here is a Toast to your Career, Maria. May it be long and prosperous," Hawk said.

"OK, I can drink to that," Maria said.

"Tonight only, though," Hawk said.

"Because your career could be over by morning after telling me about the Dragon Slayer?" Maria asked.

"Could we maybe take exception tonight only after a nightcap at the hotel if you are planning on destroying my career? Or, does that mean I would have to take you to dinner again, just to have a second date and a chance to get into your pants after that?" Hawk asked. He could see on her face that she was toying with the thought.

"Maybe," she said with a really big smile. Meanwhile, her hands were fumbling in her purse. Hawk was sure she wanted to turn her recorder off; if the talk turned to hot and sexy, that might be construed as leading Hawk on and recriminating herself. Although, Hawk was sure she knew all about the Tokyo Rose's rules of engagement.

Their salad arrived along with warm sourdough bread and butter. A casual conversation ensued over their different trips in their worlds, with laughter and touching hands and legs on occasion.

"Oh, this is nice," Maria exclaimed. She was feeling the effect of the wine.

Finally, the main course was placed before them. Too bad because Maria was already undoing yet another button on her blouse, revealing more of her already nearly bare and naked breast. *I doubt if she went to work without a bra, but somewhere along the line coming here, she had removed it.* It was very obvious what she was doing, and Hawk was having fun. Especially knowing what course of the menu was coming next.

This was the time Hawk thought to strike before things got too far down the trail.

Prior to Maria picking up her fork and knife, Hawk asked her one simple question:

"Maria, how is your father doing these days?"

"What?" Maria replied in a very surprised manner, half choking on a sip of wine. "What do you know of my father," she asked, bristling her back straight-up.

"Oh, not too much, babe, just that he is one of the Cartel Jefes. I believe his name is Arturo Beltran-Leyva? The Jefe of the Beltran-Leyva Cartel, is he not? Is he well?" Hawk asked.

"How the hell did you find that out? Who the hell are you, Hawk?" Her voice was going higher and higher, almost screaming as she spat out the words. Some people were turning heads to see who and why this woman was screaming and hissing so loud. She was shouting, demanding to know how Hawk could have found out such information. Because she had undone most all the buttons on her blouse, her breasts were now nearly bouncing out of it as she heaved one way then the other in total shock. It was a fascinating workout watching both her breasts dance and fully displayed for Hawk's viewing pleasure. After all, they were beautiful, and he was enjoying the smacking calamity.

"It is alright, folks," Hawk said, addressing the patrons around them. "This lady has been most unfaithful to me, and we are discussing her future plans and where she is now going to move. Please, continue with your meals."

Maria could no longer eat or even open her mouth without spitting saliva out onto the table in anger. Her eyes were red, and her demeanor displayed a total embarrassment of her situation and the full disclosure that Hawk presented her with. She had nowhere to run and nowhere to hide. She was caught and trapped like a big ole momma bear—checkmate, some would say.

"Who the hell are you?" she repeated again and again. "How did you find out this information? This was impossible to find out."

Hissing and spitting was about all she could manage to exalt now like a wounded snake—unable to strike or do damage; just turn and twist and hiss—because Hawk had stepped on her head figuratively.

With that, Maria got up and left the table, dragging her napkin and nearly tripping on it as she was leaving the restaurant. Hawk thanked the waitress and asked if she would box up the remaining dinners which he would take home for Annie and himself to eat later. No sense wasting two perfectly good meals.

By the time Hawk got outside, Maria's car was gone, and he knew she would be racing home to pack and leave town. Driving back to the Detective Bureau to remove the wire, Hawk could not help but gloat a little. "'The Dragon Slayer' rides again!" he yelled from the Vette as he was driving back to the office.

When Hawk walked into the office, Capt. Gee, exclaimed, "Good job! We got every word, and our Intel says she has already contacted her father and things are exploding everywhere in Santa Barbara and Mexico. I think you struck a very hot nerve, Hawk."

Misty was in the background of the office with a big smile on her face and delighting in the coming attraction of a major Cartel bust. Hawk overheard her say very quietly, "Vengeance is Mine."

CHAPTER 12

PANGA

It really wasn't too hard to convince Annie to go out to dinner this Saturday evening. It was a balmy warm December evening and night time was fast approaching by five thirty. Hawk had spent the better part of the day helping to vacuum and clean the house, and then the pool. Even though he was physically tired, he needed to have a discussion with Antonio at the Wharf Restaurant. He might just have some answers for Hawk on the gauntlet of Panga boats traveling with humans and drug cargos month in and month out. If Antonio didn't know, he could most likely point Hawk in the right direction. Hawk took Red into his confidence and swore him to secrecy. In time, he might tell Misty if she would like to get her boots wet. Misty was still on loan from the FBI and might herself have intel on the Pangas.

Annie and Hawk jumped into the Vette and headed down the freeway toward the Pier on lower State St. They pulled into the Wharf parking lot and Robert, the young valet kid that got hit on the head a couple of months back, was glad to see them.

"Parking is free, and your Vette will be right up front," Robert said.

"Thanks, Robert. Much appreciated. Bet you could still use a little change, though." Hawk slipped a twenty-dollar bill into his hand as he gave him the car keys.

"Thank you, Mr. Hawk," Robert said.

Once inside the restaurant, Antonio was very happy to see them and wanted to take them to the bar for drinks and conversation.

"My friend, Annie and I would like to sit at one of your magnificent window booths and have the special fish and chips plate but first, could you join us?" Hawk said.

"Yes, Hawk, for a few minutes anyway. Come with me, please. Here for you is the best window seat in the house. Annie, can I get a hug tonight?" Antonio asked.

"Of course, Antonio. Thank you for the beautiful seating," Annie said; she leaned over and gave Antonio big hug.

"Oh, my beautiful, for you anything. Anything at all," Antonio said.

As they were seated, Hawk wasted no time asking his question. "Antonio, I want to ask you a question about boats," Hawk said.

"Boats? Hawk, there is a harbor full of boats right there in front of you, my friend," Antonio said.

"Yes, I know those boats, but I am looking for a special kind of boat," Hawk said. Antonio's eyes narrowed a little in question or anticipation of Hawk's special interest in a particular kind of boat.

"Antonio, I am looking for Pangas," Hawk said.

"Oh, si, si. I understand what you are asking now. Must be quiet, please," Antonio said.

"Antonio, I understand quiet, but I am looking for Cartel or gang members moving people and drugs from Mexico to our coast. I really need to find out who is behind the transporting and I am hoping you can shed some light on it. Too many dead people floating in our waters and up onto our beaches. You know, Antonio, I am working Cold Case files now? I have a lot of unanswered questions about families that don't know about relatives who are buried in unmarked graves here. Can you help me?" That was partially the truth, but Hawk was really more concerned about the Pangas themselves and the cargo of drugs they were offloading on their beaches.

"Oh, Hawk, you don't know what you are asking, my friend. I owe you a big debt for saving my life, but if I tell you anything about the Pangas, I may never see you again," Antonio said.

"I fully understand, and I am prepared to meet anywhere but here," Hawk said.

"Do you ever shop at the El Rancho Market on Milpas?" Antonio asked.

"Yes, almost weekly," Hawk replied.

"Then you know Filippo, the owner, and manager, right?" Antonio asked.

Yes, he is a good friend. Does he know about such things?" Hawk asked.

"No," Antonio said, but he has a private room in the back of his store that nobody can hear or see what is going on. He is a very good friend of mine for many years now. We can meet there and talk. What do you say we meet there tomorrow around two-thirty before work?"

"Yes, I think that could work," Hawk said.

"But Hawk, I don't know what information I have for you," Antonio said.

"Antonio, anything will help and together, quietly, we can put many poor families at ease and stop them from killing our children. Agreed?" Hawk asked.

"Si, Amigo Hawk. I will find out what I can," Antonio said.

Annie reached over and grabbed Antonio's hand on the table and gave him a big silent thank you for his willingness to help Hawk. Antonio, got up and kissed her on the cheek and gave Hawk a wink and a pat on the shoulder. "Tomorrow at two thirty, my friend," he said in a low voice.

"Thank you, friend," Hawk replied.

"Well, my dear, thank you for the back-up, and now what would you like to have? The Cod and Chips or something else?" Antonio asked.

"I think I would like the Cod and Chips with a big salad, with blue cheese dressing and some of those sourdough rolls. Lots of butter and lemon for my water, please," Annie said.

"Me too. Honey and maybe raspberry ice tea," Hawk said.

They ordered their feast and enjoyed the food and the view. Hawk especially enjoyed looking at Annie this evening. All of his current health issues was very hard on her and Hawk felt like he owed her much more than just a dinner or two. His life, her care, her changing of dressings, and preparing new diets, etc. He owed Annie a lot.

The evening was perfect. Sunset was on time with two coffees after dinner and a couple of small sailboats meandering about chasing catspaws in the harbor entrance. It was just perfect. Hawk took advantage to scoot closer to Annie and whisper sweet nothings in her ear and a kiss on her cheek. "Are you, happy, honey?" he asked.

"Yes, I am. For the first time in a long time. I am so glad that you are out of the direct line of fire in the Bureau. No more gun play and stress on your stomach. I feel like we can take a breath of fresh air and not have to look over our shoulder's every few seconds. Hawk, that was horrible," Annie said.

"I know, honey. I am happy too," Hawk said. He could not afford to tell Annie what his true motives were regarding the Panga boats and chasing the Cartels all over the high seas at all hours of the night. Somehow, he had to find a way to keep the news and tenseness of the missions he would be gearing up for away from his stomach. The question was: How? If Hawk ever came home throwing up blood again, his butt would be cooked on the BBQ. But, chasing the bad guys in any venue was why he was born. Hawk, the Dragon Slayer, and the dragons were the Cartels along with any would-be jeffe who thought himself above the law or God Himself. Hawk was determined to fight the fight as long as he physically could. He just had to keep it all away from Annie.

They left the restaurant at seven in the evening and took a very leisurely drive through town, all the way toward home. Then Hawk came up with an idea: "Do you mind, honey, if we take a little trip down memory lane?"

"No! Of course not. But what does that mean?" Annie asked.

"Just you wait, babe. Maybe you can find some nice soft music on the radio while I show you our special place on the bluffs by the University. Remember our special place?" Hawk asked.

"Yes, of course," Annie said. "I could I ever forget that."

They drove up to the bluff, overlooking their old spot where they used to come for hours at a time to just talk, hold hands, and a little

REX BARTON

flirting. It was nice to return to the beginning now and again. Annie loved the sound of the small waves beating themselves against the shoreline sand and the white phosphorous bubbles glittering on the waves. It was a perfect time to steal a kiss or two and laugh at things in the beginning. How simple it all seemed back then, even though it wasn't. Hawk wasn't going there tonight; just wanted to hold Annie and maybe go for a little stroll on the beach.

Besides a few rocks jutting up through the sand because of the low tidal waves and some smelly seaweed here and there, it couldn't get any better until Hawk heard that sound—the sound of a Panga boat slipping through the rolls of the waves, looking for a beach to unload her cargo. It was a one-of-a-kind sound. This one looked like a Twenty-one-footer, with a center console and bimni top cover all the way to the bow. The engines just purred like kittens. Twin 300 hp Yamahas. Hawk knew where they were headed—just around the point about a hundred yards ahead.

When he was surfing, as a young kid, the beach was popularly called Sands Pit. Only because it was a deep trench—just offshore—where people could get big bursts of waves rolling in from the northern swells and hitting the sand bar. It would drop people into the trench with steep take offs before landing them back up on top of another sand bar. Hitting that, they would be lifted up fifteen feet or more at times. The rides were short but challenging. Fast was a better word. On the other side of the sandy trench was a nice long flat beach with access to the dirt perimeter roads surrounding Devereux School. Devereux School was where Hawk's beautiful horse Sheila and her colt Chalktaw went when Sam sold her. One of the resident kids who was boarding there year-round took them both back to the Kings Ranch in Texas when he graduated.

None of that was Hawk's problem now. His problem was, how was he going tell Annie what was going on and how was he going to make a big bust within minutes of where they were standing?

"Annie honey, do you suppose I could get you to go back to the car? Once at the car, get in and drive to the Campus police and have them call the office and send as many cars as possible to Sands Pitt behind Devereux School. Please?" Hawk pleaded.

"Why, Hawk, what's going on?" Annie asked.

"I can't explain right now, honey, other than to say I know the boat that just passed by and I need to stop it. Please, babe, just go. And go quickly; then go on home, and I will have someone drive me back home. OK? Please, because I need to go right now after that boat," Hawk said.

"How? How are you going to chase a boat that is in the water and you are here on the beach?" Annie asked.

"Honey, I know where they are headed. Please, just do it. Now," Hawk said.

Hawk watched Annie climb back up the stairs before he took off, running down the beach to make sure she got to the car safely. Then he said a little prayer: *Please Lord, give me the speed and strength to get to the drop zone before everyone is gone.*

Fortunately, Hawk still had his Glock in his back-side holster with the twelve round a clip. That should be enough if he acts conservatively and places his shots only at the hands holding the guns. He just didn't know how many trucks would be waiting or how many guards that were on the boats. There shouldn't be more than two trucks for the twenty-one-foot Panga if it were loaded with pot bales or Heroin or Crack. Probably not more than five or ten people lying down in the shallow haul. They would be walked on if a firefight began. That's only if Hawk could get there in time.

Hawk's chest was heaving, and his legs were starting to hurt. He was way past the burn. He had not done this much running since High School. Not even with all the ops training did he have to do this. Jogging, yes, but full out running? No! Hawk had to stop for a second and catch his breath. He was probably not more than thirty-five yards from the rocky point and just on the other side would be the first spot a Panga boat could drive right up onto the sand. With its shallow bottom and short shafted twin Yamaha outboards, it could probably scoot up twenty feet onto the beach. It would only take three or four people pushing the bow to get it back into deep enough water to lower the twins and take off again when unloaded. If they had to, the Cartels were willing to ditch the Pangas because, in the overall scheme of things, they were pretty cheap compared to the drug cargos they carried.

Hawk took off running again, but this time, he was being extra cautious in case he ran up into the unloading or someone's waiting arms. As Hawk leaned around the corner, he could see that the Panga boat was indeed unloading but it was still another hundred yards ahead of him on the other side of the point, and it was all open sand. He quickly looked up toward the shoreline and decided to run in the soft sand, using the weeds and brush as a backdrop cover as he ran in their direction. He felt secure to within a couple of hundred feet of the trucks and a line of people marching back and forth, from the boat to the trucks. If only his legs would stop shaking so much. Surely, Hawk's knees were knocking so loud from the running that the guards had a good chance of hearing them. The Cartel was using the innocent refugees who were laboriously unloading the heavy containers of drugs while each driver of the vehicles and the Panga boat stood guard.

Hawk's only hope of success was to sneak up as close as possible to the trucks, and then shoot at least two tires out of each truck, thus preventing them from getting away, before shooting the guards. First, he had to know that the Panga was empty; then he could charge them. Hawk prayed that the Sheriff's Department didn't show up first—which would cause everyone to panic and innocent lives would be lost. If that happened, the Cartel guards would shoot all the illegal immigrants.

How would I be able to tell Annie later tonight that a new sport coat, slacks, and shoes were going to be ruined in just a few minutes? Little did Hawk know at that moment, his clothes were the least of his problems. Walking on the dirt road toward him was a Cartel guard with his automatic rifle slung over his shoulder. He was not more than five or six feet away from Hawk when he unzipped his pants and began relieving himself within inches from where Hawk was. *Oh, hell no!* Hawk thought. *I will be damn if I am going to get pissed on too by these bastards.* An adrenalin rush enabled Hawk to jump up and crack the guy across the face, thus knocking him out cold. The sounds of breaking bones were a little harder to cover up because it brought attention to Hawk's location before he wanted it to. There was nothing Hawk could do but move as quickly as his legs would allow him. He leaned forward, looking for the gun toting guards. *God, please help my legs work again. I can barely move now.*

It wasn't as dark as Hawk would have liked for a cover, but then he would not have seen the automatic rifle swinging in his direction, had there not been a little evening sparkle. Hawk shot once, and the guard dropped to the ground. He then shot the two tires out of the first truck and ducked behind it, looking for another guard. Hawk didn't have to wait very long. The guard came around the backside of the first truck running into the middle of the road. He got a small burst of rounds off, which flew beyond Hawk's right shoulder about ten yards down range—approximately where the first guard went down with head trauma. People were screaming and running in all directions away from Hawk. The Panga was being pushed back into the water, and by the sounds of all the shouting near the water's edge, they were getting ready to drop everything else in the boat and turn tail back out to sea. Hawk's only hope was that they would not get past the Coast Guard a second time.

Hawk heard two patrol cars headed down the dirt road from the school and saw the dirt flying even higher, muffling a lot of the noise, with their red lights and sirens blaring. *Why in the hell are they boring down on all of us with the full parade of lights? Sitting targets for sure. This would be another class of proper emergency running when engaged with the bad guys and not wanting to draw that much attention to yourself. Come on, guys, shut them off,* Hawk said to himself. Now he was a better target for whoever might be lurking out there on the beach.

Hawk took a chance and ran a few steps up the road and jumped into some brush to try and hide and hope that one of the patrol cars didn't want to take a shortcut through the brush and run him over.

As the patrols cars drew nearer, Hawk figured out that the trucks were being abandoned and the Cartel hoods were re-organizing back into the Panga boat, including the truck drivers. With an empty vessel, those twin Yamaha-hoppys would assail the water at speeds up to forty or fifty knots, while barely skimming the surface of the water. They were tossing cargo out by the pounds and leaving the beach strewn with dope.

Hawk could see what he believed were refugees scattered everywhere, looking for a place to hide and take cover. He took a chance in standing up to see what had been loaded into the trucks. It was a haul. Bails of pot in the truck and Heroin; who knows what more—the beach had a great deal more.

Hawk heard the Panga boat motors fire up and he knew they would be on their way south again. He needed to flag down one of the oncoming patrol units and have them alert the Coast Guard ASAP. He started waving his hands in the air while holding his weapon, and sure enough, one of the patrol units stopped within twenty-five yards of him, and someone yelled out, "Drop your gun and turn around." *Oh crap.* Hawk didn't recognize the voice, and they obviously didn't recognize him. "OK, OK!" Hawk yelled, "I am a deputy. Detective Hawk here."

What Hawk heard afterward really pissed him off:

"I don't care who you think you are. Drop the damn gun and turn around. Do it now, or you're dead, ass hole."

Hawk swore he would remember this dumb butt head and ream him a new one.

"OK, OK!" Hawk yelled back; he didn't drop his gun, though. He took a chance that this cop wouldn't shoot him in the back; he gently laid his Glock down on the ground and got down on both knees with his hands behind his head and his fingers interlocked with each other. As the newbie was approaching, Hawk said, for the record, "I am a cop. Detective Hawk, SBSO. Who is in the other patrol unit?"

The punk grabbed Hawk's hands and pushed him to the ground, face down. "Slow up, deputy," Hawk yelled.

"Shut up, ass hole. Keep your mouth shut," the newbie said, and with one knee in Hawk's back, he put the handcuffs on Hawk's left wrist and bent his arm around to his back. The entire time, he was yelling obscenities in Hawk's ears, and then Hawk had had enough. *This punk is going down and is going to learn a valuable lesson.* The deputy was off balance to start with, having to try and hold Hawk down with one knee on his back. So, Hawk used his right leg and kicked backward, causing this newbie to fall forward toward Hawk's head. From there, it was an easy head but to his face, which just about knocked him out. It was enough of a shock and disorientation that Hawk slipped the newbie's grip, turned over, hit him in the jaw, and then kicked him off. Hawk got up, grabbed his Glock, and pointed it at his bleeding face. "Ok, punk, you want to die tonight? Or would you rather listen to me?" Hawk said.

"Listen, listen. Don't shoot please," the newbie pleaded.

"You are a real butt head, aren't you? A big tough cop. You're a piece of crap right now, boy. Did you not hear me?" Hawk asked.

"Yes, yes, sir. I didn't know," the newbie said.

"That's too bad, because this could've been your last night as a cop. When someone is waving a badge at you with a gun and yelling at you that he is a cop, you had better take an extra moment to check it out. Do you have any idea how much you cost us, boy?" Hawk asked. He grabbed him by the front of the shirt and hauled his ass back onto his feet. The newbie was spitting blood up the entire time all over Hawk, trying to answer his questions, and then fell back down to the ground to one knee. "Sorry, sir," he said.

"My suit may have been a little dirty, but you just ruined it with your stupid bleeding, butt head. Now, who is in the other unit?" Hawk asked.

"Carlos, sir," he said, spitting up more blood and falling over to one side.

"Now, that wasn't so hard, was it?" Hawk yelled amidst the screams of the refugees. "Hey, Carlos, it's Hawk. Get over here now. Forget what you are doing."

Carlos and his partner turned and ran over immediately they heard Hawk's voice.

"Hey, Hawk, I didn't know you were surfing out here tonight. What happened to you? Hey, Jerry, what the hell happened to—"

"Yes, Carlos, this idiot just wouldn't listen. We can talk about it later. Right now, I need you to get on the horn and have dispatch call the Coast Guard and the Harbor Master to intercept a white twenty-one-foot Panga boat. Not sure how many people are on board but they are armed and dangerous. What's your name, soldier?" Hawk asked.

"Deputy Marks, sir," Marks replied.

"Well, Deputy Marks, get your friend here over to the car and put your best first aid moves on him. He's hurting. I am sure his nose is broken, and he has a concussion along with cuts and bruises. Fix him up, son," Hawk said.

"Yes, sir. Come on, Jerry," Marks said.

"Jerry, when you wake up here in the next few minutes, you look me up because we are going to have a little talk, son," Hawk said.

"Aarau... umm ... aaa," Jerry groaned.

"Jerry, you just met Hawk the hard way. I told you about him, man. Weren't you listening?" Carlos said to him. "You don't mess with the Hawk. You are lucky you aren't dead right now."

"Oooo...," Jerry groaned again.

"Good enough, guys. Let's take a walk down to the beach area to survey the merchandise that the Cartel left behind. We found several more bags of drugs, bricks of Heroin, and sacks of pills. All in all, a very good bust for the night, as long as the tide didn't wash it all away. We had to move fast to get it all picked up," Hawk said, and then asked

Carlos, "Please, get on your loudspeaker and start telling the refugees that were left to gather around so we can help them. Most probably, we're going to stay hidden in the bush, and some may have already fled on foot to places unknown, but we have to try and bring them back all together.

"Marks, would you use Jerry's car and let dispatch know that we need help out here? Advise them to send the Campus police and CHP. Also, tell them they may encounter refugees walking on the side of the roads. Don't hurt them; just bring them back here," Hawk said.

"Yes, sir. Will do," Marks replied.

Hawk didn't see Jerry for at least another hour. He remained in the patrol car more or less passed out. *I guess I hurt him more than I thought.* Hawk's head was harder than most—so he learned over the years—but this time, he was sporting a nice little headache himself. He couldn't believe how painful his legs felt after all that running. His adrenalin was still pulling him through the moment, but he realized a crash of his own would be arriving after he settled down later. If there were any way for Hawk to get back downtown to the harbor, he would have loved to nail the Panga boat as it whipped over the waves in its attempt to escape the coast. *Oh, well.* Hawk knew he would eventually have his day on the high seas.

As more patrol cars were arriving on the scene, Hawk looked down at himself and couldn't believe what a mess he was. Had he known how bad he looked, maybe he would have shown a little mercy with Jerry. Then he thought again, *Hell no. He won't forget this night, and he won't forget me either.*

There was a lot of clean up to be done at Sands Pitt. Hawk let Carlos take over and organize the police evidence pick-up party. Carlos was able to gather in six refugees, though Hawk and Carlos suspected that maybe four more, at least, were missing, still hiding in the brush somewhere.

Someone shouted down at the water's edge, asking them to come down to where the Panga boat had once been. A dead body was floating in the shallow water and moving around with the tidal action. *Missing number seven refugees,* Hawk thought out loud. One of the Cartel guards must have shot him in their haste to escape. Poor guy. Came all that way from Mexico for a chance at freedom after having given all that he had to the Cartel. He was being used like a beast of burden in the field, and then shot to death because he would be a witness. Hawk dislike for the Cartel was gaining energy, to say the least. *Maybe now would be a good time to entrust Misty with joining my new task force that no one will hear about,* Hawk thought. His cold case work would be put on suspension for a while as he delved deeper into the Panga boat cases.

Hawk was calming down a few degrees and decided it was time to pay Jerry another call to see how he was doing. Not good for sure. Hawk guessed he really did a number on Jerry's head. He asked Carlos to get him to the hospital for observation. "Call a medic if you have to. Just get him driven to the ER," Hawk said. He knew Jerry couldn't hear him, but he uttered sorry to him, anyway, and patted him on the shoulder. He jumped at being touched, and that wasn't a good sign. He was really in shock. Don't let him go to sleep, guys. Keep him awake," Hawk said.

Now would be a good time to call Annie. It would also be Hawk's turn to get reamed out royally. He was sure she would jump all over his case, so he tried to put it off a little while longer. *The rest of tonight and all day tomorrow would be filled with reporting,* Hawk thought. Somehow, Hawk needed to get home, though, and shower and redress in clean clothes before showing up at the Bureau. His bloody look would have been too much, even for Halloween.

Sands Pitt would never be the same after tonight, Hawk thought. It changed to a bloody battlefield where innocent lives were wasted by the Cartel. Surfing was no longer his priority as it once was when in High School. Hawk's only thought now was the mess on the beach, and getting it cleaned up before the kids at Devereux woke up and wandered down the beach. This was definitely going to be a long shift.

And it was. It was one of the longest nights Hawk worked in a long, long time. When the reports were all written, the drugs all accounted for, and Jerry revived but in need of time off to heal, Hawk made more amends. The lessons learned this night would be building blocks for future confirmations with the Cartels. Hawk finally got the chance to leave the department and drove home. Annie was still asleep when he walked into the bedroom. Not wanting to wake her, he took a shower in the guest bathroom and then slipped his old clothes into a plastic sack and into the garbage can. Hawk's sport jacket, slacks, and shirt were all torn and blood-stained, and he knew nothing could be done to salvage them. He took a look at his shoes and decided maybe he could have them brought back to life and redeemed. *That was an expensive dinner*, Hawk thought to himself. He was still brewing on how he was going to tell Annie when he got into bed and cuddled up next to her. She made a few cooing sounds and snuggled up tighter, and together they slept another four hours. It was well into the day when the phone rang, and Hawk groggily picked it up.

Capt. Gee was asking Hawk about the Panga boat incident and how it all went down again. He was amazed and shocked at the delivery system of the Cartel. "We had only heard about the boats recently. It happened in San Diego County but not here," he said.

"Well, sir, it happened by sheer mistake and wanting to revisit a familiar haunt that Annie and I had early on in our relationship in Isle

Vista. We parked at the end of the houses next to the field and then decided to take a walk on the beach. It was then that I heard the Panga boat and its twin one Yamahas clipping along just behind the breakers. I knew the sound from live illustrations and pictures that I have studied of late. A friend down at the marina has nice a Trophy Boat with the same Yamaha set-up, and we have spent some time on it fishing. I know the sounds. The only boats cruising behind the breakers at that time of evening would have to be drug dealers, and I was right. I told Annie to go back to the car and then onto the Campus Police office to notify our office. They sent two patrol units within twenty minutes.

"I then ran North up the beach to keep track of the Panga boat and sure enough, just a little beyond Sands Pitt, they were unloading the boat. Two one ton pick-up trucks with siding and tarps were being loaded just behind Devereux school at the edge of the shore. The rest is history, with the exception of the big bertha between Jerry and myself. Just a little misunderstanding about who I was and why I was there," Hawk said.

"Yeah, I understand everything up to the misunderstanding. How come you were so tough on the kid, Hawk?" Capt. Gee asked.

"Because he was unwilling to check my identification, or look at me or follow any instructions. We all could have been killed, had I not taken enforcement action. I stood up from a hiding place in the brush not far from one of the trucks. I had already eliminated three armed

Cartel guards and several more were waiting for me to reappear. Rather than be run over by a zealous deputy, I jumped up in front of him with my badge in one hand and my Glock in the other. I was suited up and lit up by his head lights. Carlos was there as well. I just don't think Carlos saw me yet. So, Jerry forced my hand, and after he had hurt me playing the tough cop, I had to make the decision to break lose. Shooters were still on the beach and elsewhere firing and, in fact, they killed one of the refugees before taking off. If Jerry or his lieutenant want to make a big deal out of this, then I will recommend his dismissal for using excessive force. Who knows what he is doing in the field to other victims? However, I think he has learned a valuable lesson here, and I could even continue working with him and his training, if he's teachable," Hawk said.

"No, after explaining the situation, his lieutenant is not going to say anything, and if you are willing to take this kid on, then I am all for it. Does he have the qualities to make the team?" Capt. Gee asked.

"Not sure. He either folded from weakness, fear, or I am stronger than I think I am at times. I just know I didn't want to be shot or see anyone else killed. I did clearly identify myself more than once with the fear of being shot in the back by the Cartel," Hawk said.

"Understood. Will let you know after debriefing the Sheriff. Not to worry, Hawk," Capt. Gee said.

"Oh, I am not worrying. Jerry had better be the one to worry, and his lieutenant," Hawk said.

"By the way, did the Coast Guard ever pick-up the Panga boat?" Capt. Gee Asked.

"No, they never found it, and we alerted Ventura and Los Angeles Coast Guard to be on the lookout. Nothing. They disappeared like ghosts. Then my only thought was that someone else took them in at the harbor and trailered them out, or someone at sea. I will check tomorrow morning and see who or what was going on in the harbor and in Ventura last night," Hawk said.

"OK, good," Capt. Gee said. "Hawk, you might check other launch ramps, like McGrath Beach just outside of the Ventura Keys or any other similar points of entry," Capt. Gee said

"Will do, Captain. See you tomorrow, if that is alright?" Hawk asked.

"Not a problem, Hawk. Get some rest. I think your cold case files are churning up some good evidence. See you tomorrow morning," Capt. Gee said.

When Hawk turned back over, Annie was looking at him with suspicious looking eyes and taut lips. Even though her hair was all messed up, she was beautiful. Hawk thought she was ready to pounce him like a sleek panther ready to attack its prey, and her look had nothing to do with sex. She was waiting for him to say something and he knew it had better be the truth, or else... This was not play time, and he had not even tried to divert the unspoken subject. But it was hard, as she didn't have anything on. Annie was nude, sitting up in bed. Then Hawk made a stupid mistake by saying, "It was nice cuddling this morning, honey, and oh yeah, you are so beautiful this morning sitting there like that."

Annie butted in: "Go ahead and look, and I hope you enjoyed cuddling because it could be your last time, buster." Then she raised her voice, "What the hell happened last night, Hawk? Why didn't you call me? What the did you get into?" Tears of fear were trickling down her face. "Why couldn't you have just called me? I got scared, Hawk."

These were not just run of the mail questions; these were straight to the point that required immediate answers. But Hawk had to try to stave them off just a little while until he could think of good answers. "Can't it wait just a little while longer, honey? I am really tired and need a little more sleep. Or at least some coffee?" Hawk asked.

"What do you think?" Annie said. "Start talking. Now!"

"OK, OK. How about some coffee first then? You might need it. I could really use a cup myself," Hawk said.

Hawk then got up and started for the kitchen to turn the coffee pot on and noticed something hanging outside of the kitchen window on the front porch hook where a plant normally hangs. It looked like a bird. It was hanging by its neck with a miniature hangmen noose. The hanging plant was there earlier and now broken on the ground below the bird. A large bird, red in color. A Red Tail Hawk, in fact. The message was clear. The Cartel was not happy with the new turn of events from last night. They obviously didn't like losing any more men and especially the shipload of drugs. This is going to scare the hell out of Annie. *Now what,* Hawk thought? *I can't just throw it in the trash before she gets up. It wouldn't be fair to her. Annie deserves the truth. All of it.*

Hawk called Capt. Gee to send a unit with a camera to take pictures of the threat and they discussed having a guard again in the neighborhood. Hawk didn't think it was going to be that easy this time but had little choice. Something was better than nothing and running was not an option. He struck hard at the core of the Cartel last night and cost them millions and their only freedom of access to the shores. They were pissed. What they thought was an easy way of doing business just became more difficult and they were getting tired of Hawk interrupting their multi-million-dollar drug trade.

Hawk thought about Annie and how to protect her but not for long. She had her robe on and was standing behind him, listening to his conversation with Capt. Gee. Hawk wondered how she kept doing that. He thought he was a good Indian Scout but Annie always had a way of sneaking up behind him, unseen and unheard.

"OK, Hawk. Give it to me straight and without any sugar." In a raised and somewhat angry voice, she asked, "What-Happened-Last-Night?"

Hawk had to show her the dead Hawk hanging from the flower pot hook outside of the kitchen window first. "That is what happened, honey. I am very sorry. It is going to start all over again. That is a clear message to me that I hit a very dangerous nerve of the Cartel last night."

Hawk heard Annie groan deep in her throat and turn around, holding her stomach as if she was going to be sick. The full implications of last night and the last three years just came down on her like a ton of bricks. The reality of the drugs, the deaths, the fears, the threats, running, all of it manifested in one big lump in her stomach. In front of her eyes, by way of the dead hawk hanging outside of their kitchen window, was the truth. The symbol of the dead hawk was Hawk hanging somewhere dead or struggling for death over the pain they were going to inflict upon him, or them. There was no sugar coating this, not this time, so Hawk waited for Annie to come out of the bathroom to tell her the whole story.

When Annie returned from the bathroom, Hawk told her to go back into the bedroom, and they would talk. He already brought coffee and grapefruit in on a tray. She agreed with little objection, as long as he agreed to tell her everything. It was a critical time for them because as far as Annie knew, Hawk was more or less out to pasture in an easy assignment of Cold Case work. To Annie, that meant he was sitting at a desk most every day, or in the labs waiting for the clock to finally make its way to five o'clock hour. Annie liked the regular, dependable hours and the safety of the detective bureau. She thought that all the Cartel business was over and no more active gun shootings or running all over the country; no more ulcers or bleeding stomachs, and that Hawk was given a chance to heal.

"OK, honey, I am going to tell you what happened last night and anything else you want to know if I can. The Sheriff is being debriefed right now, so it should be safe to share everything with you," Hawk said.

"Don't leave out anything, Hawk. Don't even try to soften this in any way on my behalf. I want to know why you went back on your word regarding being on the front line again. You said you liked working the Cold Case files. What happened? What have you done, and does this have anything to do with Antonio?" Annie asked.

"Annie, I do like working the Cold Case department files. It gives me time in the lab to run experiments, looking back over people's lives and trying to bring closure to families and everything else. Real hardcore investigation on a different scale. A scale of Science and not just chasing people all around the countryside with a gun, as you say. Seeing justice played out at long last for some of the worst criminals in history. And I am not giving that up, Annie. However, along the way, I discovered a string of dead bodies. Most were immigrants with no names, no identifications of any kind. These were people who had been drowned, their stomachs cut open, or they were just coldly shot. It was all too familiar with the drug trades. Some of the women were butchered and left to die by bleeding to death. The pain and body mutilations were by the devil himself. I could not ignore it, Annie. When cases like that repeatedly fall in my lap, you know I cannot turn away or ignore them. I had to investigate further.

"These poor people are innocent human beings that were enlisted by the Cartels to carry drugs inside them. Surgically, the men and women were opened up or told to swallow the drugs in various types of containers. Then the drugs are cut out of them once they landed on our soil. The Cartels never told them that part, though. Most of the times, the people were shot and cut open for the product and just left to bleed out and thrown overboard in the ocean as shark bait. The picture became clear what was going on but the how was a mystery until I heard about a new kind of drug trafficking. Only then all the pieces started to come together. Boston Whalers used to be the Cartel boat of choice, but they were slow. Cigarettes were the second choice because they were so fast but hard on fuel. The Cigarettes had to carry so much extra fuel, which took away the room for drugs—the money maker. Plus, as you know from being around the boats down in the harbor, Cigarettes have a very deep haul, which prevents them from shallow wave running or being able to beach the boats and unload, and then turning them around and escaping," Hawk said.

Looking up at Annie between sips of coffee and talking, Hawk noticed she was turning shades of white. "Are you OK, honey, for me to continue?" he asked.

"Yes. Don't stop," she said.

"OK. Just recently, I ran across a new boat in my investigation called a Panga boat. That was what I heard and saw last night running along the edge of the shore. That boat is a consortium built boat between an American offshore company, Yamaha Corporation, and Mexico Cartels. They are ordered in three different lengths. The twenty-one-footer is the most popular, and that is what was running last night. They have a center console and can be tarped off from bow to stern, thus protecting both people and drug cargos. The engines are all Yamahas in the two hundred series that can move like a striped ape. The best part; they are lightweight and have a very shallow bottom for wave running and beaching. Once on the beaches, they can be spun around and floated back out to sea by only two or three people.

"That is what happened last night, babe. It was just dumb luck that we were there and I heard and saw the very boat that the Cartels are using," Hawk said.

"But how did you know where they were going, Hawk? And how did this have anything to do with us? Why couldn't you have just called for patrol units yourself to chase them down?" Annie asked.

"I knew where they were going, Annie, and there wasn't any time. When I was younger, I used to surf Sands Pitt. It was a popular surfing spot. Just around the corner is the perfect spot to unload cargo and not be seen by anyone. No one else on the patrol side has my intel knowledge, Annie. No one, except Capt. Gee. Do you remember me talking about Devereux school and my horses? That place has the roads and unique hidden qualities that no place else has. The Cartel has been using it for some time now because of that," Hawk said.

"What or who is this Jerry guy? What did he do that is causing so much fuss with the lieutenant or Capt. Gee?" Annie asked.

"Oh, that was a rookie mistake. Jerry is a yearling that thinks he is big and tough and knows how to handle himself and a pair of cuffs. He refused to listen to me, even after showing him my badge and explaining who I was. So, he got nasty and rough. After hurting me a little, I turned the table on him and gave him a concussion which put him out. It was either that or risk getting shot by the Cartel thugs still shooting in our direction. Not to worry. He is out of the picture for now. I think he learned a valuable lesson. Capt. Gee was just assuring me that Jerry or his lieutenant was not going to be a problem," Hawk said.

"Where did he hurt you?" Annie asked.

"Nowhere, baby. Not to worry about it," Hawk replied.

"Then why is your wrist so swollen and red? That indention and those scratches don't exactly look like nothing," Annie said.

"My head feels worse where I head-butted him. But really, all is good," Hawk said.

"I need to hear more about that part sometime," Annie said.

"Oh, I am sure you will. Believe me, though; he is far worse off than I," Hawk said.

"OK. I kind of get the picture, Hawk. That still does not explain what happened all of last night. How did you manage to capture all the Cartel people and all the drugs by yourself? How many were there?" Annie asked.

"Not sure, honey. Maybe fifty or hundred. Just kidding. Probably seven or eight guards and maybe ten refugees. We don't have a clear count yet. The drug hull was in the millions. A little of everything. I don't think my report is over yet," Hawk said.

"Now, tell me how many people were shot or killed and show me all your cuts, bruises, and bullet holes. And where are your clothes?" Annie asked.

Ohoo! Hawk had to avoid the last question on where his clothes were. If Annie saw them, she would faint. "No bullet holes, babe. The closest gunshot was ten yards away. Yes, I did kill at least three and beat one deputy up, but that was all. The worse problem was my legs and knees. Getting to Sands Pitt was the hardest of all. My knees wanted to give out every step of the way. Today I am going very slow, and boy do they hurt. I thought I was in good shape still, but being off that long with the stomach problem took more out of me than I thought," Hawk said.

"You see? That is why I am so worried. You can't afford to start bleeding again, Hawk. It is too soon to start in. What are you thinking? Your surgery was a serious thing," Annie said.

"I know, I know. Please, honey, it was just one of those, like I said, dumb luck incidents," Hawk said.

"Incidents? Really, Hawk? People are dead! Guns were fired! Drugs were scattered all over the beach! Panga boats! Boats everywhere; trucks and people everywhere. God! Hawk, this is not just a run-of-the-mill incident," Annie said.

"Wait a minute. You just gave me an idea," Hawk said.

"What? To retire from law enforcement today?" Annie asked.

"No, Annie. Something else you just said. I need to make a call right away. Give me a minute, OK, babe?" Hawk pleaded.

"No. You said you were going to tell me everything, Hawk," Annie said.

"I am. I promise. Just give me a minute, honey," Hawk said.

"OK, but you come back here, alright?" Annie demanded.

"Yes. I will. I promise," Hawk replied.

"Lou, it's Hawk at the S.O."

"Hi, Hawk, how are you doing after last night? And by the way, I looked high and low for your Panga boat, and nothing came off the coast. I had Ventura check every boat slip in all the Marina's between them and Channel Islands. Nothing. They just disappeared."

"I am doing good. Thanks. Regarding that; can you tell me what fishing boats, trawlers, or tankers were in the two- or four-mile range markers last night between nine and midnight?"

"Yes, I think I can. We normally get call-ins when a vessel over forty feet is in the channel. Give me a minute, and I will call you back, alright?"

"That's fine, Lou. Any information at all will be helpful. I am at home."

Hawk then called Ventura and Channel Islands Harbor Masters and Coast Guard offices and asked the same questions.

Ventura and Channel Islands Coast Guard told Hawk, "Four vessels were in the channel between the hours of eight and midnight. It was, in fact, a busy night on the water and fairly clear. Other tankers further out saw more activity than usual."

Hawk asked Lieutenant Gough of the U.S. Coast Guard in Channel Islands, "Is it possible for a Panga boat to be out that far and be hoisted up into a tanker of over fifty or sixty- foot?"

"Yes, of course. They are already rigged up with automatic hoist and wenches for just such a thing. Hawk, remember, they put smaller craft into the water to assist in untangling nets and grafting holes. Hell, those tankers and oil cargo ships have heavier lifeboats than the Panga boats," Lieutenant Gough said.

"Thanks, Lieutenant. That is what I needed to find out. Is there any way of determining if something like a tanker slowed down long enough to hoist up a Panga boat? Or did anyone see something like that going on?" Hawk asked.

"No. Not that I am aware of. Don't forget, beyond the eight-mile markers, any number of vessels could have done that and from any number of countries," Lieutenant Gough said.

"Oh, wow. I hadn't thought of that. So, a Peruvian, or Argentina, or Dominican vessel and any Mexican ship could pick-up a Panga and cover them up?" Hawk asked.

"Yes, and without ever being noticed, Hawk. They would do that at the two-mile markers and out," Lieutenant Gough replied.

"Let me ask this question, Lieutenant. What if we spot a Panga making a dash to the beach heads and then return back to the ocean and the eight-mile markers. Could one of your rotary craft observe from a distance without being seen?" Hawk asked.

"Yes, I think so. Especially if we were up wind and turned off all navigation lighting," Lieutenant Gough said.

"If I could get Capt. Gee of my department to contact your liaison officer, could we depend on the Coast Guard to agree to a joint task force with us in apprehending both the Panga and the tanker involved?" Hawk asked.

"Yes, I think we can manage that, Hawk," Lieutenant Gough said.

"Great, Lieutenant. I look forward to the day. Together, maybe we can bankrupt the Cartels by taking the big ships filled with drugs off the market as well," Hawk said.

"It would be a good exercise for us, because these guys are armed and can pretty much shoot us out of the water if we are not careful. We might even want to involve the Navy at some point," Lieutenant Gough said.

"Wow. Not quite yet. Let's leave the Navy out of it. You guys get all the glory. OK? Hawk said.

"You got it. Look forward to chatting with you later, Hawk. Take care of yourself," Lieutenant Gough said.

"You too. Be good, Lieutenant. Don't let your anchors drag. OK?" Hawk said jokingly.

"Ha ha," Lieutenant Gough laughed.

Now Hawk wanted to get back to Lou at their harbor master's office and ask the same questions. Just to keep the communication lines open and make sure they were all on the same wavelength, so to speak. Busting bad guys, not grabbing loot. Something told Hawk to watch his step.

"Hey, Lou, it's Hawk again. How did you do, sir? Any information for me?" Hawk asked.

"No, not really, Hawk. We don't have the ability to check that far out. Our navigation is limited to mainly fish and small craft. I couldn't tell you if one of your water crafts was speeding away from us or coming at us until we were basically hit. The sounders gage depth like any normal sonar has limitations. We don't have tracking devices and distance charting ability like the Coast Guard or Navy does. Our crafts are small Boston Whalers," Lou said.

"OK, Lou. Thanks for your help," Hawk said.

He might be right or not. I will check later and make sure everything matches up, Hawk thought. It just seemed strange that the harbor patrol was more concerned about renting slips and making sure no one drowned by falling off the party boats in and out of the harbor than making an arrest for drugs. Hawk thought their biggest hoo-ha was firing their flare guns to start the Wednesday sailboat races.

"Sorry, honey. I am done with the calls for now. Where were we?" Hawk asked.

"What was it that I said that made you have to call people on the phone in the middle of our conversation?" Annie asked.

"Sorry again. It was a word that you said. Boats. Big boats. That made me think how the Panga boats are getting to and from the beaches. They aren't driving at high speeds from Mexico to here. They are being lifted off large tankers vessels by wenches, and then they load up the drugs and finally do their beach runs and landings. When they are done, it's back out to sea beyond the eight-mile markers where nobody can see and either reload or are lifted back up and covered for another night. That's why they are never seen until it is too late or by accident like last night. Anyway, I will check back in with Capt. Gee later and let him know what I found out," Hawk said.

"Do you even realize what is going on, and what you are saying?" Annie sputtered.

"What do you mean, honey? Of course, I understand. What kind of a question is that?" Hawk asked.

"Hawk, you are going to see more than a dead hawk hanging from our flower pot hook over the next few weeks if you continue to charge forward like Teddy Roosevelt. Don't you get it? They are going to kill you, me, and anyone else in our families if you don't stop right now," Annie said.

There it was. Stop the fight. Retire or else... Hawk was not sure how to handle this delicate conversation any longer. He didn't blame Annie for being afraid but he wasn't sure how he could just turn this over to someone else either in the department either.

"Yes, honey, I know what you think, and I know how scared you must be. Can I promise you and the family complete safety? No, in all honesty, I can't promise that. I and the department will do everything in our collective power to position us and protect us in a safe zone if need be. At least for now, while this particular investigation is going on. Remember our Honey Moon in Hawaii? I might be able to move us there temporarily, while I finish this. Or anywhere else you want? How about Channel Islands area by Ventura?" Hawk asked.

"Hawk, I don't want anything to happen to you. But I feel you have busted open the beehive and now the bees are swarming and looking to kill all of us. There is no place to hide anymore. If the Cartel comes today or five years from now, they are going to come. Right? And I won't leave our home. Period!" Annie said.

"No, Annie. Cut off the head of a poisonous snake and throw it in the fire and it is dead, and it won't come back to bite you. That is what I am going to do—cut the head off one of the biggest poisonous snakes in Mexico. This is worth fighting for, Annie. Too many of our young children are being killed needlessly by these greedy bastards, and I have a way to stop it. Once I do, then life can go back to normal, and we can all relax. Maybe that was a stretch in my thinking. Probably a real stretch of ignorance, but worth a try," Hawk said.

"You're wrong, Hawk. Nothing will ever return back to normal. You have opened everything up, and it will never be normal. You have killed bad people, and they now want you dead more than ever. I can't stay here and watch this any longer, Hawk. I have been hoping and praying that you were changing and would be taking care of yourself when you clearly aren't. You have some kind of a death wish or something," Annie said.

The phone was ringing again, and Annie told Hawk to answer it.

"No, Annie, I won't answer it. We need to finish our conversation. You asked me to tell you everything, and I am going to. No matter how hard it is, you must know what my driving force is and why I am doing what I do," Hawk said.

"I know what it is, Hawk. You want this mythical dream of Justice, Peace, and Love throughout the kingdom. The problem is, it can never happen. The armies against you are too big and too powerful, and the king on duty couldn't really give a damn. He has other fish to fry and elections to win and so on and so on. Your life is expendable, and I guess mine too. The big Dragon Slayer is going to get us killed," Annie said.

"No, honey, I wouldn't really worry until you see a dragon hanging on the porch," Hawk said.

"Not funny, Hawk. Not funny at all. How many people got killed last night?" Annie asked.

"Four or five that we know of. Why?" Hawk asked.

"How many did you kill, Hawk?" Annie asked.

"Three Cartel guards, and injured one deputy," Hawk replied.

"Oh, you mean that killing guards is not enough, so you turned on your own deputies?" Annie asked.

"Not fair, Annie. The guards gave me no choice. Kill or be killed and I am not going down on the beach. I told you I could take care of myself. I put the deputy down on the ground because he wouldn't listen and tried to hurt me for no reason. He was out of line and could have potentially got all of us killed. The Cartel killed one of the refugees themselves. I don't really know; it could be even more immigrants than that. Are you happy now, Annie? Would you like more gruesome details?" Hawk asked.

"Hawk, I don't want you killed, and I don't want to see you hurt anymore. Is there anything wrong with that? You still have not told me why you didn't just let the Campus Police or your own department handle this case. Why do you insist on doing everything yourself? Your stomach ulcer is going to start bleeding again and then who knows what can happen?" Anny said.

"Annie, I am sorry. I know this scares you and I wish I could have called you last night but I couldn't. I was not off the beach until after one or two this morning. Large amounts of drugs, dead bodies, and refugees needed to be dealt with. Carlos helped out a lot, but it was too much mass confusion and carnage. I will try and do things differently the next time," Hawk said.

"The next time, Hawk? What if there is no next time? What if the Cartels come back today and—"

Annie began crying uncontrollably at this point. She was scared for more than one reason, and Hawk didn't think he could console her. All of his promises meant nothing to her now. All he could do was wait and plan the next step. He reassured Annie that patrol units were now in the area and no one was coming to kill anyone.

"You are safe, Annie. Do you hear me? Please understand that my life is doing what I do in Law Enforcement. I can't change that, Annie. Maybe someday, but not yet. You must get a grip on this and trust God. He is our only source of protection and comfort. Re-read Psalm 23, honey. He is our comforter. He will cause us to rest and lay down in greener pastures beside the still waters. We have it all right in the middle of the work and the battle. Trust in Him, Annie. We must put our full faith in God right now. Actually, not just now but every moment of every day," Hawk said.

Annie started to relax a little and asked if they could finish talking later. She just wanted to rest and think. Hawk agreed and decided to make some breakfast for the both of them.

After breakfast, Hawk went into the study to continue his investigation into the type of fishing boat he might be looking for in the deep waters off the coast of Santa Barbara. He came across several and took notes down and copied pictures for future reference. While thinking about how the Panga boats were coming ashore, he thought of Misty. Of all his law enforcement officers available to him, she was probably more capable and knowledgeable on the Cartel fishing expeditions than anyone. Hawk decided it was time to bring her in on his own expedition of fishing for Cartel chum.

The doorbell rang, and Annie answered the door. It was Deputy Jake Stallworth. He had been with the department for approximately five years, and Hawk had kept notes on his accomplishments. He had integrity, likeability, intelligence, good mechanical skills with firearms, an expert with the Glock, and married with two children. It was time to talk with Jake and possibly bring him onto Hawk's team. All Hawk needed to know was if he could swim or not.

"Hey, Jake, how are you doing?" Hawk greeted.

"Good, sir! I heard, though, that some old friends visited you?" Jake asked.

"If you can call them that," Hawk replied. "Have you met my wife, Annie, yet?"

"Yes, she just introduced herself," Jake said.

"Do you guys need my help with anything?" Annie asked.

"No, honey. Jake and I will take it from here. Thank you," Hawk replied.

"Good to meet you, Jake. Please talk some sense into Hawk before you leave," Annie said.

Jake looked at Hawk as Annie was walking back down the hallway.

"What's going on, Hawk?" Jake asked.

"My wife is scared of all the recently renewed activity with the Cartels. I promised her I would settle down and get off the bandwagon but the Cartels keep coming up on my radar screens. Can't just let go and write parking tickets or sit at a desk all day. I was not wired that way," Hawk said.

"I understand. This is a pretty gruesome site hanging her, Hawk. Do you remember hearing anything or seeing any activity outside last night?" Jake asked.

"No, nothing. I am of no help there. After the bust last night at Sands Pitt, and by the time I got home, I was toast. They could have put dynamite out here and lit it, and I still would not have awoken. I was dead out," Hawk said.

"You are lucky you both were not killed. This is not a light weight threat, is it?" Jake asked.

"No, it isn't, Jake. I have had many before, but this has significance because of the manner in which they did this. Yes, they could have broken in and cut our throats, but this was a different message. One of taunting and letting me know that the day is near and I won't know when. So, it is my intention to go on a full attack mode and not give them another chance. If I am running the offensive, they will be so busy trying to protect and save what they have. If I can keep them busy, maybe they will forget about me personally. My plans go deep and wide," Hawk said.

"Sounds good. What do you want me to do, Hawk, with this bird hanging here?" Jake asked.

"Take a few pictures and write it up as an unknown threat in our home. Nothing else. Keep it light weight and not much to be concerned with. You might even put in the report that it is thought to be local kids playing pranks. That way, the press won't even look at any other possibilities," Hawk said.

"Got it. And just so you know, per Capt. Joel, we will have patrols in the area at all times. Drive-by units and extra patrols within minutes. I will run plates and descriptions of every known gang mobile in Santa Barbara County. If we see anything close, you can be sure they will be jacked up," Jake assured Hawk.

"Good. One more thing, Jake. Something for you to think about. How would you like to come over to my team at the Detective Bureau? It would mean a promotion and a hell of a lot more work. Long hours and lots of practice at the range and on the matts. You also have to know how to swim. Can you swim?" Hawk asked.

"Wow. Thank you. Yes, I can swim, but I need to talk with my wife, Sharon, first. Is that alright?" Jake asked.

"That is a prerequisite with every detective in the Bureau. You can see what I am dealing with. Get back to me soon. Alright?" Hawk said.

"Yes, sir," Jake replied with a smile on his face.

"By the way, Jake, this is between us right now. I won't say anything to Capt. Joel or anyone else," Hawk said.

"Thank you, sir. I appreciate your confidence in me and this opportunity," Jake said.

"Good. Talk with you later. Thanks for coming by and handling the reports and all the drive-by," Hawk said.

Jake saluted with two fingers to his forehead as he was turning to leave. Hawk thought to himself that between Red, Carlos, and possibly Jake, his muscle would be good, and with Misty's deadly force and knowledge, the team would be almost complete. He just had to find a way to keep all of it from Annie.

Hawk checked in with Annie and let her know that she could expect to see a lot of patrol cars in and about their area, and not to get concerned; they would be fine.

CHAPTER 13

WHIPLASH

Hawk finally dragged his tail out of bed and into the shower. It was Friday morning at 0730 hours and the following night's Panga party at sea would certainly promote Cartel Whiplash. The dead hanging hawk was enough, but Hawk knew better than to believe that that would be all there is. He was almost certain to expect more. He was, in fact, reluctant to even walk by his kitchen window this morning. He wasn't sure who might be hanging around there this time. *Maybe another graffiti pictorial job lathering our garage door? No, not going there yet either,* Hawk thought. He was content to take his shower first and dress before even turning on the coffee this morning.

Well done, Hawk, he said to himself. *You, big baby, scared of a few ruffled feathers?* Hawk didn't listen to himself. It was exhaustion talk, and the hot shower was a welcome refresher to the otherwise drowsy day. He got dressed in Levi's and a surf shirt from his son Randy's printing shop. *Beautiful work. That kid is really talented. Need to call*

Randy today and thank him again for the box of surf tees he sent our way. Thank God he and his wife, Lanai, and our grand-daughter Jamie are far enough away not to be a worry. Hawaii is a great place to work and play, and Hawk was sure they were doing great. Jamie was, in fact, straight A's at the University of Hawaii; couldn't ask for more than that. Annie and Hawk were fortunate that all their kids and grandkids were doing well. The further they were from Annie and Hawk, the better for the mean time. Hawk hesitated to even think about them, for fear of what the Cartels might do if they found them. *Violet, our oldest and our family RN is too close. She is tough but not invincible like some of us, like to think,* Hawk said to himself.

Oh, what a headache. Hawk reached up to touch the top of his head; that was a big mistake. Looking back on the incident the previous night, Hawk could not believe how stupid a mistake that was—bumping into the metal door frame. *Guess that is why I never joined the Navy. Who the hell is that small anyway?* He said to himself. Looking into the mirror, Hawk swore the bump on the top of his head was larger than his head. His eyes were still crossed. *Maybe I am no longer invincible either,* he thought. *Put that on the back burner for later.*

While shaving, Hawk recounted in his head the entire night's operation and what had led up to it. All the intelligence gathering from the different agencies and people along the way. The patience and timing of the entire ops. He felt good at what was accomplished. More bad guys were down, and lots more drugs would never come to their shore. *Strike one for justice and the American way.* Speaking to himself, it all sounded a little cheesy, but that was what he thought. *Mission accomplished, and I can wear my badge a little higher on my chest today.* Hawk actually felt proud to be a cop.

For the Cartel, unfortunately, it was a rather bad day. Hawk wondered while nicking his chin a little with a sharp razor blade, shaving, not paying attention if he would ever meet any of the Cartel bosses. Not just in a line-up but face to face, look each one in the eye, spit out his name, and brand him 'GUILTY'! Off with his head, Hawk would say.

Behind him, he heard a sleepy 'good morning mister.' Annie had just awakened and was listening to Hawk's shaving rants.

"Have you heard the news on the television yet?" she asked.

"No, I haven't even turned the coffee on yet. How are you, babe?" Hawk asked.

"A little tired. The girls and I went out last night and partied with some nice guys from Mexico. They had a big boat and offered to take us for a ride, but somehow it sank before we got there," Hawk said. That is on the news?"

"All over it. Two fishing vessels sink in the channel. Both caught fire and unknown death toll. More news coming. Are you alright?" Annie asked.

"Yes. Just a little bump on my head from a small doorway made for hobbits only," Hawk said.

"Let me see?" Annie asked.

"No, no thank you; it is fine. Don't touch, please," Hawk remitted.

"Just a little bump? Hawk, that is huge. And you have a cut as well. You had better get it looked at today in the hospital," Annie said.

"I think not. Too much paperwork left to work on," Hawk replied.

"Can you tell me anything yet?" Annie asked.

"A little. The best news is, tons of drugs are either at the bottom of the ocean or in evidence and a few bad guys with guns are dead. The good guys won the battle on the high seas last night. That's what it is all about, Annie. Winning the war on drugs and keeping our streets and kids safe. That, my dear, is why I wear my badge," Hawk said.

"I know, Hawk. I am sorry for trying to take that away from you. Somehow, I will learn to get a grip on my fear of losing you. The job you do day in and day out in protecting and serving everyone is beyond belief. I only wish more people could know the risk you take every day. Just look at you. Barely out of bed and you are bleeding on your chin already. Can you even see? Both your eyes are black. Please get the bump looked at today. I will start the coffee, OK?"

"Thanks, honey. Thanks for understanding. I love you," Hawk said. "NO, don't go in the kitchen yet."

"Why?" Annie asked.

"It is my job to turn the coffee on, dear. Just let me finish shaving. I love you!" Hawk yelled.

Annie was in the doorway and already headed down the hallway.

The moment Hawk had finished saying "I love you," as if on cue, the house shook, and he and Annie were thrown to the ground. Hawk dropped his razor and crawled into the hallway, looking through the smoke and dust for Annie in a complete daze.

"Annie? Annie? Where are you? Annie?" Hawk yelled. Hawk heard her moan behind him. The blast from the explosion had thrown her backward into the hallway linen cabinets. Annie was folded up like a pretzel—covered in dirt, pieces of brick, wood, stucco, and drywall material. Somewhere in the house was an explosion that must have hit a 10 on the rector scale. Hawk screamed at Annie to stay put and not move. She couldn't have moved if she wanted to. It appeared as though she was broken into pieces. The blast had dissected her body with cuts, bruises, and blast burns so much so that she was unrecognizable. Her beautiful dark brown hair which Hawk always teased was the color of shiny coffee beans growing on Juan Valdez's coffee bean plantation in Colombia. One could say it was from the color of her hair that God got the idea for the color of the coffee bean. Now, it was ashen gray and spots of frizzy burns. Her golden tan skin was red, gray, black, and blue from an unknown bomb blast. Hawk thought that they were under siege. The whiplash that he had joked about earlier was happening for real. *An assault on my home and my family? Where the hell is our protection?* Hawk thought. *Where the hell is our help?* he screamed. *Help!* The coughing and choking was nearly unbearable, but he managed to scream again, *HELP!* Something was wrong with Hawk's hearing. He couldn't hear anything and couldn't see through all the smoke, dust, and fire. He kept seeing little flickers of bright blades of red and yellow flames ahead of him where their living room fireplace used to be. Now there was a big hole. The wall of brick was gone. As Hawk came closer, he saw more flames around their once beautiful living room. Whatever it was that caused the blast pretty much destroyed their home and subsequent garage and Hawk's office.

Suddenly, Hawk felt a pull on both his arms and a shadow of one or two people. They were jerking him forward, half-dragging him down the debris-filled hallway toward the open hole where the fireplace once stood. He could smell gas and the lick of smoke and fire still burning ahead of him. Who were these people? Hawk didn't know them. Where were they taking him? Hawk wondered between partial blackouts. He passed out at the next shock to his head. He thought he heard gunfire or more explosions. Everything went completely dark and quiet...

Hawk awoke from the shadows of minimum brain activity. Again, trying to make sense of what had just happened moments ago. "Where am I? What is this place?" he asked.

"Everything is OK, Mr. Hawk," someone said with a foreign accent. "Just be quiet while we finish our tests."

"Who are you?" Hawk retorted in a higher voice that he couldn't identify as his own.

"Hawk, it's Doctor Collins. Not to worry, you are in the hospital being evaluated. We will be done in just a moment. Nurse 20 cc's now."

"What? What are you doing?" Hawk was totally confused and choking for breath. *I passed out once again while on duty,* he thought. *This can't be happening.* Hawk's subconscious mind was repeating over and over again the same thoughts and blurred focuses. Sounds were off; the entire world was off course. He was lost somewhere between reality and never-never land.

Whatever the 20 cc's were, which was the last thing Hawk heard, was two days earlier, as he was told. Dr. Collins came into the room and began to explain all that happened. Capt. Gee was sitting in a chair opposite the room window, and all the machines making burping noises and tick-tocks as well as bleeps on a green screen of wavelengths. *What the hell? What are all these wires pulling and tugging at me? What is going on?* Then the thought occurred to Hawk, *Where is Annie?* He screamed for her. "Annie? Annie? Where are you?" Hawk's world of sound was still groggy and slurred, so no wonder he never heard an answer.

It took two nurses, Dr. Collins, and Capt. Gee to hold Hawk down. Dr. Collins kept saying, over and over, "She is alright, Hawk. She will be fine. Annie is right next door."

"Why?" Hawk yelled, barely hearing himself. "What the Hell is going on? An explosion? Voices? What? What?"

"Hawk, someone set off a gas explosion at your home three days ago. They tried to drag you off and put the burning gas line down your throat when we came in and exterminated the vermin. Two Cartel jokers that slipped in under our surveillance. We got there just in time. Annie is alright; just a few cuts, bruises, and minor burns. She suffered more shock than anything. Your kids are with her now," Capt. Gee said.

"How the hell did this happen, man? Where were the patrol units? Eating donuts somewhere like all the jokes we hear about? How did this happen?" Hawk demanded.

"Apparently, The Los Zeta Cartel didn't like the losses they sustained the other night and put the order out: Dead or alive, $250,000 U.S. dollars. They walked in, Hawk. Hidden by homes and cars, so we never saw them," Capt. Gee said.

That was too cheap, Hawk thought. "That's why they bungled the job. They are afraid of me alive, and they couldn't kill me right, either."

"They came close this time, Hawk. Another second and that burning gas line would have been stuffed down your throat!" Capt. Gee exclaimed.

"Hawk, just so you know, your hearing will return to normal in a few weeks and everything else is checking out good. I want to observe you for a few more days, but you should be good to go soon. You sustained a bad concussion on top of your head and a significant laceration," Dr. Collins said.

"Thanks, doc, but I need to see Annie right now. I need to make sure she is alright," Hawk said.

"No. It is better that you wait. She doesn't want you seeing her all wrapped up in bandages like a birthday present or a mummy. Poor choice of words. Sorry," Dr. Collins said.

"How bad is she, Doc? Tell me the truth!" Hawk demanded.

"She is absolutely going to be fine. We are just staving off infections with the burns and keeping her comfortable," Dr. Collins insisted.

"How long, doctor? How long before she can be moved?" Hawk asked.

"Tomorrow perhaps or the next day," he answered. "Why? She shouldn't leave the hospital," Dr. Collins said.

"No, I want her moved in here with me. We need to be in the same room. I can take care of her better," Hawk said.

"We will wait until tomorrow, Hawk. Just take it easy for now," Dr. Collins. said

"Bullshit! I am taking Annie, and we are leaving just as soon as I can get us dressed. Don't you see? It's not safe here. We are in danger.

Capt. Gee, what else happened? And how long ago did you say this was?" Hawk asked.

"Three days ago today, Hawk. A lot has happened. First, be advised that your home is secured and the damage areas were closed off. Your pool was drained because the blast cracked the pool in several places and the fire chief thought it best to empty it for safety reasons.

"You can't leave the hospital yet. Too dangerous for Annie and you. I have deputies posted outside of the doors. No one gets in or out without photo ID and knowledge of why they are on the floor. All nurses and doctors attending are known by every deputy," Capt. Gee said.

"Yeah, but that could pop the pool right out the ground because it is empty. Stucco pools don't do well with no water in them." That was all Hawk heard or could think of. How stupid once he understood what Capt. Gee was telling him.

"Don't worry; everything will be fine. Everything that could be salvaged was boxed up and placed in storage for you. All your valuables, guns, jewelry, cars, and so forth is all safe. The house will have to be rebuilt basically and a few new trees planted, but you are not to worry. A lot of people are out in the hallway waiting to see you, so when you feel up to it, I will let them in one by one, alright? In the meantime, you need to get some rest, and later on, we can finish our talk and debriefing.

"Oh, one more thing. Capt. Numb-nuts, as you call him, died yesterday in a head-on collision in Escondido. Apparently, he was onto us that we suspected him of being one of the Cartel insiders and he was making a run for the border the back way. Thought you might like to hear that," Capt. Gee said.

"This was his order, right? He put the hit out?" Hawk asked.

"Later, Lieutenant. Rest now like the doctor said," Capt. Gee said.

Hawk missed that last remark, as I floated off into oblivion as the shot of 20 cc's of something was taking effect.

Violet walked into the room from visiting her mother, and the whole room seemed brighter. Violet's presence actually lit everything up. Hawk's mind wandered slowly down to a normal frequency level.

CHAPTER 14

BLOOD POOL

It turned out that with the explosion, Hawk received a gold shoulder bar promotion the hard way. He had to ask himself if it was really worth it or not for all the pain and suffering caused.

0800 hrs. Monday, Santa Barbara County Sheriff's Department, Detective Bureau. Panga boat Meeting Team One, Team Two, and Team Three.

Identification Meeting followed by training at the range. Be on time. Be ready. Be prepared.

Lt. Hawk!

That was all the posting that was necessary to ready three teams for a full day of mental, physical, and emotional training. Everyone on the team knew what the words "Be Prepared" meant—everything, from a cup and canteen to full ops gear; all weapons and ammo preparedness. That would include M-16, Glock 9mm, cleaning oils and pads, 8" saw-tooth tactical knife (complete with flints, string, hooks, wire, and matches inside the handle), water, scarf, glasses, rations for three days, rope, silencer, vest, and a change of socks. Everything had to fit in a sixty-pound backpack. Anything else one elected was on one's shoulders or would be left. Anything more required, once in the field, would be made or created on the trail.

Six weeks earlier

It has been two months to the day since Annie and Hawk left the confines and protection of their hospital rooms. It was decided by the family, after learning all that Annie and Hawk had been going through over the last three years with the various Cartels, that Hawaii would be their safest rehabilitation spot.

Yes, Hawk had to agree with the family's decision and prepare himself for not only healing but healthy living. That included good food, rest, and exercise. Randy, Lani, and Jamie—their youngest and last grandchild—insisted that Hawk spend some quality time surfing the warm Pacific Ocean waters of Hawaii.

It had been many years since Hawk put his surfboard away. It was a beautiful ten-foot Yater fiberglass board. Two skags for better wave control and tight turns. When he finally gave up the sport for Special

Teams, he thought he would never use it again. Now Hawaii would be the real test of his retired surfing abilities. With a little rest, maybe, just maybe he could massage the muscles into working those paddling requirements again.

The waves were pretty much consistent on a daily basis of three to four feet just beyond the reef off Kona. The Big Island of Hawaii was far different than what Hawk had experienced on Oahu when he was younger. Even twenty years later, when Annie and Hawk celebrated their honeymoon there, the islands were now more congested. That's why Randy and Lani chose the Big Island—because it was far less crowded.

It was such a joy to just sit in the Pacific Ocean in eighty-degree water and rest one's bones. The sun, water, and island habitat were great, but it also gave Hawk a chance to regain his perspective. One day out on one of Randy's big wave boards, Hawk said to himself aloud, *God allowed the house to be blown up. I was given warnings but had ignored them all because of ego-driven vanity. I somehow thought I was invincible. Beyond getting killed or that my family might be injured. I took too much for granted and became lazy in my prayer and Bible reading time. Forgive me, God. It's me again just realizing that my thoughts are not Your thoughts and if I stray, it is not You that moved but me. Help me, Lord, to put my priorities right. Amen.*

The waves were much easier and smoother. Gentle, one may say, like the ocean breezes themselves. Along with the salty taste and ocean smells, there was more. On the soft breeze were wispy smells of Plumeria flowers on the ever changing air streams. Looking at the island from the water, Hawk could see lush plants and wild orchids in full bloom along with dozens of other flowers. The smells, the sights, the sounds were all part of God's bigger plan to bring Hawk back to Himself. Just the fragrances alone and breathing in such beautiful perfumes was intoxicating beyond one's senses. *Which way do I point myself?* Hawk thought. In every direction, there was a new experience. *North, South, East or West?* Each position was a different enchanted exhilarating moment. With new breaths, each turn offered a new delight to nearly every fiber of Hawk's body. One could not help but be delirious with excitement in each turn.

The sun, sand, surf, and family time was a healing balm that Annie and Hawk needed so desperately. It was such fun to just watch the interaction of Randy and Jamie and Lani out surfing. *One outdoing the other in some real family time competition. Not cutting each other off or trying to hurt one another like back home at work. This is what it should be like daily—enjoyment and celebration of life with God, the creator of everything. If I could smile at the employment of such family fun as this, how must God feel? He surely is smiling as well.*

Hawk looked up at the blue, blue sky and then let his sight lazily drop back down to the blue-green ocean with white bubbly waves being carved off the main body of water. Then he saw a long ago familiar sight. Not that he hadn't seen Annie in a bikini at home, but now she was so much more beautiful. The yellow contrast of her bikini against the red surfboard floating on the blue-green sea and the smells just took Hawk's breath away. Annie was not out here to surf but to allow the warm salty water penetrate her wounds and permit more healing along with the sun. It was enthralling, to say the least. Hawk's heart was captivated by the scene that he would not forget for a long time.

"Hey, babe, watch this," Hawk exclaimed with excitement. A nice five-foot wave was realizing its dream of making shore, having rolled all the way from Japan. This was not a tube ride or anything critical; just a nice easy ride from sixty or seventy yards out. Unfortunately, Hawk's dream of a long ride was cut short by muscles that wouldn't perform like days of old. As he leisurely got to his feet, after paddling a few strokes, he was headed down the face of the wave. The problem was, his leisurely mannered attempt to get up drove him and the tip of the surfboard straight down to the sandy bottom. When he arrived back to the surface, Annie was laughing her head off. After the shock and embarrassment had worn off Hawk's face, he began laughing with her. It just couldn't get any better!

Now it was time to return to the mainland and put into action the necessary plans of offense against the Cartels. Of course, and with much understanding and assurances, Hawk had to make in concrete certain concessions with his family—of what he would and would not do any longer. Most importantly was a renewed commitment to his God. Annie and Hawk wanted to stay in paradise, but too many things begged their attention, not to mention what to do with their blown-up home.

Jeff had stayed in touch and kept them advised of all the necessary things required to rebuild, but he still needed them there. Annie and Hawk said their Alohas to their island family after many tears and flew back to Los Angeles. It was depressing and fearful all at the same time. Annie and Hawk had agreed beforehand to leave a check for the kids for all they had done for them. Just before leaving the house, as is custom, Annie threw her floral Carnation Lei into the ocean, signifying the tradition of their return. They then had a little family prayer time and lots of hugs and kisses.

Tears of joy and sadness emptied from their eyes as they watched the beautiful Lei float out fifty yards or so, and then returned to the beach, floating on a small shore break wave. *Thank You, Lord, for our many gifts and blessings. We look forward to our return one day.*

Six hours later, they could see the smog on their descent into LAX. If that wasn't sad enough, the high-rise buildings and all the congestion was overwhelming after a month of near solitude on the big island of Hawaii. There was no music or dancing girls swaying to gentle Hawaiian music or Lei welcoming them back to Los Angeles. Just the hustle of everyone trying to get past before the person in front of them. People, all but running, and some actually running to beat the long lines for connecting flights. Even the luggage area was jam-packed at least four or five people deep; everyone looking for the specially marked tag or color of suitcase to signify 'it's mine.' Hawk hated what they had just disembarked into. Another sour-smelling pit of humanity. A virtual stagnant pond of filth and angry peoples. Hawk could see on their faces the lack of love or care for one another. *What did I expect?* he thought. His temperament was already changing from one of love to the mirrored running attitudes that passed by them. *Oh, God,* Hawk prayed. *Help me love my neighbor as myself.* Then, within a fraction of a second, Hawk's next thought was one of a couple of Cartel bosses. *How could I love that neighbor who was trying to kill us all? The ones who hurt Annie and blew up our home. The ones that tempered a coin with my picture and a reward on it. Wanted Dead or Alive.* Even when God said to pray for your enemies, Hawk could only pray for quick kills. Annie and Hawk had just landed one hour earlier, and already Hawk was in the mental fight and planning stages of war.

Their rent a car was waiting for them. After packing their suitcases away in the trunk of the car, they started out of the airport arena. Hawk told Annie that they needed to be thinking of a place to stay other than hotels in Santa Barbara. Too many Hispanic personnel working for the hotel trades that could alert the wrong people. Hawk didn't want to scare Annie but reality was now in front of them and what they might be headed into. Hawk asked her if she could think of any other place they could stay than Santa Barbara.

"Yes," she replied almost without hesitating. "Remember the Channel Islands Peninsula and the condos at the beach? Why don't we rent one?"

"Yes, I do. Annie, that could be perfect. On the next street over, remember the little country kitchen restaurant? If I am not mistaken, it was called Mrs. Olson's Café. A perfect area. The Harbor on one side, and the Ocean on the other," Hawk said.

"Wow, what a good idea," Annie said.

"Plus, it is less than an hour from Santa Barbara. You could continue to rest, heal, and be safe in the fenced-in pool areas that are accessible only by keys. All the stores we need are close by, and we have a wonderful beach to walk on every day," Hawk said.

"Good idea, honey," Annie said.

Then Hawk heard a loud bang. They both nearly jumped out of our skin and Hawk was looking for the nearest freeway exit when he realized it was only a car backfire.

"A little edgy, aren't we?" Hawk's skin was crawling with fear bumps on his arms and the back of his neck. "Can you believe this?!" he exclaimed. "We have not been in Los Angeles one hour, and I am ready to kill a car. This is not good, honey. Maybe we need to stop at a local hotel for one night and gather our thoughts. We might even enjoy some therapy shopping at Nordstrom's in the valley. You could defiantly use some more clothes. Right?" Hawk asked Annie.

It was only six and a half hours ago that peace of mind and heart were in their souls on the islands. Now they were back on the mainland and edgy, nervous, and, truth be told, a little scared. Neither Annie or Hawk wanted to really leave the Big Island or their respite to end. However, if legends be true, they would be back. The swapping of crappy air, the hustle and bustle of Los Angeles for Hawaii seemed like another lifetime ago.

Hawk prayed to God that the whole family would one day be blessed with another long stay in Kona, and with the youngest of their four kids. Annie and Hawk had really been blessed to have such a wonderful family that cared for them the way they all gave back love and support. *Blessed indeed*, Hawk thought to himself.

Two hours later, they arrived in Westlake, looking for a hotel close to all the big stores. Then Annie suggested they drive on for one more hour and go to the Lobster Trap for dinner and stay in the Casa Sirena Hotel in Channel Islands harbor.

"What the heck?! You're right; we really are not that much further away. Let's do it," Hawk said.

They arrived at seven in the evening and checked into the Casa Sirena Hotel. Their upper floor room deposited a wonderful view of both the Channel Islands harbor and the other side of the Pacific Ocean. The islands they were familiar with was not the Hawaiian Islands but their very own Channel Islands. Just beyond the harbor, they were looking at Santa Cruz and Anacapa islands. It wasn't Hawaii, but still a beautiful sight.

The sky looked almost the same as Hawaii. But only if one looked straight up.

If one tried to scan the horizon, it was brown. Annie and Hawk were breathing smog which blew up from Los Angles and stayed trapped inside the channel. The atmosphere pressures were perfect for holding down the heavier smog between the mainland and the islands. Hawk had almost forgotten the rancidness of the mainland. Channel Islands today and Santa Barbara the next day was predicted to be smoggy as well. Sad but true.

After a good night's sleep, Annie and Hawk decided to go apartment hunting for an ocean view condo. It didn't take long to find the right two bedroom, two-bath, two story Condo right on the beach. They felt like life was good and immediately gave thanks to God for all his help. In the next few days, Annie and Hawk spent many hours just strolling the beach shores, playing hop-scotch on the wet sand, and dreaming of their next trip. All was good until Hawk brought up having to go back to work in a couple of days. Annie groaned with sadness and cried at the mention of his return to the department.

"I have to go, baby. I have no choice. We are not done yet. I still have a job to do, and we have a home to rebuild. Jeff is waiting for me, and I must get back up there. Violet is wanting to check with us as well—as soon as we got back. The nice thing is, I will be home right here every night with you. We can go back home in a day or two and bring your car back down here so you are not stuck without transportation. Maybe you and Dorothy can plan a few shopping trips together," Hawk said.

Jim and his wife, Dorothy, were dear friends who lived in the Condos they had bought years before as a second home to escape the heat of Westlake. Jim was a senior vice president, retired, from JC Penny's. Dorothy was a very successful real estate broker, and both were so inspirational in Annie and Hawk's belief system and lives. They didn't just talk the talk, they walked the walk and lived the Word of God. When Annie and Hawk came to Channel Islands for short getaways, they always made it a point to visit and Jim and Dorothy to dinner, which they never let us pay for. No matter how hard Annie and Hawk tried to sneak the check or give their credit card to a waitress in advance of seating, Jim always took care of the bill and handed Hawk back their credit card.

"Hawk, maybe next week," Annie replied. "Right now, I just want to continue to rest. The trip was hard, and all the change is confusing and bewildering at the same time. I know we are doing the right thing, but it remains hard. That was a clue to me that we were truly doing the right thing by staying here."

"I understand, honey. Let's just take it one day at a time as the saying goes," Hawk said.

* * *

The day of infamy arrived. It was six in the morning, June 11th and Hawk had just two hours to get to the Bureau and start the training meeting. The days spent with Annie on the beach were breached at times with ideas for the Special Ops Teams and the upcoming training. He couldn't help but think about the training and the plan on how his teams could infiltrate, conquer, and extinguish the Cartel enemies of their land and return without loss. In those moments of silence, walking hand in hand on the beach, Annie knew instinctively how far away

Hawk was in his head. She was ever respectful and quite knowing the importance of what Hawk must do.

Then there were times Hawk knew not why. God would draw his attention to when he was a very young and innocent child. A time of talking with his friends—the Angelic Beings. Again, when he had accidently shot Maria, jumping down off his Grandfather's bed while holding his 22 revolver. Not many minutes later, Hawk was thinking of the time he was completely stripped of all his innocence at the Military Academy and then the drowning. A young life not more than seven, as real today as it was then. A life fully lived and yet just a child. Hawk was shaking his head as Annie was describing to him something she saw in the water just a few feet away from where they were walking. Her mention of it grabbed Hawk's attention, and they saw, to their delight, just a few feet away, a baby seal following their steps as they walked in the shallows.

"Hi, baby! What are you doing today? Where's your momma?" Hawk softly talked to the infant while looking for its mom further out. He knew its mom must be around somewhere, watching and ready to protect if need be. Hawk had seen this situation before, where a baby comes in, exhausted from swimming and wanting to just rest for a while; the infant's mom swimming just off shore, watching every human move. Should anyone reach down to disturb her baby, mother seals have been known to charge the shoreline to protect her young.

Nature is not afraid of man. Nor does it trust man. What's the lesson, Lord?

It was then that Hawk looked up to the sky. Flying in formation were a flock of California Brown Pelicans. In formation, they would skim the surface of the waves. There must have been at least ten, one behind the other, flying as if in a trance, looking for the feeding grounds. Hawk's mind was being split into two parts; one-half thinking how beautiful everything was and the other, more disturbing thoughts of war-like conditions. What was it all about? Probably the shock of being back there, on the mainland, and all that Hawk was facing. More reality was up ahead of them.

Annie grabbed Hawk's arm and pointed to something about thirty yards ahead. There on the beach, just above the lowering tide, was a mother seal. She was dead. Upon a cursory exam, Hawk could see teeth marks on the lower half of her body. It was obvious she was bitten and killed by a shark while trying to protect her baby. She fought to protect her young and then bled out. *Most likely a Great White witch is now very prevalent in our waters,* Hawk thought. He knew then that the baby was looking for its mother and was more than likely hungry and frightened. The baby seal would die very soon if not helped.

Hawk suggested that Annie call Animal Control and have them send a couple of people out to take the infant seal to a seal sanctuary facility in Morro Bay. Meanwhile, he would try and coax the baby seal out of the water.

It wasn't that hard, as long as no other humans were around. Hawk had learned, as a young surfer, to mimic seals by watching their movements and antics in the water while surfing. In the breeding waters, off of the Central Coast, seals lived in abundance. Hawk told Annie to move back about twenty-five or thirty feet from the dead momma seal. All alone now and lying down on the sand next to the pup's momma, all Hawk had to do was clap his hands repeatedly and touch the momma soothingly as the pup watched and heard every move he made. Annie was sitting down on the soft, warm sand, holding her breath. She had seen Hawk talking with animals many times before. It didn't seem to matter what kind of animal it was, but God had gifted Hawk with the ability to watch, listen, and know what animals needed or wanted most. It didn't matter the size or the type of animal. This gift was partly because of all the animals Hawk had on his Grandparents' ranch in Ventura. At least once a week, his Grandfather, who was a coon hunter, would bring something home for him to feed, take care of, and then release back into the wild if possible. Hawk read about the different animals; he studied them and their behaviors and figured out, in part, what they were trying to communicate to him. He was by no means an animal whisperer but just very observant. Just knowing what to look for made it easy. Maybe that was where he got the ability to observe people so closely in such a short period. *This gift, God-given or not, has saved my life more than once,* Hawk said to himself.

It wasn't too much longer that the baby seal pup came bounding out of the water, figuring that Hawk was another seal just like it, lying next to its mom. At about the same time as the pup was coming on shore, the animal control people were watching the pup, and then Hawk, with some amazement. They must have thought he was crazy—lying next to the seal, clapping his hands. The pup stopped a few feet short of the mom. It instinctively wanted to come closer, but its senses told it to be careful. The uniformed women put a net over the pup from behind and together they were able to place the baby seal into a cage. She exchanged phone numbers with Hawk so they could keep track of the little guy over the course of weeks ahead. At least the moment the caged pup got into the truck, it would be hydrated and bottle-fed a special baby seal formula and could make the trip north to Morro Bay.

The day ended well for all. After a nice dinner, compliments of Taco Bell, Annie and Hawk were sitting by the living room fire pit, reflecting quietly on the day. Hawk related to Annie that when he was as a little boy swimming one summer day at the Military school, he had actually drowned. On that day, he came face to face with God. This was a childhood experience that he seldom ever discussed with anyone. Without a good reason to relate his experience, Hawk never talked about it. That was what he was told as a child; threatened, one may say, not to ever discuss the incident. "My mother insisted that I never repeat such a thing. I learned later why it embarrassed her so much or was such a threat to her," he said. But now Hawk had a question for God: *Why father? Why did that happen to me? Why was I permitted to stand in front of You, face-to-face, and talk with You? Other than the obvious question You asked me, which was, if I want to stay in Heaven with You or not, the moment I turned and looked backward, I told You that my family would miss me and hurt so much. Maybe I shouldn't have turned away, because the very next moment, I was there floating over my dead body, prior to my spirit re-entering myself. Strange to have gone through such an experience and not ever share it and not ever knowing the reason why. How can that experience be of any value to me today, Lord?* Every time Hawk asked that question, the answer was always the same. *Because I know that I know who You are, God. You are for real. You do love me and want more from me than mere hellos and goodbyes. Or my so-called popcorn prayers to You. Lord, how can You help me out of this situation or that and seldom did I give you a friendly Thank You? OK, God, I get it. You really do want to be my friend and commune with me on a regular basis. To listen and hear Your voice as You have taught me to do with lesser creatures. I get it now. Even when I am broken, You love me more.*

OK, here is a question for you then, based on a long overdue conversation: How do I fight the war on drugs? How can I make a difference, Father? Right where I am, right here and now? Can I even eliminate the problem?

Not so strangely, Hawk would have to wait for an answer on that question. At least for a little while. Over the years, he learned that God always answers questions. Sometimes it is Yes, and sometimes No. Hawk even once heard very profound 'Wait.' So, he waited. Through the night of familiar unrest, streams and streams of thought came and went from his brain. Hawk had wished that somehow his mind could have been recorded. It was too much work trying to sort through all the thoughts in the morning. However, he felt that something had to be in there. His answer was coded in his unrest, but he knew it was there. Somewhere. He just needed to be patient.

Hawk gave Annie a kiss goodbye and encouraged her not to worry, and just enjoy the day of peace and rest. "Why don't you hang out by the pool and maybe feed the birds? Read or even start drawing again?" Hawk suggested. He then gave Annie a big hug, said a short prayer, and then he was on his way to Santa Barbara for the team meeting.

Hawk pulled into a packed parking lot at the Bureau. *Good, everyone is here.* He found an empty space at the end of the lot and walked up to the office front door. To Hawk's surprise, he received a gracious welcoming from everyone, which really warmed his heart. Misty brought his coffee, and Big Red just gave him an enduring hug.

"Hey, big fella, you had better let go, or these people will think something strange is going on," Hawk said. Red repeated what most everyone else was thinking.

"We miss you, man, and are glad you're back in the saddle, cowboy," Red said.

"Thank you. Thanks to all of you. Now I have some bad news. It's time to get back to work. We have a meeting in two minutes in the squad room," Hawk said. Laughter and welcome back followed Hawk into the Bureau room where their training meeting would start—with all the maps and Intel of the next couple of days' training. Hawk had only discussed the reason for the training mission with Capt. Gee who first asked him into his office. With his consent, they were able to proceed forward after he asked Hawk how he felt and how much he could honestly contribute overall.

"I was given a full bill of health. I am recovered and ready to go. No hold backs. Let's do this thing, Capt.," Hawk replied.

"OK. The Special Ops teams are all yours!" Capt. Gee ordered.

Every team member was dressed in training gear, and all equipment was compactly stowed in 60-pound backpacks, ready to grab at a moment's notice.

Hawk started out the meeting thus: "Thank you again for all your prayers. For those of you who don't believe in prayer or if there is someone up there not watching over you, just keep coming back to these meetings anyway. Warning: we pray before, during, and after every mission, so get used to it. Any questions?" Hawk didn't think the teams ever heard him start off that way, but they were intrigued and delighted that his absence had reignited something deep within him. Really, everyone except Misty. She was forever skeptical but would never reject any of it. To her, every angle was needed for her survival.

"OK, people, I am assuming that everyone has a pen and notebook. Here is your first order: Everyone, look at the person sitting next to you on either side on my mark. Write down everything you see and feel. This first test is going to last three seconds. On my mark, GO! One thousand one, one thousand two, one thousand three. STOP and face me! Now write down everything you saw and felt about the person next to you. You have sixty seconds and no looking back," Hawk said.

The intention of this test was to get the group thinking about instant sight recognition. Hawk wanted everyone to really start looking at what they saw and not go to sleep or daydream; in the field, if they were observing people, to look for specific things—bulges in clothes other than big stomachs, tattoos, hair color and length, genders, clothes and colors, heights, and weights. The more detail a team member could recall, the odds of survival for all team members increased. This was the simplistic approach to every test. The better shooter one was, the more reliable and dependable one was as a team member. Everything was a team effort and accomplished for the team's survival.

"Jake, tell me what you saw, heard, or smelled in the person on your left?" Hawk asked.

"Yes, sir. Name tag says Carlos. He is wearing a black ops uniform, and his name tag is black with olive writing. His shirt sleeves are rolled up past his elbows and on his left forearm is a tattoo of the 82nd Air Borne. His boot laces are tied in the traditional military crossover style. Carlos has black hair, thinning a little on top. Sideburns are just above his earlobes, and he is sporting a full mustache like yours, sir. Black belt, shiny brace buckle, mole on right cheek and one mole below his Adam's apple. I believe Carlos is five foot seven inches tall and approximately one hundred sixty pounds. I further noticed that when he was leaning on the desk, his hands were rough and calloused. Especially his right forefinger. I know that he is a sniper, so I would assume it was from target practice every day," Jake said.

"Thank you, Jake. Anything else?" Hawk asked.

"Well, I think I saw a bugger in his nose?" Jake said.

That caused everyone to laugh uproariously, and Carlos had to stick his finger up his nose to check; his reddening face indicating slight embarrassment.

"OK, OK, people. Let's keep going here. Thank you for that bit of information, Jake," Hawk said.

Most everyone was used to these quick tests and did well. If Hawk were to ask any one of them for a description of an intersection or a group of people, he would not get five different answers. He would only hear one answer and possibly additional information in calling attention to details that someone could not have possibly seen.

"Good. Let's move on to the reason we are here. In this group of twenty-four, Carlos, who have you spotted, could possibly be a good sniper candidate," Hawk said.

"Sir, I believe Jake is one, Donald is two, and Raymond is three," Carlos said.

"Good. That makes one for each team. Now I need three more volunteers that want to excel in long range targets. I am talking one to two miles away," Hawk said. He got three more hands, which completed the two per squad rule. It takes two snipers per team. One to obtain accurate distance, windage, unusual atmospheric conditions such as humidity, barrel heat because of the casing load, Coriolis effect, and the ability to take over—if a team member is taken out or injured.

"Thank you for generously volunteering people," Hawk said. "Alright, teams, meet all of you at the range. Sgt. Prince and Sgt. Red, would you please take charge of the shoot today while I work on our next mission ops?" Both Prince and Red acknowledged and all three teams got up to leave. "Misty and Carlos, would you remain behind, please?"

"Yes, sir!" the both replied.

After everyone had left, the doors were locked, the window shades were put down, and the wall maps of Mexico, Central and South America were lowered.

"Guys, first off, I want to say thank you again for everything you have done for Annie and I, and for continuing to keep the team ready. Capt. Gee was notified of our discussion on the plan to go on the offense and begin the attack of the Cartel Bosses. What we have come up with is the following:

"Three teams working simultaneously five miles apart, tracking Northeast, starting here." Hawk's pointer went to Guadalajara. "Every day we must make twenty-five miles until we have covered this entire area." He drew a circle around known Cartel strongholds. "We will always have the option for pick-up if we encounter heavy firepower or are in need of additional equipment, ammo, food, or evacuation.

"Our mission is simple: Avoid contact with civilians, engage Cartel only, and no arrest. We are looking to confuse and cause suspicion on our attacks as coming from other Cartels. By the time anyone figures this out, it will be too late. Without leaders to lead, the armies die, and soldiers go back home and work the fields.

"On the way to each stronghold, we will be posting flyers with names, pictures, and reward amounts. The final mission will be a C-32 dropping flyers in mid-air, covering the entire country if need be. We just need to do our job proficiently.

"Places like Colombia that supply 80% of the Cocaine today will be too afraid to go into drop zones without proper connections. They will be forced to sit on it or go to other countries to sell. That is one of our main objectives. If that should happen, we might just get a United Nations Army to jump into the havoc we started.

"We will start with the five (5) most wanted Drug Cartels. They are:

1. Guadalajara Cartel. Miguel Angel Felix Gallardo, target one. Ernesto Fonseca Carrillo, second target. Rafael Caro Quintero, third target. This Cartel deals mostly in Cocaine and takes delivery regularly from Colombia. Miguel has more than one airstrip and alternates between them. Now Miguel has a fortress in Acapulco, which we may have to visit on one of our trips out.

2. Sinoloa Cartel: Again, located not too far from Papa Miguel Gallardo. Joaquin Guzman is target one. Joaquin is the most wanted and has the highest reward on his head. Not sure who we might see there, but we know his employees—the Artist Assassins, Genre Nueva, and Los Mexiciles. At one time, brother Juarez was part of the Guadalajara Cartel before the split. The three gangs were brought in to kill and destroy the Juarez Cartel because of a territory dispute worth billions. The territory I am speaking of is El Paso Texas. Just so you know the kind of people we are talking about here, ended up killing—"

"Over 12,000 people," Misty spoke up.

"Yes, that is correct. Lives are cheap within the Cartels.

3. Juarez Cartel: Brothers to Joaquin and lives and operates out of the Jalisco area. Very much feared for what they have done to their enemies within the Sinoloa Cartel. They have no problem with decapitating victims and then mutilating the bodies and publicly discarding the corpses in the city streets and squares. Even on the Church steps or on doorsteps of relatives as a warning.

4. The Gulf Cartel. This Cartel is based in Matamoros and Tamaulipas. It is the oldest Cartel tied to Mexico's international crime groups and has no problem with assassinations of anyone in their way. Many of Misty's family, the Los Zetas, are part of the Gulf now, having brought down their numbers in our Tijuana raid. Mario Alberto Cardenas Guyillen is target one. Osiel Cardenas Guyillen, target two. Jorge Eduardo Costilla Sanchez, target three, and Antonio Guillen is target four.

5. The Tijuana Cartel. Arellano Felix, target one, and brother Luis Fernando Arellano, target two. These two perps are Misty's cousins. She can identify very fast. They have promoted a few younger brothers and cousins, plus they have been busy enlisting both military and police generals to add to their protection package. This is a case where money talks and protect and serve be damned.

"We have a big job on our hands, guys, and it goes without saying that nothing leaves this room. You are Not to share any of this Intel with friends, relatives or other team members. Those who will know answers are Prince, Red, Carlos, Misty, and Capt. Gee.

"Misty, I know you must be feeling very heavy in your heart right about now. I would not blame you for not wanting to go with us. We are talking about your family down there. Carlos, I believe you have family in every area that I just outlined. Is that not right?" Hawk asked.

"Yes, sir, but none that I know of are involved with the Cartels," Carlos informed Hawk. "Wouldn't matter, though. I have never been to Mexico. I was born here in Santa Barbara, and my parents have not been in touch with family either for twenty-five plus years."

Misty jumped in and said, "Don't even think about me not going. I don't care if I was having a baby. At jump off time; you don't leave me. This is my dream too, you know?" she said.

"Yes, I do know but just wanted to make sure. I Was thinking more about Sissy and your mom. Our mission, guys, is going to be a virtual blood pool. Do you get that?" Hawk asked.

"Yes," Misty replied.

Carlos answered by just looking up and nodding his head. No words.

"Hawk, both Momma and Sissy are a long way from Mexico. Not to worry," Misty said.

"OK, guys, get on your marks and join the teams at the range. Good job, Carlos, on assisting with snipers. Misty, do you have all you need for medical repairs?" Hawk asked.

"Yes, and so does Linda. I will make sure to double check," Misty said.

"I will see you out there then. Need to update Capt. Gee," Hawk said.

Meetings were over, and Hawk was getting a little nervous about seeing his home. Jeff had called him and left a message during the team meeting. He wanted to go over the new plans and a few changes. Hawk really didn't want anyone to know that he was back in town, especially the neighbors. It may still be too soon for that. He decided to have one of the Capt. Joel's patrol units drive him out to the house, and he would more or less wear his baseball hat down low and have Jeff talk to him from the car. Hawk could read plans as good as Jeff and would know what he was talking about.

Little talk was going on between Deputy Peterson and Hawk, which was good. He was pretty much tired out from the team meetings and Capt. Gee. Silence was golden at the moment.

But then, as if out of know where, over an unseen, imaginative airwave, a call came in over the radio—of a mid-day bank robbery alarm in Goleta.

"Oh, crap," Hawk announced. Then he picked up the radio and advised that they were en route. Peterson flipped the lights and siren on and Hawk got busy with the details of how to approach the scene. He knew that Peterson only had three or four years on patrol.

"When we get to the Bank of America branch, stay across the street and park next to any car above the bank. Do you understand?" Hawk asked.

"Yes, sir," Peterson replied.

"Once you stop, grab the car keys and crawl out on my side. Grab the radio as you get out. It does not matter if we encounter fire or not. Just do as I ask," Hawk said.

"Yes, sir," Peterson replied.

"I will grab the shotgun and pop the trunk on my way out either way. Got it?" Hawk asked.

"Yes, sir," Peterson replied.

"Is this your first bank robbery Peterson?" Hawk asked.

"Yes, sir," Peterson replied in a shaky voice.

"OK. Just stay cool and rely on your training and what I tell you to do. Keep your head down. Be a small target until we can identify the perps and how many we are dealing with. I need to know who is a perp and who is a civilian. This is a hot day, so a couple of clues might be someone wearing gloves or having a scarf around their neck. Chances are, it's your everyday bank robber," Hawk said.

Dispatch: "Unit 3. How many responders rolling and what departments?"

Dispatch: "FBI has three units en route. CHP has two units rolling and then our three. 10-4."

10-4: "OK."

"When we get there, Peterson, look for the FBI; they will be taking the lead on this because it is a federal jurisdiction situation," Hawk said.

"Yes, sir," Peterson replied.

"Good. Do as I tell you and just stay put unless I tell you otherwise. OK, we are getting close. See that black Chevy up there parked by the shoe store across the street from the bank?" Hawk asked.

"Yes, sir," Peterson replied.

"Park beside it, leaving enough room for us to get out. When you crawl out on my side, go to the front of the patrol car. I will take the rear," Hawk said.

"Yes, sir," Peterson replied.

Hawk had no idea how this kid was going to react to anything, but he just prayed to God for help and protection for them all.

"Listen, kid. I would appreciate if you would just respond with OK. Getting tired of all the 'Yes, sir's," Hawk said.

"OK, sir," Peterson replied.

Hawk's Glock was out and in his right hand while he was fumbling with the door handle and his left hand was unlocking the shotgun as the unit was partially sliding to a halt next to the black Chevy.

When they stopped and started to disembark the unit, Peterson and Hawk suddenly saw movement inside the black Chevy. Behind the wheel was a small guy with a baseball cap pulled low and a bandana mask on, just under the eyes. The driver popped up in a panic and began to back-up as Peterson was taking his spot at the front of the patrol unit. Once Hawk realized what was going on, he drew down on the perp, preparing to put a bullet between his eyes rather than get run over. He had the room to back up two more car lengths or drive forward into Hawk and then on out. Little did Hawk and Peterson realize, until it was too late, that the car they had just pulled alongside was the getaway car for the bank robbers.

As Hawk lowered his Glock at the driver's windshield, he uttered a simple prayer: *You and me, Jesus. Just You and me.* Almost immediately, the get-away car driver stepped on the brakes and put his hands up. Hawk was not even sure how his Glock was raised to the level of the windshield that fast but there it was pointed at the perp's head. The shotgun in Hawk's left hand was pointed at the ground, guarding the dirt. He had all the grim and sinful discards of cigarette butts and trash on the street below the curb well under control.

For some unknown reason to Hawk, rather than open the Chevy's door and pull the perp out of the car, Peterson reached in through the car's open side window and grabbed the only weapon he could see on the seat next to the driver. Hawk waited for Peterson to grab the weapon. Instead, the driver grabbed Peterson by the head and yanked him forward, further into the car, suspending Peterson off the ground. Now Peterson was the target shielding the punk driver, and Peterson's Glock now lay on the ground where he dropped it trying to free himself from the choke hold of the perp. No use, this was an impossible situation. The driver had both control of the weapon, Hawk's deputy, and his foot on the accelerator. The spinning tires and smoke was blinding, and Hawk no longer had a decent shot. Peterson's own body was blocking that.

First, Hawk raised the shotgun and fired one shot into the car's grill. His intention was not to disable the all-steel and chrome front end of the 1970 Chevy with a mere shotgun blast, but cause a little shock to distract the driver. Hawk figured if he could distract him long enough, then maybe he would fire a clean shot.

The moment arrived, just prior to Deputy Peterson's butt and flying legs knocking Hawk over and on the ground. Hawk aimed right at the hump in the dash where the speedometer was protected from view and lower than Peterson's head and torso. He fired twice and saw Deputy Peterson fall to the ground and heard the perp screaming. He had let go of Peterson, the steering wheel, and was trying to stop the pain, Hawk was sure. The Chevy, meanwhile, rolled up and over the curb and hit the building wall between two stores. Hawk holstered his Glock and pulled his handcuffs out and grabbed the left wrist of the driver and cuffed him to the steering wheel. He then grabbed the revolver while the driver was still screaming and did a cursory check for more weapons, and then dropped back to the ground. Hawk took note that both Peterson and the car missed hitting him. *How?* one may ask. *It was virtually impossible to have not been hit.* The truth is, the steering wheel never moved. All Hawk could think was, *God is a good driver.* He was sure that inside of the store, it must have felt like an earthquake just struck.

Deputy Peterson, now extracted from the car, fell to the street and crawled, still choking from the perp's hold around his neck. He crawled up next to Hawk. From their vantage point, they had a good view of the bank and the street. They then waited for the other patrol units and/or bank robbers to come running out.

"Peterson, you OK?" Hawk asked.

"I think so," Peterson answered. Sorry, I don't know what happened."

"Rather than open a door, you reached in, which is a no-no. I think you just learned a valuable lesson, did you not?" Hawk asked.

"Yes, sir," Peterson replied.

"Good, stay alert now in case these guys come our way. If the driver had a gun, you could bet that the others will have them too," Hawk said.

Patrol units one and two arrived at opposite ends of the street on the same side as the bank. One CHP unit drove in and stopped in the middle of the street.

As he was parking, the would-be robbers came running out. Seeing the three police cars, all three robbers began firing at the patrol units. They never even looked up to see that their black Chevy get-away car had turned into a black and white Ford patrol unit until it was too late. In the middle of the street, when they looked up and saw that their ride to freedom was gone, the next thing they heard was: "Stop. Police. Lay down your weapons. Now." One of the three perps could count, because they soon realized how many guns were pointing at them. Two of the three perps dropped their guns on the ground along with two canvas bags. They put their hands high in the air, yelling, "Don't shoot. Don't shoot!"

The third guy was unsure what he wanted to do. Hawk could only figure that he had been a visitor of the penal system and didn't want to go back. His hesitancy in giving up gave time for seven weapons to center on his chest.

"Drop the gun," Hawk yelled. "Don't be a fool. You have no place to go, man."

"Hey, is that you, Hawk? You low-life Pendejo," the perp asked.

"What's your name?" Hawk demanded without answering his question.

"An old friend, Pendejo. Sergio. I am the one that is going to kill you, Pendejo," the perp said.

"Put the gun down, Sergio, you will gain nothing but hell. You have no back-up, no car, nothing. Give it up, man. Seven guns are pointed at your head right now," Hawk said.

"I heard that there is some money on your dumb ass, man. Where you been hiding, Pendejo? Nobody can find you. Yeah, I will stay alive just to take you out, man," Sergio retorted.

"Good for you, Sergio," Hawk said. "Drop the gun. Drop it NOW."

"I would be famous, wouldn't I, man?!" Sergio exclaimed.

"Makes no sense, Sergio. Too many guns on you. Why don't you drop the weapon and plan for another day? I can meet you in the desert someplace after you get out. Then you might get lucky and be famous, as you say," Hawk said.

Hawk didn't think he believed him or wanted to go back to a cell because his next move was pure suicide.

"Screw you, Pendejo," Sergio shouted.

Sergio raised his gun part way in Hawk's direction and took a half step toward Hawk when he was cut down by four officers. He never even got a shot off. He was dead before he hit the ground. Hawk never took a shot at him. He didn't have to. He had a chance but his timing was off just a fraction, and all the other officers were just waiting for that extraverted move that the perp made. *Oh, make no mistake, I would have killed him, but my hopes were, he would just give it up,* Hawk said to himself

As the FBI was rolling in, Hawk yelled for everyone to stay in place. "Don't move!" They didn't know if there might be more inside the bank with hostages.

The FBI took up a stance behind the other units and observed the carnage in the street and on the sidewalk behind Hawk and asked who was senior.

"Hawk here," Hawk said and raised his hand, not knowing who else was on the scene exactly.

"Hawk, what's happening? Come on over here and brief me," Mr. FBI agent man said.

"Why don't you get your ass into your little black car and drive over here? That way no one else gets shot. Especially me. It is unknown how many more perps we are dealing with inside the bank. One dead in the street, you can see from all the blood, and the other two perps are waiting for you to cuff them. Can you do that for us? It is customary that the last one on the scene does a little of the dirty work. We are just a little busy with other things right now Mr. FBI agent man," Hawk said.

Before Hawk could get an answer, another deputy closest to the front door of the bank yelled that he could see a white shirt being waved inside the bank near the door.

Hawk yelled once again for everyone to stay put. "Peterson, stay low but go get the perp closest to you in the street. Cuff him and drag his ass over here," Hawk said. Is that you Ronnie, across from me?

"Yeah, Hawk, it's me. What do you need?" Ronnie asked.

"Peterson is going to meet you in the street. Cuff the perp closest to you and drag him back behind your car. Ask how many more are inside," Hawk said.

One of the perps laying in the middle of the street yelled back, "No one, man. Just us!"

"Go, Peterson. Go, Ronnie!" Hawk yelled. "FBI, why don't you check out the white flag in the bank. The street gang says there is no one else inside. If you believe it, go in the bank and look. It might be the safest thing for you right now," Hawk said.

"Roger that," one of the FBI agents said.

"Peterson, did you hear what I just heard? Roger Rabbit?" Hawk asked.

Peterson, who was half-laughing, said, "No, Sarg. I didn't hear; Roger that!"

"Oh, alright then. No wonder we never have any parties with the FBI. Roger that, and Roger and out, Roger all you boys now. Peterson, I think his tie is too tight," Hawk said.

Coughing and choking, he acknowledged Hawk's joke while kneeling on the perp he had cuffed in the street. He was securing his prisoner like the guy was a special birthday package.

Hawk watched intently as the FBI moved into the bank. A few minutes later, one of the agents came back out and yelled that the bank was all clear.

Hawk yelled back, "Roger That," to which Peterson cracked up completely.

"You see, Peterson, you can do your job and still have a little fun," Hawk said.

"Yes, sir. I see how it is done," Peterson commented. "Thanks for your help, sir. Sorry for the secure up. Won't happen again."

"Good, because you might not live through it next time. Teach someone else someday, OK? Now, we had better see how the driver is. He may have bled out by now. Have you been watching him?" Hawk asked.

"Yes, sir. I know he is still alive and in a lot of pain because he is still screaming. You just can't hear his voice. I think he lost it," Peterson said.

"Check lost and found when we get back. Meanwhile, I will take care of him, and you put your guy in the back of your car," Hawk said, and then walked up to the black Chevy and asked, "What's your name, boy?"

He could only moan with an open mouth while holding his inner leg. Hawk could see two wounds. "Slight hole in your pants near your crotch, and your left leg. Looks superficial. Don't think you lost your manhood yet. The other wound you are holding on your upper right leg could be a broken femur. Lots of blood there. Looks pretty messed up. But you're lucky. That wasn't what I was aiming at. OK out of the car," Hawk said.

Hawk released the steering wheel cuff and pulled the perp out of the car and face down on the sidewalk. Grabbing his right arm, Hawk placed both arms in the cuffs behind the perp's back and rolled him over. Now he was screaming real loud. After checking for any weapons on his back, Hawk rolled him back over and checked his front pockets. "What a bloody mess you are, man!" Hawk said. Both of his hands were blood red after checking the perp's front pockets and inside belt area. It seemed to Hawk this kid had been working out a little. He was sure he felt something larger than two normal size male boobs. Hawk then frisked both legs. The perp found his voice, which was elevated as Hawk quickly went over the wounded areas on either leg. "Wow," Hawk told him. "You scream pretty good for a guy." Hawk had been joking, but when he removed the baseball cap from the perp's head, lo and behold, shoulder-length brown hair cascaded out. Hawk took a hard look and then opened up the cowboy shirt the perp had on. Sure enough, there were two small woman's breast staring back at Hawk, tucked tightly in a white bra. "What the hell!" Hawk muttered. "What's your name, girl?"

"Lola. Please help me. My legs hurt really bad. I can't walk," she said.

"How old are you, Lola?" Hawk asked.

"Seventeen," she replied.

"What the hell?!" Hawk exclaimed.

"How did you get mixed up with this gang, girl?" Hawk asked. He ripped the legs of her Levi pants open, with the assistance of my pocket knife. He tore all the way up to her crotch. He had to see both the front and exit wounds of the bullets. She was bleeding pretty bad from the thigh wound. Then Hawk made two tourniquets using both sleeves of her cowboy shirt. The blood stopped for the moment, and he sat her up against the rear of the front door.

"I know it hurts, honey, but I need you sitting up right now to put constant pressure on the wounds until the ambulance gets here," Hawk said.

Grabbing the patrol car's microphone, which was laying on the ground, Hawk contacted dispatch to send two ambulances and let them know that the scene was under control. His radio report was brief but to the point: "One perp dead, three arrested, one of which is a female, age seventeen. FBI is on the scene, no other injuries to report at this time. FBI is now inside the bank and conducting the investigation. Over," Hawk said.

Dispatch: "10-4 unit 3. Ambulances and tow trucks rolling. Should be there any time now."

Unit 3: "10-4."

"Peterson, go inside the two business here and make sure everyone is alright. I see faces down low in the windows but we need to secure the scenes," Hawk said.

"Yes, sir. How's the driver doing?" Peterson asked.

"Well, Peterson, the girl is doing alright for having been shot twice," Hawk said.

"Is that a Roger that or is it really a girl?" Peterson asked.

"She's really a girl," Hawk replied.

"Hell, she is as strong as an ape. How old is she?" Peterson asked.

"Seventeen, five-foot-five and one hundred pounds," Hawk replied.

"No way. What the hell! I feel like a professional wrestler choked me," Peterson said.

Hawk watched as Peterson was checking out the two business. The entire time he was talking, he was shaking his head in disbelief. Hawk knew he was probably thinking how in the hell would he ever live this day down. Dragged through a car window and nearly killed by a seventeen-year-old girl not more than five-feet-five tall and one hundred pounds.

REX BARTON

Hawk felt sorry for him, but that kind of thing can happen to anyone. When the adrenalin is pumping, anyone, any size, can do unbelievable things. Hawk had had too many experiences proving it.

When Peterson was finished with checking the folks inside the stores to make sure they were alright, Hawk asked him to get unit two to transport the perp in back of their car. Once that was accomplished, Hawk got back on the radio.

"Unit 3 Dispatch, would you please contact the range and have team one medical ops officer meet me at Valley Hospital ASAP?" Hawk asked.

"10-4," Unit 3 Dispatch acknowledged.

The ambulances arrived, and the first one on the scene picked up little Lola. "Guys, I am riding with you. This is a collar, not a civilian witness. Got it?" Hawk said.

"Yes, sir. Understood. Why don't you sit over here on this left side so I can check vitals and administer first aid to the victim?" the ambulance attendant asked.

"Will do. Thanks," Hawk said.

They arrived first at the Valley Hospital and shortly after, Misty came rolling in and parked next to the ambulance. Hawk told the security guard to let the car go, as the car and driver was one of them.

"OK. Here is what we got, Misty. Bank robbery downtown Goleta. Three perps inside and get-away car and driver outside. The victim inside ER was the driver. A little girl who said she is seventeen. She is small and Spanish-looking. A couple tats but nothing major. A few hands, arms, and body scars, again nothing major. Burn marks on wrist most likely cigarettes. The one dead perp in the street was Sergio. Remember him and Flavio from the airport showdown?

"Yes, I remember very well. It was Flavio who got the drop on me and nearly wasted me in the process," Misty said. But what was Sergio doing back here? I thought he was still in prison?"

"Apparently not. He just got out and recognized my voice and wanted to be famous. I didn't kill him, but seven other guns nailed him. I tried to talk him down, but he just wouldn't have it. His life ended in a blood pool just like his cousin Flavio. So, I need you to talk to this girl and get all the information you can from her," Hawk said. "Word is going to travel fast on this one, and I don't want our ops compromised. This little girl, her name is Lola, by the way, needs to be put under wraps until we get back. No contact or phone calls, nothing. Understand?" Hawk said.

"Got it. When she is able, I will secure her at Juvenile Hall myself," Misty said.

"Don't think she will make Juvie tonight. She has one bad bullet hole with a possible broken femur in the right leg. The other hole was a crotch shot that hit the upper left leg with minimal damage. In and out of the inner thigh. I will let you handle the chaperons while she is here. Remember, no public contact. Watch out for sympathy nurses, etc. I don't trust anyone here at this hospital. Too many Hispanic non-English speaking people roaming around in scrubs. Make sure that the female deputies are in the room at all times and have knowledge and understanding of Spanish. Get her out of her as fast as you can," Hawk said.

"Have a good evening, Lieutenant. I will call you later when she is out of surgery or whatever happens," Misty said.

"OK, thanks. I still have to get to Goleta and see my son about our home if he is still there," Hawk said.

Before starting the car, Hawk took a moment and gave thanks for his team's protection. *Thank You, Lord, for loving me so much.* Then he thought of Annie. *What if she hears on the radio or television about the attempted bank robbery at our old bank in Goleta? She might panic, even though she knows I wasn't really working today. Better call now before leaving to find Jeff.*

"Misty, wait up, I need to make a phone call to Annie. She might hear about the robbery before I get home tonight," Hawk said.

"Where's home for you guys now?" Misty asked.

"Don't know yet. Just hoteling it," Hawk said. He felt bad for not telling Misty exactly where he and Annie were living, but after Sergio recognizing him and this little girl open to talking, he was a little shy of explaining too much just yet.

Hawk decided to give Jeff a call at his office and left a message at his home telling him what his hold up was. Hawk then decided to drive back to the condo in Channel Islands. After all, for his first day back to work on what was to be light duty, he was exhausted. Once again, he found himself in a position of *what could I have possibly done differently given the same circumstances?* His life as a cop was operating at full tilt. No reservations required, just all out, every day—protect and serve the public at large. Hawk never had the option to think twice about what or why he was going to do something. He just did it. If God or life's circumstances presented him with a problem, his job was to solve it. Deal with it and bring closure to families in need, help when asked, politic for peace, and harness the bad elements. Laugh and cry and love with all those close to him. That included the wonderful animals in his life as well.

Hawk was feeling pretty good on his drive home. His priorities were straight, he thought, and God had definitely given him his expressed protection and showed him the power of prayer. It wasn't hard. He was driving home to his wife, and another man was dead. That man was lying in a bloody pool on the street far far away from his home. Unfortunately, there were going to be more in the weeks and months to come, just like Sergio. Greed, drugs, and lawlessness abounded in third world countries where most people spent a lifetime, short or long, just trying to survive. A little bread on a rickety table. Keeping clean a dirt floor, and barely any running water to drink. Hawk could understand wanting to get out of that type of life and environment when one knows nothing else that is home. *That's the way it is, and a man's family is what he loves. Toiling all day long in a field, under the hot sun, is life, and God fills that man with the measure of success and happiness just like he does mine—having, by standard, a fortune.*

Hawk's thoughts were running far ahead of him in his discussion with God. Philosophically, he was thinking of missions. *How could I give back something good to a people after removing bad cancer growing around them?* At the moment, he could not think of any way other than fostering children in their own homes. *Maybe patching a broken roof. Buying a cow or goat. Anything to help educate and bring a little celebration of life in the form of love.*

The reality of the thoughts streaming through Hawk's brain was impractical. One can't kill off a family and then provide for the laborers who depended on them.

He left his thoughts with God and decided that Annie and he needed to take a walk on the beach this evening. It was just too nice out, and he needed to be close to her.

Hawk's life was feeling a little out of control after the day's events and the drive home. Soaring on the airstreams of life was over for the day. He needed rest.

This was probably the first time in a long time that Hawk was driving and never paid attention to the drive. He wondered, *How did I get here? How did I know where to turn? How long has that car behind me been tailing me?* It looked like the same car that followed him out of the hospital parking lot in Goleta, but he wasn't sure. *Oh well, a simple test would tell me soon enough.* Hawk initiated an old law enforcement maneuver that he had used many times before. It wasn't pedal to the medal, although that was always an option, but rather something much subtle than that. He just put his turn single on and pulled off the freeway and parked on the side of the road, overlooking the Pacific Ocean.

Was Hawk just being a little paranoid? Maybe, but he took note of the white caddy as it passed by and jotted down the license plate. The people didn't seem out of place, but he wasn't taking any chances. He watched the caddy drive until it disappeared into the glare of the sunset. *OK, take a breath and put the Glock back in the holster. Enough already,* he thought. *The day is done. Well, almost.* Hawk was looking forward to taking Annie out to dinner this evening and that walk on the beach.

CHAPTER 15

IN THE EYE OF THE HAWK

The days that followed were labor intensive and grueling for the most part. Tending to all the little details of a well-planned out operation is not easy. Arranging transportation from Santa Barbara to undisclosed airfields in foreign countries for one thing. Because Hawk had three teams, all the personal and ops materials required, plus food, water, and oversight requirements were monumental. Then extraction points and personnel with trucks, choppers, horses if need be, and the list went on. Maps, all the correct coordinates, time zones, fly zones, equipment required for that, tested and readied. Right down to the little AAA batteries that keep the one piece of equipment that was so important working—their radio. *Bring extra AAA's in watertight containers,* Hawk thought. There was a virtual mountain of needs and requirements, not to mention paperwork and written permits where possible from government officials that were really untrustworthy. Any connection made by any outside person was a possible breach of this mission. Everything and everyone could be lost by one mistake in judgment on any of the team's foreign connections. Hawk was getting a little uneasy with this operation, and he needed to listen to what the message was or who it was that was talking inside his brain. Was it common sense, God talking, which He often did, experience, or the enemy of his soul? Hawk Couldn't tell at this point. He needed to off brand himself from all the running thoughts and discuss with someone that had as much, if not more, experience than he does.

"Why, in God's name, is it really necessary to acquire travel and landing permits when we are not even supposed to be there in the first place? Why can't we just go?" Capt. Gee asked. "So we didn't see the no trespassing sign or avoided the border checkpoints because we were chasing dirt devils? So what? It could happen innocently enough. Killing big wigs—that might be another problem, but one we were trained to do and do very well."

"The war on drugs was called a war for a reason. If it is a war, you don't give out your mission statements to every tom, dick, or harry, do you? Or in this case, Tobias, Ricardo, or Horho. You don't ask for permission to bomb, destroy buildings, and blow people up. So why in Heaven's name are we asking the very enemy, and most likely the very people that will profit and could stop our mission dead in its tracks, or every deputy involved, at any given moment for the sake of the very thing we are trying to stop? Makes no sense, Capt. Gee. Just let us go down there and do our business. Maybe reduce our numbers. Put us on dirt bikes and let us ride down Baja and put an end to the Drug Cartels," Hawk said.

"Because alone, you can't, and you know it," Capt. Gee said. "This is a cooperative effort on a lot of people's parts and requires diplomatic effort and permissions. You just don't walk into a country and start killing its citizens that help support the economics and its political parties like that. The ramification of this ops is so monumental that other governments are watching and learning from us. You are not alone, and at some point, we must trust someone," Capt. Gee.

"I disagree." Hawk switched tactics in midstream with Capt. Gee, using their experiences together. "With a party of six and a little help from the underground mercenaries and our own transportation, I could do what an infantry division couldn't even accomplish. Smaller numbers and a well-developed plan is better than all we are going through now. I just don't trust our would-be supporters down there if they are in any way politically or economically motivated or attached to the Cartels. In fact, we both know of several people in the parties that are Cartel leaders, holding offices. High ranking officials, they are. The decision makers and the very ones that would kill us all.

"Captain, you and I have traveled many, many miles together. We have made it on foot, by bicycle, motorcycle, horseback, car, plane, and so on. Always, the simplest was best. Anytime we put more men or power into the equation, it got screwed up, or someone got hurt. Smaller tactical groups are faster, easier to maneuver and extract. A smaller contingency is faster and more motivated to succeed than an army. We both know that, because we have done it together many times over the years," Hawk said.

"I agree with what you are saying in part, and I understand your reason for hesitating in the eye of progress, speed, and need. But—" Capt. Gee was interrupted.

"Excuse me, Capt., but I can do it with five or six better than with three complete teams. All I need is a couple of drop zones for additional equipment and or extraction, and really not even that. We can get the hell out of there, with mission accomplished, with a smaller group. And I, alone, understand about not disclosing our mission. I know we are truly alone. Our Country, our State, our county and our Department wouldn't even know who we were if captured or killed. No identifications, no ranks, no mess, no fuss. Clean and simple. Just pay my wife my retirement benefits.

"The only way to clean house is clean house where the mess is. Let me take two snipers, Misty and Robert," Hawk said.

"Robert's wife is about to have a baby, so he shouldn't be going at all. Carlos has a wife and kids that need him. Jake, maybe. Recently married, no kids, and equal in sniper skills as Carlos. How about Red?

Or even Sgt. Prince? He has older kids but now divorced. So, it would be you that would lose the most, Hawk," Capt. Gee reminded Hawk.

"No, you're wrong. I don't lose anything. I have God, and so does Annie and all my kids. You know the old saying, 'Absent from the body is home with the Lord.' I have no fear of that. I have died once, and I should have died so many more times that I have lost count. Just don't scare me, Capt., by terminating the mission. Nothing scares me more than mission failure. If we don't go now, we have failed," Hawk said.

"Let me think about it, Hawk," Capt. Gee said. "This is a real switch, and I understand why you are leaning this way in your thinking. Maybe we shouldn't even plan taking such a big bite out of the apple? Keep things status quo? Work the streets smarter and try and get ahead of the problem. What do you think about that, Hawk?" Capt. Gee asked.

"We have tried that, Capt. In fact, we retool all the time. The problem that we are facing is budget cuts and restraints from the courts. Every time we make a good stab at the heart of the enemy, it ends up nothing more than a stupid, vain wound and nothing more. What I see is, the longer we keep doing the same old thing, then we will continue getting the same results. You know that. We have been here so many times in years past. However, if I can actually cut the throat of the Cartel and bleed him out in his own house, we dry up the drug problems for years. It will never end, but the slowdown would save money, and we could concentrate on cleaning up our local gangs and meth houses. We have more than enough personnel to handle our own area but throw in the open ocean, cross-county's party raids, then we are just playing games. That is what the Cartels are counting on. Always playing defense," Hawk said.

"Ok, let's think about it a day or two and let me work on the problems. I will keep you informed. Where are you and Annie staying? Do you have all you need?" Capt. Gee inquired.

"We are staying in the Channel Islands area near the beach. And yes, we have all we need. Thanks," Hawk replied.

Why, in the hell, did I say where we are? This is so wrong. I need to have my head examined! Hawk thought.

Capt. Gee thought for a moment, then related to Hawk, "Channel Islands is outside of our county. That is against the Sheriff's Office rules and regulations and your contract agreement. Deputies must stay in the county jurisdiction for response times. That is in your employee contract as well," Capt. Gee said.

"But Capt.," Hawk said, "in light of our situation, don't you think the Sheriff will give a little here? If we come back to Santa Barbara, I am afraid that something more might happen. Plus, we are not taking up time and money on watchdogs," Hawk said.

"Again," Capt. Gee said, "let me think about that one too. Good points, all, but the employment rules contract is the Sheriff's Waterloo. You know what he will say," Capt. Gee said.

"Then don't tell him. You didn't ask, and I am not repeating it," Hawk said.

* * *

Hawk went back to his desk with a big distraction on his mind. He began to pray for a little help when Misty and Linda walked in and surprised him with their new uniforms. Nothing out of the ordinary because they always wore Levi's, and tee shirts with the Sheriff's logo on it and most always had shoulder holsters strapped on. Somehow, in Hawk's intense thinking, after leaving Capt. Gee's office, the two of them crossed his eyes. Seeing them walk in with both of their chests pointing out in too tight of tee shirts and their butts bulging in too tight of Levies. Both of their guns were moving slightly as they swayed over to Hawk's desk. They were saying in effect, *"Here I am"* and very tauntingly so. *"Reach for me, touch me, and you're dead."* All of that in a whisper of their walk. "Go ahead, perp, if you're feeling lucky today."

Hawk had to shake his head to clear it and get the images brought on by these two beautiful women out of his mind. "Sorry," he said, "I don't feel lucky today. I was just going over some plans here on my desk."

"Oh, really?" Misty chirped. "You don't feel lucky? What is that all about? What plans? Did you lose something between us walking through the door and now?"

Hawk smiled as he looked up at both girls who clearly never missed a beat of anyone's drum. "OK, so I was preoccupied a little. Trying to figure out all the details. My mind is full of details and plans," Hawk said.

Linda smiled at Misty, both knowing what had just happened. "Like our new tee shirts, Hawk? The Sheriff just authorized them and signed them just for us. See the little 'T' with a circle around it under the logo?" Misty asked.

"Sure. What else do you girls have for me? Any real tea from China perhaps? Maybe a fortune cookie? You are both trademarked now. Wow! Owned by the establishment," Hawk said.

"Maybe," Misty said. "I know what the fortune cookie would say, though—all you want all day long." Then she blew a kiss at Hawk and stuck her chest out further while standing directly in front of him about two feet away. Hawk could smell her perfume and knew it wasn't legal. Just too sweet of a smell.

"I should arrest you both for smelling too good, and sticking your chest out too far in my presence," Hawk said. "What are you two children thinking? Are you testing me? Back it off, please. Come on;

why are you here?" Hawk said this in as harsh a tone without cracking a smile. Nor did he look up to see what they were doing.

"Just loving you, Hawk boy. Linda had an idea that might work in the upcoming ops. Thought you might like to hear it." Misty was standing up proudly, ready to volunteer her thoughts.

"OK, I will bite. What are you two dreamers thinking?" Hawk asked.

Linda responded first. "Well, sir, I think we should parachute into a very remote area of Mexico and set-up a base camp without the help of any lobos and wait a week or two before starting the operation. Make sure we have no busy eyes or people looking for anything before striking our targets. Maybe even cut down the teams to smaller amounts?"

"Good idea. Thought of that already, though. You girls are getting slow," Hawk said.

"I thought so. But going off the radar for a while and really taking our time, watching the targets prior to the fireworks, puts us at the surprising advantage. Don't cha think?" Misty asked.

"You are right. I kinda brought the same idea to the captain, and he is not for a smaller contingency. Nor does he want us dropping in unannounced. Nor will your signed tee shirt fan (the Sheriff) give us that much time off. Sorry, ladies, but I feel this mission is going to be scrubbed. I don't feel good about it at all now. Too many eyes and too many people will know where we are at every moment, which puts the entire mission and our lives at risk," Hawk said.

"So, what do we do now?" Misty asked.

"Continue playing defense. That's all we have. Hit more big ships carrying drugs, and Panga boats. Keep the pressure on in every area. Start hitting the gangs and robbing them of their supply chains," Hawk said.

"But Hawk," Linda said, "We don't have the manpower to do what you are saying on the streets."

"No, we don't. However, we can incorporate other agencies and take more risks. Just have to watch each other's backs a little closer. Any organization or group outside of our own teams is reason to be suspicious," Hawk said.

Misty asked Hawk, "Would you like me to pay Antonio another visit, and keep the pressure on him for information?"

"Yeah, go ahead and take Linda with you. Between the two of you, Antonio won't know whose specially signed tee shirt to look at first. Just don't let him drool over police property. And if the two of you keep sticking your chests out too far, you might hurt something. Or something(s). Now go. Please," Hawk said.

Linda began to laugh. "Ha ha. Don't be surprised if we come back with a treasure chest of Intel," she said.

"Hey, go for it, girls. I am serious. I can call the coast guard and get our special ops teams ready within an hour. How's that?" Hawk asked.

"That's taking the bull by the horns," Misty reminded everyone. "Let's do this thing."

"Do it. Talk to me later and let me know what you find out. Then both of you hit the range and the pool. I have a feeling we are going to be busy, and we all need to be in shape," Hawk said.

"I thought I was shapely," Misty teasingly replied as both she and Linda turned toward the door, sticking their chest out or breasts out as far as they could. They could be heard laughing all the way down the hall.

God help me, Hawk muttered.

It was time for a command meeting to clear the record and reestablish the teams' position before anyone else did, so Hawk called Capt. Gee back and told him his thoughts. Capt. Gee agreed so fast that Hawk knew he was on the hot seat and what political nightmare the original operation was doing to him. Hawk then told him his misgivings and the risk was just too high. *No more cross country lines. We work and enforce in our own back yard.* Hawk and Capt. Gee agreed to move on. Hawk folded all the current Intelligence information he had been working, as well as the Cartel family albums, and put everything into a legal box and placed it under his desk for the moment. It was not the sort of thing he wanted to leave out, but he didn't have time to walk it down to the evidence room.

With the time left on the clock, which Hawk never really looked at nor did the time ever run the narcotics bureau, Hawk started making phone calls to the Coast Guard and the Harbor Patrol. He related to Lt. Gough and Capt. Lynch the need for their services again if they were able to move out on short notice. Both said yes, and the plans were in the making.

Hawk's next call was with Lt. John Johnston, Navy Seal and friend, who was assisting in the teams' upscale training camp. They were trying to build on seal training along with endurance and strength training. Hawk's teams were going to be the best—they felt that if they were the best, they had the greatest chance of survival. Hawk let John know what he and his teams had planned and what they were now going to do. Lt. John Johnston agreed that the Mexico trip was ill-fated from the beginning. Too many eyes on the plan. He would meet Hawk and his teams at the range anytime. He was always ready, able, and willing to train and teach. The end game, of course, was to rid their country of the drug trades, however it got there.

Hawk felt that John was going to be a close friend one day as they had much similar interests, including their love for God. Plus, John was married with two teenage girls. John was strong, and had earned his first degree, a black belt in Jujitsu and Karate. He was one lean, mean machine packed into a six-foot frame. Hawk was not really sure what color his hair was because he always kept his head shaved. Part of the Navy Seal way of doing things. John was as comfortable in the water as he was on land like most Navy Seals.

Hawk guessed it was the similar training and ideals that drew them to talking about the long term goals one day while watching the sailboats in the harbor. Both of them wanted to leave a legacy of truth, courage, and love of country behind in a safer world for their families. How to attain that was the problem they were training for. They both knew it wasn't just the Mexican Cartel that was their problem but several others. John not only spoke Spanish but he was fluent in Russian as well. He had met the Russian Mafia's top aids on other government ops and knew all the right sources. Hawk knew it was only a matter of time before they would have all-out gang wars over the county turf.

John would be a help one day as their department expanded and their education of their community needs demanded. Unfortunately, those demands were on their doorsteps already. Hawk thanked God for John's Christianity because Misty and Linda were on the prowl and he was getting weak in dealing with them all the time. Hawk's defenses were getting beat-up, and John gave him permission to call at any time. He knew Hawk's plight and shared when a woman entered the one-time all men's seal division. "It was hard," he said, "and is hard watching half naked woman doing the same thing we have to do. In the Seals, there is no division of humanity. We used the same bathrooms and showers in the beginning and still, when doing water rescues or change over drills, we are all in the water at the same time, changing or naked, trying to re-outfit." Personally, John admitted to Hawk that he still and probably never will get used to the combos. "About the only time it changes is when someone gets hurt. Then it doesn't matter male or female. Life and death is on your doorstep, and you do what you are trained to do. We leave no one behind. Ever! I have carried one of my best friends five miles to get first aid. That is what we do, and that is what your teams need to learn. Man, woman, whatever, you must have each other's back. Everyone must feel like he or she is covered and protected, no matter what," John said.

Hawk warned John about Misty for one reason. "If you ever meet her on the mat or in the ring, watch out. She is one of the best athletes I know. She, too, is a black belt in Karate and a few more disciplines. Truth be known, if I ever blinked, she could kick my ass. And you have seen her. She is only five-foot-five and one hundred twenty pounds. Pure dynamite and a trained killer. She was number one at Quantico. She is our team's medic and one of the best snipers you will ever work with. But never forget who she is and what she is," Hawk said.

"Wow. OK. I will remember that," John commented. "Thanks."

Hawk's mind was filling with more information and current trends than he could afford to think about. He had to get back to the moment and look over the lists of ships sailing their channels on a regular basis to see if there might be a pattern.

Within an hour, Hawk had nine vessels that were frequently sailing from South American ports, Acapulco and on up the Santa Barbara Channel to Canada.

He wondered what would be going to Canada, but didn't have the time for that research. He was half expecting to hear from Misty and Linda at any moment with some good news.

All nine ships were more than capable of placing Panga boats in the water without hardly slowing down. *Smooth operation*, Hawk thought, then his eyes landed on a familiar vessel, The Dawn Star. *Oh, yeah*, he thought, *I know this boat. Its owner is Mr. Ernesto Carrillo of the family known as the Guadalajara Cartel. This tied in the Colombia connection of Cocaine to Mexico. Why stop in Acapulco?* Hawk asked himself, and then he remembered the crime boss himself, Miguel Gallardo, and his brothers who had a lavage Hacienda in Acapulco. The Guadalajara Cartel was known Worldwide, and now the pieces of the puzzle were falling together. *Stop this one boat, and we would stop half of the drugs floating into North America.*

Hawk's research told him that the Dawn Star was over eighty-five feet long with a big draft, numerous holds, and outfitted with heavy artillery. A takedown or sinking of this ship would not be easy, nor would sneaking up on her. She most likely had all the latest sonar equipment available on the market that only the Navy possessed—so they thought! Cartels love buying the World's newest and most secretive black market equipment and weapons available. If it's not available, they just steal the shipments and obtain the latest for free—compliments of lazy governments. Or money paid to the outstretched hand.

The Solis was another large one-hundred-thirty-foot container ship that has been running back and forth for some time now. *Worth monitoring her travels and port of calls,* Hawk thought. The captain was listed as Juan Moreno. Funny, his name was familiar too, but Hawk couldn't place it at the moment. The vessel was a Brazilian purchase. Hawk opened his Who's Who three-ring binder in a locked desk file, and opened it to Juan Moreno. *Cross reference, Sinaloa Cartel. Oh yeah,* Hawk said to himself. Sinaloa was advertised as part of the top thirty-seven Cartels, with wanted posters averaging thirty million peso's rewards. That's a lot of money. Approximately two and a half million U.S. dollars. Just then, Hawk had a strange thought: *I should be a professional bounty hunter. I could get rich really quick. Well, maybe not really quick but quick enough.*

Back to the drawing board. What about these ships? How do we safely find, stop, and board them without being blown out of the water ourselves?

It was then that Hawk thought of maybe using balloons. *Why not? We could go as high as we needed to, and not be heard or seen. Only in the eyes of the Hawk could I see for miles and miles as we silently floated above what would seem like the world, silently spying on the entire channel. Would have to bring the idea up to Capt. Gee. It felt right.*

But then Hawk asked himself, *How could I leave my teams to fight the fight and not be there with them?* Delegate was a word that came to mind. *But who? Then there is the problem of aircraft.* Hawk couldn't give locations to airports or military for fear of espionage. He feared that the Cartels would know before he even got off the ground.

He got up to get a cup of coffee in the break room and looked at the color of the dark brew in his white Sheriff's cup with his badge logo and name on it. Hawk's mind tripped back to just weeks ago when he and Annie were floating in the water at Kona Beach Hawaii. The dark coffee bean hair that flowed all the way down her back to her waist. *How beautiful those moments were! I will cherish them forever in a special place in my heart. I especially remember the pink hibiscus flower resting on the side of her head and the stem behind her ear. How could we have left that moment behind?* Hawk wondered. *We need to go back; that is for sure.*

Hawk heard someone from down the hallway yell out to him, "Hey, Hawk, you have a phone call. Misty, I think!"

"Misty, is that you?" Hawk asked.

"Yes. Linda and I had a good meeting with Antonio in the grocery room. Seems that several ships are sailing on a weekly basis, dropping Pangas and loads of drugs up and down our coasts. From there, as we know, it is being trucked to other states. Big operation and lots of money on the line," Misty said.

"Did Antonio mention any ship names or Cartel names?" Hawk asked.

"No, not this time," Misty responded. "He said he didn't really know but just that they were coming in."

"OK, ladies, good work," Hawk said. "Get back here and let's put this new Intel in writing and have it submitted. I have a feeling; we might need to get out on the water very soon. Maybe even in the next couple of nights."

* * *

Hawk walked back down the hall and knocked on Capt. Gee's office and told him his latest idea regarding the use of hot air balloon to establish a silent observation point. Hawk was obviously excited and wanted to get authorization as soon as possible. "Captain, we would be able to see the entire channel, all the traffic lanes and if any one or more vessels are dropping Panga boats into the water. One or two people in the balloon could control the entire Navy below. What do you think? Oh, and by the way, our latest intelligence from Antonio is, three ships are running the channel this week. All Cartel-owned. Big shipments of narcotics," Hawk said.

"Don't know where you come up with all this stuff, Hawk," Capt. Gee uttered, "but I understand the conception. Provided you have a clear night, that balloon idea could be a good one. However, we have a couple of problems. One is money. We are not budgeted for that. There is no way I can get clearance for that and/or endanger a pilot's life in the process. In short, our special team's operations are now suspended due to loss of budget.

"Number two, and the only way we can work as a team when Intel comes in, is to stay on the beaches and wait for the Panga boats to land. Then we can affect an arrest and detain the refugees.

"Number three, you will have to move back to Santa Barbara. The Sheriff will not allow anyone to live outside of the county for any reason. Sorry, Hawk, but that is an order," Capt. Gee said.

"What! What the hell just happened? You finished saying less than an hour ago that other cities and counties were watching our tactics and methods of engagement. I thought we were good to go," Hawk said.

Capt. Gee then reminded Hawk that such was not the case. "No is your final answer. The Sheriff does not want to run his department on a lopsided budget basis anymore—where we get the majority of the pie. Sorry. We are now back to old fashion enforcement with an eye on exercising patience. No more special teams. Everyone other than homicide, burglary, special crimes, and a skeleton crew in narcotics will take up the detective bureau. Everyone else is back on patrol.

"The Sheriff wants all of the teams promoted to corporal status and/or Sargent, if they are not already in those ranks, leading the patrol units. He wants experience in the field, and you and your teams have it," Capt. Gee said.

"In other words, wait until someone is killed, or the problem gets too big, and politics begin to complain before ramping up again? Is that what it is?" Hawk asked. "This is crap, and you know that, right? Our duty is to protect our citizens, which includes the kids trying and dying from the Cocaine and Heroin coming in here. The parents are going to raise hell when they realize nothing is being done to curtail the problem. What is the Sheriff going to say then? *Sorry, folks, we are out of money? Take care of your own kids. We didn't cause the drug problem. Therefore, we are not going to budget for it any longer?*"

"You have a right to be upset," Capt. Gee said. "This was not what we originally talked about. You were going to have a free hand, and now that hand has been cut off. Nothing I can do about it. I have seen this type of thing happen over and over. Especially in election years."

"Did you tell the Sheriff why Annie and I are in the Channel Islands? Did you happen to mention the Cartel and death threats and almost being killed? Our home being blown up and having to get away from Santa Barbara for more than a month?" Hawk asked.

"Of course," Capt. Gee said. "He is concerned, but his hands are tied. The rules are for everyone, not just a few. I told you it was his

Waterloo. Had to tell him, Hawk. Rank means more responsibility and more ramifications when things go wrong," Capt. Gee said.

"Well, the Sheriff is causing me to have to lie to my wife about protecting her and keeping her safe. There are no safe places here in Santa Barbara. You can't protect us. You can tell the Sheriff that I won't sacrifice my family for his stupid ass election or a stupid ass rule book. I am done here. You can have my badge, but the gun is mine. As I see it, and from what I really heard, the Cartel has gotten to someone higher up and is now compressing the Sheriff downward. The Sheriff is a pawn in a hideous game of death. All inspired by money and greed," Hawk said.

"Hold on, Hawk," Capt. Gee said. "We can work something out, I am sure. Give me a few days to look into a few things. Please. I am sure we can find something."

"I am not sure you are right with your assumptions. This is all about policy," Hawk said.

"Go home early today and don't worry about any of this," Capt. Gee told Hawk. "I will handle it."

"I hope you can but believe me," Hawk said, "I will not have my family slaughtered, or the Cartels rampage over the walls of our city because of budget cuts. Tell the Sheriff to find the money someplace else. Hell! I have given millions of dollars in cash from all our drug raids to this department. Has the city council allocated the confiscated drug money back to the department that earned it? Pay the taxes on it then spend it the right way. Better equipment for future busts which will bring in more millions of dollars. Ever think what could be done with some of the drugs? Save the pharmaceutical companies money and sell for less the drugs we confiscate. That way, they don't have to spend time and money in manufacturing what we already have. Plus, their main suppliers are the very same the Cartels are going to. Think about the power we already own in our evidence rooms and how it can increase good law enforcement. I don't want to hear that the council will put it in the next quarter's meeting, though. We need answers now. They can do it if they are not already bought off too. And if that is the case they can stick this job up their ass."

Hawk left the Captain's office sick to his stomach and went back to his own office completely rejected. *Now what? I can't go back to the way things were, and I can't move back here. What do I do Lord? Where can I go? How do I protect Annie and my family?*

The facts were, someone got to the Sheriff. Someone in the counsel or higher up who promised him another win at the election polls. All he had to do was clip the wings of the hawk. Apparently, Hawk has flown too high for too long and costing the Cartel empires too much money, drugs, and manpower.

Hawk was tired of this rodeo ride. *Just about to put the cuffs on crime and I discovered a very weak link in the chain. The top dog sold out and probably a quarter of his pups as well. Certainly, someone or more of the city council members have been bought off. It wouldn't be that difficult to find out either. Just run bank accounts and spending habits.*

Maybe it was time to kick it up a notch and see what the FBI has or what Hawk could do in a solo career. In the eyes of this hawk, Hawk could see very well. Perhaps his personal friends, Troy Anderson or Rocker, and several other rich friends who were wealthy banking and newspaper moguls would fund his personal Black Ops Organization. He could continue fighting organized crime and doing protection details for the rich and famous people. Private businesses were willing to pay the price for protecting individually and corporately. Anything was possible, including going to work for another department.

Hawk was an FBI trained and had an open job offer from agent Kevin Butler, but with that comes even more restraints and red tape he feared. *The government is not our friend. I could be tied up for months trying to move forward in the war on drugs.* National security was more of the FBI's playbook. Federal took precedence over all cities, counties, and states, but with that kind of power, it took time. Time Hawk was running out of.

San Luis Obispo Sheriff and Ventura County wanted Hawk as well, but what difference would it be? Same situation as Santa Barbara. If he ruffled too many feathers, then come election time, there would be more wing feather cuts. It was hopeless trying to keep from making a change. Hawk was a creature of habit, and change was difficult.

Go out of state? Texas Ranger Perhaps? No! Texas was too far and too hot, but they did have a big drug problem. The Cartels loved Texas and the Billions of dollars extracted from there.

The one idea that kept flashing in Hawk's brain was becoming a mercenary soldier bent on destroying the Cartels himself. Hire a few good men and women and do it all underground. *Annie would be sent back to Hawaii to live with our youngest son and family,* he thought.

Hawk decided to take Capt. Gee's advice and go home early. He needed more than his own whirly thoughts rummaging around in his head, kicking him out. He remembered he said something about patience. He also recalled his thoughts on the council and running backgrounds. *Maybe, just maybe, I could end this problem by going through the back door.* Hawk gave Kevin a call and made an appointment for the following morning. He didn't tell him why; he just needed to talk to him as a friend.

Hawk walked into the FBI office on Anacapa Street and asked the secretary that he had an appointment with agent Kevin Butler. She looked at him with anticipating eyes and asked, "Your name, please?"

"Hawk," he replied.

"Mr. Barton, Agent Butler is waiting for you. Nice to meet you, Hawk," the cute looking secretary commented with a smile.

Hawk took a more interesting look at the woman behind the high counter desk. He was sure she had more buttons she could push and guns in drawers in the event anyone who was unknown and suspicious in nature walked into the building. He wondered even more how many people had been jacked up onto a wall with hands behind their back, surrounded by FBI agents, because of the panic button the very pretty lady commanded. *How many times had she been wrong? Some poor nerd dressed down and scrubby because he wanted to apply for a job and probably was qualified?*

"Thank you," Hawk said as Kevin walked up to the counter where he was standing, with his hand outstretched. Hawk was grateful for seeing agent Kevin. He shook his hand vigorously. He had learned, even as a young boy, that anytime one shakes a man's hand, it should be done with gusto and firmness. *Never offer a limp wrist handshake. You're a man,* Hawk's uncle would caution, so he always shook hands firmly to a point many a man complained, or nearly took a knee. With women, it was different. *Never limp, but not too firm, just enough to guarantee that they had a strong man in control of their immediate presence.*

"Common in Hawk," Kevin said. "What a pleasure to have heard from you last night and then see you today. What brings you into my sanctuary today?"

"Oh, just checking on your security systems. Wanted to see how long it would take that pretty lady out front to determine if I was friend or foe," Hawk said.

"Ha ha," Kevin laughed. "She knew who you were when you walked in. Our doors are rigged with a system that someday will be used everywhere. She actually did a body scan which determined that you were carrying a 9mm in a lower back holster, handcuffs, extra ammo clips and a badge in your left rear pants pocket. Had she not seen the cuffs or badge, she would have pushed the panic button alarm, which would have brought all the agents out with guns pointed at your head.

"You are kidding me? A full body scan? How much can she really see?" Hawk asked.

"Most everything if she were looking, but her job is not to hold a tape measure with you but look for metal, like guns, wires, dynamite, and the like," Kevin replied.

"Well, I guess I will have to be a little more prepared from now on," Hawk said.

"One more thing," Kevin added. "Along with the scan machine, everyone has their picture taken, which is immediately sent through NCIS, our own FBI files, and even the international databases. Oh, yeah, Lori not only knew what you were carrying, she knew who and what you are. Name, date of birth, address and phone number, married or not, etc. No surprises."

"I need one of those secret door cameras and magic wand scans. I had no idea that every time I walked in here, that was going on. No wonder I never set off the alarms," Hawk said.

"So, my friend, what is happening?" Kevin inquired. "How can I help you?"

"Well, sir, I almost quit the department yesterday after a very disappointing meeting with Capt. Gee. Our drug Cartel war has been canceled. Not by the Cartel but by the Sheriff. Seems to me, but not confirmed yet, that someone higher up in the political food chain is on the payroll and I need to find out who. Either I leave the department because they have canceled the war on drugs or I find out who is responsible," Hawk said.

"You know that either way you lose, right?" Kevin responded.

"Yes, I do. Have not told Annie anything yet because I don't know which way to go. Back on patrol with my teams or go rogue around the world," Hawk said.

"Listen, my friend," Kevin said, "if you go out in a worldly fashion, all of the alarms will go off wherever you are. Everyone knows that when the hawk takes flight, they have to watch out. Your reputation is worldwide, my man. Not many departments would take you in. Oh, they all would want you, but the price would be too high.

"Following you is a path of destruction a mile wide. Thus the wanted posters and silver coins. There is a hefty price on your head, and the price keeps going up. Do you realize that? Every failed attempt the Cartels make, the price goes up and up and isn't it all the Cartel money?" Kevin asked.

"No. What the hell?! What are you saying?" Hawk asked.

"The Cartel wants you bad, anyway they can carve you up, dead or alive," Kevin told Hawk. "But so do many other organized crime groups that can see you stand in their way. In fact, you and your teams are probably responsible for the slow growth in drugs and street crime at least here in Santa Barbara. The Mafias are scared of you. Nobody wants to lose good men or product, and they know that you are in the mix of it all. In fact, case in point. Do you remember your little rattlesnake incident out on the Ceilo's last year when you and John Blood got into it? Remember what I told you?" Kevin asked.

"Yeah, that I was the only cop that could bring him down; you had your chance, but I was the one that knew how to do it best." One on one, Hawk reminded him.

"Point taken," Kevin said, "but I told you that he was a one-man army hired to kill whoever was in his way. You were the target, Hawk. You were always the target from the start. I told the Sheriff, and he backed you and told me, 'If anyone could get our man, Blood, it would be you.' He was right, but he also knew the odds that were in Blood's favor. Blood actually led you to the mountain top where he had planned to kill you. Never did he expect that you were a race car driver and could maneuver him off of the road. Your little maneuver probably saved a lot of lives, including your own.

"That was not the Mexican Mafia Cartels that hired John Blood but the big New York crime family Mafia. They were looking to claim their share of the pie out West, and you were a known target in their way.

"Hawk, we even have the intelligence on parts of the Middle East that are keeping track of you. We do not have all the facts yet, as to why, but we are watching you too just for those reasons," Kevin said.

"Oh, great, just when in the hell was I going to be told about all this? I Have been worried sick about Annie and our family, and you have known this from a year ago, and you didn't tell me? I came here today to maybe even ask you for a job, in that I am so qualified. But why? Even the FBI can't protect me, and according to you, you and your teams have been trying to keep up? This is crap, Kevin," Hawk said.

"I am truly sorry, Hawk, that I didn't share everything with you. But why? You are a virtual, one-man army. Coming to work here would be a real slow down for you. Frankly, I don't know where to tell you to go. Unless you are somehow neutralized or slowed down, you are the hunter that is being hunted. There is no win-win here. All and everyone will, at some point, be extinguished. The flame will go out, and crime will continue on its way as always," Kevin said.

"Kevin, is my phone tapped?" Hawk asked. "Are there any listening devices being used?"

"Not that I am aware of," Kevin replied. "We didn't order anything like that."

"Can you have one of your phone trucks come by the condo and check inside and out, please? Maybe do the old house as well—just to see who might be getting a heads-up on all my activity? Also, what Intel are you sitting on now that could be beneficial to me? Need to know all you got, Kevin," Hawk said.

"We here at the FBI are not all that powerful or rich to keep up on all worldly chatter or keep a contingency or small army watching you. One man shows. Wish I did have you, Hawk. What a team that would be. But, if the Sheriff can't control your moves, no one can. You are always a step or two ahead. I even heard about your balloon idea of going after the Cartels. Brilliant! We have a pilot that is on our payroll. I even offered it to Capt. Gee but he turned us down. That is what I am talking about. Always a step ahead of the curve," Kevin said.

"So, Capt. Gee called you and shared my ideas and requests? Wow, at least he tried to help, maybe," Hawk said.

"No, he didn't," Kevin replied. "He was just wondering how to ease you down a little and get you back on patrol until things quieted down. He wants to keep you, Hawk, but he can't buck the challenge of the political enemies that you mentioned. All hell would go up in flames," Kevin said.

"It already has, Kevin. It already has," Hawk replied.

"Hawk, just so you know, I could give Gee and the Sheriff a call and get your mission approved for this week if intelligence is correct and I have knowledge that it is. It would be your last, but I might be able to encourage our Chief to help out as well. What do you say? After that, make your choice," Kevin said.

"Does that include the balloon too?" Hawk asked.

"Yes," Kevin responded, "because that is a damn good idea. A spotter that high up would be invaluable. You could see everything," Kevin said.

"That was what I said. John is all ready to go as is our teams," Hawk said.

"OK, let's do it and show the Cartel we ain't afraid of them," Kevin said. "Plus, after this is over, if you chose to leave, I will give you a golden goose from the left wing," Kevin said.

"Thank you, Kevin. Much appreciated. Call me if you get Gee's approval and I'll gather the litter," Hawk said.

When Hawk got back to the office, he called Annie and asked, "Would you like to go to dinner tonight? How about the Whales Tale?" Annie agreed, so Hawk wrapped things up at the office and started driving home. Home to Channel Islands.

* * *

About half way home, Hawk noticed out of the rearview mirror once again that white colored Caddy following him at a respectable distance. He slowed down and pulled over to the right shoulder of the road and waited. The Caddy did likewise. Hawk, too, pulled over to the right and parked approximately one hundred yards back. *OK!* Hawk thought about it for a minute and decided that the best way to find out who these characters were was to play a little game of chicken. Whoever these fools were, they had better be able to drive. But just to make sure, Hawk started up one more time and jump quickly up to eight miles per hour. Once Hawk saw the Caddy follow the bait, he slammed on the brakes and waited for a reaction from the Caddy. The Caddy braked and pulled to the side of the road, determined not to pull too close to Hawk. The Caddy's reaction time was slow, and Hawk figured the driver might know how to drive on dirt but not pavement. Hawk could see two, if not three, people in the car just like before. *OK, chicken time.*

Hawk waited for a break in the traffic and started backing up fast, and then did a backward one-eighty and spun the tires, headed straight into the Caddy. The driver tried to back-up to avoid a head-on collision but failed to maneuver fast enough. Hawk's front end smacked his front end and began pushing him backward. Now was the time to find out how good the driver really was. He would have to make a quick decision to either turn into the oncoming traffic lanes or better yet, turn into the curb and over the embankment right into the sea. He was a good driver and kept the Caddy going backward in a straight line. Hawk's only choice now was to brake quickly, detaching their front ends, then speeding head-on, knocking the driver up and over the curb by hitting him in the driver side front fender and the tire area on his speed up.

The driver would either bottom out on top of the curb or go completely over and into the ocean.

The screeching of tires, the mashing of metal and honking horns from oncoming traffic was enough to distract anyone, but Hawk knew to get ready to brake hard again once the Caddy was on top of the curb. Otherwise, the driver would pull Hawk with him right over the curbing and into the ocean. At the exact moment, the Caddy jumped the curb, going backward at forty-five miles an hour, a bullet came crashing through Hawk's windshield, just missing his right ear by inches. Hawk slammed on the brakes, dislodging the Caddy and waited for him to plunge backward into the sea, but instead, he swung around and into the oncoming traffic behind him. For a second, Hawk worried for the other drivers until a big semi-truck hit his passenger side door, ramming the Caddy out of the traffic lanes and back over the curb and into the sea. The semi driver was good as was all other cars and drivers. Unfortunately, the Caddy was taking on lots of salt water and would soon sink and be pulled out to sea. One person was trying to get out of the passenger side door and was pulled under the car from oncoming waves hitting the car and the rock embankment. The driver was unconscious and sprawled out on top of the steering wheel. The perp in the back seat was screaming his head off, trying to get out of the car somehow without drowning. He saw Hawk and took aim with the pistol still in his hand when another wave hit the Caddy from behind and tossed him forward. With that action, his gun went off, most likely killing the driver. It wasn't much longer when the Caddy was pulled out to sea with its roof bobbing up and down. Hawk never saw anyone in the water swimming or getting free from the Caddy. All the participants were assumed to have drowned or have been shot by their own friends if they had any such thing.

The CHP was on the scene, watching the Caddy and looking at Hawk's car with the bullet hole in the windshield, then at the long trail of dual black tire marks leading up to the Semi-truck which had hit Caddy over the embankment. Hawk was relieved that the chase was finished and just sat down on the curbing and took a deep breath.

Thank You, Lord, He said, *for once again saving my life, not causing innocent people to get hurt and another day to live. Amen.*

The CHP officers walked over and asked if Hawk was alright and asked for license and registration cards. "Right," Hawk muttered, "which first? My license or my registration cards?" Off in the distance, Hawk heard more sirens blaring en route to the accident location.

The CHP officer was not very happy with Hawk's reply and asked if he had been drinking or using drugs.

"No and No. What else you want to ask?" Hawk asked.

"OK, smart-ass, get up off the curb and stand up next to your car. Put both hands on the hood when you get there," ordered Officer Walker.

"Sorry, Walker, I am too tired to jump right up just yet. But here is my license, badge and Identification cards."

"Barton?" Walker said. "Hawk Barton?"

"In the flesh; at your service," Hawk replied. He was tired and just realizing that everything Kevin had told him today was true. *I am a target and will be as long as I am here in California,* Hawk said to himself. This wasn't fair to Annie, and he needed to make other plans. Plans to escape and fast. He was then motivated and ask Walker to look up and down the freeway to see if he could spot any other cars or trucks stopped alongside the roadway. Any parked cars could be possible chase cars to lend the perps a hand or finish a bungled job. Hawk just felt the cash register bells go *ka-Ching* as his reward went higher. *It is true,* Hawk concluded, *the target on my back is big, and I am too popular amongst too many factions, and that is only going to get worse as time goes on.* It was time to move again, only this time to a safe zone. An Island perhaps. An island in the Pacific Ocean named Hawaii.

"Sorry, Hawk, I didn't recognize you. What the hell happened here?" Officer Walker asked.

CHP Johnston was walking up after taking a statement from the truck driver and two other car drivers. "I'll tell you what the hell happened here," Johnston said. "This idiot was pushing that car backward and—"

It was time for Hawk to step in, and he asked, "What car, Officer Johnston?"

"Shut-up and stand up now!" Officer Johnson ordered.

Johnston was about ready to pull his revolver when Walker held his arm to his gun and said, "Back-off. You have no idea who this guy is. If you don't want to die right here and now, back it down. Way down."

"OK, then who the hell is he?" Officer Johnston asked. "He sure as hell isn't the president of the United States or the governor of California now, is he?" He was so angry that the veins on his neck were bulging out and his eyes were the color of an angry volcano.

"I said back it down, Johnston. This here is Hawk," Walker said. "Hawk Barton of the Sheriff's Department. You remember me telling you about him. This is the guy that is bringing down the Cartels around here almost single-handedly. He just may have saved a lot of lives here today," Walker said.

"Guys, guys, that is not true. I have a lot of help from every department, including yours. By the way, where is Rob working tonight?" Hawk asked.

"Got your back, cowboy. I am walking up right behind you," Rob said.

"Yes, I know. Heard you coming, you big ox." Hawk turned around and shook hands with Rob they and hung on to each other for a moment. CHP Johnston was calming down, but still pretty miffed at all the circus act on the freeway, which was displaying car parts, metal, rubber, and glass all over his road.

Rob had gone through one of Hawk's early driving academies at the Santa Barbara Airport. He was a good officer and loved working the freeways. He came back to Santa Barbara after a short stint in Lancaster and a promotion.

"Good to see you, Hawk," Rob said.

"Yeah, as I remember, the last time was at the Jail when you brought in that meth-head from Isla Vista. That kid was as calm as could be until you jacked him up the wall as you were leaving," Hawk said.

"Oh yeah, the Kennedy kid. Spooky, wasn't he? Kinda hard to handle as I recall. Did you get your daily dose of exercise that night?" Rob asked laughingly.

Laughing right back, Hawk said, "Oh, it wasn't too hard after calling four other deputies to help sit on him. I meant to thank you for your contribution to a bloody uniform that day and a real workout."

"No problem, Hawk. Loved to help keep you boys stay in shape by wrestling with dope fiends," Rob said.

"So how did all this fun driving stuff begin today, Hawk? Reminds me of the driving academy you put on out at the airport in Santa Barbara. 'The Fun Zone.'"

"It took a few minutes to lead up to the actual reverse one-eighty and then pushing the Caddy backward. The perp in the back seat was the shooter. The driver was doing what he could to keep the car from going over the curb, and the passenger was holding on for dear life and both feet up on the dash, bracing himself for hell itself. It was the Semi-truck that did us all a favor and hit the Caddy off the freeway and up and over the curb and into the ocean depths. The same thing I was trying to teach you in the early seventies, only doing it backward," Hawk said.

"Yes, I see the tire mark patterns. What a ride that must have been. Wish I could have seen it. You OK, though?"

"Oh, sure," Hawk said. "Just getting tired of all the attention. Do you mind if I get on home now? This was one of those days that had just a little too much vinegar," Hawk said.

"No, not at all Hawk. We can take over from here. You take care of yourself," Rod said. "Alright?"

"You bet, Rob. Good to meet you, Walker. Johnston, hang in there," Hawk said.

It was no lie. Hawk was very tired all of a sudden. Life was getting more complicated and dangerous every day. This was not what or how Hawk wanted his life to be but backing down was not an option either. Making a decision was not going to be easy, but something Hawk knew he must do, and soon.

In the eye of the hawk, there was No Fear, just tired of winging it without the needed support. Hawk was getting tired mentally, and that is a danger and a pull on the physical aspect of the whole person. He determined that another vacation would be nice right about now. He needed to contemplate the new reward poster stuck to his backside. Plus a million now, according to Capt. Gee. Every want-to-be hero and bandit looking to get rich quick was coming after Hawk.

On the rest of the ride home, all Hawk could think about was taking Annie and going back to Hawaii. The problem was, he didn't think she would like leaving Rainey her sister and all her friends. This move would have to be sold as temporary until retirement. At the rate things were moving, retirement might not be that far off.

If everything went right, Kevin would have talked to Capt. Gee and Hawk would have a return call to make when he got home for the following night's last Panga boat ops for a while.

* * *

"Hi, honey, I'm home. How did it go today?" Hawk asked.

"Peaceful and quiet," Annie replied. "Dorothy and I got caught up on things, and we have been invited to Church tonight. Would you like to go?"

"I would, honey, but we can't. We need to talk. Some things went down today that require immediate discussion. That's why I mentioned the restaurant and a quiet evening in the booth, talking about our future," Hawk said. "Did I get any calls this afternoon?"

"Yes, as a matter of fact, both Capt. Gee and agent Kevin called. What's going on?" Annie asked. "It sounds serious, Hawk."

"I have to make those two callbacks, and then maybe we can go eat? Will that work? Can you call Dorothy back and explain to her and Jim that we have a very important meeting that came up late, regarding work and God's Will?" Hawk asked.

"Should I start getting worried, Hawk? Or start packing again?" Annie asked.

"No on both counts for now," Hawk said. He then picked up the telephone and dialed Kevin first to see what he found out about the following night's mission. Kevin must have been sitting on the phone, waiting for Hawk. "Kevin, it's Hawk. How did you do with Capt. Gee today? I have a call to return from him, but I wanted to call you first. You had sounded pretty sure that you could convince him to tango."

"I wish I could have, Hawk, but he said no. The Sheriff is tied into his decision. I understand it, but I don't. From what I hear from you, and can paste together, your assumption is correct. It's a shame because you trained a damn good team. What are you going to do now?" Kevin asked Hawk.

"After today's ride home, I have no choice. Quitting tomorrow, Kevin. I am done with the chicken crap. Time to move on," Hawk said.

"What happened on your ride home, Hawk? Oh, wait a minute. Thanks, Cheryl. Give me a minute, Hawk," Kevin said. "Oh, shit. Oh, my God. Ha! Oh, shit. I can't believe this report, but then I do. Nice going, Hawk. Just received the brief on your trip home. What the hell, man? You OK after a few spins?"

"Oh, yeah. I am fine, but the three perps are now fish bait. The bottom fish and crabs have got to be enjoying a feast tonight. Eyeball to eyeball. Would have got more if law enforcement, in general, weren't so clueless. I am sure they had a chase car covering and following us close by. Don't think they would have missed yet another opportunity. Capt.

Gee told me that a new poster was coming out soon for more than a million. Not paseos either," Hawk said.

"This really isn't any laughing matter, Hawk. They will find you. You know that, right? Please be careful. We need you, Hawk. You are the only Law Enforcement hunter that can truly finish the job. I wish you could hang in at the Sheriff's Office but understand why you can't," Kevin admitted.

"You sound like a riddle talker tonight. I fully understand the target on my back, Kevin, and all the implications it carries. Everyone close to me will be a target if I am around. I don't want to tell you your job, Kevin but, why don't you pull Misty back into the Bureau?" Hawk asked.

"Not yet, she has her hand on the pulse of the core issue here, and she might just fish out the joker in the counsel. You know, Hawk, don't you—how much she loves and respects you?" Kevin implied. "By the way, this is not a simple traffic accident report. The CHP put together a fifteen-page report, mostly how you could have endangered innocent drivers. They aren't saying a whole lot on the danger factor that the perps put the public in with the flying bullets that could have killed innocent drivers. What a crock. How close did that bullet come to you, Hawk? Kevin asked.

"Inches. Just a couple inches. I didn't take the time to measure, but it was close. The fool was trying to shoot through the Caddy

Annie was a little suspicious of their date and was hoping that Hawk would have told her more information before dinner while walking. That was not going to be the case. First, Hawk had to make sure that they saw eye-to-eye on the new developments and pending move back to Hawaii, not to mention what he would be doing next.

After being seated in their favorite booth, they told their waitress to hold off on any food for twenty minutes.

Looking Annie in the eye, Hawk related to her his meetings with Capt. Gee, Kevin and the problems with the teams. To Annie, it was a big relief not having heard the final incident that nearly cost Hawk his life on the drive home. That was going to be the hard part.

OK! Hawk took a big breath and told her all about the hit on him while driving home, and how he drove the Caddy into the ocean.

Annie nearly broke down into tears. She was visibly shaken up. Now for the big bang and their immediate moving situation, Hawk said, "Honey, the only safe place for us now is back to the islands. Unfortunately, we can no longer stay here. It has become entirely too dangerous."

"I can understand that, but what about Violet, Jeff, the grandkids, and all our friends? What about Rainey and Tom? What about your job?" Annie asked.

Hawk butted in to help calm her down as her voice was exalting higher and higher.

"It will be alright, babe, trying to convince myself at the same time. We will get our insurance money from the house and take it with us to buy a new home in Hawaii. And we have a nice retirement package waiting from the Sheriff's department, so we can put round trip tickets in the mail every year for family visits. I know that Violet and all the grandkids will love coming over every year. Maybe even more often than that" Hawk said.

"Hawk, you know that type of thing rarely works. This is devastating news," Annie muttered while trying to catch her breath and talk about all the ramifications involved with what she just heard him say and the impact of his job.

"It doesn't matter, honey. It is my promise to you. I haven't called Randy or Lani yet, but I will when you say the word. I just know that every minute we stay here, we are at risk. I am not saying that to scare you, but it is true. My ride home today proves that. The reward on my back went up a lot higher. My work here in Santa Barbara is over. The Sheriff has made that clear by not standing up to the Council. He is allowing himself to be bullied for whatever the reason. It is time for me to go. He won't even protect us any longer. We are on our own and would be forced back to Santa Barbara, thus making it easier for the Cartel to achieve its reward," Hawk said.

"I am in shock, Hawk. Don't know how to process this. Just can't believe it," Annie said.

Tears were now streaming down Annie's face. She used the cloth table napkin to dab her cheeks and dry her tears. For the remainder of the dinner, they mostly sat in silence. It didn't matter how good the fish was; everything tasted bad in both of their mouths. Even if they both had drunk rum, the bitter taste of their dilemma was too fresh, and nothing would have helped settle their stomachs. This was a final blow. Their entire lives, their families, Hawk's career, and their home was now being tossed onto the fall fire of burning leaves. Everything they had worked so hard for. This was a terribly depressing situation right now. Hawk grabbed Annie's hand and held it. After kissing her delicate hand several times, he reassured her that everything would be alright. He had calls to make in the morning and encouraged her not to worry. "We need to thank God for the trouble we are in. Give Him a chance to work on our behalf by giving Him our problems. OK, honey?"

Annie didn't say anything. She just nodded her head but avoided Hawk's gaze for the moment.

* * *

Hawk got up early in the morning at about six a.m., showered, and dressed in Levi's and a dress shirt. He gave Annie a kiss goodbye and headed north to Santa Barbara for possibly the last time. It was both alarming, frightening, whimsical, borderline maddening, and intense. The radio didn't help; neither did the sun in his eyes. Coming up to the incident the previous day and passing all the tire marks on the pavement, Hawk's mind did backflip tricks, which made driving all the more difficult.

As he was easing up the Rincon grade, he took a look to the right at the frontage road leading up to the time where he chased that assassin Larry Blood north on this very stretch of highway. A flood of memories began to attack him—how many times he had been shot, knifed, and beaten up by perps of all sizes, shapes, and colors. Hawk was always the Hunter, and now he was the Hunted too.

All his life, the ocean was south, and the mountains that nestled next to the city was north. The plains of Santa Barbara, however, was built in an east and west mode. It is the only way it would have worked. So, heading north on the 101 Freeway was actually going east and west. Thus the sun was in Hawk's eyes the entire drive, coming or going. He then realized how tiring it was and how much concentration it took to just go to work and come home again. That was different for sure.

Hawk was at the office one hour after he left the condo and pulling into the parking lot. In the street parking was their local radio and TV networks. *Why are they here?* he wondered. *What happened last night?* He got out and walked into the main office and bumped into Red and Misty.

"What is going on, guys?" Hawk asked.

"You tell me, cowboy. What the hell is going on?" Red asked. "I heard you were leaving."

"How did you find that out so soon? I just made the decision last night at dinner," Hawk said.

Misty had tears in her eyes and moved in close and gave a great big hug and squeezed real tight. Her whisper was barely audible, but Hawk heard her say, "No matter what, Hawk, I am with you. Call me, and I will be there. Without you, there is no job. You and you alone make all the difference."

Hawk nodded and said, "Thank you. I will call at some point. Appreciate all you are doing to unfurl the truth. Please keep working at it. No matter where we end up, your Intel is going to make all the difference. We are tied together, Misty. Red, you and the rest of the team, are going back to patrol duties until Capt. Gee finds new money and allocates everyone back in. I have to go, my friend, but know that this business is not over. We are going to reunite real soon."

"Wait, cowboy. Why don't we go to the big trout lake and spend a little saddle time and fish a couple of days?" Red asked.

"Wish I could, buddy, but I have to go. It just is no longer safe here for my family or me. First things first. But just remember that we are not giving up. The fight will go on—only in a different town," Hawk said.

Red and Hawk hugged, and then Hawk turned and walked into the Sheriff's Department. Down the familiar hallway straight to Capt. Gee's office.

"Capt. Gee, may I come in, please?" Hawk asked.

"Yes, of course, Hawk. I know you want to hear the Sheriff's new command orders. Sorry to say, but he is just not in a position at this time to allow anymore Panga boat missions in the deep water. That does not mean that you and your 'one' team cannot score, still, on the local beachheads. Once the boats land on the beaches, they belong to us. Also, the Sheriff wants to give new ranks to some of your team members as well as you. Hawk, I am proud to tell you that you are going to the rank of Captain. Congratulations!" Capt. Gee said.

Capt. Gee stuck out his hand to shake Hawk's hand in a congratulatory way.

Hawk took a quick moment to pause and take a breath as the Captain's hand stuck in midair.

"Thanks, Capt. Gee, I appreciate the Sheriff's gesture and rank increase. However, my answer is no. I quit. Here is my badge. I hope that somehow you and the Sheriff continue to increase the ranks of my team's deputies. They worked hard to get to where they are, Captain. I will be cleaning out my desk in just a few minutes," Hawk said.

"Oh, hell no, Hawk. Come on. The Sheriff does not want you to go and is doing everything within his power to keep you by giving you a promotion and keeping your team together. You are too good, Hawk, to just up and leave. Way too valuable of an asset. The Sheriff has spent a lot of time and money to get you and your team to where you are. Please, reconsider what you are saying," Capt. Gee said.

"No, I spent the time and money to get to where I am today. Not him. If the Sheriff were serious, he would have taken measures to protect my family and me. Hell! He would do more for a perp being relocated than his own personnel. If I am so valuable as you say, then let me stay in Channel Islands or, at the least, give us some protection here at home. But you know he won't, right? Thus I am forced to quit," Hawk said.

THE END

Is it really the end? I think not. Hawk had some thinking to do. He had options. Hawk always had options in reserve. He was thinking about maybe:

1. Transferring to another department in or out of state
2. Joining the FBI
3. Becoming a Mercenary Solider
4. Starting his own Black Ops Company

Which option would he take? Not sure yet, but The End? Hell No.

ABOUT THE AUTHOR AND STORY TELLER:

Rex Barton, now retired from the Military, Law Enforcement, Mortgage broker and real estate businesses. What's next in his seemingly dull life? I guess it would be his enjoyment of writing about the many years of his wild and adventurous lifetime in service and the world we live in.

Rex enjoys his retirement with his beautiful wife, Antoinette, in the Northwest and has completed three additional books, all due out this year. They are sure to excite.

Look for: *The Mongoose Diaries* (fiction) 2017

The Panga Wars (fiction) 2017

What If (non-fiction, biography) 2017

1849 - About the hard life of Barton's forefathers going West (fiction)

The Depths of Hell (fiction) - *Hawk finds himself in the fight of his life*

CPSIA information can be obtained
at www.ICGtesting.com
Printed in the USA
BVOW10*0431080617

486212BV00004B/13/P